DEEP COVER

A TRIGGER MAN THRILLER

AIDEN BAILEY

INKUBATOR
BOOKS

Published by Inkubator Books
www.inkubatorbooks.com

ISBN (eBook): 978-1-83756-348-7
ISBN (Paperback): 978-1-83756-349-4
ISBN (Hardback): 978-1-83756-350-0

For Bec, with love

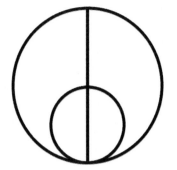

PROLOGUE
THREE MONTHS EARLIER...

Bayanga, Central African Republic

With his hands tied tight above his head, and as his sweat mixed with his blood flowed hot across his face, neck and bare back, Mark Pierce wished to die.

Not die, perhaps. Passing out would be enough.

"Tell us what we want to know, Pierce, and this all ends."

He hurt all over from the months of beatings, forced stress positions and waterboarding, and was weak from lack of food and water in the incessant tropical heat. The electric cables adhered to his nipples and toes were today's torture. His captors were ready to go again, but he was too weak to fight them. They had brutalised him like this for too long, until he had no fight left in him.

"The numbers, Pierce? Tell us the numbers. The bank accounts and their passwords?"

His torturers were two masked men who spoke with Aussie accents. They never hurt him enough to maim or permanently cripple him, but they hurt him well enough, and did so every day. The rope around his wrists suspending him from the wooden ceiling was all that kept him upright.

"Come on, mate, tell us?"

Pierce whispered his response, but he lacked the energy to give his words volume.

"What was that?"

He whispered again. This time his voice released as an indecipherable rasp.

"Pierce?"

The red-headed Aussie leaned in close to hear better.

Near enough so that Pierce could feel the torturer's hot breath on his face.

"Tell me?"

"Fuck... you!"

The man stepped back, and Pierce could make out the sneer behind the masked eyes. "Very well, fuck you too, Pierce."

They placed the wooden rod back into Pierce's mouth.

He bit down just before the electric jolts surged through his atrophied body. Pierce convulsed as spit and blood dribbled from his lips, and his muscles spasmed while his eyes rolled into the back of his head. He'd known what was coming, but knowing didn't lessen the agony that surged through him.

But this time, blissful unconsciousness found him again.

Just as he'd hoped it would.

PART I

OLD SOVIETS

1

PRESENT DAY...

Aral Sea, Kazakhstan

Consciousness returned with a jolt.

After a moment of disorientation, Mark Pierce opened his eyes, but he couldn't see. When he felt rough hessian on his face, he realised he had a bag over his head. It stank of another man's vomit, so he was not the first to wear it.

Police handcuffs bound his wrists in his lap. It felt like he was wearing a T-shirt, loose-fitting jeans and running shoes one size too small. He recognised he was in the back seat of a moving car, shared with four other occupants. One burly man on each side. Two in the front.

This was not the Central African Republic of his nightmares. It was too cold here, and the air was too dry. He remembered the torture he had dreamed of had been from months back, and in the last few weeks, his captors had allowed him time to recover and recuperate. But why?

The men in the car grumbled and snorted snot back into their nasal passages.

Pierce feigned unconsciousness and listened, sensing they were about to speak.

When they did, it was a mixture of Russian, which Pierce followed, and Kazak, which he did not. The gist of the conversation centred on one key fact. They were driving Pierce to a remote location where they would put a bullet through the back of his head.

While the news was disheartening, especially after seven months imprisoned in a dirty and decrepit cage inside a Congo rainforest-shrouded war camp, death was not inevitable.

The men laughed, settled into speaking Russian and shared a joke about a prostitute they all knew, whom they liked to keep naked.

"How soon before we kill him, Sanzhar?" asked the man in the front passenger seat. He sounded young, and he was a fidgeter, judging by the rustling noises he made. Perhaps this outing was his initiation into the profession of killing and torture.

"Soon, Amir. We do it quick and clean, like I told you earlier, and as my cousin asked us to do it," answered Sanzhar from the driver seat next to the young Amir. The older man sounded world-weary, yet confident, sensed by the inflection in his voice that only experience and age could carry. "You can pull the trigger if you desire. You're the only one of us who needs practice."

"*Squeeze* the trigger, Sanzhar?"

"Of course, my boy, *squeeze*."

The other men laughed.

The man on Pierce's right had barely moved since Pierce

had regained consciousness, suggestive he was an opponent practised in calm and controlled responses to stressful situations. He now spoke in a deep, guttural voice. "Boss, he's awake."

Sanzhar cut his laughs short. "Are you certain, Erasyl?"

"His breathing changed. His muscles are tight."

Pierce was not aware his body rhythms had given away his ruse. Too much time incarcerated in his filthy prison had dulled his abilities and weakened him, so he was no longer able to control his formerly honed body as he once had. At least in his last few weeks of imprisonment they had fed him sufficiently and not tortured him, so he had some strength again, which he would no doubt need soon.

"And what do you think, Kemhebek?" Sanzhar asked the man to Pierce's left.

Kemhebek grunted an unintelligible response as he played with a set of keys for a moment. Pierce felt his hand brush against Pierce's leg as he placed them in his pocket.

Erasyl then punched Pierce hard in his side. The blow was painful, but Pierce had expected it and had already tensed his abdominal muscles to protect his organs. The shudder was involuntary, but the coughing and spluttering into his bound hands was deliberate misdirection. He needed the men to believe he was weak and pliable.

"See, what did I tell you?" Erasyl reached under the hood and pressed a finger into Pierce's ear canal. Pierce reacted as if terrified while he concentrated on shaking the hood free. It dropped to his feet as Erasyl removed his hand.

With his visual senses returned, Pierce studied the four Kazakhs, men who were unperturbed that he looked upon their faces, as he would soon be dead. Together they were five bodies packed into a Russian Lada 4x4. Pistols bulged under their tight leather jackets. Ears jutted from shaven heads, and their flashy gold neck chains were almost laughable in their stereotypical representation of Russian or Kazak mafia. These men were criminals, not soldiers, which would make his escape easier. Pierce's only concern was Erasyl, who, Pierce guessed, knew how to fight and had learned through soldiering. Erasyl must be his first target.

The four criminals were sizeable men, their limbs thick with muscles. Amir was the thinnest and youngest, but only compared to the others, and he couldn't sit still. As the novice of the group, Pierce would kill him last.

It was daytime outside, and the sky was a clear blue. The landscape was flat grassland and wide patches of sand in every direction. The air presented a natural crispness, suggesting they were far from any urban settlement.

Three rusted fishing trawlers appeared on the horizon.

There was no water anywhere.

Kemhebek laughed as he nudged Pierce. "This is the Aral Sea, fuckhead, or what's left of it. The fucking Russians have drained it since the sixties, to irrigate their useless cotton fields."

Pierce resisted a nod, for the information was useful. He was in Kazakhstan, a country many thousands of kilometres from his last memories in tropical Central Africa, and a little too close to Russia for his liking.

"Enjoy the view, American. It will be your last."

Pierce pretended not to understand.

Sanzhar took a smartphone from his jacket. From Pierce's position in the middle of the back seat, it was a simple matter to look over Sanzhar's shoulder to watch him key in the PIN to unlock it: 614-479. Pierce memorised the number while Sanzhar made a call. He listened as the ringtone repeated twelve times, then dropped out. Whoever Sanzhar had expected to reach, they didn't answer. He returned the phone to his inside jacket pocket.

Soon the three fishing trawlers loomed larger on the horizon. Stranded for decades, their hulls were copper-red with rust. The two closest boats were side by side, with the nearest angled at sixty degrees to the horizon. The trawlers must once have been loved, providers of food and a livelihood. No one had loved them for at least a generation.

Pierce sensed their drive would end here. The men would shoot him and hide his body in a hull. He had to act in the coming minutes or die. The problem was Erasyl. The former soldier watched Pierce like a hungry bird of prey, expecting Pierce to fight for his life when he came for him.

Amir's legs jittered with excitement. "He's not begging? Sanzhar, why isn't he begging?"

Once out of the Lada, all eyes and weapons would be on Pierce. He had to act as soon as Erasyl looked away...

"Relax," Sanzhar said through a long, lingered breath. "He'll beg soon enough."

They hit a rut, and the Lada dropped.

Pierce took his chance. With his cuffed hands clenched together, he struck Erasyl's windpipe. The criminal gasped for oxygen as Pierce leaned left, pulled the .380 Makarov semi-automatic pistol from Kemhebek's shoulder holster, pressed the weapon against the man's chest and fired. The Kazakh's ribcage instantly ruptured with blood and meat.

Amir, in the front, screamed with rage and fear as his face turned crimson, but he did little else.

Sanzhar reacted fastest and yanked on the wheel so inertia pulled them all in unexpected directions. The manoeuvre saved the crime boss's life, for Pierce would have shot Sanzhar next while Erasyl recovered from his throat punch. Now Pierce couldn't get the muzzle lined up on any of the men.

While the car spun, a recovering Erasyl reached for his pistol.

Pierce used the inertia to his advantage. He reached over Kemhebek's corpse, pulled on the door handle and, since neither wore seat belts, the two of them flew from the vehicle. Erasyl didn't follow, as he held his position by pressing his free hand and knees into the seat in front of him.

Holding Kemhebek's corpse tight, they tumbled together and landed with the Kazak impacting first, cushioning Pierce as they hit the grass hard.

Grunting, Pierce rolled, then came up on his feet. As the Lada swerved erratically to gain control in the flat semi-desert, Pierce felt in Kemhebek's pockets until he found the keys the man had held earlier. As Pierce had hoped, they were handcuff keys. Then he sprinted to the first angled fishing trawler.

Bullets flew by him.

Within seconds, he was behind the closest rusted trawler and safe for the moment. He looked back, briefly noticing that the men had stalled the Lada and were now out of it. Pierce ducked further around and behind the rusting trawler, where he was outside of their firing range.

"Fuck!" Sanzhar yelled in Russian, his voice carrying over the flat grasslands. "How the fuck did he escape?"

"It wasn't my fault," Amir moaned. "I was up front with you, remember?"

"Of course I fucking remember."

Sanzhar and Amir continued their argument, revealing their location to Pierce.

Erasyl was silent. He would not give away his position so easily. This was confirmation of Pierce's earlier assumption that Erasyl was the most dangerous of the four.

After removing the handcuffs, Pierce used the cover of the first trawler to run for the second. He spotted a hull breach where two sections of the metal exterior had long ago shifted and split. Within seconds he was inside, but not before bullets pinged off the nearby hull.

The trawler's interior was dark and dusty. He fired two bullets back out of the breach he had entered by, pinning down whoever was shooting. While he couldn't see the details of his pistol in the dark, he knew the .380 Makarov carried eight rounds in the magazine. He'd used three already. Not great odds against three armed men with multiple magazines at their disposal no doubt, but his situation had improved compared to the circumstances he'd endured the last seven months.

Time to use that advantage.

"He's in the second boat!" Erasyl yelled in Russian. He switched to Kazakh and spoke again, perhaps sensing Pierce could understand Russian. Sanzhar argued with him for a moment.

In the darkness of the rusted hull, with only narrow hull breaches allowing slivers of light inside, and standing in the centre of its near empty hull, he couldn't see the three men. He needed to move soon because they would quickly pin him down if he did not, but what was the optimal path to take? Pierce still wasn't certain.

Suddenly the boat shuddered, suggesting in its rusted state the hull was no longer structurally sound and was now unbalanced and near to collapsing as he moved across its shuddering hull interior. These boats could have been here for half a century or more, slowly disintegrating as time ravished them. It was not safe to be inside, when his movements might be the final edge it required to collapse completely. Noticing another tear in the hull at the opposite side of the boat, Pierce used the gap to step out to the other side—

Behind him, bullets flew through the gap he'd entered, missing him but penetrating the trawler's rusted metal shell. The noise was louder than a normal gunshot in the echoing chamber. He'd remained standing in its centre too long, and now it was time to move.

With his ears ringing, Pierce ducked for cover.

Amir stepped inside the boat, seen as the light from outside silhouetted him, but he couldn't properly see Pierce because he was completely shrouded in shadow.

On a hunch, Pierce ducked outside through another hull breach on the opposite side, then leaned against the hull. It rocked, for its balance, now that he had disturbed it, was precarious like he had suspected. As he made out Amir's silhouette venture further inside, he pushed hard, and the entire boat shuddered. Then to Pierce's amazement, the whole front half of the boat toppled over as Amir screamed before the many tons of scrap metal crushed, then silenced him.

"What the fuck—!" Sanzhar yelled, giving away his position again.

Pierce raced round the collapsed trawler with his gun raised. He fired a single bullet into Sanzhar's head.

Three dead.

That left Erasyl. The professionals had to play their game as single participants, ready to hunt, seek and kill.

2

Pierce's first thought was to run to Sanzhar's body and take the fallen opponent's weapon, which was a mere five metres from him, but he knew Erasyl would guess that course of action and would wait in ambush, as the body lay in an open patch of the dried seabed. Instead, Pierce sprinted for the third rusted trawler, which offered better cover than the boat that had collapsed. He just hoped this third boat was more structurally sound than the one he'd escaped from.

To Pierce's relief, he soon saw that the elements had been kinder to the last boat, for it was mostly intact. Pierce ducked behind the propellers half buried in the sand. From their cover, he glanced back. Through the settling dust cloud of the collapsed second boat, he could see Erasyl hidden behind a torn length of hull from the first boat Pierce had entered. His Makarov was out in front of him as his eyes stared down the length of barrel, but he hadn't yet seen Pierce. At the distance of the fifteen metres now separating them, and with his near-effective cover, Pierce wasn't certain he could fatally shoot Erasyl with an accurate grouping of shots using his pistol.

"You have four bullets, my friend," he yelled in Russian. "I have forty."

Erasyl had been counting bullets, speaking to his professionalism as a killer and exactly what Pierce would have done if the situation were reversed, but to respond to the killer's taunts was to give away his position, so Pierce ignored him. He examined the landscape instead. A flat grassland that had once been a sea. Only three places to hide, a trio of rusted boats, with one a collapsed wreckage of metal.

Knowing that Erasyl would advance on Pierce, with his weapon firing to force Pierce into returning covering fire until his Makarov emptied, Pierce raced further behind the third trawler and hoped he could find an alternative plan to beat this man. He pushed his weight against the hull, found it securely embedded in the dirt, for this trawler, in comparison, was solid and mostly intact. Rusted handholds provided a means to the top. Pierce figured height was better than his current predicament, so he scrambled up to the deck. Several rungs snapped as he climbed, and the clanging noise they made as they bounced down the hull gave away his position.

He heard Erasyl grunt as the killer sprinted towards him.

Pierce climbed up onto the deck.

He had planned to sprint across to the other side of the trawler, ready to shoot Erasyl, but the wooden decking had mostly collapsed, and what wood remained was incapable of supporting his weight. Hearing further grunting, Pierce glanced back over his shoulder. Erasyl was on the underside of this trawler's hull before Pierce could act, closing the distance between them considerably.

"You're trapped," Erasyl yelled. "I know you're on the deck, fuckhead. It's only a matter of time before I kill you."

Crouched low, Pierce ran close along the edge of the hull to the rusted remains of the bridge. The stairs up had disintegrated long ago, so he climbed to the top using the broken remains of the railing. The bridge was higher and commanded a greater view of the battlefield.

Once on the bridge, Pierce searched for items that could help him. He quickly discovered three five-litre drums of engine oil, and while rusted on the outside, each was structurally sound and contained hydrocarbons within.

He moved quietly so he could listen for Erasyl and soon heard him shuffling below. Erasyl was inside the boat, had entered through a gap in the hull Pierce hadn't noticed.

Pierce lifted each drum and threw them through holes in the hull, hearing them break in the darkness due to the force shattering them from a long fall. Once he'd dropped the third drum, he fired a single bullet into the splashed hydrocarbons. The fuels ignited, as Pierce had hoped, and a fire soon raged below.

Erasyl's screams echoed. Caught in the flames, he ran in multiple directions, smashing into metal panels over and over in his frantic and desperate race to escape. Then he was outside, sprinting through the sand and clumps of grass, the top half of his body alight.

Pierce climbed from the bridge, then lowered himself over the hull, dropped the last two metres into the sand and rolled when he hit the ground to absorb the impact. The rusted boat was soon an inferno. Pierce had escaped just in time.

He followed Erasyl across the sand and grass. The Kazakh rolled in the grass, trying to extinguish the flames, but his blackened skin was raw, and his fingers, ears and nose destroyed. He screamed, and his eyes were unable to close. His eyelids had burned away.

"Kill me!" he pleaded.

Pierce held out the Makarov and aimed at Erasyl's wailing head. Pierce's teeth clamped tight. His every muscle tensed in anticipation of executing this opponent.

As he lined up the suffering man in his sights, Pierce remembered his days of torture in the Central African Republic, so far away from this inhospitable place to find himself, where he had been bound naked to a chair while men electrocuted him, beat him or waterboarded him until he revealed the secrets they wanted to hear.

Memories returned of the starvation diet he'd endured, and when he almost died from malaria until his captors deemed him sick enough to treat him humanely, but only until he recovered, healthy enough to torture again.

Erasyl was complicit in Pierce's pain, because the Aussies who had tortured Pierce had obviously hired this man to bring him to the Kazakh desert to kill him. But why bring him thousands of kilometres across the globe when a bullet in the head in the Congo jungle would have been a far simpler solution?

"Please!"

Pierce stared at his hands.

They trembled.

His legs jittered too.

"I would have killed you quick, American. I swear."

Before rage blinded his mind, Pierce shot the blistered man through the forehead. Whatever Erasyl's sins, he didn't need to suffer as retribution for Pierce's pain. Yet Pierce watched without feeling as blood flowed fast from the Kazakh's wound and soaked the sand red.

For a long moment, Pierce stood without moving. Introspective contemplation consumed him. Killing these men, he felt nothing when he thought he'd might. Had he hoped for satisfaction, retribution, a balancing of the wrongs inflicted upon him?

Why was he wasting his time trying to understand emotions that wouldn't serve him?

Now that his melancholy bored him, Pierce returned to Sanzhar's corpse. The man had nicer clothes, a lined jacket and desert boots.

Pierce stripped the body, used his old clothes to try to wipe away Kemhebek's blood that had splashed on his skin, and then dressed in the warmer outfit. While he'd been unaware of the weather until now, and despite the sun being high in the sky, the air carried a mild chill. The dead man's clothes warmed him.

He stood, recognised the involuntary shakes across his body. Were these the ongoing neurological impacts of a head injury from years ago, or his subconscious telling him to right some wrongs?

It was probably both.

Trying to ignore his condition, Pierce took Sanzhar's Makarov pistol and the three spare magazines, pocketed the Lada ignition keys, then checked the dead man's wallet. He found no identification but a million tenge, which was worth about two and a half thousand US dollars. He pocketed the money, then examined the cell phone. Pierce keyed in the PIN, 614-479, and checked the call history. The phone must have been a burner because it contained two numbers, both of which Sanzhar had called frequently over the last three days.

Pierce activated the phone's audio recording app and called the first number.

It came back with a message that the number was no longer in service.

He called the second number.

It connected after three rings.

"Is there a problem?" The man who answered spoke Russian, but his accent was Australian.

"No," Pierce answered in the same language, but with perfect Russian enunciation.

No response.

"Then what do you want?"

Pierce's free hand tightened into a fist. This was the voice of the masked man who had tortured him for months in the rainforest war camp.

"You call me tomorrow, when it's done. Not before. That is what we agreed."

"Yes." Pierce used few words so as not to betray who he was. He wanted the Aussie to talk, to give something away before he realised Pierce was not one of the Kazakhs hired to kill him. "Understood."

"Where is he now?"

"With me."

"He's still unconscious?" A long pause followed. "Wait...?"

Pierce said nothing, sensing that the Australian had just detected that Pierce's accent was not right, and that he was not Sanzhar. His teeth clenched, and his legs shook. He imagined pressing a pistol against this man's forehead and blowing out his brains. This was the lead torturer complicit in his prolonged suffering.

"Fuck me, Mark Pierce, you are one slippery bastard." The Australian spoke English now.

Pierce switched to the same tongue. "You got me. And you are?"

The Australian laughed. "Nice try."

"I'm guessing you wanted me drugged a little longer."

More laughter. "Fuck you, mate. As long as you are dead, I don't care."

"I'm not dead."

"Yeah, I fucking guessed. But that will change soon enough."

Pierce closed his eyes and focused. Seven months imprisoned in Central Africa had been a hell like nothing he had ever experienced.

Pierce's hands gripped the phone so tight the screen cracked through the middle. "'Hemsworth'," he said, using the nickname Pierce had called him during their sessions together.

The Aussie snorted. "You thought you were in hell before, Pierce. Your suffering has only just begun."

The line went dead.

Pierce took deep, controlled breaths until his hands stopped shaking and his muscles relaxed, dissipating the tension they had been holding across his body.

He halted the recording and replayed the conversation. Once satisfied with the quality, Pierce saved it in a draft email in one of his many Gmail accounts. He then loaded Google Maps to find his exact location, discovering he was indeed inside the former Aral Sea, well inside the Central Asian nation of Kazakhstan.

The Caspian Sea lay four hundred kilometres to the west. If he reached its coast, from there he could secure passage on a boat and reach neighbouring Azerbaijan, the safest of all the countries for him that encircled the inland sea but still far from ideal. At least Pierce had contacts in Azerbaijan's capital, Baku, he could call upon for support.

Memorising the required information, Pierce removed the SIM card and the battery from the phone, then smashed the device under his new boots.

Next Pierce collected the dead Kazakhs' possessions, which didn't equate to much more cash and three further Makarov pistols and a half dozen loaded magazines, each with .380 rounds. Keeping one weapon, he dismantled the others and scattered their pieces across the former seabed.

He approached the Lada, figuring it would get him away faster than walking could. The burning trawler still spewed a dark black cloud into the sky, which would soon draw attention.

Then the car rattled.

Someone inside banged against the trunk.

Pierce froze, then drew his Makarov from his jacket pocket and approached.

The captive inside was trying to jimmy the trunk open.

Pierce unlocked the trunk with the keys and stepped back.

A young, slim, and naked Asiatic woman stared up at him. "Who the fuck are you?" she exclaimed in Russian.

Pierce kept his weapon trained on her. "I was about to ask you the same question."

3

The slim woman raised her arms and sat up in the trunk. Pierce noticed the red blotches around her lips and similar markings around her wrists and ankles, and a large bruise on the side of her forehead, though elsewhere her flesh was untouched. Torn strips of gaffer tape lay on the trunk's floor. She appeared to be a prisoner as much as he was, but this could be a deception.

"Are you going to kill me?"

Pierce's brow furrowed. "Do I have reason to?"

She made a face. Her demeanour projected calmness, which made Pierce suspicious.

"Who are you?" He noticed an old scar above her left hip, which had once been a serious wound, and wondered how she had received it.

She covered her breasts with her arms. "I'm nobody."

"Everybody is somebody."

"Can I get out, please? The smell is horrible."

Pierce nodded. He kept the Makarov trained on her long limbs as they lifted her from confinement. He wasn't a

trusting individual, even in the most benign of circumstances. There was no reason to be cold towards her, but the
rage burning inside prevented him from offering any sign
that he wouldn't harm her.

"You thirsty?" he asked with effort.

She nodded. "I'd also like clothes, if you've finished
checking me out."

As Pierce studied her, he ensured his stares didn't linger
from her neck down. She was attractive, with a long slim
neck and defined jawline. Her dark straight hair reached to
the point between her shoulder blades, and her eyes were an
emerald green. Old scars patterned her body, suggestive that
she'd been beaten badly at least once in her past.

With effort, he asked, "Did they... hurt you?"

She shook her head. "Not like that! But will you?"

"No. Stand there for a minute."

"Why?"

Pierce straightened his gun arm and kept the barrel
pointed at her head. "Because if I know where you are, I
won't shoot you accidentally, thinking you are a threat."

"Charming." She tightened her arms over her breasts,
perhaps now because of the cold rather than the fact she was
naked.

With sufficient distance separating them so she couldn't
rush Pierce without him raising his gun to shoot her in
time, Pierce searched the Lada, finding several water
bottles. He took one and threw her another. They both
drank, with Pierce finishing his bottle in seconds, his gun
again aimed at her in the other hand. He would have been
unconscious for some time while his captors transported
him from Central Africa to Central Asia. His thirst wasn't a
surprise.

"What about clothes? I'd feel more comfortable if we could talk with clothes on."

He nodded. "I'm getting to that."

"You were their prisoner?"

"Yes."

"So was I."

"Turn around and look away for a moment."

"Why?"

Pierce shook his head and didn't bother to explain. If she couldn't look at him, she couldn't judge the best time to run or attack him while he wasn't concentrating on her. "Just do it."

With a snarl, she turned in a half circle, facing away from the vehicle.

"I won't shoot you."

She nodded. Her long slender back twitched while she shifted her weight from one long leg to the other, but none of her movements suggested she was about to attempt an attack on him.

Pierce found a plastic bag on the back seat, with tight jeans, a grey sweater, a white T-shirt, sand shoes, and black practical underwear. He checked the clothes for concealed items she could use as a weapon. Satisfied they were harmless, he threw them to her. "You can turn around now."

"Checked me out enough?" she said with a sneer, picking up the sweater.

"You still haven't told me who you are."

"You first, mister."

She was only marginally shorter than him, which made her tall for a woman. He guessed her age to be late twenties, so not much younger than him. Her body was fit and toned, and he would have guessed her to be Chinese if her Russian wasn't perfect. Once she'd sorted through her clothes, she dressed.

"What did you do to upset them?" She gestured to the burned Kazakh corpse as she pulled on her jeans.

"Good question." He waved the Makarov, forming an imaginary circle in the air with the barrel. He speculated who she might be: a girlfriend of the Kazakh thugs, a CIA spy, a Russian spy, or a prostitute. The latter seemed likely, as the four Kazakh criminals had talked about a naked prostitute during their drive to the rusting trawlers. "What did you do to upset them?"

"Who knows, with angry men like that?"

"You have a name?"

"Irina."

"You have a last name?"

She laughed, but he sensed she found no aspect of their situation amusing. "In my profession, clients have trouble remembering my first name, let alone a second." She glared as he remained stoic and unresponsive. "I'm an escort, okay? Does that bother you?"

"Not in the slightest. How did you escape your bonds?"

Her eyes were like icicles. "Do you know how many times fuckers like to tie me up? I've had to learn a trick or two in my time, to escape when I need to."

"Why were you in the trunk?"

"Why does it matter? And why so many fucking questions?"

Pierce had a dozen reasons "why" it mattered, but no explanation would make sense to her unless he revealed he was a former CIA paramilitary operative who, while escaping the Aussies who had tortured him in Africa, was also on the run from his own people because his torturers had tricked the CIA into believing Pierce had turned rogue. Anyone he encountered could be an American or foreign nation operative sent to kill him. But he had no intention of telling her any of that.

She tucked her hair behind her left ear. "The men you killed; they came into some money. They wanted to celebrate, as men with money and no skills in talking to women do, so they hired my services. After I stripped for them, they insisted we go for a drive, to finish some business I couldn't witness. They tied and gagged me and left me in the trunk. It's not the first time."

Pierce nodded and said nothing. The tremors in his hands returned, mild and slight so only he would notice.

Irina snorted. "Like I said, it's happened to me before. I suppose they brought you out here to kill you, but you killed them instead." She pointed to the burning boat and the dead corpses within visual range. "I understand why you are angry."

He nodded, recognising that the spoken emotion still consumed him. He asked, "Does it bother you? That they are dead?"

"Of course not. They were assholes. Except I won't get paid."

Pierce nodded and asked himself why he was being cold towards her when she was supposedly as much a victim as he was.

"Are you going to kill me?"

"No."

"Are you going to fuck me?"

"No!"

"Are you going to tell me your name?"

"Viktor Sarkisian."

"Yeah, like that is your actual name."

"Is Irina real?"

She lowered her arms. "Viktor will do, but it doesn't suit you. So what's the plan now, *Viktor?*"

Pierce scanned the horizon. Nothing but flat expanses of grassland and clean blue sky. "We leave before someone comes looking. Gunshots will have carried far, and that smoke is visible for kilometres."

"I guess that's a plan. You want to drive, or you want me to?"

"I'll drive."

"I thought you'd want to keep that gun pointed at me." Her eyes rolled as she climbed in the Lada. "Typical man, always wanting to control everything."

Pierce slipped the gun into the back of his trousers, slid in behind the wheel and started the engine. Irina didn't look at him and seemed in no mood for further conversation. That suited Pierce for the moment while he settled his rage and planned out his next moves. Soon they followed the only track out of the sea that was not a sea.

As he drove, Pierce thought upon the men who had imprisoned and tortured him and destroyed his reputation within the CIA.

His thoughts turned not to the masked Australians, but their boss, the CIA spymaster who had first betrayed Pierce seven months earlier...

4

SEVEN MONTHS EARLIER…

Bayanga, Central African Republic

Consciousness returned in short pockets of time. Pierce tried to speak, but his words were slurry. When he opened his eyes, they were unfocused, and his muscles barely responded to his mental commands. He looked down along his body, stripped of clothes. Someone had applied fresh bandages to an injury in his leg he'd received in North Africa weeks earlier.

The air felt humid, and sweat drenched his skin. As his eyesight focused, he saw that his new cell was a wooden bungalow with mosquitos buzzing in the heat. Outside, thick tropical foliage grew close to the windows. He tried to sit, only to discover that handcuffs restrained his wrists and ankles to a metal-framed bed.

A man in his mid-thirties stood over Pierce. His surgical-gloved hand explored the insides of Pierce's wound. Pierce screamed when he registered the pain.

The man removed his finger and placed his other hand

over Pierce's forehead. The bloodied hand he held close to his mouth to make a shushing noise. "Be still, Mr Pierce," he said, speaking English with an African accent. "In the tropics, your wounds risk infection. Nobody wants you to die. Not yet anyway."

Pierce looked down and examined his leg. The thigh was red and raw where a foe had impaled him with a screwdriver. Pierce tried to sit, but he felt weak from pain and the drugs in his system. He fell back onto the uncomfortable bed.

"Where...? Where am I?"

"Central African Republic, Mr Pierce."

"Who...? Who are you?"

"No one you need to concern yourself about. Except that I am a doctor. I'm here to make you better."

"Better?" Pierce's throat felt parched. A headache stabbed at the insides of his skull. He turned left and right, noticing a saline drip in his arm. "Why?"

The doctor stood back, grabbed a bottle of water, unscrewed the lid, and held it to Pierce's lips. Pierce drank fast.

"Feeling better?"

Pierce nodded. The headache's intensity dropped away, but the pain in his leg still ached.

"The men who brought you here, they want you to make a full recovery."

"I bet... they do..."

He guessed his captors would heal him for a single purpose. He imagined a future of prolonged interrogations and torture, because with the current state of his wounds, Pierce wouldn't last long under those ordeals.

"It is unfortunate you are awake. I need to attend to your

wounds again, Mr Pierce. It will hurt, but I need to clean out any foreign debris that might be inside. You're drugged up on antibiotics, if you are wondering."

Pierce lay back on the bunk. Breathing was difficult, and his muscles felt weak. He would attempt to escape, but that was only possible if his physical condition improved. If his captors planned to repair him, he would let them. But healing would take time. With time he could plan.

The latex-gloved hand again explored the wound, searching for debris to remove.

Pierce cried out.

5

SIX MONTHS EARLIER...

D ays became weeks. Weeks extended into a month. His wound healed. As Pierce gained mobility and no longer faced death from infection or a weak constitution, paramilitary soldiers took him from the bungalow and locked him in a cage outside in the jungle camp, forged of strong wooden planks interlaced in a grid on four sides and the roof.

The muddy wooden floorboards crawled with insects. The men manacled his good leg to a chain attached to a post positioned several metres outside his cage. His only possessions were a camp bed, bottled water, and a bucket for his personal needs.

More days passed.

It rained often, and with the latticed wood-framed roof, Pierce was soaked most of the time. When it wasn't raining, the hot sun burned down on him. His only clothes were his cargo pants and an olive-green T-shirt. He changed position often to avoid sunburn.

The camp was a quasi-military establishment, mostly

single-room houses with thatched grass roofs, stores for weapons, including rocket launchers and AK-47 rifles, and tents. Under covered veranda areas, soldiers drank beer and palm wine, played cards, and slapped the bottoms of prostitutes. Armed children were plentiful, young boys slinging real weapons far too large for effective use in their tiny hands. Adult soldiers with better boots than the children wore watched over the youngsters and would occasionally teach lessons on how to fight and kill. At night men and boys played hate rap and heavy bass Afropop through loudspeakers and boom boxes.

The camp languages were French and presumably Sango — the official languages of the Central African Republic — or one of the many local dialects of the Congo Basin. Much of the camp activity centred on the collection and sorting of diamonds sourced from various nearby mines and all of them dug by hand. Sorters and collectors constantly smoked marijuana and popped pills. Soldiers with guns watched over the sorters, while the soldiers had further soldiers with bigger guns watching them. Nobody trusted anybody in this hellhole.

After two weeks in his cage, Pierce witnessed a dispute turn ugly. An older soldier accused a teenager of swallowing a diamond. The soldier proved it by shooting the boy in the head, then cutting open his gut. Pierce had hoped the boy proved to be innocent so as to become a perverse sense of justice from the grave. To Pierce's disappointment, the boy had swallowed a diamond to presumably smuggle it from the camp and make his fortunes further afield.

After that incident, everyone watched everyone else just a little closer.

Other than to bring Pierce scraps of food and water, no

one came close enough to strike up a conversation. Of the two Australian men who had captured him in Europe, there had been no sign.

He tried to escape many times, but with nothing to break the manacle, his efforts always ended before they truly started. Yet despite the futility of his situation, escape was his only thought, and he'd developed many plans for freedom. The major problem with all his schemes was his health, for he'd lost most of his muscle mass during his recovery. With the insufficient food they were feeding him, he wasn't getting stronger, but weaker.

He suspected he was somewhere in the country's south-west because it was the only region of the CAR with tropical forests. A triangle wedged between CAR's international borders with Cameroon, the Congo, and the Democratic Republic of the Congo. One of those nations had to be within thirty kilometres of his position. If he ever discovered a realistic means of escape, it was a distance he could manage, and he would head south.

Four weeks passed, during which he endured a starvation diet. The food was enough to keep him alive, but low on protein, and left him with only enough strength to watch and observe. If he somehow escaped his manacle and cage, and overpowered the guards, and found boots and food and a compass, and then overpowered more guards, he wouldn't have the strength left to run more than a kilometre. He doubted he could even achieve that.

All day and all night, Pierce rarely moved. He let insects crawl on him without bothering to swat them away. Mosquito bites covered his skin.

In those moments when escape no longer occupied his

thoughts, he reflected on why he was here, and why he was being kept alive. His only conclusion was that someone connected to this primitive diamond mining and smuggling operation needed Pierce and his particular set of skills. If it was information in his head they sought, they would have interrogated, tortured, and murdered him already, and his body would have now fed the worms making a home in his shallow jungle grave. He was here because of what he could do for these people at some future time.

One morning, during a particularly misty day in the jungle, Pierce experienced another near-delirious state and didn't at first notice the doctor standing just outside his cage. Like Pierce, the man had lost weight. His limbs were long, gangly sticks, and his clothes were dirty, threadbare, and too big on him. He used rope to hold up his pants.

"Mr Pierce?"

Pierce looked up at the man. "Haven't seen you for a while."

"I've been in a prison of my own."

Pierce shrugged. "My condolences."

"You can be sarcastic, but I'm here to help you."

"Sure you are."

"Men are coming. Today. They will take you away. I do not know their plans for you."

Pierce rattled the chain attached to the manacle around his ankle. The skin was raw and welted where it had rubbed incessantly. "Not much I can do about that."

The doctor crouched low so he could look Pierce in the eyes. "See that hut?" The doctor motioned to a small wooden building with a thatched grass roof.

Pierce nodded.

"Inside is a cardboard box, with a pair of boots and some food."

"That's all?"

"Unfortunately, yes. I'm a prisoner like you. It's taken me weeks to gather that much."

Pierce shrugged. "Yet you are on the outside, looking in at me on the inside."

"Mr Pierce, my name is Derek Kiambi. I'm a doctor, or was a doctor in my home town of Berberati, north of here along the Kadei River. Two months ago, the men who kidnapped you came for me, took me from my wife and children. Said they needed me to fix a man who was dying. That man was you, Mr Pierce."

"I wasn't dying—"

"I don't care about semantics, and you were. Without antibiotics, the infection in your leg would have killed you. Then you got malaria, but luckily that was a mild case. I cared only that if you died, the men would kill my family. That single threat compelled me to save your life. I don't expect thanks. I did it for myself." The doctor reached inside the cage and pretended to test Pierce's pulse rate. "When you recovered, I thought they would release me. They didn't. When they put you in this cage, they put me in a cell too. Admittedly, my cell is better than yours, but it is still a cell." He touched Pierce's forehead, checking his temperature. "The warlord who controls these lands, he's a soldier. His men are always getting shot, burned, cut, drunk..."

"You fix them? You're the warlord's enslaved doctor?"

Tears ran down his cheeks. "I haven't seen my wife and daughters in two months. I don't even know if these soldiers have hurt or raped or killed them. But I can't escape. I don't know how, and I wouldn't get far, but you might. What I know is what kind of man you are. I bribed soldiers for the boots and food in return for medical treatment against the diseases they catch from the prostitutes, but I dared not bribe them for weapons."

"What are you asking, Kiambi? If I somehow escape, you want to come with me?"

The doctor sobbed for a few seconds, then regained his composure. "No. I'm never getting out of here. I want you to promise me, Mr Pierce, that if you can, you'll help my family." He told Pierce the names of his wife and daughters and the address for where they lived in Berberati, a large town in the CAR's southwest that Kiambi believed was close to their location, undisclosed to both of them. His hand reached inside, pretending to check Pierce's ears and throat while passing over a metal file, which Pierce quickly concealed under his shirt. "Can you promise me that?"

Pierce held Dr Kiambi's stare and, realising this was the best chance he had of escape, said, "Whatever I can do, Doctor, I will do. I promise."

Wiping tears from his eyes, the doctor stood. He'd noticed soldiers approaching with AK-47 assault rifles, interested in what Pierce and Kiambi might be doing.

"The men coming to take you will be here soon. Good luck. Hopefully you will be long gone before they arrive."

"Australian men?"

Kiambi nodded.

"How long have I got?"

"Hours. Maybe less." Kiambi turned to the soldiers standing behind him now. He spoke in French, which, with Pierce's minimal knowledge of the language, he interpreted as the doctor saying, "I've checked the prisoner. He's healthy. Weak, but healthy."

That seemed to be the response the soldiers expected.

As the three men walked away from the cage, Pierce got to work with the metal file.

6

Pierce had no means of assessing whether this was an elaborate scheme orchestrated by his captors to test him, or if the doctor was genuine, but Pierce knew this was his best opportunity to escape since his incarceration. He had nothing to lose by trying.

The steps were simple. One, detach the manacle. Two, break the lock. Three, reach the hut and secure the food and boots. Four, find a weapon and flee into the jungle. From there he'd just keep going until he reached a town in another neighbouring nation.

The file proved sturdy enough. He tested it on the chain, finding its hardness was greater than the links, so it cut. Because Pierce could no longer bear the manacle grazing his ankle, he worked on the pinning bolt. While he sawed, he often watched the men patrolling the camp, but no one was interested in or suspected him of anything but suffering in silence.

It took him more than an hour to weaken the pin enough that it popped out. With his leg free, he rubbed the rawness and welts around his ankle and grinned. He had accomplished the first step of his plan.

But the work was exhausting. Before Pierce felt able to begin with step two, he drank the last of his water rations and rested. He wanted nothing more than to flee now that escape was a real possibility, but he was weak. His muscles had atrophied. The food rations provided barely enough energy to get through a day of inactivity, let alone prolonged physical activity.

Pierce closed his eyes for a few minutes, just to rest...

When he opened them again, the sun was close to the horizon.

The fool that he was, he must have slept for hours, even knowing that the Aussies were coming for him.

Willing himself to move, he worked the file on the wood around the bolt securing the cage door. This proved faster than working the lock itself, and within ten minutes he'd disengaged the mechanism.

Step two.

Pierce stood to test his strength.

His hands and legs shook, but considering the conditions he'd endured since his capture, he had expected this. Pierce told himself if he reached the food, he'd regain strength, and his shakes would vanish.

The hut was about thirty metres distant on the edge of the low-lying mist that often appeared in the camp at random times. His first thought was to sprint there, but no one in the camp paid him any attention. Most soldiers played cards. Girls danced in skimpy outfits. Child soldiers rediscovering their lost innocence competed in a game of chase in the mud. Pierce unlatched the door and walked into the hut with purpose. No one saw him as being any different to anyone else in the camp. No one stopped him.

Once inside the hut, he discovered its interior was damp, dark, and smelled of mould. A storeroom, it contained old blankets, shovels, picks, bags of cement and handyman tools such as nails, saws, wrenches, and hammers. The cardboard box was where Kiambi said it would be. Inside was a pair of worn but sturdy boots, which Pierce laced to his cut and welted feet. He pocketed a screwdriver and a hammer as a weapon. Then he devoured the cold stew of rice and what was probably goat meat.

No food had ever tasted this good to him.

He felt his strength return. His spirits lifted.

Step three complete.

Pierce considered that securing a firearm was an optional step for his long-term survival, but his priority in the immediate moment was to flee, and securing a weapon would expend energy he didn't have. So he snuck a look through the hut door to assess his situation. He saw nothing out of the ordinary, but in the distance, he heard cars approaching.

Vehicles were a rarity in this outpost.

Pierce stepped out and walked with purpose. When he passed a clothesline with drying quasi-military uniforms, he snatched a mottle green camouflage shirt and an olive-green cap, which he donned.

The car noises grew louder.

"Hey! You!" someone shouted in French.

Pierce kept walking.

He heard a slide being pulled back on a weapon. He'd been identified already.

Pierce halted and put his hands to his head.

"Turn around."

Pierce obeyed.

He faced a boy, only ten, pointing an old Browning Hi-Power 9mm pistol at Pierce. A bandolier of bullets over one shoulder weighed him down, and his gumboots were several sizes too big for his feet. The boy did a commendable job of projecting a tough, aggressive exterior, but he couldn't completely mask his fear. The trembles in his facial muscles and shoulders gave it away.

"What happened to you?" Pierce asked, but he had already guessed the boy's story. Adult quasi-soldiers would have taken him from his family, brought him here and terrorised him, trained him as a soldier and forced him to kill prisoners tied to posts on a firing line. Far too much trauma for an adult to endure, let alone a child. "Are your parents alive?"

"Shut your mouth!"

Pierce noticed the boy hadn't called for help, so he said in a low voice, "Come with me. I'll get you out of here."

The boy gritted his teeth and lifted the weapon. His thin arms could barely hold it steady. "No!"

Pierce took several steps forward, knowing the longer this situation stretched out, the greater the chances someone would see him.

"I can get you to your parents—"

"NO!"

"What's going on?"

An adult soldier appeared from the mist and approached. The boy turned his attention away for a moment, so Pierce took his chance. The boy was close. He snatched the Browning from the tiny hands and in a prac-tised, fluid motion, flipped the weapon around so it pointed towards the adult soldier. With the safety already off, Pierce squeezed the trigger, peppering the soldier with three bullets. The noise was loud in Pierce's ears, and man was dead and drenched in blood before he splashed face down in the brown, watery mud.

But it was the recoil that surprised Pierce, which knocked him back on his feet. He recognised how heavy the weapon felt and how much of himself he had lost since his capture in Italy.

Then Pierce heard a commotion where the men were playing cards and eyeing prostitutes.

"Come with me." Pierce spoke to the boy.

The child swore and ran back to the soldiers.

Several adult soldiers with their military assault rifles raced at Pierce.

He returned fire. Three men fell, but so did Pierce, as the recoil knocked him to the muddy ground this time.

With the magazine empty, Pierce dropped the Browning pistol and scrambled to his feet. His breath was out of control. His shakes intensified. Pierce could barely stand and run, but he did.

The cars he'd heard earlier appeared. Two Land Rovers churned up the mud ahead of him and came to a stop. The two Australian soldiers who had captured him in Italy stepped from the cabin, again with their concealing ski masks, but this time armed with 7.62mm FN-FAL assault rifles. If Pierce kept running, they would cut him down before he made his first step. He halted and raised his empty hands in surrender.

The masked man with red hair showing at the back of his head rushed Pierce and jabbed Pierce hard in the gut with the stock of his rifle.

More from surprise at how weak he was than from the

pain, Pierce dropped to the mud and doubled over, gasping for breath.

The second masked man cuffed him and dragged him to his feet.

The first Aussie captor said, "Pierce, I know you're thinking your situation can't get any worse. Believe me, it can, and it will."

"Why?" Pierce asked.

The man didn't answer. As they both led Pierce to the first Land Rover, the slimmer soldier opened the back door. The red-headed soldier whacked him across the back of the head. Pierce tried to fight the signals firing in his mind, but lost consciousness and fell into darkness.

7

FIVE MONTHS EARLIER…

Over the next month, incarceration, starvation and boredom turned into a hell far worse than anything Pierce had ever experienced in his life.

Pierce's new prison was a dark wooden cell lit by a single overhead lightbulb, and it was the only light he had known for weeks. Today, he sat emaciated and naked on a metal chair with his hands and feet bound. The two black-clad Aussies who still controlled him wore their full-face ski masks. The red-headed masked man, whom Pierce had nicknamed "Jackman", held electric cables connected to a battery used in heavy construction equipment. The second slimmer and dark-haired Aussie, whom he'd nicknamed "Hemsworth", stood close to Pierce near an empty chair he could sit in when he occasionally needed to rest his weary legs, and was the man in charge who asked all the questions.

In this momentary lull between electric shocks in today's torture session, Pierce realised he had grown used to the scents of sweat, mould and humidity that seemed to ooze from the wooden walls and roof of his cell, but the lingering heat that hung like a stagnant fog was always unbearable. There never seemed to be enough oxygen to breathe, and the stale air always drained him of his energy even before the physical pain sessions had begun for the day.

"Jackman" placed a wooden guard in Pierce's mouth, then prodded him with the electric cables. Pierce tensed and shook with seizures for many seconds. The mouth guard protected him from biting off his own tongue, which would have been counterproductive to their needs. The pain surging through him felt as if his muscles were cooking from the inside out.

When the cables were disconnected from his bare chest, many seconds or perhaps even a minute later, Pierce slumped into his chair and feigned unconsciousness. With his eyes closed, he sensed his body glistening with sweat, but it barely cooled him. Bruises and cuts ached on his face and arms from an earlier beating, and it was difficult not to flinch at how uncomfortable they were, but he tried because he wanted this day to end. He would have given anything in that moment for a cup of water to drink.

The Aussie who always asked the questions waved smelling salts under Pierce's nose, which caused him to jolt and reveal his pathetic attempt at feigned unconsciousness. "Come on, Pierce," "Hemsworth" said with laboured breath. "You're not cooperating. You know this won't end until you tell us what we need to know."

Pierce panted. His burning eyes felt vacant and couldn't properly focus on anything. Spit dribbled from his mouth. If he told them what they wanted, they might stop. But when he told them everything they needed to know, they might kill him outright too.

"We've drained three of your secret bank accounts

already. We've stolen two of your false, CIA-manufactured identities, and we know you have more of each. All we need today is one further account number and password, or ID, and this all stops."

Pierce nodded. He tried to speak, but with his parched throat, no words came forth from his mouth. Involuntarily, his bloodshot eyes motioned to the water bottle next to the laptop that "Hemsworth" occasionally tapped away on, to test each bank account and password that Pierce reluctantly provided on those days when he had no will left in him to resist their pain sessions.

"You thirsty?"

Pierce nodded again.

"You can drink when you give me an account number."

"Hemsworth" sighed theatrically, an often-used expression for his frustration with Pierce.

Then the only door to this room sprang open, and Pierce's old boss at the Central Intelligence Agency, Idris Walsh, entered the torture room.

Unlike "Jackman" and "Hemsworth", Walsh made no pretence by hiding his identity. Pierce already knew the spymaster had betrayed Pierce two months earlier and was behind his kidnapping and imprisonment. Walsh's deception had involved framing Pierce for the theft of eleven million in CIA funds during an operation in North Africa, which had forced Pierce to go on the run across Morocco, Spain and Italy, both from his own people and Walsh's mercenaries. It had been "Jackman" and "Hemsworth" from the latter group who had tracked Pierce in Siena, had then cornered and drugged him, and brought him to this awful warlord camp in the African jungles, where he had been tortured incessantly ever since. Pierce only knew that they wanted access to his bank accounts and his many CIA-forged legends, because they asked him for nothing else.

After a minute passed enduring Pierce's unresponsiveness, Walsh grabbed the water bottle next to the laptop that was always just out of Pierce's reach and sat close to him on the empty chair normally reserved for "Hemsworth". They locked eyes for a moment, like high-stakes poker players looking for a tell. Then Walsh lifted the water bottle to Pierce's lips and let him drink. For a few seconds, Pierce felt a modicum of relief.

Walsh took tablets from his pocket and popped two in his mouth before washing them down with a drink of his own. "No one is coming for you, Pierce."

His throat no longer like sandpaper, Pierce laughed as he struggled against the handcuffs securing him to the chair. "Well, I have you to thank for that little fact, Idris Walsh."

Walsh leaned in and whispered, "You think this is personal? It was never personal. Sure, it was about vengeance. But not against you, Pierce. I learned long ago that vengeance, retribution, revenge, whatever you want to call it, is a hollow motivation. You torture and murder the people who wronged you, but when you're done, what do you have to show for it? Nothing. Revenge is pointless without progress." Walsh offered Pierce more water, which the prisoner drank in large gulps. "Vengeance should not be personal. It should be a tool for achieving power. I'm surgical in how I use retribution, for it is sweeter when the parties that wronged me suffer while I make a gain."

Liquid dribbled from Pierce's mouth, and when he tasted its saltiness, he realised the water he'd been drinking had mixed with his own blood. Pierce laughed again, and it sounded pathetic. "Okay, I'll bite. If it wasn't me, who wronged you, Walsh?"

Idris Walsh rubbed his chin and stared at Pierce's naked, bruised, cut and bound body. "Perhaps I should tell you a little about myself, Pierce, for context. That way you might understand why I am here. And why you are here. And why you need to answer my men's questions." The late-middle-aged spymaster's eyes motioned to the two masked interrogators, who now stood in the cell's dark, dank corners, waiting patiently and to attention until they were summoned into action again.

Pierce looked only at Walsh. "I guess a space just opened in my schedule."

Walsh laughed. "Even now, you have a sense of humour. You are like my sister when I'm trying to help her with business decisions. She thinks my help is a joke."

Pierce chuckled. "Is your sister even real?"

Walsh grinned, then massaged his greying goatee with his thin fingers. "You'll never know. But where to start with my story? I know, it begins in the eighties. I joined the CIA straight out of college after majoring in Eastern European politics and mastering my fluency in Russian and German. I was the perfect Cold War rookie operative. Nothing could go wrong, I thought. But I was very wrong. The Berlin Wall fell. And suddenly my skills weren't so useful for the CIA. In their wisdom, my superiors sent me to Central America, where for years I lived in jungle hellholes fighting communists and narco-traffickers. They didn't even care that I couldn't speak Spanish, but I learned to in time, mind you. It should not have surprised me when the CIA ordered me to smuggle drugs from Nicaragua into America, to fund covert Middle Eastern operations of the era. I performed my duties without question. But you know what? That cost me, because suddenly, with the Iran-Contra affair exposed and the morality of the CIA under public scrutiny, the fiasco tainted me too. I only kept my position with the Company because I was young."

"Has this story got a point? Because I'm thinking I'd prefer the electrocutions."

"You jest. That means my men haven't broken you, yet." Walsh wiped his sweating head with a handkerchief. "But I digress. My story is interesting. Despite not losing my job, the Iran-Contra deal still tainted me, so my superiors left me in Central America with nothing interesting to do, waiting for me to quit. I was too proud to resign and stayed in Central America for two fucking long decades in that point-less hellhole, and my career quickly stagnated as a result."

Pierce snorted coagulated blood from his nostrils. "Am I supposed to feel sorry for you?"

"No, Pierce. I don't expect you to feel any more pity for me than I do for you. That isn't the point, as I'm trying to explain."

"The point?"

"That I do feel the need for retribution. It is human nature to want revenge against those who hurt you. We deny our own emotional well-being when we ignore the base desires of retribution. But I don't feel any need to make you suffer, other than to meet my ends, because it wasn't you who ruined my career. I should have been deputy director of Operations by now, the most powerful non-political position one can achieve in our organisation. It took me a while to realise that would never happen, because the CIA fucked me over with the wrong career assignment. So, I decided, when I was ready all those decades later, when I was finally being recognised again for the skills I now possessed, I'd make my own fortune. My own covert retribution, and you just happened to be the unlucky pawn I required for my plan to succeed."

Pierce struggled against his bindings, but his limbs carried little muscle, and his depleted constitution soon forced him to abandon his efforts. He slumped to catch his breath. Then he motioned to Walsh for more water. The spymaster obliged and allowed Pierce to drink the entire contents.

Pierce said, "You sure this isn't personal, Walsh? I shot you in Morocco. I shot you so well, I'd presumed you'd bleed out and die. My mistake, and one I won't make again. But look at you now. You are like how you've made me, thin and haggard and weak. You've lost ten years. Your movements are stiff, and I'm guessing by your constant, glum expression, you endure constant pain. Those tablets you took earlier. Is that for the pain? So perhaps I just think your story is bullshit. You hate me for everything that I took away from you. I would understand that rather than this shit you are trying to feed me."

Walsh smiled, though the rest of his face remained cold and expressionless. "Yes, it's true, Pierce. You shot me through the liver. I spent weeks in hospital recovering, but not before needing a liver transplant. Now I'll spend the rest of my life on anti-rejection medication — that was what I took just then — which increases my risk of catching other diseases and infections. The doctors told me my life expectancy was likely reduced. So yes, you have cost me."

Pierce flinched, unable to ignore the itching burns spread across his scarred body from his earlier electrocutions and beatings. "Good!"

Walsh snorted. "But I survived, Pierce, and during my recovery, I remembered again that the purpose of all this is not to make you suffer, but for me to become stupidly rich. I want to live my remaining days on a yacht, sailing the Mediterranean and enjoying beautiful sunsets, gorgeous women at my side, and elegant cuisines. But to do that, I need to disappear and ensure the CIA never come after me. The easiest way to achieve that is to frame you as the villain."

Pierce chuckled with a raspy voice. "So that's why you've got 'Hemsworth' here torturing me—"

"Yes. I have a plan. But you have to be complicit in that plan."

Pierce wished to pass out so he could get some relief from the pain and discomforts he suffered, but they had not tortured him enough for him to reach that point yet. "You want my bank accounts so you can spend the money in various locations across the globe. Make it look like I'm still out there, causing havoc like the good rogue operative you want me to be. A ghost for the CIA to hunt while you get on with your own plans, using those eleven million dollars that you actually stole. I know why. You're afraid of the CIA figuring out that you are the real traitor here, and that when they learn the truth, they'll come after you. I don't know what you are up to, but whatever it is, I can see that it is far more traitorous than anything I can imagine you doing, and if you and your Aussie mates fuck it up, the CIA will be on your asses so fast you'll never shit again. I can see that you are scared, Walsh, and I'm glad."

Walsh's eyes darkened as he frowned, and Pierce saw that he had guessed right.

"You'll fuck up eventually, Walsh, and then when the CIA come after you, you'll be as dead as I am."

Walsh licked his lips, then nodded. "You're probably right, but you'll be inside a forgotten grave much sooner than I ever will."

Pierce said, "I'm guessing you're still with the CIA? That they haven't yet worked out what a sociopathic, traitorous asshole you are yet?"

Walsh nodded. "Ironic, really, that I am, while you suffer here unnecessarily for such a minor thing that we need from you." He glanced at "Jackman" and "Hemsworth" and, turning his finger in a circle in the air, said, "I'm not getting through to our guest. I'll leave it to you both and your proven methods."

The Aussies forced the wooden guard back into Pierce's mouth.

Then the electric shocks started up again, and he wished only to be non-existent, because nothing was the only place he knew of where pain couldn't exist.

8

PRESENT DAY...

Aktobe Region, Kazakhstan

After following the track leading out of the Aral Sea, Pierce discovered a gravel road and drove west. The recurring memories of his torture and incarceration in the Central African Republic had upset him, so he pushed them from his mind and focused on the present situation, where he finally had the chance to be free again. The Lada had a full tank of gas, so he had no intention of stopping until he put significant distance between him and Irina and the four dead Kazakh criminals.

The drive featured long periods in featureless, flat landscapes. Grass was abundant, and trees were rare.

With nothing to occupy his mind, Pierce's often returned to the same thought: after so long imprisoned in a filthy jungle camp, he was free. His mind had trouble accepting this fact, that his escape was real.

The question remained, however, had Pierce escaped on his own merit, or was his release part of a larger conspiracy planned by Idris Walsh and his two Australian henchmen? If the latter, then was it to frame him for a heinous crime here in Kazakhstan? Until he figured out why, his only option was to create as much distance as possible between himself and the former Soviet State.

At a truck stop on the outskirts of a small town, Pierce noticed a parked Skoda sedan. He turned the corner and parked the Lada in a narrow street out of sight. As he engaged the handbrake, he turned to Irina and said, "We're changing cars."

She shrugged. "Whatever you say."

After wiping down the Lada to remove fingerprints, Pierce and Irina walked a hundred metres back to the truck stop. Although Irina moved slower than he would have liked, she had accepted his tradecraft antics without question.

Pierce realised her demeanour was boredom rather than fear. During much of their earlier drive, she had focused on fixing her hair. She'd asked him if he had found her make-up bag, and he'd laughed. She hadn't laughed with him.

At the Skoda, Pierce picked the lock and hot-wired its ignition in under thirty seconds, and they were on the road again.

As before, the roads were mostly empty, and what traffic there was consisted of trucks traversing the Silk Road, a famous trade route dating back to antiquity that linked Asia with Europe and still remained operational today.

"You from Kazakhstan?" he asked.

"No."

"Russia?"

"Yes."

"Which part?"

"Why so many questions?"

Pierce shrugged. He didn't have a handle on Irina, and this bothered him. He also didn't understand why Sanzhar and his criminal gang had brought her to Pierce's execution. There was a real possibility she was a Russian, American or Chinese spy also scheduled to be executed after Pierce. Or she was exactly who she claimed to be, and had become embroiled in a dangerous situation not of her making.

"Irina, those men who kidnapped you today, they took you to the middle of nowhere to rape and murder you. Most people would be a nervous wreck if that happened."

"A 'nervous wreck'? What does that mean?"

Conversing in Russian, Pierce realised he had not translated the English expression well. "I thought you would be more nervous? Distraught? Scared?"

Irina laughed. "My life is not 'sunshine and rainbows'," she said, using the English expression. "I'm a prostitute. I've sat naked on the laps of Russian mafia bosses at their private parties, watched while they've tortured and murdered their enemies. Men have beaten me during sex or humiliated me for their pleasure. I once had to screw a Russian mafia hitman while his victim bled out in the same room. What I saw today, Mr Viktor, it was nothing!"

Pierce nodded and kept silent and wondered if that was how she had obtained the scar on her hip. His life had been difficult and not without trauma, but he'd been privileged compared to her. While Irina's explanation could be an elaborate ruse, her contained rage suggested that she told the truth.

Soon they drove through one of Kazakhstan's many oil and gas fields. Flat and dusty lands with thousands of onshore derricks and electric power lines. Automated pumps continuously drew the black gold from deep underground, then pumped it through oil and gas supply pipelines that would ultimately link up to major transnational pipelines destined for Europe, Russia, and China. The scene was a wasteland, and Pierce identified many areas where oil had spilled from ruptured pipelines and broken pumps, contaminating the soil. Maintenance crews operated here and there, not to clean spills but to ensure the pumps functioned as designed. He noticed separate security teams armed with assault rifles and sub-machine guns. So as long as Pierce kept their Skoda on the transit road dissecting the fields, the guards would leave them alone.

"Irina, where do you want me to take you?"

"Oh, so you are being civil with me now?"

Pierce shook his head.

"'Civil'? Did I use the correct word?"

"Yes."

Since switching cars, Irina had spent most of her time staring out the window and had said little. Now she turned to Pierce and looked at him suspiciously. "Why do you want to know where I live?"

"I don't want to know where you live, just where you want to go." Every muscle in Pierce's body ached from tension. He couldn't get the thoughts from his mind on how he would hunt down and murder Walsh. "I'm driving to Aktau. From there I'll cross the Caspian Sea to Baku." He didn't say this was his escape plan to get out of Kazakhstan, and to find contacts who could get him out of Central Asia altogether. "I'm not sure if I'm taking you closer or further from where you want to be."

She shrugged. "I don't really have a home. I go where the work is." When Pierce didn't answer, she said, "Baku is fine, but how do you intend on getting us across international borders with the Kazakh authorities pursuing us?"

"Why do you think we are being pursued?"

"Because you killed four men. I thought it was obvious?"

"Nobody saw us. We were in the middle of nowhere."

"This is Kazakhstan. The secret police are everywhere. They will find the bodies sooner than you expect, and work out it was us."

Pierce shrugged, but he didn't disagree with her. "That is why I'll get us to Baku, quickly."

Although he couldn't determine if she was a spy or a prostitute, he sensed Irina wished to escape Kazakhstan as much as he did. Despite her brave, dispassionate exterior, Pierce sensed her kidnapping and bearing witness to the aftermath of a quadruple murder had rattled her. If the Kazakh authorities caught them as she suggested...

He didn't want to think about that. Kazakhstan was a nation known for its poor human rights record and corrupt legal system. If caught, the local authorities would incarcerate, torture, and then execute them in the space of a few days, a week at most. Better to run and start afresh somewhere new.

He noticed how tightly his fists gripped the steering wheel, and how his jaw hurt from clenching his teeth. He kept imagining Idris Walsh and the two Australians as corpses, and a smoking gun in his hand short of three bullets.

She turned to him. "Why are you helping me, Viktor? Are you my new pimp?"

"No!" he answered through gritted teeth.

"You don't want to sleep with me even though I saw how much you enjoyed looking at my naked body. You don't want to control me either, hiring me out so other men can enjoy my naked flesh. Do you want to sell me off?"

Irina kept saying the word "naked", and each time her use of the word felt erotic. Was she deliberately manipulating him to lower his guard around her?

"No!"

"Then why are you helping me?"

Pierce shrugged. "It's the right thing to do."

This response seemed to startle her; then her expression became a mask again. "You must want something?"

"Safety," he said, letting out a long breath. "Mine. Yours. Even if it is only temporary. I need time to recuperate, think and recover."

"Recover from what? Are you physically wounded?"

"No!"

"Then what do you mean?"

He didn't answer her. He couldn't relax his tense body and was in no mood to explain to her his distraught state of mind. The only thought on his mind was murder.

She crossed her arms and slunk into the passenger seat. "You are a strange man."

9

For a time, Pierce and Irina again drove in silence. The landscape transformed from grasslands into arid semi-desert. Mountainous ranges appeared on the horizon. Soon they passed through another expansive oil field with its hundreds of pumps and drilling towers.

"Irina," Pierce said, ending the silence, "if I get us to Baku, what will you do from there?"

Irina shrugged. "I don't know. What else is there to do?"

Pierce felt sympathy for her plight. He sensed Irina was an intelligent woman, with an attractive face and body, but uneducated and forced into prostitution because life had offered her no other choice. Under different circumstances, the world might have treated her as she deserved. He felt compelled to help her, but in his current predicament, he was not sure what he could do or if she would even accept his help.

A police car overtook them.

A minute later, a second police car followed the first. It slowed long enough for the officers inside to get a good look at Pierce and Irina. Then the driver accelerated and raced ahead of their Skoda.

Pierce counted four men in each vehicle, all wearing blue uniforms and American-style police caps with red bands. At least two officers held Beretta ARX160 modular assault rifles, serious weapons for deadly gun battles. There was no doubt in Pierce's mind the second car had gotten a good look at him.

Irina's eyes widened and she sat up straight. "What's going on?"

Pierce braked and pivoted, drove off the road and into the new oil field with its hundreds of pumps and power lines. A maze of rusted but functional technology in a lifeless land.

He glanced backwards through his side window. The police cars had slowed, performed U-turns and were now coming after them, churning up a dust cloud behind them.

"How did they find us?"

"That's a good question, Irina." He didn't want to say but suspected the Australians "Hemsworth" and "Jackman", or Idris Walsh, had tipped off the Kazakh police to their whereabouts. Why incarcerate Pierce for seven months only to help him recover his strength before releasing him in a country in a far-off continent? Only a single answer made sense. Whoever sent him here did so to frame him as a murderer and a terrorist, distracting the local authorities while his enemies performed an even more heinous crime somewhere else inside Kazakhstan. The Kazakh mafia were like Pierce and Irina, unimportant pawns in a bigger game Pierce could not comprehend... yet. But now that Pierce had made his escape, they still needed Pierce out of the picture because corpses don't talk like living bodies do, and the local police could be bribed into executing Pierce and Irina if the price was right.

He drew the Makarov pistol he'd tucked into the back of his trousers, so it was within easy reach. Not an ideal weapon against police armed with assault rifles, but better than nothing. He wished he had kept the three other pistols, but not trusting Irina, it would have been inadvisable for her to find one and use it against him. He'd kept the spare magazines, so he had plenty of bullets.

He glanced at his companion. Irina's eyes were wide and focused behind them at the advancing cars. "If they catch us, they'll kill us!"

Pierce nodded and pressed his foot down on the accelerator. The pursuing police cars with more powerful engines soon gained on Pierce and Irina. Dust and spilled oil sprayed behind them as their respective cars sped on.

The oil fields hadn't helped Pierce gain distance from the police because the landscape was open and flat ground despite the hundreds of derricks and pumps as obstacles in their path. But oil fields carried different risks Pierce could exploit. Dirty puddles of water and hydrocarbons lay everywhere, as did high-pressure pipes, pumps, and fuel storage vessels. A firefight here would invite flames and destruction, or produce a firebomb of devastating capacity. For the first time, Pierce was thankful for environmental pollution.

The two police cars closed the gap. Sirens sounded, and lights flashed. Officers leaned out of windows and aimed their ARX160 assault rifles in the Skoda's general direction. They hadn't fired yet, and Pierce hoped it was because of the hydrocarbons.

Irina gripped the dashboard and clenched her teeth, but otherwise kept her cool. "What's the plan?"

Pierce saw an oil slick and showed her the Makarov. "Once we're through..."

"You are crazy! The entire field could ignite!"

"Not the entire field, but enough of it."

Pierce aimed for the slick and sped through the oily sludge. The Skoda lost traction, forcing the car to glide through the hydrocarbons, but Pierce expected this. Once on the other side, Pierce applied the brakes and slid through a mud puddle, mixing any remaining oil on the tyres with non-flammable liquids. He then turned the Skoda so it skidded to a stop with the driver's side — his side — facing the slick.

He fired three rapid shots from his Makarov.

The field ignited and soon became a roaring wall of heat and flames.

Pierce floored the accelerator, shifted gears, and sped the Skoda onwards. He'd heard stories about how easily oil spills could ignite in the poorly maintained fields of Azerbaijan, and his hunch had paid off.

Meanwhile, seen through the rear-view mirror, the first police car failed to slow, raced through the thick fire and hit a derrick. Officers screamed as they leaped from their burning vehicle. They rolled in the dust until the few fires burning their uniforms extinguished. None seemed to have suffered serious injuries.

The second police car, avoiding the wall of flame, soon found a path around the burning slick.

Pierce increased their speed while avoiding derricks in their path ahead.

Behind them, the out-of-control flames soon consumed a fuel pump. As the oil inside ignited, the sudden explosion that ripped fifty metres upwards into the sky provided further cover.

"Fuck!" Irina tensed as she gripped the dashboard and looked back. "The other police car is gaining. You'll destroy something else to stop them too?"

Unsure whether she was serious or being sarcastic, Pierce didn't answer. He concentrated on the new road ahead that led them out of the oil fields and into rising foothills.

The dusty, desert landscape ahead featured low mountainous peaks. The road passed between peaks of the low-lying mountains, which meant windy and elevated driving conditions. Skill would be more important than speed.

"You can't shoot and drive at the same time."

"You ever killed a man?" he asked. She looked away, and he guessed that she hadn't. "It's more difficult than you might imagine." With the pistol back on his lap, Pierce switched through the gears as the Skoda traversed up through the mountains.

With its more powerful engine, the second police car gained on them. The officers in the back leaned out and fired their ARX160 assault rifles.

Pierce turned a tight corner in a rapid but controlled spin, burning tyre tracks in the compact earthen track.

The officers fired again. With their speed and erratic turns, they couldn't get a bead on Pierce and Irina.

"Keep your head down."

She ducked as instructed.

Pierce turned a sharp corner, placing them out of sight from their pursuers, then slammed on the brake. He was out of the car in seconds as the police car turned the corner.

The officers weren't expecting him to have stopped, so they braked and skidded to a halt.

Pierce shot out the front tyres. The driver, seeing Pierce aiming his weapon at him, accelerated again, but unable to control the police car with wrecked wheels, rammed into a rocky embankment. Assault rifles flew from the officers' hands. Steam gushed from the radiator. The driver touched his head where it now dribbled blood.

Pierce raced closer and grabbed the closest ARX160, then advanced on the officers.

Dazed and concussed, the men raised their hands in surrender.

"Throw down your guns!" he commanded in Russian.

They did as he instructed. Their pay wasn't sufficient to risk death attempting to capture or kill him, not when he held the advantage.

Pierce lost control of his mind. Rage consumed him. He almost squeezed the trigger, peppered the men with bullets, and ended their lives. They would have killed him if the circumstances were reversed, so the morality of the situation placed him in the clear.

Then the fog cleared, and Pierce could focus his thinking again.

He didn't need to kill them. They weren't his enemy.

"Get out of the vehicle, and run."

Surprised at his sudden compassion, the officers scrambled from the wrecked police car.

"Keep running," Pierce yelled again as they took off down the road they had just driven up.

When the officers were a few hundred metres distant, Pierce checked the police car.

Irina was well ahead of him and had already found the wanted poster with his prominent photograph. She held it high for Pierce to see. "It says you are an American terrorist, wanted for procuring and trading in nuclear materials."

Pierce stopped dead in his tracks. Not at all what he was expecting.

"It says your name is Mark Pierce?"

He nodded. There was no point pretending otherwise. "Yes, that's me. But the rest, it's a lie." He held out his hand for the wanted poster, and she passed it over. The first aspect that struck Pierce was that the ink was fresh, as if it had been printed in the last few hours, suggesting it had been issued not long after Pierce and Irina had driven out of the Aral Sea. Pierce read it quickly, for the same information had been presented twice, once in Russian, and once in Kazakh.

"What are you looking for, Mark Pierce?" she asked.

He pointed to the fine print at the bottom of the page. "The officer who issued this order is one Colonel Mikail Drossanov, of the Ground Forces of the Republic of Kazakhstan."

"How does that help us?"

"The order was issued in the town of Beyneu, less than one hundred klicks west from here, which we planned to pass through anyway. The instructions are to bring me, alive or dead, to Drossanov in this location. I should have a chat."

"Are you insane? Why would you want to go to this colonel when he wants you killed?"

"Because of this," Pierce said as he pointed to further fine print on the document. "This initialisation here, KATEP, next to Drossanov's name, it means Kazakhstan State Corporation for Atomic Power and Industry. He's connected."

Irina folded her arms together and shook her head. "I still don't understand. It all sounds like utter madness to me."

"Because if I'm wanted for nuclear terrorism, this man Drossanov will know who set me up and why."

"But you *are* a nuclear terrorist. That's what it says."

Pierce shook his head and tried not to express his frustration. "I'm not. Trust me on this. And Drossanov will prove it, even if he doesn't want to."

"How will you make him prove it, and not get caught in the process?"

Pierce suppressed a grin, finally feeling a modicum of power back in his life again. "Don't worry about how. I have skills he won't be expecting."

10

Beyneu, Kazakhstan

Pierce and Irina drove through the rest of the afternoon and into the early evening before they arrived at the outskirts of Beyneu, an unimposing drab town built on a flat expanse of the desert that expanded across most of this part of Kazakhstan. Buildings were utilitarian with washed-out yellow walls and blue roofs, while most surfaces, including the roads, were compacted sand awash with dirty puddles. The only trees were leafless, stark, and resembled inverted witches' broomsticks, but were everywhere, as were chaotically designed power lines. A few citizens wandered the streets in caps and dark jackets, and none of them expressed any emotion on their faces.

"Charming place," said Irina. "What's the plan now?"

"I'm working on it," Pierce said as he drove them through several streets that all looked the same as each other, until they came across a two-storey hotel near the town's railway station, painted a sky blue with an octagonal front section. Outside were parked two Humvee armoured cars with Kazakhstan insignia and three soldiers, illuminated under a lit streetlight, standing guard next to them but also chatting rather than observing, and drinking from half-empty bottles of vodka. Pierce didn't slow and kept driving for another hundred metres, turned a corner so they were out of sight, parked and killed the engine of the Skoda. "Did you see all that?"

Irina shrugged. "A hotel, with military vehicles out front. You are crazy if you think I'm spending the night there. The colonel will be there for sure."

"I'm counting on it," said Pierce. "But we're not staying long enough to need a room."

"That was an American joke, about sex?"

Pierce shook his head. "Anything but."

It was dark out, and the first stars had filled the sky. With the engine stopped, the outside chill seeped in. He turned to Irina and wondered again if she was a spy or merely what she said she was, a prostitute caught up in a dangerous situation not of her making. What he planned to do next would either benefit them both, would put both of them in danger or — if she were a spy for the people acting against him — would give her great advantage in bringing him down. No choices were good, but Pierce figured it was better to gain intel than to run blind.

"Why are you looking at me like that?"

"I need to leave you here, alone. But only for a few hours at most. You okay with that?"

Her eyes grew wide as her back stiffened. "What? Why? This is a dangerous place for us to be in."

Pierce nodded. He sensed her fear, but was it genuine? He didn't wish to leave her alone for any length of time, in case she was a spy and would call in their location given the opportunity, but he felt he had no choice. They had no means of communication or weapons in the vehicle she could easily access while he was gone. "I agree, we are in danger here. But I need intel, and it's in that hotel. Without it, our situation is far more precarious."

She crossed her arms as all the muscles in her face tensed. "What am I supposed to do while you're gone? What if they find me?"

Pierce searched the back of their Skoda, where he had earlier found a blanket during the switch with the Lada. There were plenty of cars in the street, and theirs didn't look any different to any of the others. "Hide under this and wait until I return."

"And what if you don't come back?"

Pierce paused and sat motionless for a moment. There was a real possibility he might get killed or captured in the coming hours, which left Irina in a vulnerable position. He was reluctant to leave her their cash, which would help her to escape if he were compromised, but would also allow her to easily return to her superiors if she were acting against him.

"Don't you trust me, Mark Pierce?"

"Just Mark is fine."

"You don't trust me, Mark?"

"No!" he said without hesitation.

Irina shrugged. "I wouldn't trust me either, in your position." She grabbed the blanket off Pierce and snuggled under it. "I'll wait here. Two hours. If you are not back by then, I'm driving off."

"Fine. Keep your head under the blanket while I'm gone. You'll more resemble luggage than a person by doing so, should anyone peer inside."

She nodded. "They want me dead too, Mark. And so far, and as much as I hate to admit it, you are my best chance of getting out of this alive."

Pierce nodded. "Thank you, Irina, for saying that."

"You really need this intel?"

"I do."

"Then be quick about it."

He nodded again, then stepped out of the car and walked into the night back down the puddled road to the hotel, where the soldiers drank and talked.

As Pierce slinked closer, he kept out of the beams of the streetlights and watched the men from the opposite side of the road. Inevitably, one of them needed to pee, and wandered off into the darkness to do so. Pierce took his chance, snuck up behind the soldier and forced him into a chokehold and, with the blood no longer reaching his brain, rendered him unconscious in ten seconds.

Dragging the body further into the darkness, Pierce stripped him of his coat, military cap and AKM assault rifle, then dressed in the same gear.

Using slurred words, one of the two remaining soldiers yelled back from where he stood by the Humvees to his peeing friend. Speaking Kazakh, Pierce didn't understand the meaning, but guessed it was checking on why the soldier was taking so long to empty his bladder.

In his limited disguise, Pierce stepped towards the soldiers using a staggering gait, suggesting drunkenness, and kept his head down and cap over his face until he was standing between them. Only then did they recognise that

Pierce was not their comrade, but it was too late. In their drunken state, they could not react fast enough as Pierce clobbered them both unconscious with the stock of his AKM.

With both men down, he dragged the three unconscious bodies to the first Humvee, then rolled them all underneath so they were out of sight. He removed all their weapons, dismantled them, and threw the parts under the second Humvee. Then Pierce advanced on the hotel.

Once inside the stark hotel interior, Pierce discovered that the building was low-lit with blank walls and an absence of furniture. Sitting at the reception desk on the room's only chair behind the only desk was an old man in a cap, woollen coat and scarf, the concierge no doubt.

Pierce said in Russian, "I need to speak to the colonel urgently. Which room is he in?"

The old man stammered when he answered, "Room twelve, on the first floor."

Pierce nodded. "Good. I will see him now."

He found the hotel's stairs and advanced up them quickly, the AKM at the ready for action, but he also tried to make it seem it was held casually, because the soldier's clothes he wore still offered a disguise from casual glances.

In the upstairs hall, Pierce noticed another soldier seated outside room twelve. He stood when Pierce approached, rubbing his eyes as if to fight off his need for sleep. Then when Pierce was almost upon him, he yelled out further words Pierce didn't understand.

Pierce rammed the AKM barrel into the soldier's gut, then spun the stock in a fast circle, connecting with him across the jaw and sending him down onto the ground fast.

The door to room twelve sprang open, and an angular-faced man with a bald head, wearing only a dirty white singlet and pants, stepped out. He held a Makarov pistol in his hand down by his side, but Pierce was faster and already had his AKM pointed at the man's gut while Pierce's boot simultaneously pressed the guarding soldier face down into the concrete floor.

"Not so fast!" said Pierce in his calmest voice, using Russian.

The singlet-wearing soldier hesitated and, while still holding the pistol, seemed to consider his options. Pierce didn't sense fear in this man, as he'd sensed in the other soldiers he had fought this night, and this could be a problem.

"Don't even think about it. You'll be dead before you get your first shot."

"And my men will kill you seconds later," said the singlet-wearing man in a deep voice that was accustomed to giving orders and not receiving them.

"Then we both lose."

The man hesitated again as his eyes darted in many directions, assessing his odds.

Pierce didn't hesitate as he stepped off the supine soldier and smashed the AKM onto the waving hand holding the Makarov pistol. They both heard his finger bones break and watched as the pistol dropped to the floor. Pierce then spun the singlet-wearing soldier around, then kicked his leg hard behind the knee, forcing him to kneel. Then Pierce twisted his right arm up behind his back until he knew it would surge with agonising pain, while Pierce scooped up the fallen Makarov with his other hand.

In the meantime, the first guarding soldier, whose jaw Pierce had broken, now staggered to his feet. Pierce immediately had the Makarov pointed at this foe's head and said, "Now it's your turn not to do anything stupid."

The guard raised his hands high and nodded slightly, which brought him further pain with his broken jaw jiggling unnaturally in his face.

"Both of you, inside."

The broken-jawed soldier did as he was instructed, while the commanding officer resisted, so Pierce had to drag him inside.

With the hotel room door shut behind them, Pierce forced them both onto their knees and had them face the wall. He levered a chair under the door handle to slow anyone that might try to force their way in, then used electric cable from the bedside lamp to bind his captives' hands behind their backs.

The soldier in the singlet stiffened and said to the wall, "I know who you are, American. You are the terrorist Mark Pierce."

Pierce huffed as he closely examined the room and noticed a colonel's uniform hung in the wardrobe, and a colonel's hat rested on a side table. "If you know that, then you must be Drossanov."

"You won't escape. My men will respond imminently, and you'll be dead within the hour."

Pierce pressed the barrel of the Makarov into the back of Drossanov's skull, which caused him to flinch. "So, the plan always was to kill me. I think I'm going to need a little more detail."

Drossanov snarled. "What makes you think I'll talk?"

Pierce pushed the barrel further into Drossanov's shaved head, forcing his face to press up against the drab concrete wall, squashing his nose into the coarse concrete. "Because the alternatives aren't pretty, that's why. I know this, and you know this too, so start talking."

11

W hen Colonel Drossanov mumbled a response through lips pressed into the wall, Pierce released the pressure of his weapon pressed up against the back of his head. Drossanov then growled like a dog. "Your situation is hopeless, Pierce."

"I agree, but that makes me desperate." Pierce still held the pistol at Drossanov's head should he need to quickly shoot the man despite his superior position. "We both know more of your soldiers will investigate further, as you said, especially when they find the unconscious bodies I left outside. So I need to be quick with my questioning."

"You should shoot yourself now, because if you don't, the pain my men will shortly subject you to will be excruciating."

Pierce glanced at the soldier with the broken jaw. He was all teary and had closed his eyes as if expecting to have his brains blown out at any moment. The underling would not be a problem for Pierce, but Drossanov, projecting a simmering anger ready to boil over at any moment, would.

"We're going to play out the situation like this, Colonel. You've already figured it's only a matter of minutes before your men arrive, and then I'll need to fight my way out. But to avoid me executing you in the meantime, you need to keep me talking until they get here. We both understand this. So, from my point of view, I need answers, but the questions I'm about to ask, some of the answers I already know. My deal with you is this, the first question I ask that is answered with a lie will result in a bullet exploding the insides of your brain all over that nice drab concrete wall you are staring at. Do I make myself clear?"

Drossanov was motionless for a moment before he nodded.

"Good." Pierce listened for noises inside the hotel, but so far, everywhere outside of this room was silent. "First question: Why do you want me dead?"

"Because you are a nuclear terrorist. You stole nuclear waste."

Pierce smacked Drossanov hard across the back of his skull with the pistol, which had the desired effect of causing the man to cry out a whimper of pain, because for a second, Drossanov had thought Pierce had shot him. "That's not strictly true, is it, Drossanov? You know I'm innocent of that crime. You know it is a set-up."

Drossanov nodded, then hung his head.

"Tell me."

"Six months ago, I was approached by an American wanting to buy six canisters of highly irradiated nuclear waste from our old Soviet nuclear test program, conducted in Semey in eastern Kazakhstan decades ago."

Pierce remembered that Semey was where Russia had once built, tested, and stored nuclear rockets and bombs back during the Cold War when Russia was known as the Union of Soviet Socialist Republics, or the USSR. Back in the days before Pierce was born, when the collective global psychosis believed all life would end in nuclear war and not through collapse of the earth's environmental systems, which terrified the world today.

"The American, what did he look like?"

"Late fifties. Blue eyes and grey hair."

The description immediately fitted the profile on Pierce's primary nemesis, so he described Idris Walsh as he remembered him from the torture sessions in the Central African Republic. "Was it the same man?"

"Yes."

"Where is the nuclear waste now?"

"Two Australian mercenaries and a British nuclear scientist took it off our hands earlier this morning. It's on a plane already, headed out of the country."

"What were their names?"

"I don't know. No names were ever used. The mercenaries were men, and the scientist was a woman."

A pause followed, so Pierce said, "Go on?"

Drossanov looked to his underling. They exchanged glances, and the broken-jawed man nodded.

Pierce said in a quiet but firm voice, "Don't even think about moving a muscle. I only need Drossanov alive to answer my questions."

The broken-jawed man nodded, then cast his eyes downwards.

"Go on, Colonel. No more interruptions."

"You already know what I'm about to tell you, Pierce. You can't sell nuclear waste and not have the world's intelligence and military services hunt you down and execute you as a result. We needed a stooge. Someone to take the fall. Someone for the CIA to come after so they wouldn't come after us."

Pierce recalled how in his torture sessions, "Jackman" and "Hemsworth" had only wanted information on his bank accounts and many false identifications. On reflection now, this must have been so they could set up a trail of purchases, travel itineraries, and meetings that made it look like it was Pierce who sought to purchase nuclear waste when the CIA later investigated his spending and travel habits. It also explained the eleven million dollars Walsh had stolen and framed Pierce for, because that money would have been used to purchase the irradiated waste, and was also linked to Pierce.

Pierce sighed. Despite himself, he realised Walsh had done a commendable job of framing him. "That's why you needed me fit and strong again and alive in Kazakhstan just long enough for the deal to go through. So my body could be found here, and with the waste vanished."

"Sanzhar, my cousin, and his syndicate were supposed to execute you tomorrow. But then you had to escape and fuck everything up."

Pierce smirked. "That's because they fucked up, not me. They decided to take a shortcut and execute me this morning, which would have thrown out your timeframes if they had succeeded. And if they failed, which they did, left me running around and spoiling all your plans."

"You outsmarted them."

"Of course."

Drossanov nodded. "When I learned what had happened, I moved quickly to have you arrested."

"Yes, I guess I'm a liability, being alive and all." Pierce

again pressed the Makarov hard into the back of Drossanov's skull. He felt his anger surge in him again, and it took his every effort not to beat both these men to death after the tortures he had suffered this last half year. Instead, he drew in a deep breath, calmed his mind, and said, "What is the nuclear waste's destination?"

"I don't know."

Pierce shook his head and made a "tsking" sound. "That, Colonel, we both know is a lie."

The singlet-wearing man sobbed, then yelled out, "It's not, I swear."

There came a forceful knock on the door.

Drossanov's demeanour suddenly changed, and he bellowed, "Shoot high! Twelve o'clock!" His face was now beetroot red with the anger exploding out of him that he had contained until now. "The fucker's here!"

Pierce dropped suddenly as the air above him filled with fast-moving bullets, which shattered the door and disintegrated the only window. In the noise and confusion that followed, as soldiers burst into the room, Pierce rolled onto Drossanov, gripped his foe by his singlet and spun them both so the colonel became a shield. The two overkeen soldiers storming the room quickly peppered Drossanov and the broken-jawed soldier with sprays of bullets from their AKMs, with their barrels licking flames in their full-automatic fire settings.

With a sudden, sinking feeling in his gut, Pierce presumed he must have taken a bullet with all the shooting, but with the adrenalin surging through him, he felt nothing for the moment. While he was still operational, he aimed the Makarov and shot the two soldiers three times each, killing them both.

After the bodies dropped lifeless into the carnage building in this confined room, Pierce staggered to his feet, then felt all over his body for sticky wetness. Miraculously, he felt nothing and realised he was unharmed.

Deciding it was time to make his escape, Pierce entered the hallway to discover three more soldiers advancing up the stairs. He released the entire magazine of his AKM, killing them all as blood splashed across a wall and the stairs, and sent them tumbling down the stairs together. Pierce reloaded his assault rifle using magazines sourced from the dead soldiers, then pocketed two more and kept moving.

In the reception, the old man cowered under his desk.

"Are there any others?" Pierce shouted at him, keeping his assault rifle aimed at the main entrance should anyone surprise them.

The old man raised his arms in surrender and shook his head.

"Keep your head down for two minutes, then get yourself as far from here as you can. Understand?"

The man nodded as tears gushed from his eyes.

Outside, Pierce found the three soldiers he had incapacitated earlier and left under the closest Humvee. One was stirring, so Pierce put a bullet through the back of his head. He had tried not to leave them with lasting damage earlier because they were enlisted men, but after learning the truth from Drossanov, he didn't believe this any longer. These men were nuclear terrorists after all, so they had death coming for them. He shot the other two men as well, to ensure none of them would come after him later.

Pierce jogged back to where he had left Irina, while always checking his back and corners in case other soldiers were on his trail or lying in ambush, but no one came for him. But when he found the parked Skoda, he looked inside and discovered that it was empty.

His heart racing, Pierce glanced up and down the streets. Someone had taken Irina, and there were no signs as to what might have happened.

Then he heard footsteps as someone approached.

Pierce raised his AKM in the direction of the sound, ready to shoot them dead, until it became evident that it was Irina who had materialised out of the darkness.

"What are you doing?" he asked, unable to keep the concern for her well-being out of his voice.

"Men were checking the cars. Not breaking into them but looking in with flashlights. I slipped out and hid in the darkness before they found me in there." She nodded to their car.

Pierce nodded, as he realised this meant there were still more foes to deal with in this town, and that they had stayed longer than they should have already. "Are you okay? You're not hurt?"

"I'm fine! But this is a terrifying situation."

"Then let's leave. Now."

Pierce removed his uniform and threw it into the darkness, lobbed his AKM into the trunk of the Skoda, and when they were both inside and buckled in, drove off with speed into the night.

When they were on the road, it occurred to him Irina might have stepped out of the vehicle to make a phone call to her superiors, but he would never know until it was too late.

"Did you get what you wanted, Mark?"

Pierce clamped down on his teeth. "I did. Do you have any reason to stay in Kazakhstan?"

She shook her head vigorously.

"Good, then I'm getting us both out of here."

12

Aktau, Kazakhstan

After an uneventful sprint out of Beyneu, Pierce drove through the night, stopping only once for gas and a moment to stretch their legs and relieve cramping muscles. When they were back on the road again, Irina slept.

With a quiet moment to himself, Pierce wondered why she had stuck with him this long. The only plausible answer was fear. Complicating circumstances associated her with Pierce now, and local authorities would blame her for the Kazakhs' murders and the death of Drossanov and his men as much as they would blame him. In her mind, was it a preferable alternative that she run with Pierce, escape to another country, and start afresh with a new identity? He knew he would have done the same in her situation, and this was true whether she was a spy or a prostitute.

Hours later, they arrived at Aktau as the sun rose behind them. The modern but bleak city built on the edge of white cliffs looked out across the lapping inland ocean of the Caspian Sea. All streets had numbers instead of names, a practicality since Aktau had begun its life as an oil workers' camp some seventy years ago.

Parking on the road encircling the cliff, Pierce stepped out and stretched. The lined jacket warmed against the cool, dry air, and he was grateful he had kept it. Three hundred kilometres over the water to the west lay Baku, their destination. But until they reached Azerbaijan, they could face further complications with the local police, the military, criminal gangs, and anyone else chasing them.

His thoughts turned again to Idris Walsh, the man who'd ultimately framed Pierce as a nuclear terrorist. Intelligence services and police forces across the globe always placed instigators of nuclear terror at the top of their capture or kill lists, and now the most active of those agencies hunting him would be his old employers, the CIA.

He looked at his hands.

They shook.

No matter how often he focused and stilled his mind, he couldn't get his shakes under control.

Tremors were an infliction that had troubled him for over a year now. Early on, he'd believed these were the symptoms of neurological damage sustained during a grenade blast deep inside insurgent territory in Yemen. Then a nurse who'd treated him on a past mission believed they were psychological, convinced him they would "disappear" when Pierce "did the right thing", aiding the less fortunate against tyrants. He had done little of anything for seven months, and nothing good, so the tremors had stayed.

Pierce closed his eyes, and when he did, he was immediately back in the dark, dank torture shack. Naked and strapped to a wooden frame. Electric volts surging through his body...

Pierce opened his eyes.

Irina stirred in the passenger seat. After stretching and yawning, she stepped from the Skoda, wrapped her arms around herself against the cold, and joined him.

"You sleep all right?"

She poked out her tongue. "I've had better nights' sleep, Mark."

He nodded and stared out over the inland sea with its many distant lights denoting offshore oil drilling platforms. The serenity of the scene calmed his mind, which he found to be odd, considering how much inner turmoil he'd been experiencing since his freedom. "That is my name, but I'm not a terrorist."

She shrugged. "I was angry yesterday, but what do I care? You haven't hurt me or tried to sleep with me or pimp me out. Hell, I have my own secrets too, some of which I'm sure would disgust you. So who am I to judge?" Irina turned and stood with her back to Pierce's chest, so he was protecting her from the wintry winds blowing off the desert behind them. She too stared out across the water. "This is my first time seeing the Caspian Sea."

"It's an impressive view."

"It's ugly. See those lights; they are oil rigs. They pollute the water, kill the fish, and kill us." She turned back to him. "Just so Russians and the Europeans can drive nice cars."

Pierce raised an eyebrow at her activist spirit. Not what he had expected, not this clarity of thought, especially after the three violent encounters they had barely survived in the last twenty-four hours.

"If you are not a terrorist, Mark, what are you?"

He held out his hand, testing to see if he could control the tremors, but couldn't.

He imagined those shaking fingers around Idris Walsh's neck, tightening, strangling the life out of the man central to Pierce's incarceration and torture, and wondered if doing so would cure him of his festering hatred for the man. Dark thoughts and wild emotions had never driven him before, but he had never endured prolonged and intense torture either. He also realised in that moment that he had trouble believing he was free again. "Men held me prisoner for seven months in a warlord's camp. Possibly a black prison site."

"Black? Prison? For African people?"

He shook his head. Irina might not be who she claimed to be, so he would be careful with what he told her. She could work for the Kazakh criminal gang, or for Walsh and the Australian, reporting his every move. She might even be CIA. But she could also be an innocent, in which case it was his duty to do everything in his power to protect her and remove her from further danger.

"No, I mean an off-the-books prison, but in Africa." He saw she didn't understand his Russian translation of a well-known English phrase. "A secret prison. A concentration camp."

"Ah... A concentration camp... in Africa?"

"I don't know where." This was a lie. He knew the prison was on the Kadei River in the Central African Republic's southwest region. Irina would benefit from that specific piece of information only if she planned on passing it on to someone else.

"What was it like?"

He shuddered, but not from the tremors this time.

"Horrible."

"Did they torture you?"

He nodded. His shakes grew in intensity.

"Do you have scars?" Her question wasn't unkind.

Pierce lifted his shirt, showed her the burn marks on his abdomen and chest where electric prods had singed his skin, leaving several small circular scars. Some of those scars were fresh.

Her eyes widened, as if this revelation had truly shocked her. "I'm sorry."

"You don't have to be sorry. It wasn't your fault."

She wiped her eyes. She empathised, and this was unexpected.

He turned to her and willed himself to maintain eye contact. "Did something similar happen to you, just as bad?"

She shook her head, then nodded. "Not me. My mother..." She looked away and said nothing more.

"You don't have to tell me. I understand."

She hugged herself tighter against the cold. "Can I ask you a question?"

He nodded.

"The policemen at the oil fields. You didn't kill them?"

The tremors in his hands spread to his legs. "No."

"Why not?"

Since their escape, Pierce had fought to become the man he had been before torture and incarceration had nearly destroyed his mind. His old self had a much better grip on what was right and what was wrong. "They were just doing their job. I would never let them arrest me, but I would not hurt them anymore than I had to. They'd all have families who depend on them. They deserve to live as much as we do."

"What about the soldiers and Drossanov? I heard gunfire. Lots of it."

Pierce shrugged. "They were different."

"How?"

"They were nuclear terrorists, who if left alive would cause suffering and death for hundreds or thousands more. It was them who framed me."

Irina frowned, then said, "I thought you would kill me, eventually."

"Then why did you stick with me?"

She shrugged. "If I tried to run, then I definitely thought you would kill me. But if I stayed, I feared my complicity in all the men you murdered would cause the Kazakh authorities to execute me too if they caught us. Both impossible choices. I don't want to end my life in prison. I don't want to die either. You were my best option, but only if you were a 'good' man."

Pierce nodded. Perhaps she was who she claimed to be. "I won't kill you. I won't hurt you. That is my promise, Irina."

She nodded and turned her gaze to the burning lights of the offshore oil drilling platforms. "That is where we're headed?"

He nodded.

"Good. Then what are we doing standing around here?"

13

Pierce and Irina found a café, where he drank his first coffee in more than seven months. Black and strong, with rich beans; coffee had never tasted this good. He soon consumed the first and ordered a second.

Lunch was lamb kebabs with bread and onions. Flavours weren't strong, but the food was nourishing. It too was the best food he had eaten in a long time.

The café sat on a cosmopolitan street near the central business district. Men and women wore western attire decades out of fashion. Many women wore hijabs, reminding Pierce that most Kazakhstan citizens were Muslim. Several men had holstered pistols in their belts, but that was not uncommon in this part of the world.

While they ate and drank, he monitored the patrons for anyone with unusual characteristics and focused on any repeat appearances. So far, nothing alarmed him.

"We have better food in Russia."

Pierce shrugged. "I'm sure." In his past, conversation

came easily to him, but he had trouble engaging with this woman. He knew the problem lay with him and not her.

"You really were in a prison?"

"Yes. Well, more of a military camp, but a prisoner nonetheless."

"Did you escape Africa on your own?"

"No. I don't even know how I got to Kazakhstan. I woke in the same car I found you in. Prisoner of the same men who took you."

"And yet you overpowered them. Killed them all."

Pierce finished his second coffee. "I guess I had better training."

"In fighting?"

He nodded. "And other skills. You ask a lot of questions."

Irina looked away. "Most people are under this misconception that men — and sometimes women — hire prostitutes just for sex. But that's untrue. Most people are lonely. They just want someone to listen to them, make them feel understood, empathised with, even if it is only for an hour and all an illusion. Helping others express their emotions and to feel heard is the most important skill I've mastered. Asking questions is something I do out of habit."

Pierce lowered his utensils and leaned across the table. "Who looks after you?"

Irina flinched. "Now who is asking lots of questions."

Finished with his dish, Pierce pushed his plate from him. "Too personal?"

"Yes."

He nodded, not wishing to push her on a subject that made her uncomfortable. "If you've finished eating, we need new clothes and provisions. Then we secure passage to Baku."

"That's across the Caspian Sea. How, with the authorities looking for us?"

"Bus, ferry and car."

"You've thought this all out."

He was about to say "trust me" but considered the statement unfair, when Pierce himself had only trusted a handful of people in his life. He stood and paid the bill. "Let me show you."

They spent the morning shopping for clothes, including long jackets and knit caps, to protect against the cooling weather. At a drugstore, Pierce bought scissors and trimmed his scraggly beard and hair to less than a few millimetres all over. Next, they purchased tickets for the ferry to Baku, a bus ride through Russia and Georgia taking them around the north end of the Caspian Sea, and another set of tickets for a different bus taking them south through Iran. By midday he'd used most of the Kazakh gangsters' money.

"We're not taking any of those routes, are we?"

"No."

At the bus station, Pierce identified two German backpackers searching for cheap passage to Baku. He sold them his tickets at a discounted price. He did the same with an Iranian couple returning home to Tehran, and the ferry tickets he sold to two Kazakh men looking for work in Baku.

"Why are you doing this?" she asked when they were alone.

"To throw the police off our tracks, forcing them to investigate multiple escape routes. Police will interview these ticket vendors and discover conflicting stories."

"But now we have no means of transport ourselves?"

"I'll get us to Azerbaijan."

"How?"

"You'll see."

During his career with the CIA, and his time before working deep undercover on a highly classified and protracted mission, Pierce had established multiple bank accounts through various tax havens across the globe. Funds that protected him in circumstances like this, where he needed to go dark and operate with no external support. In his time, Pierce had accumulated over three hundred thousand US dollars in a dozen accounts, but his incarceration had changed that. His savings were now considerably less. Still, there was enough money to cover short-term expenses.

No person can sustain torture forever, as Pierce had discovered. His captors had pressured him with burns, poison, electrocution, stress positions and waterboarding until he gave up account after account. When his torturers drained eight secret stashes, Pierce finally convinced them that was all he had. Unfortunately, his four remaining untouched accounts had less than fifty thousand dollars between them. The money was more than sufficient to secure them passage out of Central Asia, but it would quickly be depleted during any sustained action required to stay ahead of his enemies.

Using the last of Sanzhar's cash, Pierce called his bank in Panama and arranged for a transfer of funds to a local bank in Aktau. The process took two hours to complete, but resulted in Pierce pocketing ten thousand US dollars in cash.

Pierce had been reluctant to bring Irina with him to the bank. The more she discovered about him, the greater her betrayal would be if she were an operative for an enemy opponent, but a greater risk was leaving her alone, able to contact her people unnoticed, therefore allowing forces to move in to kidnap or murder him. The same risk had been there in Beyneu, but in that smaller town, there were less opportunities for her to find a means to contact her superiors. If her plan was to betray him, she showed no sign of bother as he dragged her from one financial institution to the next, never allowing her an opportunity to call in.

By late afternoon, he had everything they needed.

"What now?"

"Now we escape."

They took a taxi to the port. Many fishing trawlers chugged in and out from their moorings. The stench of fish was overpowering. Weather-hardened men hauled buckets laden with fresh catches. "Beluga caviar," he said as a way of explanation when Irina peered into one bucket. "Fished to near extinction and smuggled between the various nations of the Caspian Sea."

Irina nodded. "Yes, I know all that. A kilogram of caviar can sell for up to a thousand American dollars. You think women like me don't know such things?"

He smiled. "I never take anything for granted."

Pierce and Irina asked around until they found a trawler preparing to depart.

"Can you take us to Baku?" Pierce asked the captain of the trawler that other fishermen had directed them to.

The short, squat Kazakh with a bald scalp and long white hair shook his head and answered in the same language Pierce had spoken, Russian. "I can take you half-way. We can rendezvous with a Baku captain willing to take you the rest of the way. But it will cost you." He winked at both Pierce and Irina. "You don't want to involve the authorities, do you?"

Pierce handed over fifteen hundred dollars. "Half now,

half when we transfer to the next boat. We pay the next captain the same."

The old fisherman raised an eyebrow. "So, you have at least six thousand in cash. What's stopping me from taking it all and throwing you both overboard?"

Pierce opened his jacket, showing the captain the .380 Makarov tucked into his belt. He had left the AKM in the Skoda, as the assault rifle was too conspicuous a weapon to carry around in the streets of a populated town. "Believe me, it will be me throwing you and your crew overboard if it comes to that. I'd rather you just got paid, and we depart on amicable terms." Pierce maintained eye contact, didn't blink as he stared down the older, shorter man.

The captain looked away, took the money, and said, "Follow me. You need to stay out of sight, at least until the coast is beyond the horizon."

"Suits us fine." Pierce grabbed Irina by the arm and led her into the boat. Together they followed the captain into the hull and into a bunk room.

For a moment the captain lingered, as if he wished to reconsider his deal.

Pierce's hands trembled, so he clasped them together.

"We don't want any trouble," Irina said, taking the captain's hand, pulling him close and giving him a big, beautiful smile. "My boyfriend is nervous. He got me... you know..." She glanced meaningfully at her belly. "My father will kill Viktor if he finds out. My father doesn't think Viktor is good enough for me. But it is love. What do you do?"

She turned and kissed Pierce on the lips. He reciprocated, and not unwillingly.

Irina turned to the captain and held his hands again. "Sir, were you young and in love, once upon a time?"

The captain's eyes drifted back and forth between his two passengers.

"My boyfriend is impulsive. He thinks he needs to prove all the time he is a man. I promise he won't threaten you again."

The captain made a dismissive gesture, then turned to leave. "No sex, not on my boat. And if you want my advice...?"

"I do." Irina nodded.

"Get married as soon as you are in Baku. Fathers are more forgiving if you honour the old, traditional ways."

Irina gave another big smile and whispered, "We will. That is why we are eloping to Baku."

When the captain left and they were alone, Pierce said, "Well done."

"Thank you."

They sat on a bunk next to each other, not moving.

"What now, Mark?"

"Call me Viktor. You've used that name now, so we'll stick with that."

"Okay, Viktor," she said with a grin and nudged him with her elbow.

"We wait until the boat is on the water; then we get some sleep."

She nodded and shifted closer to him. "Your actual name, Mark Pierce, is it English?"

"American."

"Why do you speak Russian so well?"

"I studied Russian and economics at college. My first job was a venture capitalist working from the Moscow office of an American firm."

"Working in Russia, is that how you became a terrorist?"

"I'm not a terrorist."

Noticing his shakes, she glanced at his hands.

Pierce clasped them together. He didn't want Irina to see how bad they were. "Get some sleep, Irina. We'll be busy when we reach Baku. I'll get you some money once we are there, set you up for a new life. Then, if it is safe to do so, you can go your own way."

She leaned close and opened her lips. "What if I wanted to stay with you?"

He returned her stare but kept his expression devoid of emotion. "That's not a good idea."

"Why?"

Pierce shook his head. She wanted him to trust her, but he couldn't.

"Get some sleep. We'll talk again after we switch boats."

14

Caspian Sea

Pierce drifted between waking and sleeping, his mind foggy as it went back and forth between the long days constrained in a dark and humid cell, interspersed with prolonged beatings and electrocutions.

For a moment, the memories were so sharp that he was back in the jungle camp, and the escape across Kazakhstan was a dream...

When he finally jolted awake, sat upright, and opened his eyes, Pierce remembered he was on a boat. Gentle rolling sensations were waves. Not waterboarding.

He sighed, expecting to feel relief but felt only exhaustion.

The only light was from lamps in the hall outside. Irina slept in the same bunk, curled up beside him. He hadn't remembered her joining him during the night.

The dredged memories clung to him.

The dank cell.

Naked.

Bound to a wooden rack while masked men fried him with electric currents.

Another man, on a laptop, opening Pierce's various bank accounts.

Balances turning to zero.

Sometimes the torture continued for days. He'd passed out often, but they always brought him back, ready with more pain.

Another image came to him of the past.

The man seated at the laptop...

Demands for Pierce's account numbers and passwords followed...

The same voice as the man on the phone...

"Hemsworth."

Pierce remembered. He'd watched "Jackman" transfer the money to a different account.

Up on his feet, Pierce searched various lockers until he found a pen and paper. Long ago he had memorised those account numbers and passwords but had forgotten that he had. He closed his eyes and remembered them again.

As soon as his recall felt accurate, he committed the numbers and letters to paper, then pressed the paper into his pocket as he left the cabin.

The torture was months ago. The Australians had never changed the passwords, even after multiple torture sessions. A mistake they would soon regret.

He found the galley and made himself a hot black coffee.

Not long after, Irina joined him. She too moved through the motions of waking from an exhausting sleep. "Nightmares?" she asked.

He nodded.

"You kept calling out. You settled only when I slept next to you."

Pierce said nothing, uncertain how to respond.

"I hope you didn't mind?"

"No." He shrugged. "I don't remember you joining me. But if you calmed my mind, thank you." He sipped his coffee and looked to the kettle. "You want one?"

"I'll get it." She refilled the coffeepot and set it to boil.

Soon the rich aroma of coffee scented the galley. Pierce was growing to love the smell.

"You kept screaming about the CIA."

"CIA? Are you sure?"

Irina nodded casually. "Betrayed... by the CIA. Is that what you really are? A spy?"

Pierce looked at his hands. They shook like pistons, firing through his fingers and wrists.

She took his hands and massaged them. Then her eyes looked up into his and held his stare. Her perfectly structured face mesmerised him. He couldn't remember the last time he had looked upon a beautiful woman who didn't want to look away either.

Then he remembered who she might be.

"I thought, perhaps, that you had made it all up to impress me?"

"Being CIA?" He tried to imagine what other secrets he might have revealed during his sleep. "What else do you think I made up?"

"Being a prisoner? Being betrayed?"

Anger overcame Pierce, and he didn't understand why. After tensing and pulling back from her, he suppressed his feelings before he acted impulsively or spoke words he would later regret. "Let's get to Baku, Irina; then I can be out of your life forever. You don't need my problems complicating your life."

Irina's eyes flashed before going blank. Standing up, she went back to the simmering coffeepot, then without looking at him, poured one black coffee. She took hers and disappeared from the galley without looking back.

She didn't join him that night either, sleeping by his side, calming his troubled mind.

15

Baku, Azerbaijan

Pierce and Irina stepped onto the docks of Baku three days after their departure from Aktau, took a moment to breathe in the air and silently acknowledge they had so far evaded their pursuers. Baku gave them options not previously available in Kazakhstan.

During their journey across the Caspian Sea, they changed boats three times, with each transfer draining more of Pierce's funds to pay off the next crew. The last captain only delivered them to Azerbaijan because he had searched Pierce and Irina at gunpoint to discover — after they had paid him — that they were penniless. He'd taken Pierce's pistol and spare clips as the last payment but had delivered them both unharmed to Azerbaijan's capital. Pierce didn't bother to fight or argue with him.

Baku was a refreshing destination compared to the drabness of Kazakhstan. The city was a mixture of European and Middle Eastern architecture overlooked by glitzy skyscrapers that resembled space needles and blue flames. Streets alternated between old, cobbled stones or modern asphalt surfaces. A heavy smog hung in the air, its source a nod to the overexploitation of the country's oil and gas reserves. Women wore hijabs and long shapeless robes or designer jeans and short skirts. Men dressed in denim jeans, T-shirts and open jackets. Baku felt like a mixture of Dubai, St Petersburg and Prague, but without the grandeur or glitz. At least it felt alive compared to the sleepy towns they had encountered in Kazakhstan.

"You know Baku?" Irina asked.

"Yes."

"You going to elaborate on how you know it?"

Pierce watched the crowds, searching for a tail, but noticed nothing out of the ordinary. An absence of surveillance bothered him more than if he were trying to shake enemy operatives. Perhaps Walsh needed Pierce to run for some time, as a distraction, while he enacted another horrendous crime involving nuclear technology, which they would later frame him for.

"We need money."

"I don't have any, Mark."

"Well, I do."

They entered a pedestrian-only mall in search of banks Pierce could use.

"Oh," she said after they crossed several blocks.

"What?" Pierce asked. His senses alerted, he searched again for threats.

"That man?"

Pierce looked to where she gestured. A fortyish, over-weight individual with a moustache and thick black hair perused magazines in a shopfront. He didn't look their way, but his posture seemed stiff. He carried a gun in a holster under his left armpit, but like Kazakhstan, guns were common here.

"What about him?" he asked.

"Oh, nothing. Just thought I saw him at the docks."

Pierce grabbed her by the arm, and they marched towards denser crowds.

"What's going on?" Irina protested, resisting his pull.

"He's a tail," Pierce said through gritted teeth. He recognised he was angry, but he couldn't get his emotion under control.

"Tail?"

"Yes, and he won't be the only one. I don't know who they are, but you must follow my instructions. I need to identify who they are. Then we need to shake them."

"How do we do that?"

Pierce noticed an elderly couple. The man held an older model digital camera in his shaky hands, ready to take holiday snaps of his wife, who stood vacant-eyed next to him. He angled the camera to include chandelier-style lighting hung between three-storey shops in the backdrop of his photos. Shop windows held black-and-white posters of models promoting perfumes, watches, and diamond jewellery.

Pierce approached and said in Russian, "I can take your photo? The two of you together?"

The man nodded, and Pierce took the camera, pocketed the SD memory card while he snapped images that would go unrecorded. Irina and Pierce had featured in the backdrop of earlier photos, therefore so might the assailants who had followed them.

The old couple thanked Pierce. He and Irina then took off before the man discovered his memory card was missing.

In the next street, Pierce knocked into another man, apologised as he slipped the man's wallet into his own pocket, and kept walking.

"What's going on?" Irina asked, her voice raised, and her face flushed.

"The people who wanted us dead in Kazakhstan..."

"What about them?"

"They're trying again. To kill us."

They marched through a less busy road. Pierce stopped in the middle, turned, and embraced her. "Keep your eyes open," he spoke in a low voice. "See if anyone is watching."

She nodded. "You look one way? I look in the other direction?"

"Exactly."

Pierce studied the thinned crowd for individuals changing their behaviour, such as stopping to check the time, to tie shoelaces or answer a fake phone call. The narrow lane was to trap anyone following them, forcing their exposure.

He saw nothing.

He felt Irina tremble against his chest.

"It will be fine," he whispered. "No one has moved on us yet. It means they don't have the resources to take us down."

She held his stare. "You sure?"

He nodded, but he didn't believe it. Their enemy waited only for the opportune moment to strike.

"What do we do?"

Pierce spotted a sign leading to a station of the Baku Metro rapid transit system. "I have an idea."

As they took the stairs into the subterranean station, Pierce checked the wallet he had pocketed earlier. There was plenty of cash, some of which he used to buy two tickets, one of which he gave to Irina. They passed through the turnstile and entered the white polished interior, with more chandelier-style lighting hung over every platform. Pierce couldn't read or understand Azerbaijani, so he followed the sound of an approaching train.

"I just saw him!" She spoke out of breath.

"Who?"

"The man from before. The one I pointed out."

"Where is he now?"

She studied the crowds, her lips open and her eyes unblinking. "I don't know. I've lost him."

Pierce rushed them to the crowded platform. A utilitarian train painted pink and grey pulled onto the platform and slowed. "Irina, we get on when it stops, but stand by the doors. Different entrances for each of us. As the doors are about to close, we jump off."

"What will that do?"

"Expose whoever is following us. They must jump off too."

She nodded, her chest rising and falling as she breathed. "Okay. That sounds sensible."

The train squealed to a stop. They separated and moved with the mingling crowds, allowing Pierce to watch commuters as he stepped into a carriage and waited by the door. He memorised faces, particularly individuals who glanced at him. It took about thirty seconds for the train to load.

As the doors slid shut, Pierce leaped from the train.

He was the only person who did.

Irina stared at him through the train's window as the carriages sped away.

She smiled, then waved to him, and finally disappeared into the dark subterranean tunnel.

Pierce tightened his fists.

Irina, or whatever her actual name was, had just played him. The prostitute story she had spun must be a legend, a fabricated identity. He thought of many possibilities as to what might have just occurred, but the only one that made sense to him was that the woman was an intelligence operative. She had duped Pierce into believing they were under surveillance and used his distraction to slip away. If she were an intelligence operative, this also begged the question, which one did she work for?

Then it occurred to Pierce that she might have led him into a trap, where other operatives from her organisation waited and now descended upon him, to kill or capture.

Pierce turned and marched to the next platform, stepped onto a train headed in the opposite direction to build as much distance between himself and the agent code-named "Irina". He changed trains several times, walked up and down stairs and doubled back multiple times until he felt certain no one was about to make an immediate move on him.

He headed for the surface.

What the operative formerly known as "Irina" didn't know was that Pierce had her photograph saved on the SD card he'd snatched earlier.

16

B ack on the Baku streets again, Pierce first checked himself for obvious bugs and, finding none, then ran a lengthier and more thorough surveillance detection route. He walked, jogged, took taxis, and caught further rides on the Metro. He stopped often, turned and doubled back, spent minutes in shops pretending to browse, but at all times he kept his eyes and ears open, ready for any sign he was under surveillance. While he concentrated on people, he also watched for surveillance cameras — which he avoided to the best of his abilities — and drones, of which he saw none.

He passed Turkish baths, traversed wide parks dominated by olive and palm trees, walked beside medieval walls with old turrets and fortified battlements, and disappeared under the shadows of utilitarian skyscrapers and ugly apartment blocks.

Three hours later, Pierce was sure no one was following him.

The only conclusion that made sense to Pierce now was

that Irina, or whatever her actual name was, had tricked him into believing they were under surveillance so she could escape from him.

He found an internet café, used up more of his cash from the wallet he had pickpocketed earlier, and bought an hour of screen time. He selected a monitor positioned towards the back, but close to a group of about ten-year-old boys immersed in a multiplayer first-person shooter game who had no interest in anything Pierce might browse, and their energetic antics kept other adults from sitting too close.

After downloading a reliable encryption program, and then hacking the operating system with codes and passwords taught to him by CIA cyber-threat experts, Pierce felt comfortable that his digital trail was better hidden than it had any right to be.

He took the paper from his pocket with the Australians' bank accounts and passwords he had recalled on the Caspian Sea, then used them to log on to the bank's website.

Pierce was surprised to find a numbered account with almost four million US dollars.

Stunned, Pierce leaned back and took a deep breath. This was unexpected.

In five seconds, he had a plan.

First, he transferred two and a half million dollars into one of his holding accounts. Although "Hemsworth" and "Jackman's" password was complex, the men should have changed it more often. Stealing the money seemed too easy.

Once the money was in an account Pierce controlled, he broke the sum into three separate amounts and transferred them to three more accounts. There was, unfortunately, nothing in any of the accounts that provided names or other details about Idris Walsh and his Australian accomplices except for an email address comprising random numbers and letters, which Pierce copied into a temporary text file.

He next downloaded a CSV, comma separated values, file of all the torturers' bank account transactions — essentially a Microsoft Excel spreadsheet, but with all the fancy coding and graphics stripped out. The CSV file contained thousands of debit and credit entries, with account and bank numbers, and a host of other financial information. He knew he'd scored a mother lode of intel on his enemy's operations, but what should he do with this information?

He'd worry about that later.

Pierce returned to his four intact bank accounts, broke the sums into smaller quantities and, leaving small values, transferred the funds again.

It would be difficult to trace the money, as his were also numbered accounts, established through fake shell companies operating in half a dozen tax havens across the globe, and each account had a long alphanumeric password. Even if someone traced the transfers, recovering the money would be nearly impossible and would likely draw attention to the "Hemsworth" account, which Walsh and the Australians wouldn't want anyone to examine too closely considering their scheme in play involving nuclear waste.

Pierce left close to one and a half million in the "Hemsworth" account because he had a plan on how to use it against his torturers.

He then logged into the Dark Web and searched through assassination services until he found the one professional killer he was looking for. The deactivated account of an assassin Pierce had fabricated during his missions with the CIA in Yemen, one that Idris Walsh should know nothing about, as he had had nothing to do with Yemen, nor did he have clearance to access any of Pierce's mission profiles during that time. The fake assassin went by the name of Gulzar Zam, whom Pierce had used to make contact with actual jihadists and insurgents active in the country while Pierce served there.

Pierce sent Gulzar Zam a message, using the Australian's email address as his username:

WISH TO RETAIN YOUR SERVICES. THREE MILLION FEE. ONE MILLION DOWN PAYMENT. TARGET TO BE ADVISED.

The Zam account wouldn't reply because the account was unmonitored and, as far as the CIA were concerned, deactivated.

Pierce still had access to the account and, with Zam's IP address masked, logged on, then responded to his own query. By doing so, if the CIA found this account and hacked it, they would see a message trail requesting an assassination connected to "Hemsworth" and "Jackman's" bank account and email address. This information could also get back to Walsh, sowing the seeds of distrust between the CIA spymaster and his underlings. It was a long shot, but took little effort to set in motion, so Pierce considered it worthwhile.

But there was another reason he'd created the correspondence, which he would come to later.

He typed:

WHO IS THE TARGET?

Pierce responded using the Australian's email identifier.

TO BE ADVISED. DO YOU WANT THE $3M OR NOT?

The fictious assassin responded with:

VERY WELL. PAY INTO THE ACCOUNT FOUND IN
THE FOLLOWING LINK.

Pierce transferred the one million dollars, leaving just over four hundred and seventy thousand US dollars as change in "Hemsworth's" account. A fully rounded number would look suspicious, so this random number made it look like the balance after normal transactions. He messaged back.

I'LL BE IN TOUCH. WHEN TARGET IDENTIFIED,
I'LL SEND DETAILS. CODE WORD
"HEMSWORTH".

Pierce changed the password of the drained account to "hemsworth81", then logged out. Then using the email address connected to Gulzar Zam, he emailed a confirmation email to "Hemsworth's" and "Jackman's" accounts, certain that when his adversaries received it, they would realise they had been framed for setting up an assassination attempt unauthorised by Walsh, which would hopefully create distrust among the three, giving Pierce time to locate his adversaries while they bickered.

He deleted his browser history, then set the encryption software to copy useless data across the entire hard drive multiple times. The machine would require rebuilding when the software completed its task, but Pierce would be long gone before anyone noticed.

He ran another surveillance detection route as he walked the streets.

When convinced he was still alone, he found an ATM. Using one of his newly topped-up accounts, which only required keying in an account number and PIN code — a set-up for situations where intelligence officers and covert operators like himself were without a bank card in a foreign and hostile environment — and withdrew ten thousand Azerbaijani manats, the equivalent of just under six thousand American dollars.

At a convenience store, he purchased an international phone card for Nigeria.

Then, at a telephone box, he dialled a number he hadn't called in five years.

While the number diverted through the Nigerian telephone system, it linked to a VoIP, Voice over Internet Protocol, system, transferred his call across a dozen cities around the planet, then back to Baku.

"Speak," said a voice, modulated, so it revealed nothing of the caller's identity, including their gender.

"Grey rabbit. Sad owl," he replied in the same language. Russian.

There was a pause. "*Arkady?*"

Pierce grimaced at the use of an old cover identity. "Yes."

"I thought you were dead?"

"I still am, but this ghost needs a favour."

"That's... How can I help?"

"I'm local. I need to meet."

"You mean...? Here...? In this city?"

"Yes."

Another pause. "Okay. Tomorrow we can meet. There is a flower shop." The modulated voice provided an address.

"The proprietor will tell you where to go next. No tech. That's non-negotiable. Nothing that can track you."

"I have a SIM card and an SD card I need analysed."

"Okay, but not the devices themselves. Arkady, I can't believe you are alive."

Because of the modulation, Pierce couldn't gauge the responder's emotions. He or she could have felt elated, terrified, or angry. Pierce would only know the answer to that tomorrow. "We'll talk soon."

"We will."

Pierce hung up, then hurried on.

He had money and intel. That put him in a far preferable position than he'd been in a week ago, so now he would use that advantage.

17

Tbilisi, Georgia

Her name wasn't Irina. It never had been. Irina was a legend, a false persona created in an instant when Rachel Zang realised Mark Pierce had killed the four Kazakh criminals and would kill her next.

Zang was the opposite of Irina in every way. She was an American, educated, confident, a proficient paramilitary operations officer of the Central Intelligence Agency, and her career was going places, or had been until this botched operation. Her mission in Kazakhstan had been to find and apprehend Pierce, then return him to the United States for interrogation and incarceration as a nuclear terrorist.

But the day before she met Pierce, the Kazakh criminals had stormed their operating base, killed the rest of her CIA team and took her hostage. The men dragged her away, and when she came around and discovered she was naked, Zang had believed Pierce was the mastermind behind the attack.

Now that Zang was free of Pierce, she reflected on the last five days with the disgraced CIA paramilitary operations officer who'd turned nuclear terrorist, and now questioned her earlier supposition.

She had expected Pierce to see through her ruse at any moment and then kill her as coldly as he had murdered her friends and colleagues. Zang had worried that when she had silently dispatched the two Kazakh soldiers snooping around their Skoda while Pierce confronted Drossanov in Beyneu, and then hidden their bodies in a nearby and open drain, that Pierce might have found them and exposed her subterfuge then. She had also experienced concern that Pierce might be a superior soldier to her, and that, despite her many skills, she would not be able to defeat him in close combat if it came to a direct confrontation, so she pretended to be an innocent until she could escape from him through trickery instead.

Pierce had been busy since his fall from grace, with sightings in Algeria, Belarus, Ukraine, Syria, and Iraq. The body count he'd left behind would have been impressive if the killings didn't sicken Zang to her core. Nuclear scientists, arms dealers, fundamentalist Islamist terrorists, and many of their families slaughtered with them. The photographs of the children Pierce had butchered frightened her the most.

After escaping Pierce in Baku, she'd hid in the back of a semi-trailer truck as it drove west. The border crossing between Azerbaijan and Georgia had been a formality, and the guards on both sides failed to check the crates that concealed her.

In Tbilisi, the Georgian capital that resembled a fairy-tale village with its narrow streets and small shops, she paid the truck driver with the rest of the cash she had stolen on the fishing trawlers, and walked off into its cool, sub-zero night streets.

Mountains surrounded Tbilisi, and a cityscape built on both sides of the meandering Mtkvari River gave Tbilisi a cosy, protected feel. Zang knew this was an illusion. She might have tricked Pierce in Baku and escaped him there, but that didn't mean he hadn't figured out where she had gone and wouldn't come after her.

With her feet on the ground, Zang ran a surveillance detection route. When she felt confident no one was tracking her, she found the CIA's Tbilisi resident safe house and knocked on the back door.

A man yelled abuse at her in Georgian.

"I've brought peppers and sauerkraut and good Russian brandy, as you ordered," she yelled through the door in Russian.

The entrance sprang open. The old man, with white hair and a beard like Santa Claus, greeted her. Dressed only in pyjamas and a threadbare dressing gown, he let her inside without question. She'd remembered the correct code.

"Russian or English?" the resident operator asked in the first language.

Zang went to where a log fire burned and stood next to it, warming her hands. "I don't mind. Whatever is easier for you."

"English, then. I need to practice. Coffee? Tea? Hot milk?"

She smiled at his kindness. "Tea, please. Just black."

"I'll put some honey in it. You look like you need a sugar hit."

Zang nodded and sat next to the fire. This was the first

moment since the deaths of her colleagues Julie, Brad, and Yousef that she felt safe again.

She thought about Pierce. Had he told the truth about being incarcerated in an African paramilitary camp and also about being a prisoner of the Kazah criminals?

Pierce had said it was the CIA who had betrayed him, but Zang found this difficult to believe. The CIA — her people — had been desperate to find him since his disappearance in Morocco and had chased his ghost and a trail of dead bodies across North Africa, Europe, and Asia to achieve that end. To bolster efforts, Zang's boss had transferred her to the team hunting him. Three months ago, they had almost caught Pierce in Montenegro, and she had been the mission lead on that failed effort.

Then again, until Kazakhstan, she had never actually laid eyes on Pierce.

No one had.

When Zang realised Pierce had killed the four criminals in the Aral Sea, she knew he would finish her next. Already free of her bonds, and without anything she could use as a weapon, she pretended to be the naked prostitute the Kazakh men had talked about. Zang hadn't believed her ruse would hold up for long, but to her surprise, it had.

And Pierce had treated her with kindness, or was that a ruse too?

Nothing about the last five days made any sense to her.

The resident operator returned with her tea.

She took it and held it in her hands, warming them. "Thank you."

"What else do you need?"

"Passport, with the right visas. Money. A secure phone I can call out on."

The old man nodded. "I'll take your photo first. I will arrange passport and papers through the CIA Station. Might take twelve, maybe twenty-four hours."

"That's fine," she said, sipping the tea.

Once he'd photographed her head and shoulders against a clear background, he pointed to a door. "Through there is a phone where you can speak without interruption, or being overheard. There is a laptop too. I'm presuming you know passwords to log in?"

She nodded. "Please, if you are able, some food would be great too. I haven't eaten all day."

He nodded. "I have some khinkali. Steamed dumplings stuffed with meat and spices?"

"Sounds wonderful."

When the resident operator disappeared, she asked herself, who should she call first?

18

Z ang entered the secure room and fell into the chair by the desk. Exhaustion overcame her, but so too did a sense of relief. So many people had died around Mark Pierce, yet she had survived.

Zang knew she was a competent operator and skilled in tradecraft, subterfuge, and combat, and was able to handle most situations thrown at her, but she had also been lucky. Pierce was the "Trigger Man", a code name applied by his CIA handlers before he had gone rogue and adopted a nomadic, terror-fuelled existence chasing nuclear weapons across the globe. But the code name seemed more appropriate now than when Pierce had been a trusted paramilitary operator. He had survived this long not because he was lucky, but because he was good at what he did. Pierce was at least her equal, and perhaps more so. It also bugged her that the CIA gave code names to male operators, but not female operators like herself. She was just "Zang".

With the door closed, she took the secure satellite phone and dialled CIA headquarters in Langley, Virginia. She coded in and asked for the active-duty officer on the Trigger Man task force.

"Zang? You survived."

It was Aaron Stone who answered. A former Navy SEAL special forces veteran with three tours in Afghanistan, one in Syria and four in Iraq. Now with the CIA's Special Operations Group as a respected paramilitary operations officer, he operated under the code name Night Viper. Many considered Stone to be the CIA's best and most successful tier one operator. He would be the man who would execute Pierce when they found him. The two men were the same.

Despite his reputation, Zang didn't like Stone because he never treated her as an equal. He didn't see any woman as being as competent as him and his other special forces buddies.

His bias was institutionalised too, for the CIA would never consider her tier one, and both internal and external prejudices had hindered her career. Tier one was a capability acknowledgement reserved only for ex-special forces types like Stone, and America's Special Forces never recruited women, so that opportunity would forever be beyond her reach. She should have been born in Israel.

"Stone, good to hear a friendly voice again."

"You made it. Thank God! When we got news that the rest of the team were dead, we feared the worst."

Zang sighed. "We lost three outstanding officers."

"We did."

"Stone, do we have concrete evidence who killed them?"

"'Concrete'?" Stone asked. "Mark Pierce. The Trigger Man. Who else? Hired four Kazakh criminals to take out a hit on you all. Must have known you were onto him."

Zang drew in a deep breath. Stone was confident in his

supposition, but she didn't feel the same certainty. "I'm in Tbilisi. At the local safe house. I'm unharmed."

"Good. Let's get you out of there."

"I've been with Pierce these last five days. We were together yesterday, in Baku."

"Impossible!" Stone said. "The asshole is in Tehran, been there for three days now. Spending money like he's just won the lottery, using old accounts he thinks we don't know about. He's ready to talk with Iranian Quds Force intelligence officers, whom we presume he is about to sell the nuclear waste to, but we'll move on him soon enough."

Listening to his words, she drew a deep breath, held it, and couldn't speak.

"You there, Zang?"

"Yes." He had dismissed her intelligence out of hand, and not for the first time. "I'm here."

For many months she had studied Pierce's files, memorised every non-redacted detail. She knew his face, his personality, and all his traits and skills. It was not possible that the man she had spent the last five days with was an impostor. This implied Stone was chasing a ghost.

"Zang?"

"What if *you've* got the wrong man?"

"What? No way. What are you saying, Zang?"

"I spent five days with him."

"How could you possibly do that? You're mistaken."

She sighed. Stone had dismissed her again. "I tricked him, Stone. Made him believe I was an innocent mixed up in his world. We were in Kazakhstan together, crossed the Caspian into Baku. We were together in Azerbaijan less than twenty-four hours ago."

"No, I mean, how can you be with him if we've been tracking him?"

Zang massaged her forehead. "I'm not lying."

"I'm not either. We have photographs from yesterday. In a café in Tehran with a Quds Force officer known to us."

Zang shook her head and tried to understand what was happening. Did some unknown party feed fake intel to their team? Was Pierce doing this? Whoever was doing so was an expert if no one had picked up on it yet.

Pierce's story that he had been a prisoner for seven months and was now on the run seemed more credible.

"Okay, Zang," Stone said, interrupting her thoughts. "While we've been talking, I got word from the boss. He wants you on the next flight to Langley."

Zang nodded. The head of their task force had spoken, and no one argued with Idris Walsh. She'd been on the wrong end of one of his rants in the recent past when she'd questioned a decision on an active operation, and he had constantly belittled her intelligence as well.

"Okay," she answered in a soft voice.

"It seems your RO has the arrangements in hand. Get back here as soon as you can."

"Sure." Her voice sounded ethereal even to her ears.

"This is serious, Zang. Pierce just secured himself a mother lode of radioactive materials. He secured it from a Kazakh colonel by the name of Mikail Drossanov, who's connected to Kazakhstan's nuclear program. If a dirty bomb is Pierce's intention, he has it now; all he has to do now is detonate it. So get back quickly!"

Again, the dismissal. Stone didn't believe her.

"Stone, for fuck's sake, check your situation reports from Kazakhstan and read about what happened to this Colonel

Mikail Drossanov you just mentioned in Beyneu a few days back! The man is dead. Pierce did that! I was with him when it happened!"

There was a pause on the line, and Zang could hear her peer breathing heavily. Eventually he said, "Okay, I'll look into it, Zang. But in the meantime, get back here quickly! Walsh won't be happy if you don't."

"Of course he won't!" she almost yelled down the line.

"Zang?"

"Yes, I'm on my way."

She ended the call abruptly.

In the silence, Zang took a moment to process the conversation's progression. Stone had been hostile towards her. Or was Walsh pulling at his puppet strings? Her real superior had warned her about Walsh, how manipulative he was. Apart from the single berating, Zang had never seen that side of the spymaster and had dismissed those warnings as rumours spread by personnel who felt he didn't respect them.

She didn't feel that way now.

Something was rotten inside their task force.

Zang would return to the States, but there was one avenue of investigation she had to follow before Walsh debriefed her.

That line of investigation was Pierce's former case officer. Mackenzie Summerfield.

Walsh had fired Summerfield from the CIA when Pierce turned rogue in Morocco. She was in the private sector now, a research specialist for a geopolitical analysis group, operating from offices in London. Zang had interacted with Summerfield a few times in the past, so a meet would be simple enough, without Summerfield worrying that Zang was an enemy operative seeking intel from her.

Standing and stretching out the tension in her muscles, Zang returned to the safe house's living area. Seeing her, the resident operator pointed to fresh tea and dumplings on the dining table. "It's late," he said. "I'm off to bed. Unless there is anything else you need tonight?"

"No, thank you." She sipped the tea, which warmed her insides. "You've been very kind."

He shrugged. "It's my job."

"Regardless, thank you. But there is one more thing. In the morning, can you secure me tickets to Washington, DC. It's likely already in the system."

"Certainly."

"Can you make sure it includes a stopover in London?"

He nodded and grinned, knowing she was up to something.

"And can I use the secure room again? I have one more call to make."

19

Baku, Azerbaijan

Mark Pierce knew he was walking into a past he had hoped to keep buried forever, but he had no choice.

On his way to the apartment block in an old Soviet-era section of town, he discovered grey concrete buildings and streets with as many wrecked cars as there were functional vehicles. Most residents were Muslims, identified by women with hijabs and the occasional man with a skullcap. Children chased each other up and down the stairs and across the external communal balconies of the apartment block he was here to visit. A scrawny tabby cat watched him like it was a surveillance camera, gave a stare that said Pierce wasn't welcome.

All morning, Pierce had followed his contact's directions, first to the flower shop, where the proprietor handed him a card with another address. At the next location, a young, thin taxi driver of Asian complexion and with a thick beard met him. The taxi driver patted Pierce down, checking not for weapons but tech that could be trackable, such as cell phones. Pierce had nothing on him that bothered the young man, so they took to the roads. The drive was uneventful except for the Turkish techno music playing on tinny speakers. They drove for fifteen minutes before entering a garage, where they parked the taxi, then walked three residential blocks before transferring to an unmarked civilian car and driving again for forty minutes. Finally, they reached the apartment block and stood outside.

"That building." The Asian pointed as he spoke Russian. "Level five, number fifty-eight."

Pierce nodded and thanked him.

He took the stairs, passing some children, who asked for money. He gave them the change in his pockets and moved on.

When he found apartment fifty-eight, he knocked on the door. He knew a tiny surveillance camera would be watching him, but he couldn't see where it was.

A mildly overweight man with slim arms and legs, with his hair and beard shaved down to a millimetre all over, opened the door wearing a black Miss Monique T-shirt and black jeans. His eyes seemed too large in his head, but not threatening. The tension in his body was noticeable, but controlled, like he was deciding whether to slam the door in Pierce's face or hug him like a long-lost brother.

"Arkady," he said, using a code name from a past mission in Russia. "Come in. Come in!" He embraced Pierce and kissed him on both cheeks, as was the custom for his culture.

Pierce stepped into the rather drab apartment, with old threadbare furniture, patchy carpets, a tiny television set, an eighties kitchen and faded curtains that had once been a bland shade of green. Pierce suspected the look and feel was intentional, to match the economic limits of their neighbours.

"I thought you were dead, Arkady!" The man's smile grew larger with each passing second. "The SVR files I hacked said you were."

"I still am." Pierce spoke Russian like a native. "And I'd like to stay that way, Yebin."

"Of course. Of course. Your face, it's different. I almost didn't recognise you."

"Minor facial reconstruction surgery." There was a story behind that he didn't wish to share, so he didn't elaborate.

"That makes sense after what my people tried to do to you. I owe you my life. We both do."

"You and Valeriya still together?"

Yebin smiled. "We are in love, Arkady. It might be tragic Russian love, but love nonetheless. When everything in the world seems fake and disposable, emotions hold a truth that despots and murderers can never sully."

"You're still partners in crime?"

The young man's body shook before he performed a tiny dance. "Come and meet her. It is so good to see you again, my friend. Valeriya, she too is excited to learn that you are not a corpse buried in a shallow grave somewhere and are here to visit us."

"This isn't a social call."

"Of course it isn't, but we both feel joy, nonetheless."

Pierce glanced around the empty flat. "You seem to be the only one home."

"Looks can be deceiving. You taught me that, Arkady."

Yebin led Pierce to the kitchen. The stained benches held burn rings from hot pots, and all the metal cupboard handles had rusted. The man rolled out the oven from under the kitchen bench, revealing a manhole and a ladder in the floor. "Climb down. The real action is downstairs."

Pierce took the secret entrance to the lower level, and Yebin followed him, pulling the false oven back into place to complete the illusion of a poor and empty apartment upstairs.

Downstairs was a different world, more resembling a CIA operations room with low lights, computer monitors and servers everywhere. Cables crossed the ceilings while dismantled computer parts lay stacked in crates. Pierce heard the low hum of the fans needed to prevent the tech from overheating. There were no windows, and the room held a faint aroma of sweat, coffee, and sex.

The layout was the same as upstairs. In the downstairs bedroom, Pierce noticed an unmade Japanese-style futon with discarded lacy underwear from an earlier romp. It seemed Yebin and Valeriya Radanovich maintained a passionate relationship.

He was almost jealous.

Then he saw her, the thin dark-haired woman with a Marvel Avengers T-shirt tight around her firm breasts, and denim shorts cut so high Pierce could see the shape of her ass. Valeriya's most striking feature were her tattoos, long curls of barbwire that started from her toes, then curled up around her shapely legs and presumably across her body, joining at her neck then down her arms to her fingers.

She stepped close to Pierce, embraced him and kissed him on both cheeks. "Arkady, I'm so pleased to see you are not dead."

"I'm not dead, but I am, if you know what I mean."

"I do. But you look different?"

"Some minor facial surgery, so it was harder for the FSB to find me when I had to escape," Pierce said, remembering a past mission that involved Valeriya, Yebin, and his hasty departure from Saint Petersburg.

"Well, you look better for it." She turned to Yebin and blew him a kiss. "Lover, have you offered our guest a drink?"

Yebin scratched his head. "No. What is your poison, Arkady? We have coffee. Coca-Cola? I have some sake."

"A coffee would be fine."

"He drinks it black." Valeriya spoke with authority. "No sugar."

Valeriya glanced around their abode, noticing piles of clothes scattered on a burgundy sofa, removed them, and offered the seat to Pierce. He obliged while she sat cross-legged on a wool-pile carpet across from him. Pierce noticed how warm the air was. He slipped off his jacket. In the kitchen, he heard Yebin change the filter on a coffee machine.

"I never got the chance to thank you, Arkady. If you hadn't smuggled me and Yebin out of Saint Petersburg when you did..."

"You don't have to thank me," he said, not wishing to relive the traumas of a past mission before he "officially" joined the CIA.

"But we do. The SVR would have killed Yebin and me, or banished us to a Siberian concentration camp, which is the same thing. And then I remember it could have been far worse for us... if you had not killed that assassin..." She shuddered at the memory.

Pierce nodded. "You both helped me when I was in a difficult situation. It was the least I could do." He glanced at the various high-tech computers that crowded the apartment and wondered how they'd smuggled the parts in. "Business doing well?"

She laughed. "We still have back-door hacks into all the major intelligence services, so we sneak around their servers where we can. There is an unlimited supply of buyers who will pay good money for the scraps of information we steal. One very good client, too. Consistent work that pays well. They are powerful enough to keep the Russians from finding us."

Pierce raised an eyebrow. "Sounds like a client you wouldn't want to cross either, Valeriya."

"No. We are careful. You know that about us, Arkady."

"Aren't you a little close to Russia to be taking risks against the FSB and SVR?" Pierce said, referring to both the domestic and foreign intelligence services of the Russian Federation.

She shrugged. "Maybe, but like you, Arkady, we are Russians. There are many Russians in Azerbaijan. We blend in. We don't look out of place here. And with Russians bogged down in a never-ending war in Ukraine, they have bigger problems to worry about than two missing hackers."

Yebin returned with three mugs of coffee, one black and two cappuccinos. "So why have you returned from the dead, Arkady? Why are you here? We never expected to see you again."

Pierce removed the SIM and SD cards from his pocket and held them in his palm. "I was in hiding too. Now men are hunting me, so I've had to run. I need your help to discover who these people are, and why they want me dead."

20

As day turned to night, Pierce watched Valeriya and Yebin run their trace programs. Together they searched for both "Irina", using the photos the elderly couple had snapped of her, and "Hemsworth" using the recorded audio files captured during their brief phone conversation while Pierce stood in the middle of the empty Aral Sea. Their programs automated much of their work, but still required continuous human refinement with fresh algorithms and search parameters as the two lovers trawled through various American, European, Russian, and Australian espionage organisations.

Hours later, they still had nothing. Yebin disappeared to prepare a noodle, beef, and vegetable broth.

Twenty minutes more passed, and still with no hits, they ate together from bowls resting on their laps, for there was no clear surface anywhere. The food was tasty and nourishing, and Pierce devoured it all.

"I'll make a camp bed," Yebin said after they'd eaten, and disappeared again.

Pierce watched Valeriya step into an alcove of servers, where she adjusted cables and swapped two circuit boards. The work took time, and she was in no hurry. In the soft blue light that lit her up, Pierce noticed a fluorescent tattoo on the inside of her upper arm. A circle within a circle, both dissected by a single straight line through their centres.

"I've seen that before," he said.

"Seen what?"

Pierce pointed to her tattoo. "Only shows in ultraviolet light?"

She covered it and stepped back to her monitor. Under normal light, the tattoo vanished. "Pretend you didn't see it, Arkady."

"What does it mean?"

She shuddered. Her face turned white. "It's a brand," she whispered. "It denotes ownership."

Seven months ago, Pierce had seen that same symbol on a man he'd killed in the Sahara. A member of an extraction team working for an unknown organisation he'd never had time to investigate. That tattoo hadn't been ultraviolet light sensitive, but was still hidden.

"Ownership by who?" He kept his voice low, sensing that Valeriya did not wish for Yebin to overhear them.

She hugged her arms across her chest. "Please don't ask me that question, Arkady."

He nodded, suspecting the symbol represented the well-paying client she had mentioned earlier. "Does Yebin know?"

She shook her head as tension gripped every facial muscle. "You can't tell him. Promise me you won't?"

He nodded. "Valeriya, I promise."

"It means I made a mistake. But the organisation behind

this symbol, they have nothing to do with your current situation, or Yebin and my current situation. Please don't ask me about it again. It is a past I wish to forget."

Nodding, he and Valeriya returned their gaze to her monitor to check how her last trace program had fared.

They had a hit on Irina.

"She's CIA." Her voice again at normal volume, Valeriya's fingers now raced across her keyboard. Now that the symbol was no longer a topic of conversation, she had relaxed.

"How do you know?"

"See that marker." She pointed to a line of code moving across the screen. "Only the CIA use that."

Pierce felt hopeful. Finally, he was gathering intelligence he could use. "What can you tell me about her?"

With lightning speed, Valeriya pulled up files drawn straight from the CIA's human resources database. "Rachel Zang. Twenty-seven. Born in New York City. Chinese father and American mother with Asian ancestry."

Pierce noticed she had taken her mother's name. One file said Zang's mother had died many years back, but gave no cause for her passing.

Valeriya sat taller. "Oh, that's interesting."

"What's that?" Pierce scanned the files she was pulling up, but he couldn't read as fast as Valeriya did.

"Her parents' address. It's in a wealthy part of New York. Her family must have money. I mean real money, the kind that doesn't require you to take a shit government job to get by."

He nodded. "What else can you tell me about this... Rachel Zang? What happened to her mother, for example?"

"Even with our skills," Yebin yelled from the kitchen,

betraying that he could hear them, "we can't reach every database in every intelligence agency."

Valeriya stiffened but remained focused on her work. She yelled, "Lover! Where are you with that camp bed?"

"Getting there, my love. Arkady knows we don't have full access to all networks. Only files that aren't as tightly locked down as they should be."

"Thank you for making that crystal clear, lover!" Valeriya said in a raised voice, then forcing a smile, flitted through several more files until a photograph of Zang in a US Air Force dress uniform appeared. The insignia on her uniform was that of a second lieutenant.

She was Irina. There was no mistaking that in Pierce's mind.

"Zang resigned her commission with the Air Force three years ago. Then..."

"Then... what?"

Valeriya shrugged. "Not one hundred per cent clear, but it seems the CIA recruited her. Provided her specialist training. Look." Valeriya pointed to a line in her file. "That would be why. Other than English, she speaks fluent Mandarin and Russian. With her military training, she'd make a perfect paramilitary operations officer."

"CIA paramilitary training?" Pierce asked.

Valeriya tucked a loose strand of her raven hair behind an ear. "Can't tell which outfit. Did you stand her up, Arkady? An enemy agent you seduced on a covert mission?"

Pierce shook his head, remembering that to Valeriya, he was a former and very much disgraced SVR operative. "Actually, she stood me up."

"You were *pumping* her for information?"

He laughed. "Not like that."

"She's hunting you?"

Pierce nodded, not sure what he should reveal about his current situation. During his time with Zang, Pierce almost believed the woman was who she claimed to be, a tragic Russian prostitute named Irina. The success of her deceit was testament to her skills in creating and maintaining a believable legend. He'd admired her spirit, a tough exterior but with a sensitive side buried deep beneath the fear she projected. Pierce asked himself how much of her personality had she invented, and what of her true self had she revealed to him?

Zang intrigued him.

"Your expression tells me you think about her a lot."

"Maybe," answered Pierce, surprised by his transparent emotions. "But she is not my friend."

"Do you have a girlfriend, Arkady?"

"No." He turned and caught her stare.

Valeriya shrugged, the barbwire tattoos twisting on her pale skin. "You always look sad, Arkady, even when you smile. I would be sad too if I didn't have my lover boy. We complete each other."

Pierce blinked, not sure what to say.

She looked away. "I didn't mean to embarrass you, Arkady."

He shook his head. "You didn't, Valeriya. But can we get back to work?"

Valeriya returned her attention to the monitor and sighed. "I'll keep digging. See if I can find recent missions. That might reveal more about this mysterious woman who has you blushing."

21

Pierce watched Valeriya work, the muscles in her bare limbs tensing each time she struck the keyboard. He looked again for the dual circle tattoo, but without the ultraviolet light shining on her, it left no mark. He asked, "Do you worry, Valeriya, that the SVR or the FSB might find you here?"

The hacker shuddered. "Yebin and I will never let them take us. After we last saw you, we made a pact. If the Russians find us and there is no escape, we will take our own lives. We have the means. You already know how they tortured us when you saved us from those unspeakable horrors, but I will never let that happen again."

Pierce remembered back to the incident Valeriya referred to, and felt a pang of guilt, even though it was a situation not of his making.

Yebin returned, halting Pierce from pondering further. "The camp bed is ready when you need to sleep, Arkady." He kissed Valeriya on the lips, then slouched into the desk chair next to her and checked his progress on the audio file analysis. Half a minute later he turned from the monitor and said, "Mark Pierce? Is that another code name?"

He nodded. Hemsworth had used his name during their brief phone conversation, so there was no hiding it. Now there was a link between his old life and his new one. "Another name I'll ask you to forget, if you don't mind."

"Sure." Like his girlfriend's, Yebin's fingers flitted like ghosts over the keyboards as he loaded data files faster than Pierce could absorb the information. "Looks like we have a hit here too." He pulled up a photograph of two grinning Australian Special Air Service Regiment soldiers standing in what looked to be an Afghani desert. Each man was muscular with a thick beard and sun-weathered skin. "The one on the left," Yebin pointed to the ginger-haired soldier. "His name is Alex Trager. Former SASR sergeant."

Pierce studied the eyes.

The same eyes as his torturer in Central Africa.

The same man who had hunted him in Spain and captured him in Italy.

"Hemsworth".

"That's him." Pierce's gaze moved to the second soldier. He recognised those eyes too, for this man was "Jackman", and pointed to his photograph. "What about him?"

Yebin flipped through several files. "He's Javor Terzic. A former corporal from the same outfit. Looks like the SASR dishonourably discharged them both. They spent four years together in a Kabul prison for smuggling heroin on military flights into Australia, incarcerated with two more Australian soldiers from the same regiment." Yebin pulled up the files on the last two soldiers.

Pierce recognised the last two as members of Walsh's team who'd hunted Pierce in Morocco seven months earlier.

Pierce had eliminated them both. This explained Trager's and Terzic's personal investment in Pierce's suffering, as he had killed their mates while they had tried to kidnap him.

Trager and Terzic had been more successful in Italy, capturing and subduing Pierce there before drugging him and moving him to the Central African Republic warlord camp.

Yebin said, "Looks like Trager trained with Navy SEALs before he turned dirty. Jungle warfare unit."

Pierce grabbed a chair and sat between the lovers as an idea formed. "Valeriya, Yebin, your work is impressive. Thank you."

Yebin chuckled. "The trick is to look, but not touch. If we change nothing in the networks we hack, no one knows we were there. Isn't that right, my love?"

She leaned over and kissed him. "Except in your case, touching is acceptable."

He giggled, and they laughed together.

Pierce crossed his arms and leaned back. "I'm presuming Trager and Terzic are no longer in Afghanistan?"

"No, they aren't," said Yebin. "Let me investigate where they are now. Might take a while."

Pierce scratched his chin. "While you're at it, Yebin, see if you can find connections between Zang, Trager, Terzic and nuclear weaponry."

The hackers looked to each other and then to him.

"Nuclear weaponry?" Valeriya asked. "You must be in a world of trouble, Arkady?"

He didn't answer, and that told them everything they needed to know.

Their online searches continued for another hour while Pierce drank his coffee and tried to keep his eyes open.

Exhaustion was catching up with him, and if Valeriya and Yebin didn't come up with actionable intelligence in the next five minutes, he'd excuse himself and get some sleep. Learn what they had discovered in the morning.

"This is interesting." Valeriya pointed to a file on her screen. "An ASIS report from two years ago."

Yebin glanced at Pierce. "ASIS is Australian Secret Intelligence Service."

Valeriya playfully punched her boyfriend in the arm. "You need not explain, lover. Arkady is a smart man. He knows who ASIS is." She turned to Pierce and winked.

"What does the file say, Valeriya?" Pierce asked.

"Let me see... When Trager and Terzic and two of their fellow Australian soldiers disappeared from their prison in Kabul, an ASIS team investigated how. These are their findings." Valeriya read further before speaking. "It seems a CIA operator bribed the prison authorities to secure their release. No name for who that CIA visitor was, but descriptions are of a handsome man in his late fifties or early sixties. Blue eyes and grey hair. That's not enough to run any identifier programs to determine who he might be."

The description matched Idris Walsh, or how the spymaster had looked before Pierce's altercation with him in Morocco. "That's fine, Valeriya. Can you also check on any intel linking Alex Trager and Javor Terzic to the Central African Republic?"

"Sure. Why there?"

"Can you indulge me for the moment?"

22

Valeriya nodded to Pierce, and the couple went to work. Pierce sensed their competitive streaks in who could get the requested information first.

"Here we go!" Yebin exclaimed a minute later, then leaned back in his chair to stretch his arms over his head in a salute of victory. "Video footage from four months ago, taken from an American RQ-4 Global Hawk surveillance drone. Flown from a secret US base outside of Kasese, Uganda. You want to watch?"

Pierce nodded.

"Of course you want to watch. Who wouldn't? It's very intimate watching someone who doesn't know they are under observation."

Yebin played the drone footage. The scene was a high-altitude view of thick jungle. Open cut mines broke the natural landscape where hundreds of thin men and boys dug for diamonds and gold, using shovels and picks or their hands. Other men in green uniforms armed with AK-47s watched over the workers. These were conflict-diamond mines, a few of the many thousands operational across much of war-torn Africa, including where he had been held captive. Pierce memorised the latitude and longitude coordinates from the drone data feeds and noted the location was somewhere near the Central African Republic border with the Republic of the Congo and Cameroon.

The same location Walsh, Trager and Terzic had held him prisoner.

As the drone footage played, facial-recognition software soon identified targets of interest, and a camera zoomed in on three men. Two of the figures armed with FN-FAL assault rifles wore military fatigues. Target designators identified them as Trager and Terzic. The other man in a grey suit and gumboots had no marker. The sneer on his soft face suggested living in the jungle was not a regular experience for him.

"Who controls that territory?" Pierce asked.

Yebin and Valeriya went to work, then soon pulled up a series of news articles from the International Criminal Court in The Hague in the Netherlands, and from Amnesty International and a series of other human rights groups.

Valeriya said, "Can't be one hundred per cent certain, but a CAR warlord by the name of Captain Daniel Eloko operates in this general region."

Pierce had heard the name but couldn't recall any details. "Who is he?"

Yebin pulled up a photograph of a middle-aged man in green military fatigues and beret, who wasn't much to look at, and wasn't tall nor muscular nor good looking, but there was an unsettling aspect to his stare. He holstered a Beretta APX semi-automatic pistol secured in a leather holster on his hip, and an AK-74 assault rifle slung over his back.

A dozen bodyguards with older version AK-47 rifles and battered American M16A1 assault rifles stood in the background of the photo. Their uniforms, while green, were a mismatch of styles, and odd T-shirts of beach holiday destinations from across the globe, superhero characters, or Tintin comics adorned them. Where visible, each man wore gumboots instead of military lace-up boots to keep their feet dry in the muddy jungle.

Yebin said, "Eloko is the leader of an Anti-Balaka paramilitary terrorist group. That mean anything to you?"

Pierce nodded, as he recalled situation reports that he had occasionally read during his time with the CIA regarding the CAR. Landlocked with a population of five and a half million people, Central Africa was a tropical, impoverished and highly underdeveloped nation located just north of the Democratic Republic of the Congo.

In 2012, a predominantly Muslim rebel coalition from the northeast, Seleka, marched on CAR's capital Bangui, supported by thousands of Chadian and Sudanese mercenaries, who overthrew the then president without facing much resistance, and then launched a transition phase but failed to keep its fighters under control. Faced with the rebels' brutality, local populations formed self-defence militias, known as Anti-Balaka groups, mostly comprising Christians that targeted Muslim communities. This soon blew out to fighting across the country, turning Christians against Muslims, and resulted in widespread killings, pillaging, rapes, and enslavement of captured prisoners, and the rise of the already systemic use of child soldiers on both sides. International forces deployed into the CAR had worked to secure the country to some success, while Rwandan and Russian soldiers and mercenaries such as the Wagner Group had also embroiled themselves in the conflict, causing more harm than good. The country was a mess, for the war had already resulted in the deaths of tens of thousands and had displaced hundreds of thousands more, and there was no end in sight.

Currently, the Seleka Muslims controlled the central north of the country, while the Christian Anti-Balaka controlled the west and south. But that was a simplistic understanding of the situation, for there were many other groups also at war with each other in this failed nation, and Pierce couldn't recall all their names, allegiances, and ideologies at this moment. Not that it mattered; all he needed to know right now was that Captain Eloko was Christian Anti-Balaka, and where he was located, for he felt certain this man was involved somehow regardless of never having seen him during Pierce's incarceration in the warlord camp.

Yebin skimmed an article sourced from the International Criminal Court. "Says here Captain Eloko is wanted for a very long list of war crimes, which includes genocide, murder, terrorism, use of child soldiers, slavery, and smuggling. The latter predominately involving ivory and gold, but in the majority, diamond smuggling."

Pierce felt he had missed something, then remembered what was on his mind. "Pull up the drone feed of Trager, Terzic and the other man again, please?"

"Sure."

"What's that?" Pierce asked as he pointed to a blurred bulldozer in the background. It looked out of place in a warlord camp.

"I'll see if I can clean the image." Yebin ran a program,

and soon a logo appeared out of the haze. A stylised diamond with the word Polytope in a bold serif font.

"Polytope?" Pierce asked.

Valeriya already had the company website up on her browser. "Polytope Diamonds. Mining company founded in 1961 by British entrepreneur Martin Ponsonby. Now managed by his children, Rupert and Clementine Ponsonby." She loaded all three executives' bios from the company's website. "Ha! Would you believe the man talking to Trager and Terzic in the drone footage we looked at earlier is Rupert Ponsonby?"

Pierce sat straighter. "This just gets more and more interesting."

Yebin laughed. "I would ask what have you got yourself involved in, Arkady, but perhaps I shouldn't ask."

"Don't ask," Pierce said, meaning it. He'd got the two hackers more involved than he should have. If he'd had other options, he would have left Valeriya and Yebin well alone and ignorant to him still being alive. It would have been safer for all of them if he had.

More information on Polytope Diamonds came up as the hackers found several related articles on mining industry news sites concerning Polytope. After reading a few, they learned that the private British company had made its money in mines in South Africa, Botswana and Namibia in Southern Africa in the second half of the twentieth century, but most of those mines were now depleted and decommissioned, or coming to the end of their productive lives.

There were, however, two new Polytope mines that Rupert Ponsonby oversaw. An operational site extracting marine diamonds from the seabed off the coast of Angola, and another that was in the development phase, with

infrastructure and processing equipment still to be
constructed on site, and that second one was in the Central
African Republic. The same location that Pierce had been
held captive for those seven horrific months of his life.

Yebin smirked, crossed his arms, and leaned back in his
chair. "Did you notice, Arkady, that in all the Polytype news
articles, the father and the daughter always appear together,
and only they give the statements and quotes, looking
important, while poor old Rupert is not in any of them?"

Pierce bit his lip. "So Rupert Ponsonby is on the outside,
the embarrassing son?"

Yebin flicked up a few more articles that were
disparaging in their assessment of the male heir. "Considering Rupert's reported spending habits — dozens of high-
end sports cars, a mansion in the posh London suburb of
Kensington with multiple basement levels, many wardrobes'
worth of designer suits, watches, shoes and technological
gadgets — I'd suggest Rupert is more interested in his image
and having fun than actually doing any work. No wonder
father and sister want nothing to do with him."

Pierce tried to stifle a yawn. He looked at the time on
Yebin's computer monitor and saw that it was well after 0200
hours in the evening. But they had more to do before any of
them could sleep. "I'd say your assessment is valid, Yebin."

Valeriya nodded. "That would also explain the articles
we read about the Polytope operations in Angola and CAR
being unfeasible and unprofitable, suggesting Rupert doesn't
know how to manage them properly."

Pierce said, "So Polytope is in trouble?"

Valeriya almost jumped out of her chair when she found
something new. "Look at this! Recent news from the Polytope website. Four days ago, Martin Ponsonby died of a heart

attack. Also here, it says Rupert Ponsonby took over the controlling shares of the company a few days later, and that his sister, Clementine, stepped down."

"Interesting." Pierce pointed to Polytope's most recent news article, posted only a day ago. "Can you open that one?"

Valeriya complied. The article included another photo of the well-dressed Rupert Ponsonby with too much hair product and a conceited smile, announcing his presence in Cape Town, speaking at the World Annual Diamond Industry Conference in three days' time, replacing his sister, Clementine, who was now unable to attend. Valeriya said, "That can't be a coincidence, can it?"

"No, it can't." Pierce couldn't have felt happier. "Valeriya, Yebin, can you prepare me an intel package on Polytope, Ponsonby and the Australian Special Forces men?"

"Easy. Will have it ready for you in the morning. Do you need fake passports and a plane ticket to South Africa?" Valeriya asked with a smirk.

He smiled back at her. "Yes, thank you. Two passports with unique identities if you can manage it."

"It would be our pleasure."

He studied the loving but broken Russian couple. A plan was already forming in his mind. "Since you've both been so helpful, you wouldn't know a reliable arms trader in South Africa? I believe I'm going to need a sniper rifle."

PART II

THE INVISIBLE WORLD

23

Bayanga, Central African Republic

With weeping eyes, Dr Derek Kiambi stared down at his hands, drenched in blood, where they had pressed down for what felt like hours, but was probably only minutes, on the chest of the dead Anti-Balaka soldier laid out on his ineffective operating table. Three bullets lodged in his abdomen, which were too complex to remove, had also shredded his intestines, so it had been inevitable that the shock and blood loss would kill him. Endless compressions to keep his heart pumping had achieved nothing.

The soldier standing behind Kiambi had wept earlier and for far longer, but not anymore. Now he growled, pulled a pistol from a holster on his belt, then forced its muzzle up under Kiambi's jaw. "You fucking killed my brother."

The doctor closed his eyes and willed the man to shoot him, permanently ending his endless misery and suffering. When nothing changed, and he remained alive, Kiambi spoke softly to his tormentor. "Mamadou, I did everything I could for Lembe."

The soldier cocked the weapon's hammer and pressed it harder into Kiambi's neck. "The hell you did!" he shouted.

"But he did do everything in his power to save your brother!" boomed a voice from across the decrepit surgery. "So lower that weapon."

Both Mamadou and Kiambi turned to find their camp's leader, Captain Daniel Eloko, standing in the open-air entrance, with a cold expression etched across his still face. How long had he been there, watching them both, Kiambi could only guess.

Upon seeing his commanding officer, the demeanour of the fit and muscular Mamadou — who always only ever wore an open vest, shorts and boots to display his visual strength and manliness — suddenly switched from aggression to submission. A younger pup heeding the will of the pack leader. "He killed my brother."

"No, he didn't, Mamadou. Where is your brother's magic bullet?"

Mamadou frowned, then checked Lembe's neck for the pendant that all Eloko's soldiers wore, with an amulet of a bullet. But it was nowhere. The man found his rage again as his face twisted and tensed into unnatural shapes. He pointed to Kiambi with his pistol and said, "This fucker took it. He wanted my brother to die."

"He doesn't know," said Eloko, without explaining what he meant. "Your brother lost his protection charm during your battles with the ungodly Seleka terrorists. That is why Lembe is dead."

"But—?"

Eloko raised his voice, but his commanding words

remained controlled and precise. "But nothing, Mamadou! Continue to disagree with me, and I'll take away the magic in your bullet charm. You won't last long in the battlefields if I do."

Mamadou subconsciously fingered the bullet amulet around his own neck. Then, as if sensing the evils spirits that Eloko claimed to command as having just entered the room with malice intent on their minds, he switched his weapon to safe, lowered his head, and nodded.

"Good. We have work to do." Eloko glanced around the surgery, which was little more than a wooden-framed building with insufficient overhead lights, sewn-together mosquito nets where there should have been glass windows, and old fuel drums boiled in the campfires to provide a modicum of sterile water. Then, perhaps bored by what he saw, he said, "I need you both to come with me."

Kiambi shuddered. Of all the many insane and power-hungry soldiers who lived in their camp, he feared Eloko the most. While Walsh, Trager and Terzic were all cold-hearted killers, they were at least all rational. Eloko was the same, but he was also a megalomaniac, a narcissist, and utterly unpredictable. They could be off somewhere to reward Kiambi with palm wine and good food, but it was also just as likely they were about to strap him to a post while they beat him with sticks for an hour or so's amusement.

"Yes, sir," said Kiambi. He quickly removed his blood-drenched smock and washed his hands.

"We bury Lembe's body later, when I can ensure his soul is properly guided back into the spirit realm and doesn't become trapped in the endless nightmare realms of the jungle. Is that understood, Mamadou?"

"Yes, sir."

Outside, they looked out across the camp's nearby paved airfield, which was one of the few local infrastructure projects Polytope Diamonds had completed here. It was the first of many in an ambitious program of expansion works required before they could industrialise the camp's existing hand-dug mines.

Kiambi had understood from overheard conversations between Walsh and Rupert Ponsonby, when the Englishman occasionally visited his investment, that the intention was to build a modern mass-haul mining operation here. When complete, they believed it would result in millions of carats of gem-quality diamonds lining their pockets rather than the tiny quantities they secured now, but only if the Englishman could present his scheme as an attractive offer to investors. With the misery and destitution that he saw everywhere here every day, Kiambi couldn't understand how any of this was possible.

They walked to another wooden-framed building, a bungalow where Sergeant Alex Trager and Corporal Javor Terzic sat on the steps, both of them cleaning and reassembling their modern-looking military rifles. Both men were muscular like the Bollywood actors he had seen in the cinema back home, and sweat glistened off the skins of their broad, sleeveless arms. Trager's ginger beard and hair was thick and unruly, while Terzic kept his dark scalp neatly trimmed and his face clean-shaven.

Then Kiambi watched as Molly McEwan, the slender red-headed Scottish scientist who seemed completely out of place in this hellhole, with her long frizzy hair tied back in a ponytail and wearing a man's shirt and pants too large for her, stepped out of the bungalow. She leaned down and kissed Trager on the forehead. He took her hand and squeezed it affectionately. Kiambi knew that the three foreigners lived in that building when they were not on missions requiring them to scour the globe.

"Sergeant Trager!" Eloko's voice boomed as he, Mamadou and Kiambi approached. "You are back again! Where were you this time?"

Trager and Terzic both stood and saluted.

Trager said, "Yes, Captain. Back from Botswana. Kazakhstan before that, as you know. The first radioactive drum is in place. Secure, hidden and ready for detonation. South Africa tomorrow."

"Good! Good!" Eloko embraced Trager with a rigid hug. "Walsh's plan is working, then?"

Trager nodded, but Kiambi could see hesitation in his expression, as if all was not well but he fought to hide this from Eloko. "Yes, everything is proceeding as planned." He turned to Molly, who had crossed her arms and stepped back behind Terzic.

But that didn't stop Eloko as he embraced Molly and kissed her on the cheek. She tensed as Eloko touched her, his mouth lingering longer than it should. "I missed you, my dear. You're always a pleasure for my eyes."

"It's good to see you too, Captain," she said through a mouth that barely opened.

Seemingly unaware of her barely suppressed fear of him, or perhaps ignoring it, Eloko turned to Trager. "You, my friend. You need to come with me, Mamadou and the doctor, now."

Trager checked that he had a loaded pistol in his belt holster, then said, "Where are we going?"

Eloko grinned. "It's a surprise." His eyes looked Molly up

and down. "She must stay here, and the corporal here can finish cleaning your weapons. I only need you."

Trager nodded to Molly, and she returned the nod. Then her hand gently touched his chest. "You don't look well, Alex?"

He pressed a hand against his gut. "I'll be fine, Molly."

"Talk to the doctor," she whispered while she glanced at Kiambi for the briefest moment.

"As I said, I'll be fine." Then Trager said to Eloko, "I'm ready. Let's go."

Kiambi, Trager, Captain Eloko and several of his most trusted protective guards climbed into three army trucks. Each vehicle was fitted with mounted .50-calibre machine guns capable of shredding any opposition they encountered into tiny pieces of meat with only a few seconds of controlled, full-automatic fire.

When Mamadou made to join them, Eloko said, "On second thoughts, you stay here. Bury your brother. I sense his spirit is already where it needs to be."

Mamadou saluted, then wiped tears from his wetting eyes. "Thank you, sir." He turned on a heel and marched back to the surgery.

The trucks' engines roared into life, then followed a dirty orange-brown track through the jungle. The tallest trees grew at least fifty metres into the sky, and soon their canopies of thick leaves and branches obscured most of the sunlight. Kiambi sat between Trager and Eloko in the back tray of the second truck with three other local soldiers and wondered what this could all be about.

During the drive, Trager kept clenching down on his teeth and holding his stomach, and the sweat coming off his face seemed profound, even considering their constant need to sweat in this permanent tropical environment.

"Are you ill?" Kiambi asked.

"I'm experiencing nausea and vomiting."

Kiambi nodded and was about to ask about further symptoms when Eloko spoke over him. "You know my country's story, don't you, Trager?"

The Australian soldier turned his attention to Eloko and shrugged. "Some of it. Why?"

"You should know our story, particularly now that you've been here for some time. CAR is my home. The beautiful Central African Republic. A God-fearing Christian country. We are pious and united in our faith except for the minority Muslims, who think they have rights to worship their heathen gods alongside us."

"You are talking about the Seleka Muslim rebel groups controlling the central north?"

Eloko smiled. "It's good to see you listen when I speak, my friend."

Trager was silent for a moment, then said, "I'm listening now, Captain."

"Good. Then you should know we will drive out the Muslims wherever we find them, or enslave them, to work in the mines until they die from their labours." The captain raised his eyebrows and grinned, showing his teeth. "Muslims get what they deserve."

Trager nodded and kept silent.

"You've never told me, Sergeant. I had presumed, but I don't know, and now I am curious. Are you a God-fearing Christian yourself, like me and the good doctor here?"

Trager shrugged and wouldn't look directly at their

leader. "I fear people more than anything else, Captain. Only people fuck up the world."

Eloko grinned like he knew a secret.

"What has changed, Captain? Why are we having this conversation?"

Eloko belly laughed. "You will see, Sergeant. You will see."

24

The long drive through washed-out roads took the truck convoy far from the ineffective Polytope camp to a secluded, hand-dug diamond mine deep within the jungle. Barefooted Muslim men and boys, in dirty and torn clothes, dug a deep terraced cut into the side of a hill. Additional enslaved workers panned mud in the wide river below. Eloko's soldiers watched over both groups with keen eyes and the business ends of antiquated Russian and American rifles. Kiambi had never seen these mines before, always contained in his surgery or the main camp, and estimated at least five hundred Muslim slaves and about fifty Christian soldiers lived and worked here.

The convoy pulled to a stop, and everyone except for the .50-calibre machine gunners jumped down into the mud, establishing a protective perimeter around Eloko. Kiambi had climbed out behind Trager and now stood towards the back of the group, where he hoped to remain invisible. Trager lit a cigarette and placed it in his mouth and didn't seem to care who looked at him. Then he glanced around at the soldiers who had accompanied them, and noticed something that caused his eyebrows to rise.

Kiambi looked too until he understood what had unsettled Trager. Eloko and his men had all their weapons raised, and several exhibited nervous tendencies, like they expected battle. Kiambi's instincts warned that Eloko was here to resolve a problem with the mine, and the solution would involve blood and violence.

"Where is Pious Ibaka?" Eloko screamed across the camp. "Where is my mine supervisor?"

A tall, old man with a bald head stepped forward. His clothes were the same mismatched green uniform as the other soldiers, with mud splashed up his gumboots and onto his trousers. An antiquated revolver rested in a worn leather holster on his belt. "Captain Eloko." He snapped off a salute. "It is an honour that you have come."

Eloko returned the salute, then leaned in close to Trager and had a whispered conversation that Kiambi could only just hear, but pretended not to. "Sergeant, I told you about Muslims and Christians, but monotheism is not this continent's true faith. Real African power is in witchcraft, sorcery and communion with ancient spirits that exist in great numbers perched on the edge of the material world. The spirit world thrived here long before the Europeans and Arabs invaded our lands. They will thrive long after the Muslim and Christian faiths are dead and forgotten." He twisted and stepped away from Trager to embrace Ibaka with another of his invasive, manly hugs. "Ibaka, my friend, you are looking good."

The older man gave a slight bow. "I have you to thank for my fortunes, Captain."

Eloko slung his arm over Ibaka's shoulder and leaned in close. "So what is this problem you need help with?"

Ibaka lowered his eyes. "I would not normally trouble you with such trivial matters, but seven Muslim workers have betrayed us."

"How so?"

"They panned an enormous diamond from the river but hid it. One of my men saw them. I've questioned the Muslim dogs at length, but no one has confessed."

Trager watched as Eloko's expression switched from joy to rage. "I should not have to deal with these problems myself, Ibaka."

"I am sorry, sir, but I felt it was better that you knew now before you heard from someone else. No one can become so emboldened to believe they can steal from us."

"'Us'? Or 'me'?"

Ibaka trembled. "I mean you... My... Captain. Let... let me show you."

Eloko waved his hand to usher Ibaka into action.

Together with Trager, Kiambi and a half-dozen soldiers, Eloko and Ibaka marched along the muddy river's edge until they reached a series of thatched huts. Soon Kiambi spied seven men chained and beaten and kneeling in the mud, lined up in an executioner's row. He wondered how they remained upright with the severity of the injuries on their faces and arms. Was this why he was here, to treat their injuries? The doctor's instincts, however, told him that he was not.

"Are these the thieves?" asked Eloko.

Ibaka nodded.

Eloko drew his pistol and waved it in the air. His voice boomed again, "You all know my reputation, yet you still betray me!" He walked the line of prisoners. "Let me tell you my story, if you don't know it already, because you should know it." Eloko paused, sensed the silence and stillness gripping the mine. He grinned at the power he commanded. "I don't believe in your Muslim or Christian bullshit. They are not real faiths. I believe only in our ancestral traditions. For a hundred generations, the Elokos were sorcerers, and I am one too."

Kiambi shuddered. He'd witnessed Captain Eloko's fickle faith in Christianity before, which, when convenient, he trumped with his stronger belief in magic and sorcery.

Sweat running off his forehead, Eloko turned and caught the stares of Ibaka, Trager, his combat-ready men, and the chained slaves. "I will prove it to you all, again, so there is no doubt in any of you of my power!" He held his pistol high above his head. "I cast spells over my weapons. You want to know what this pistol does? It fires justice bullets. Only justice bullets. If you are pure of intent and loyal to me, the bullets cannot harm you. If you are my enemy, or there is deceit in your heart, the bullets will kill you and send your spirit into darkness, where it will become lost forever in the nightmare realms of the great Congo, where demons will feast on your soul for eternity. Are you ready for my bullets to test you?"

One prisoner sobbed as tears gushed from his eyes.

The other six remained still and silent as their bodies tensed.

"I'll take that as a yes."

Captain Eloko pressed the weapon against the head of the first slave and squeezed the trigger. The noise of the bullet sounded loud in the otherwise silent mining camp as the dead slave fell face first into the mud.

Eloko stepped up to the second man, squeezed the trigger, blowing apart another skull.

Kiambi had witnessed plenty of Eloko's executions during his incarceration, but nothing prepared him when Eloko spun around and placed the weapon against his own sweaty skull, like a man ready to commit suicide, and fired.

The bullet sounded.

The casing ejected from the chamber.

Smoke spewed from the muzzle.

Yet Captain Eloko remained unharmed.

The warlord returned to the line and fired the weapon into the back of each slave's head, executing them all.

Or so Kiambi thought. One fallen slave struggled up out of the mud. He was not dead or even injured, for the bullet intended to shoot through the back of his head must have been a blank or a misfire.

Eloko grinned and lifted the slave to his feet and shook the already shaking man. "I know it wasn't you. I know your so-called friends made you do it. So, you will tell me where you hid the diamond, as a loyal subject would."

Kiambi couldn't hear what the prisoner mumbled, but he witnessed plenty of nodding from Eloko as they conversed. Then the warlord marched over to one of his soldiers, who then disappeared into the jungle for perhaps fifteen minutes before returning with a largish, rough diamond wrapped in cloth.

Eloko smiled again. "Ah! See, that wasn't so hard." He beckoned for Trager, Kiambi and Ibaka to step close to him.

They all complied.

Ibaka was trembling, and so was Kiambi. Trager must have felt fear too because of all the tensing and eye-flickering they were witnessing in Eloko, but Trager hid it well if he did.

Eloko switched magazines on his pistol. His movements were slow and careful. "Do you three now believe that I am a sorcerer? That I control real magic? That I can make any of you die with a click of my fingers?"

Ibaka nodded. "I never doubted you, my Captain."

Kiambi nodded vigorously in agreement. The doctor was a pious Christian, had been his entire life. Had he expressed too many opinions concerning the love of his god towards all people and his faith in this higher power, and had this displeased Eloko? Kiambi knew he was about to find out in the coming seconds. "I believe you too, Captain. I always have."

Kiambi felt sick when he spoke those words, denying his faith in this public scenario just to save his own pointless life in this moment. He knew this was trickery, and the simplest solution was a pistol loaded with both blank and live rounds. It took nerves that Kiambi could never possess, to point a weapon at one's own head and pull the trigger, hoping that you had remembered the order of rounds correctly.

Eloko turned to Trager, and the two men locked stares. He waited impatiently for an answer.

Trager just stared back into Eloko's dead eyes and spoke using careful, controlled words. "Your powers are impressive, Captain. I've never seen their like before."

Eloko's hand shot up, and he fired his pistol three times, once at Trager, once at Kiambi, and once at Ibaka.

The mine supervisor dropped dead into the mud.

Trager and Kiambi, however, remained upright.

Kiambi touched his chest.

No blood decorated his fingers, and there was no pain.

He checked his shirt, pulled open the buttons, finding no entry wound.

Trager too appeared as equally baffled that he was not dead.

"See," Eloko said with the practised grin of a madman. "Guilt is very easy to determine. Let this be a lesson for you, Sergeant Trager and Dr Kiambi. Today I've proven both your loyalties. Don't let that loyalty falter, because when you betray me, I will know the truth. And so will my magic bullets."

25

The return drive to the rebel camp seemed to make Trager sicker than he had been when they had first arrived at the mine. The rough road, erratic speeds and stop-start motions caused him to vomit often, and soon his bile streaked down the outsides of the truck. When he wasn't spewing, he closed his eyes while trying to take in deep breaths.

Kiambi sat on the floor between Trager and Eloko. He looked at his limbs, which were like twigs. He felt the tears as they streamed down his sunken face. Sometimes when Eloko or other soldiers pressed their weapons against his head, ready to execute him, he wished that they would so this could all end. As a Christian, he couldn't commit suicide, as that was a mortal sin, so his ending, when it came, would always be tied to the will of others.

Then he would remember his family and his daughters, lost to him, and how he might one day get back to them. And he also remembered the women, boys and girls of this camp, forced into soldiering and prostitution, and how he'd helped them with their ailments when they arose. It was only the needs of the innocents that he could serve with his skills, which kept him going.

"We're here," said Eloko as they arrived back at the camp.

Trager stepped onto solid ground and seemed to recover a little from his nausea now that he could stand straight again and was not confined to a vehicle roughly traversing a potholed muddy road.

Eloko grinned at Trager when he saw the man was in pain, but his eyes were like shadows. "You didn't shit in my truck?"

Trager frowned. "No. I shit in the jungle like everyone else."

"Runny shit, no doubt." The warlord belly laughed as he pounded Trager on the back, a gesture designed to appear friendly, but was a reminder of Eloko's physical power and his ability to hurt anyone whenever he chose to. "You are sick, my friend. You have angered the spirits." Eloko gestured to Trager's vomit trails staining the outside panels of his truck. "I have good reason to believe that maybe you've lost control of all your orifices."

"You're not worried about my well-being, Captain." Trager couldn't hide his sarcastic tone.

"I don't worry about anyone. I don't have to. Because I know everyone. I see all your souls, better than you see them yourselves. I know who is sick, who is healthy, who will live to the end of each day and who will not. Your spirit selves cannot hide their truth from me. The invisible world is mine to control."

Trager snorted a laugh.

"You don't believe, Sergeant. I see that. You pretend you

are better than all this, but you pass like a shadow through a material world of falsehoods."

"What do you care what I think?"

Eloko's eyes stared unblinking. "I will give you some peace of mind, Sergeant. You *will* die soon enough, and so will your friends. I've seen the future. But you will not die today, and not from the evil spirits that made you vomit all over my beautiful truck." He again slapped Trager hard on the back. "Smile, Sergeant. Enjoy what life you have now. Live in the moment, because here and now is all that matters. Go pound that beautiful piece of ass you keep locked up in your cabin. Enjoy your passions with the delightful Molly McEwan. I tell you this, Sergeant, because joy never lasts forever. Not for you, at least." He looked over to his own hut, then grabbed his crotch. "Speaking of living in the moment..."

Trager and Kiambi watched Eloko stride towards his harem. When the warlord was beyond their sight, Trager grabbed Kiambi and dragged him through the mud to his bungalow.

"What's happening now?" Kiambi asked, intensely feeling the fear that was always with him.

"Nothing sinister." At his bungalow, Trager pounded on the door. "Molly, it's me. Alex."

Several seconds of fumbling passed before the locks unlatched and Molly stood before him, with a pistol tight in her sweaty palm. Her eyes were red and her nose runny.

"You okay?" Trager asked.

Molly nodded and hugged him.

"Where is Javor? Why are you alone? Don't you know you can't be alone in this camp, with these crazy drug-addled soldiers wandering around taking whatever they want?"

She shook her head, then sobbed. "Mamadou insisted Javor help bury his brother. I should have gone with them, but... I was scared to leave. Then they kept... Peering through the windows."

"What? Who?"

"Eloko's men. Came right up to the windows. Demanded I... perform."

Trager snarled as his face twisted into ugliness. "But no one touched you?"

Molly frowned and withdrew from him. "No! Didn't make it any less scary."

Kiambi shrank into a corner of the bungalow, feeling that he didn't belong as a witness to this intimate conversation.

Trager pulled her close and hugged her again, his personality switching from anger to compassion in a single moment. "I know, and I'm sorry. I'll deal with this. But first, I need to deal with my illness."

He turned to Kiambi, stared him down, and the doctor finally understood why he was here.

26

A fter checking the Australian's temperature, blood pressure, throat, eyes and ears, and asking various questions about his diet, aches and pains, sexual appetite and other bodily functions, Kiambi said, "It's food poisoning."

"You sure?"

"Yes, or it's a stomach bug, which is essentially the same thing. Either way, nothing to worry about, and you'll recover in a few days. You just need rest and lots of fluids."

Trager tensed, then said, "Mate, could it be something else?"

The doctor shrugged, then noticed Molly's worry, equal to Trager's. Then Kiambi remembered Eloko's quasi-prophetic words concerning Trager's impending death and immediately dismissed it from his mind as folly.

"Radiation poisoning?" Molly spoke before Trager could say what was on both their minds. "Could Alex's symptoms result from exposure to fissile materials?"

Kiambi stared at them both for a long ten seconds. This

was not at all what he was expecting, and he wondered how this connected to any of the horrors they experienced in this camp on a daily basis. "Why do you ask that?"

Trager grimaced. "The places me, Molly and the corporal visited while we've been away this last week, there was nuclear waste."

"You were both exposed? And Mr Terzic as well?" Kiambi asked as his body tensed. He wondered if there was nuclear waste in the camp, and if they were all being exposed to it even now.

Then he remembered a week ago, Trager and Terzic had lowered a metal-framed contraption containing six oil-barrel-sized drums into the Kadei River. He had not understood why at the time, but now it made sense; this was the nuclear waste Trager and Molly were talking about. He remembered his studies on nuclear medicine, which didn't amount to much in the CAR, but knew enough to recall water was a highly effective means of halting gamma rays emitted from radioactive isotopes.

"The drums in the river, they are the source of the radiation?"

Molly nodded.

"Do you have any symptoms, miss?"

She shook her head.

"What about Mr Terzic?"

"He hasn't mentioned anything."

"Has Mr Trager spent more time near the fissile material than either of you?"

Another shake of the head.

"If exposed together, you should both have the same symptoms. Take off your shirts please, both of you?"

Molly looked to Trager, and he nodded that it was okay

to do so. When they stood topless, him bare-chested and her in a bra, Kiambi examined their skin. Both bodies featured plenty of cuts, mosquito bites and sores that came from living rough in the jungle, and old scar tissue from past wounds, but nothing unordinary.

"You're both okay." Kiambi motioned they should dress again. "There would be blotches on your skin, burns and sores, but there is nothing. It's food poisoning. At worst, dysentery."

Trager nodded as his breathing slowed to a more normal rhythm. "Thank you, Doctor."

The doctor sighed and smiled. "Mr Trager, Ms McEwen, now that I've helped you, can you please help me? You are both kind people, and I am desperate for your assistance."

"What kind of help?" Molly buttoned her shirt.

Kiambi sobbed. "My family. I'm worried about them."

Trager said nothing as he dressed and wouldn't look at Kiambi. Then he caught Molly's stare, and her eyes told him it was his duty to aid the doctor.

"I didn't know you had a family, Derek," she said.

Kiambi clasped his hands together as if in prayer. "My wife and three daughters, Alzina, Edmee and Saforah, I haven't seen them in seven months. I don't know if they are safe or hurt or dead."

Molly touched him on his bony elbow. "I'm so sorry."

"That's enough," Trager interrupted. "Kiambi, your situation is no different than anyone else in this camp."

"Please, Sergeant. I'm worried sick for my family. I've done everything I can to help Eloko's men when they fall ill or become wounded. I proved that again today, with Mamadou's brother, trying to save him even when it was hopeless. How long must I prove my loyalty?"

Trager circled the doctor, like a lion stalking a frail impala. "We are all prisoners here, Doctor. If you wish to have benefits, you need to prove your value, not your intentions."

Kiambi couldn't help himself and sobbed. "How? How else can I offer any more value than I do?"

Molly gave Trager a disapproving stare. He ignored her. "There are three types of people in this world, Kiambi. The first are the powerful men, who control money, resources, corporations, countries, and armies. The second are people like us." He waved his hand to include Molly, Kiambi and himself. "We are skilled individuals, valued by the powerful people because our qualifications and experiences aid them in maintaining and enhancing their powers of control."

"And the third type?" Molly asked.

Trager waved his hand towards the camp. "The men and child soldiers, the enslaved miners, and the girl prostitutes. Replaceable in an instant by more of the fallen who line up by the thousands, waiting for an opportunity not to starve to death with the pitiful resources powerful men will throw their way."

"What is your point?" Kiambi wiped away more tears that streamed down his face. He didn't like Trager's tone, for he sensed no compassion in him.

"Life is a struggle, Doctor, and the world order is always trying to pull you down. The only hope for people like us is to work hard and become one of the powerful people; otherwise we might fall forever into that endless pit of hopelessness you can never escape from. Pull yourself out of your misery and become like Molly and me, closer to the higher rungs of life's ladder. When you do, you won't need to ask us for help. You will no longer beg for reuniting with your family, but demand it."

"So you won't help me?"

Trager shook his head. "Only one man can help you now, Kiambi, and that's you. Help yourself."

The door burst open, and Corporal Terzic stormed inside. He was out of breath, and his eyes were wide with fear. "Fuck! Sergeant. Sir, we're in serious fucking trouble!"

Trager pulled his pistol from his belt holster. "Are we under attack?"

"Negative!" Terzic ran a hand through his hair. "Sorry, sir, didn't mean to surprise you like that. We are not under attack, but the news isn't good."

Trager nodded. "Then what the hell is going on, Corporal?"

The colour quickly drained from Corporal Terzic's face. "Sir, three and a half million dollars just disappeared from our operational account! And it looks like someone has used that money to hire an assassin. And who that assassin is targeting, I have no fucking idea!"

27

Cape Town, South Africa

Baku to Cape Town via Istanbul proved to be an uneventful flight. After a routine customs check using the first of two fake passports, Mark Pierce took a shuttle bus from Cape Town International Airport into the city's business district. The sunny weather lifted his mood, and so did the view. Cape Town was modern and picturesque, featuring a magnificent vista over the Atlantic Ocean and the powerful Table Mountains backdrop behind him. For Pierce, the South African metropolis was one of the most beautiful cities in the world, rivalled only by Sydney, Rio de Janeiro, San Francisco, and Hong Kong. He realised he'd missed vibrant and cosmopolitan culture — not that he could afford time to relax. A busy schedule awaited.

In a hotel on Main Road overlooking Victoria and Alfred Waterfront, Pierce downloaded and installed a sophisticated encryption program on his burner phone. A single message waited on the fake Gulzar Zam Dark Web contact page, requesting a change of target, to that of Pierce himself. This proved that Sergeant Trager and Corporal Terzic had discovered their missing money and learned of the assassin they had unwittingly paid for. Hopefully this had caused confusion and would support Pierce's plan in the coming days. He smiled and posted a reply message, saying the target would only change if accompanied with the correct password. He imagined how Trager and Terzic would sweat when they read this reply, and wondered how long it would be before Idris Walsh learned of their fabricated deception towards their boss.

After showering and shaving, then dressing in jeans, desert boots and a navy long-sleeve shirt, Pierce headed to the lobby where he ordered a steak, chips and beer, and ate in the restaurant. He kept his back to the wall with an uninterrupted view of the concierge's desk and the elevators, but didn't notice anyone suspicious coming or going. Once he had eaten, he asked for the bill and paid with cash. As he stood, he wrapped the sharp steak knife in a serviette and pocketed the weapon.

After lunch, Pierce visited several banks until he'd withdrawn the equivalent of a little over one hundred thousand US dollars. He then purchased a large sports bag and a tarpaulin, each item secured from separate shops, and both paid for in cash.

At sixteen hundred hours he returned to the hotel and rented a Suzuki Vitara four-wheel drive, then drove south towards the township of Khayelitsha on the Western Cape. Halfway, Pierce stopped and temporarily disabled the Suzuki's GPS tracker, then kept driving. Counted amongst the world's largest slums, Khayelitsha was home to some of the poorest Africans on the continent, and a risky locale for an outsider like himself. In a country that already suffered from extreme murder and assault rates, Pierce kept vigilant at all times.

Khayelitsha was a township of chaotically arranged shacks and plenty of churches. Power lines ran like nets cast over the streets, and tall grass grew where human settlement had not encroached. Only black faces looked back at him.

At sunset he found the bar where Valeriya and Yebin had told him it would be. Several large, muscular men guarded the entrance. AK-47s slung over their backs, while bored expressions masked attentive eyes.

Pierce parked and locked his Suzuki on the opposite side of the compacted earthen road, stepped over strewn litter and approached like he belonged here. "I'm here for Uuka. The name's Arkady."

The heaviest guard stared Pierce down for a long moment, then nodded to his underlings. Two men patted Pierce down. He'd left the money and the steak knife in the Suzuki, so they found nothing. Satisfied Pierce was no threat, they pushed him inside.

The bar was close to empty, with plenty of sharp-edged shadows. Two old men in fedoras played backgammon in a corner while a young man in a loose T-shirt cleaned plastic cups behind the bar. A bald, muscular man sat in a chair by a table towards the centre. A naked light bulb above him cast shadows over his eyes, which focused on the laptop in front of him. He nursed a half-finished beer. From Pierce's angle, he could not see what was on the screen. Then the man closed his laptop and looked up as Pierce approached.

"I take it you're Uuka?" Pierce spoke English but with a Russian accent.

The man nodded and shook hands with a firm grip. "And you are Arkady?"

Pierce returned the nod. "I'm presuming there'll be no problem with our transaction?"

Uuka laughed. "Not if you have the money. One hundred thousand US dollars, and the weapons are yours."

"Can I see them first?"

Uuka nodded to his men. One brought forth an oilskin and unrolled it on top of an adjacent table, revealing a Glock 22 semi-automatic pistol with three spare magazines, a grappling hook with Kevlar rope, and the most important item of the collection, a Heckler & Koch HK PSG-1 semi-automatic sniper rifle with three magazines and a scope.

The bald criminal took a pack of cigarettes from his pocket and lit one. He offered the pack to Pierce, who declined. "The weapons are old, my friend. Well used, but in good working order."

"Fine by me."

"The price is low because serious criminals used the weapons in Cape Town, and the police are investigating. I hope that won't be a problem?"

Pierce shook his head. He was paying far more than the weapons were worth, but he needed firepower fast through a supplier that the world's various intelligence agencies could not easily trace. If captured by the South African authorities, Pierce would face far more serious charges than possessing weapons connected to a murder, so the risk was acceptable. "The money is in the car. I'll go get it."

Uuka nodded.

The transaction occurred smoothly with no haggling, threats or renegotiations for more money. Sometimes, Pierce mused, shady transactions went as planned.

Their business concluded, he thanked Uuka and drove out. Dozens of young kids with dust caking their skin watched him suspiciously as he vanished in the setting sun.

Returning to Cape Town late into the night, Pierce refitted his GPS tracker and parked in the hotel car park. He placed the weapons in the sports bag and took the collection to his hotel room. After room service, comprising a spicy Malay dish of coriander, rice, lentils and lamb, and a refreshing lager, Pierce set about cleaning and prepping his weapons.

Tomorrow would be a busy day.

28

Langley, Virginia, United States

As Idris Walsh wandered the secure halls of CIA headquarters in Langley, Virginia, he realised he was playing a dangerous game, but he also knew he was excited by it. Finally, after decades of underappreciation from the executive suits that occupied the hallowed seventh-floor offices, Walsh was about to become richer than he had ever imagined possible. He also appreciated that the irony of his current position was not lost on him, in that he was in charge of the very task force chasing Mark Pierce across the globe, when it had been Walsh himself who had framed Pierce in the first place.

The Trigger Man, of course, was integral to Walsh's nuclear waste scheme, and the fact that the former CIA operative was still alive was a problem. The constant stabbing pain in Walsh's gut, where Pierce had shot and almost killed him, was a reminder of just how bothersome Pierce was, but Walsh was an expert at fixing problems, and his pawn would soon be dealt with in a permanent way.

Walsh keyed in the PIN to the Trigger Man task force's operations room, then waited as the iris scan confirmed his biometrics, then stepped inside.

He passed dozens of desks where analysts, operations specialists and tactical officers ran through the intel coming in on the Trigger Man's latest movements, and made a beeline for the only tier one operator on his team, Aaron Stone.

"Looking for me?" The spymaster spoke from behind Stone, who was on the phone and asking to be put through to Walsh.

The former Navy SEAL turned to find his superior officer standing behind him, then hung up. He stood and saluted. "Sir, we have a problem."

"The Trigger Man being in two locations at once?"

"Yes, sir. You saw the report?"

Walsh nodded. After Stone had spoken to Rachel Zang in Georgia, Night Viper had become far more suspicious than Walsh would have liked, for Zang had provided him with clear evidence that Pierce had been in two locations at the same time. Stone's report had showed clear photo-graphic imagery of Pierce in a café in Tehran, sharing a coffee and paying off a known Quds Force operator. The other was CCTV footage of Pierce running a surveillance detection route through the streets of Baku.

Yesterday Stone had sent both packages to Forgery. Eventually the nerds on the second floor would tell him which video was real. Walsh knew this would be a problem and might ultimately expose his conspiracy, so he had to deal with it quickly. Why Zang hadn't just died with the other bothersome CIA operators he'd sent to their deaths in Kazakhstan still eluded him.

"Yes, I saw your report, Stone. I take it you've sent both intel packages to Forgery?"

"Already on it, sir."

"Good." Walsh adjusted his wire-frame glasses as he beckoned Stone to a conference room. "Let's talk in private."

"That sounds like a plan."

Once inside the meeting room, Walsh flicked a wall switch, polarising the glass walls so no one outside could look in. He gestured that Stone should take a seat, but Stone remained on his feet.

Walsh clenched his teeth. "I've been standing all day, Stone, and this liver isn't my own." He pointed to his abdomen, where it never ceased aching.

Stone nodded and took a seat. He wasn't a man who liked being confined to an office, where Walsh had deliberately kept him.

"What do you know about the Trigger Man?"

Stone shrugged. "Not nearly enough."

"Summarise what you know."

"Three and a half years ago, Pierce appeared from nowhere. He's American, but there is no history of him anywhere before that, so the name isn't real. He's definitely ex-special forces and battle-hardened. You can tell by his fitness, skills, situational awareness and — reading between the lines — subtle details in his after-action reports. Operations in Greece, Yemen, Mali, Niger and a few other places. For almost three years, Mackenzie Summerfield was his case officer, whom you rightly fired after her involvement with

Pierce's theft of eleven million in CIA funds. I know Pierce shot you in Morocco, sir, and killed six private contractors you had tracking him there. I also know you were lucky to escape with your life. Since Morocco, Pierce has been on the run in North Africa, Asia, and Europe, with the clear intention of securing himself a mother lode of nuclear waste, presumably to build dirty bombs. For whom, and why, we don't know, but intel suggests it is for the Iranians. That was until today's conflicting information."

Walsh nodded. "That's a succinct summary there, Stone."

The tier one operator leaned forward and tensed. "What I don't get is, if Pierce is such a dangerous terrorist, why have the higher authorities not released his redacted records to us?"

Walsh shrugged. "I wish I knew. The associate deputy director, Special Activities Centre, he still thinks the sun shines out of the Trigger Man's ass and won't release that information."

"The AD/SAC, sir?"

"Yes. That pencil-pusher believes that what Pierce did in the past, if disclosed, could compromise ten years of quality intelligence."

"You believe that, sir? There are many in the CIA who say Pierce's field abilities are average at best."

Walsh shook his head. "I'm with you, Stone. AD/SAC and his other higher-up buddies are feeding us bullshit. I'm not even allowed to know who in the CIA knows Pierce's secret."

"I've made enquiries of my own. Put the hard word out on my old network. Pierce isn't Navy SEAL, Force Recon, Marine Special Operations Command, US Army Ranger or

Green Berets. He's not from any American special forces outfit; otherwise I would have discovered so already."

Walsh nodded. "My own investigations concluded the same."

"Then who the hell is he?"

Walsh shrugged and rolled his eyes upwards, towards the seventh floor, where the CIA directors kept their offices. "Someone in the know up there with more power than the AD/SAC looks over our daily reports. I've been told that if worrying details come up, they will inform us of a pertinent connection."

"His past should be relevant now." Stone tensed his arms. "Particularly when some third party is feeding us false information on Pierce's movements. Someone who might know far more about Pierce than we do."

"I agree. That's why I want you to concentrate on the Tehran intel. I'll take the lead on Baku. I know it frustrates you, Stone. I know you wanted to be in the field with the Kazakhstan team, but I need you here."

Stone nodded as he tensed and grimaced. "They wouldn't all be dead now, sir, if I'd been with them."

Walsh nodded. "That is probably true. It's my mistake. I Trusted Zang and overestimated her abilities."

"No disrespect, but I'm better."

"How did Zang survive?"

"That's unclear. She claims to have spent five days in Pierce's company, suggesting he had reason to keep her alive."

"To interrogate her?"

"Unclear, sir."

For a moment Walsh mentally focused on the lead he had recently secured in Baku from his contacts in Azerbaijani intelligence, concerning two hackers Pierce had spoken to there. Now Walsh needed to shut down that connection quickly before anyone on his team investigated that link too closely, and he would do so personally. "This suggests the Baku intel is the real Pierce, so I'll take responsibility for that fuck-up. Where is Zang now?"

"Flying back. She should be in Washington in the morning."

"Should?"

Stone frowned and made no attempt to mask his frustration at the unravelling situation. "Zang's like me, an operator even if only second tier, so I know her type. She'll want to gather her own intel and may be 'delayed' coming in."

"She's not as good as you, though."

Stone nodded, conceding Walsh's observation as the spymaster hoped he would, by pandering to the operator's ego.

Walsh stood, concluding the meeting. "Pick her up when she passes through immigration. Then we'll debrief Zang together, find out exactly what she knows."

Stone tensed. "Are you now assuming she's compromised?"

"I assume nothing, Stone, but I suspect a lot until proven otherwise. Zang disappears for five days when we believed she was dead. While indisposed, we receive two intel packages, one of which is obviously a fake. Tell me, are you not suspicious?"

Stone frowned, which suggested he hadn't thought through the many implications their new intel now implied as deeply as Walsh had. But then Stone was an operator, not an analyst, and in his frustration, when Walsh finally sent

Stone into the field to tie up loose ends, he would do so eagerly and without questioning why.

"That makes a certain..."

"Sense?"

"Yes, sir."

"Make the arrangements. Let's find out what Zang really knows."

29

Fifteen minutes after his conversation with Stone ended, Walsh was outside the CIA headquarters, driving southeast along George Washington Memorial Parkway. He crossed the Potomac River and then the Anacostia River until he reached the neighbourhood of the same name. A light snow had fallen during the night, dusting the pavements and lawns outside the many run-down houses. Maple trees devoid of their leaves lined the streets, as did overhead power lines. Houses were red brick or old timber. The few people on the street were African American in cheap clothes.

Walsh parked his grey SUV. Earlier he had disabled the GPS tracker and applied false number plates so no one could track him. He pulled on a knit cap and his old over-coat, then pocketed his unregistered SIG Sauer P227 semi-automatic pistol with a suppressor already fitted. There were no activated smart devices on his person, such as his cell phone with the batteries and SIM already removed, and the phone wrapped in tinfoil.

He found the run-down two-storey apartment he had come for, with overflowing trash cans out front, offending with their stench of rotting food.

Walsh pounded on the door.

The twenty-something Latin man who answered featured the whiskers of a beard and scraggly hair. Clothes were a hooded sweater, loose-fitting jeans and bony-toed bare feet. He stank of cigarettes and sweat.

"You? I thought we should never meet?"

Walsh pushed his way inside. "Shut the door."

The Latin man did.

"Raoul, who told you to put Pierce in Baku?"

"Baku?" He shook his head. "No one. Why?"

Walsh kept his hands in his pockets to ensure he touched nothing.

"You want a coffee? I was up all night, rendering Pierce onto those Iranian photos you sent me."

"No coffee. I'll make this quick."

"Good, because I'm tired—"

"I don't care about your sleeping habits, Raoul. Just show me your workspace."

Raoul looked at Walsh suspiciously through red eyes. "What is going on? I thought we would never meet face to face again?"

"So long as everything ran like clockwork, that was the deal, but you've compromised yourself."

Raoul frowned. "No way. The laptop where I create my fake intel, it's not even connected to the internet. Everything I create I copy only onto data sticks, left at the dead drops as agreed. Or upload them to the servers require only through internet cafes and libraries, and never from the same one twice. If it's compromised, it's because of you."

Walsh looked around. He acted nervous, suspicious that they might be under observation. "Well, compromised we are. Security is inefficient here; someone could have broken in. Show me where you work."

Raoul led Walsh into a bedroom converted into a home office. There wasn't much to look at except a desk, a chair, a laptop and a sizable external drive. Walsh saw no signs of data cables or wireless connectors, which gave him confidence Raoul had told the truth. On the wall hung a tattered poster of Rupert Rodriguez, the superstar soccer player from Raoul's home country of Colombia. Walsh could see nothing else that was personal.

"Everything you've created for me, it exists only on that laptop?"

Raoul shrugged. "Sure, that's what we agreed. You keep me away from the Bogota drug cartels, I create false intel for you. We both benefit."

"Good. Delete it all."

"What?"

Walsh said nothing.

"That's months of work I just can't recreate in a hurry if you change your mind."

Walsh leaned in close and breathed hot air on the young forger's face. "Yes, Raoul, I'm very serious. The FBI, they might be onto you. Delete the hard drive. Copy over everything multiple times. You don't want federal officers questioning you with that kind of intel in your possession, do you?"

"I'm compromised? You said you'd protect me."

"I am protecting you. Get to work."

Panicked, Raoul jumped on his laptop and proceeded as Walsh instructed. "What's going to happen to me?"

"Once you're done here, we leave. I have another safe house you can hide out for the short term. We'll work out the rest from there. Hurry, Raoul."

"Okay, okay. I can only work so fast. Do you know how I was compromised?"

"Are you done?"

The forger nodded, sweat beading off his head now. "Yeah. If anyone tries to rebuild deleted files, all they'll get are junk images of cats, dogs, mountains, memes... That kind of thing."

"Good." Walsh motioned that Raoul should return his attention to his laptop. "What about your recycling bin? It says there are files in there."

The forger looked back at the monitor and pointed to the screen. "Junk files, as I said—"

While Raoul wasn't looking, Walsh shot him once through the back of the head with his suppressed pistol. Blood sprayed the computer screen as the man who was now a corpse fell forward, his nose and jaw crunching onto the keyboard.

Walsh loaded a data stick of his own onto the laptop and let it run its own data-scrubbing software. Once the program had done its work, he pocketed the data stick and checked the apartment, still careful not to touch anything. Raoul was alone, no girl- or boyfriends asleep in the bed upstairs to surprise him.

Next, Walsh ensured all the windows were closed, then opened all the gas outlets on the stove, put a *WIRED* magazine into the toaster, engaged the heating mechanism and set it over the stove. Then he was on the streets and driving. He would be far away before the house incinerated, scrubbing all evidence of what had occurred here.

Raoul had fucked up. Walsh had informed Raoul not to release the last data package of Tehran, as Pierce was on the run now, but the fool hadn't listened. He liked his artistry too much, wanted to show it off. Now there would be questions, an investigation, which might lead back to Walsh. If that happened, it was all over for him.

Everything had been proceeding to plan until Pierce had escaped and met with Zang, who should have also died with him. Walsh should have travelled to Kazakhstan and killed the rogue CIA operative himself, but he had spread himself too thin, trying to control too many elements of this delicate operation. He should have followed his instincts and trusted no one else to be as thorough as himself. Perhaps that was how he should play this dangerous game from now on.

At least one of the nuclear devices was in play, and a second should be too in a day or so, so that counted for something. Everything else though was a mess.

It was time to get the team together and work out an altered plan of attack.

The centre of that plan had to be Mark Pierce's and Rachel Zang's quick deaths.

30

Cape Town, South Africa

Clean shaven, with pomade to slick his hair flat against his head, and dressed in a mid-priced charcoal double-breasted suit, striped-blue tie, and Oxford leather shoes, Pierce stepped into the foyer of the International Diamond Conference underway at the Cape Town International Convention Centre, or the CTICC as the locals referred to it. He carried a large, overstuffed leather laptop bag over his shoulder, but it didn't contain a laptop. In his pocket, he carried a cell phone and headphones.

Pierce bought an entry ticket at the door under the alias of Dimitri Levendis, signing in as an investor from Moscow, providing Pierce with a pass and lanyard. After quickly scouting the crowds, he checked his tie remained neat and presentable, because he'd cut it down to a few threads behind his shirt to foil any potential foes who might try to strangle him with it should he get himself into a fight.

Mingling amongst the trade stands, Pierce saw they promoted products and services ranging from mining software, to X-ray technology for sorting diamonds, drilling equipment suppliers, and engineering consulting services, and this was where most delegates mingled between industry presentations. The crowds were a mixture of executives, mining engineers, geologists, operations and logistics managers, and sales and marketing specialists. Most men were dressed in suits and ties like Pierce, and the women in conservative business attire.

Pierce purchased a black coffee, then stood for a moment watching the crowds while also skimming today's lecture program.

A talk scheduled to occur shortly was originally to be presented by Clementine Ponsonby, Rupert's sister, on the technical details of the *Cancri*, Polytope Diamond's marine mining ship currently extracting diamonds off the coast of Angola. Topics Ponsonby would cover included the complexities of *Cancri*'s undersea horizontal crawler, the challenges faced in operating the sediment pipe of the dredger, and the vibrating racks and rotating drums of the onboard diamond recovery treatment plant. The online version of the same lecture that Pierce had read this morning in his hotel showed that Rupert Ponsonby would now present the talk, as his sister was unable to attend due to last minute restructures in Polytope's senior management. Pierce felt certain Walsh was behind these sudden changes, but the reasons why were not yet clear to him.

It only took Pierce a few minutes to find Rupert Ponsonby, for he'd made no effort to hide or change his appearance from how he appeared on the Polytope website. He was middle aged, clean shaven, with thinning hair full of hair product to give it bounce. The two-piece business suit, tie, shirt and shoe combination looked to have cost in the tens of thousands of dollars, but no amount of money could hide Ponsonby's rounded gut.

Pierce watched from the half dozen metres separating them. Ponsonby checked his cell phone for messages, and Pierce memorised Ponsonby's PIN as he unlocked it. Whatever message Ponsonby read caused him to tense and hold his breath until his face turned red.

A curvaceous events coordinator in a tight skirt and blouse, whose name tag introduced her as Jasmine, approached Ponsonby. Her sudden appearance, from Pierce's perspective, seemed to calm Ponsonby, and he was suddenly all charm.

Pierce stepped closer and approached the trade stand next to where Ponsonby and Jasmine talked, and with his back to them, listened to their conversation while pretending to watch a corporate video running in the stand. The video promoted a firm in Mumbai with expertise in sorting and classifying diamonds, not that this interested Pierce.

Jasmine commented that she looked forward to Ponsonby's speech. They talked for several minutes on how sad it was Clementine had to cancel; then she offered her condolences on the recent death of Ponsonby's father.

"Yes, well," said Ponsonby in a gruff tone and a posh English accent. "I told dear old dad to stay off the booze and cigars. But he never listened to me."

Pierce found himself frowning at this, for there was no emotion, not even sadness, in Ponsonby's reply at the recent loss of his father.

"Yes, well. Very sad nonetheless." When Ponsonby said

nothing, Jasmine cleared her throat and said, "Attendees are looking forward to your talk on the *Cancri*. I understand many of your competitors are also looking to invest in marine diamond mining?"

Now Ponsonby became animated and passionate when he said, "That's because there are no more diamonds to find on the surface world anymore, Jazzy. The ocean is the future."

"Is that so?"

Pierce heard the strain in the coordinator's tone and mused that he wouldn't like the nickname Jazzy either.

"Yes, I'm very correct. De Beers co-owns the largest diamond mining ships in the world — to date. They are well-established in this business — for now."

"They are. Their diamond mining ships are the SS *Nujoma* and the MV *Mafuta*. I understand they are both very profitable."

Pierce grabbed a brochure from the stand next to the playing video, then casually turned so he could watch as well as listen to the interaction. He noticed neither of them were looking at each other now. It was like watching two individuals on a blind date who had quickly discovered they detested each other and couldn't wait to make the first move to get out of there.

Too many further seconds of silence passed, when Ponsonby again said nothing, which prompted Jasmine to say, "Well, good luck on your speech, Rupert."

"I won't be speaking about the *Cancri*."

"Oh, what topic, then?"

"It's a surprise, Jazzy. I need to prepare, so if you don't mind tottering off now and leaving me to it?"

As a near-fuming Jasmine disappeared, a large man built

like a wrestler who had put on too much weight approached Ponsonby, carrying two coffees in disposable cups.

"Thank you, Khawuta," Ponsonby said, taking one coffee. "You can return to security duties now."

Pierce suppressed a frown of surprise at this revelation, on just how lax and unprofessional Ponsonby's security detail were. "Yes, sir."

"No threats I should know about, my man?"

"No, sir."

"For fuck's sake!" Ponsonby exclaimed loud enough for everyone within ten metres to hear him clearly. "Khawuta, this coffee is fucking awful."

Deciding this was his moment, Pierce turned suddenly and almost knocked the coffee out of Ponsonby's hand while his left hand subtly slipped Ponsonby's cell phone from his pocket into Pierce's own.

"Bloody hell!" Ponsonby exclaimed again, not noticing the theft.

"Moi izvineniya," Pierce said, using Russian to apologise. Then switching to English, said in a thick Russian accent, "I didn't see you standing right behind me. I am sorry, yes?"

"I wasn't standing right behind you, you cad! Look at this suit! This is a Brioni, and it's worth ten thousand pounds! You're lucky I didn't get any on the fabric; otherwise..."

"Yeshche raz proshu proshcheniya," Pierce apologised again, then quickly disappeared into the crowds before Ponsonby could berate him again.

Once he was alone and Ponsonby and Khawuta were beyond his line of sight, Pierce headed to the men's bathroom and entered a cubicle. After unlocking Ponsonby's phone with the PIN he'd memorised earlier, he downloaded a mirroring app provided by Valeriya and Yebin onto

Ponsonby's phone. The app now allowed Pierce to hear the executive's every telephone conversation and passively listen to surrounding conversations via the phone's microphone. Pierce then tried to download Ponsonby's emails, but the Russian hacker's tech couldn't bypass the encryption software on the mail app. The software was state-of-the-art and reeked of CIA tech. One more link between Ponsonby and Idris Walsh.

Satisfied that the mirroring app was working properly at least, Pierce returned to the conference and found Jasmine.

"Hello!" Pierce said, using stilted English in the same Russian accent. "I found this cell phone on floor, yes? I think it fell from pocket of Englishman with the..." Pierce pretended not to know the English word he was searching for as he made shapes with his own hands around his hair.

Jasmine suddenly smiled and said, "You mean the big hair, with lots of product?"

"Yes. That is what I mean. The man with the thinning hair."

Jasmine nodded and read Pierce's name tag. "Thank you, Mr Levendis."

"Yes, not problem."

"I hope you are enjoying the conference?"

"Da spasibo."

The event coordinator disappeared.

Pierce headed up to the second level, with balconies allowing him to look down at the crowds in the main trade display hall. From his near-hidden vantage point, Pierce watched as Jasmine found Ponsonby, stepped up behind him and touched him on his sleeve.

"Mr Ponsonby? Sorry to bother you, but you are needed on stage now."

"Yes, of course."

Pierce concentrated hard to make out the conversation from his distance of a half dozen metres above them and with all the other conversations going on around them, but he got the gist of it.

"Oh, and you dropped your phone." She handed over the device Pierce had given her earlier.

Ponsonby felt in the pocket of his jacket and expressed shock when he discovered it wasn't there. He checked his phone as she handed it to him, then keyed in the PIN code, and it unlocked. This seemed to bring him relief.

"A young man saw you drop it. Then he couldn't find you again. He apologises it took so long to return it."

Ponsonby's fury grew; then he squashed it down and composed a fake smile. "Thank you, Jazzy—"

"Jasmine."

"You said the auditorium is ready for me?"

"It is."

Ponsonby summoned Khawuta with a two-finger signal, then said with a sneer, "Then let's go kill it."

31

When Ponsonby, Jasmine and Khawuta vanished from sight, Pierce returned to the men's bathroom, secured another cubical and changed into black jeans, a light blue shirt with the sleeves rolled up over a grey T-shirt, and sturdy hiking boots he'd stashed in his laptop bag. The suit, tie, Oxford shoes and laptop bag went into a garbage bag, which then went into a bin in the bathroom, which Pierce covered with paper towels.

As Pierce stepped outside and crossed the road to a corporate office block overlooking the CTICC that he'd scouted out earlier, he slipped on a black cap and sunglasses. Clothing and accessories obscuring his face limited the effectiveness of any facial-recognition software that might catch him today.

While Pierce walked with his earpiece in his left ear canal, his cell phone relayed Ponsonby's activities, including a visit to the men's bathroom and a moment of self-praise, presumably to a mirror. Pierce guessed it was in one of the other men's bathroom within the CTICC because Ponsonby's microphones were advanced enough to pick up the noise of toilets flushing and hand driers blasting out their hot air.

Acting like he worked there and bypassing the reception in an adjacent corporate office tower who barely glanced his way, Pierce called the elevator using his knuckle so not to leave fingerprints on the button. He ascended to the third floor, entered the men's bathroom there, and waited until he was alone. Then, slipping on leather gloves and jamming the door shut, he climbed up on a toilet seat and opened the ceiling partition, took down a sports bag with the sniper rifle, the grappling hook and rope, and his Glock 22 with a full magazine of fifteen .40-calibre rounds he had hidden there yesterday.

More sounds filled his ear canal. He heard Ponsonby take the stage, discernible from the murmuring crowds Ponsonby's phone picked up. The master of ceremonies introduced the new CEO of Polytope Diamonds, then mentioned the tragic death of Rupert Ponsonby's father only last week. Pierce couldn't see the scene, but it wasn't difficult to imagine in his mind's eye.

While Pierce listened, he unlocked the bathroom door before anyone noticed, and stepped out.

The crowds clapped as they welcomed Ponsonby to the stage.

At the door to a vacant office, Pierce picked the lock and stepped inside. The interior included empty desks, chairs and workstations, curtains, and fluorescent overhead lights.

"Thank you, ladies and gentlemen," Ponsonby addressed the delegates. "It's great to be back in Cape Town. I love this city and its people. South Africa is truly blessed."

Removing his cap and sunglasses, Pierce took a tarpaulin from the sports bag and laid it across the carpet, away from the window. He pulled over two chairs, one to sit on and the other to rest the Heckler & Koch HK PSG-1 semi-automatic sniper rifle, which he removed from the sports bag and assembled.

Ponsonby droned on in Pierce's ear canal. "My sister apologises for not being with us today. Clementine is too distressed about our father's passing and asked that I come in her place..."

Pierce fitted the Hensoldt ZF 6x42 scope with an illuminated reticle. The distance to the CTICC's main entrance was two hundred metres, the point where he hoped Ponsonby would appear at some time during the day. Pierce adjusted the built-in drop compensator for the fall of the bullet due to gravitational pull over that distance. There was no wind.

"When I last spoke to my father, God bless dear old dad, he said to me, 'Rupert, there is no one I trust more than my only son. I want it to be you who continues the proud legacy of Polytope Diamonds I established. No one understands my vision like you do, my only son. That's why I'm leaving you all my shares in the company...'"

There was a pause, and the room fell into silence. Pierce suspected Ponsonby was waiting for applause, but it never came.

"Anyway," Ponsonby continued, "I have great things planned for Polytope..."

Pierce stepped to the window and looked out through the blinds onto the street below. A busy, sunny day in Cape Town with clean streets and well-maintained pavements. Normal people walked those streets, both dark- and light-skinned. Modern cars drove at respectable speeds and obeyed the traffic laws. Very different to most African cities

Pierce had operated in during many past operations across this continent.

Ponsonby rushed through Polytope's corporate history, detailed its various small-scale diamond mines and larger operations in Angola and the Central African Republic, reported on capital investment projects, environmental compliance targets, quarterly performance figures and mining production rates.

For an unnatural length of time, Ponsonby focused on his various mines' tailings dams and how clean they were compared to those of his competitors. Pierce wasn't certain what a tailings dam was and made a mental note to investigate this later. The way Ponsonby kept droning on about them, they seemed important to him.

"So, what is a diamond?" Ponsonby's energy lifted as he changed topics, alerting Pierce that the CEO might finally say something that was at least mildly entertaining.

"Distinguished guests, you all know that a diamond is nothing more than carbon, a base element. Exactly what we find in coal and the building blocks of humans and all other life on this planet, and as the backbone of hydrocarbons, which fuel our world. Carbon is one of the most versatile elements in the universe, able to bond with all other elements to create the most complex and dazzling molecular structures possible. When carbon bonds with carbon, however, as a sheet, it becomes graphite, which we find in pencils, or as a lattice, and then it becomes a diamond. Carbon is why we are all here today..."

He cleared his throat. "But science and engineering can do great things with carbon. Buckyballs, as an example, are carbon atoms arranged in the molecular shape of a football, or soccer ball for all you Americans out there who think I'm talking about grid iron." He chuckled and waited for laughter, but none came. "Buckyballs are excellent inventions for increasing the efficiency of solar cells, able to transform sunlight directly into electricity. But my favourite molecule is the carbon nanotube, a long chain of bonded carbon wrapped as a tube that can stretch for thousands of kilometres. And what would we use these for, you ask?"

Pierce checked the sun's position, still high in the clear blue sky. In an hour from now the sun would be behind him, making his position more difficult to see from the street below.

"Space elevators, ladies and gentlemen. Cables one hundred thousand kilometres long, stretching from the equator to beyond geosynchronous orbits, allowing us to transport materials into space cheaply. Gone will be the need for expensive rockets. No other material is strong enough to withstand the forces that would otherwise tear a space elevator's cable into shreds. Only diamonds are that strong."

Pierce opened the window and positioned himself. He counted on Ponsonby stepping out of the front entrance at some stage today, and when the man appeared, Pierce would be ready. Now all he had to do was wait, and waiting would be easy, because in sniper school he had learned to sit and wait like this for periods of up to forty-eight hours until his target appeared. Ponsonby was only hours away from appearing at most. Inside the building, Pierce would be invisible to the commuters on the streets below.

"What I'm telling you today, distinguished ladies and gentlemen, is that the future of carbon and diamonds won't be as precious gems, but as a construction material that will revolutionise everything. And I mean everything. The tensile strength of diamond is like nothing else on this planet. With carbon, even buildings like the Burj Khalifa in Dubai — the tallest building on Earth — will pale into insignificance to what we can achieve with diamonds, for it will replace steel and concrete. That, ladies and gentlemen, is my vision for Polytope. My company won't be about gems, but the foundation of construction into the future. We won't pull diamonds from the earth, but manufacture them as sheets, columns and beams."

Ponsonby paused, then cleared his throat. "How will I achieve this, you ask? Well, through research and development, funded through Polytope's largest diamond leases in the Central African Republic and marine diamond mining off the coast of Angola. There are six major producing diamond mines in the world today, in Botswana, South Africa, Angola, Canada and two mines in Russia, producing more than eighty per cent of the world's diamond outputs. But when Polytope completes construction on our new processing technology at our Central African mines, there will then be seven major diamond mines. With the profits we make, we will invest most of it into new technologies to manufacture rather than mine construction-grade diamonds. At that point there won't be seven major mines. There will be none. Our productive and revolutionary diamond manufacturing plant will become the sole source of reliable diamond manufacturing worldwide. Ladies and gentlemen, I present you with the future of diamonds. Polytope Diamonds."

A long pause emanated from the audience.

Pierce heard Ponsonby breathing. It seemed the attendees hadn't realised his speech had concluded ten minutes earlier than his allotted time slot.

Somebody onstage clapped, the events coordinator perhaps, so the audience followed without enthusiasm.

Ponsonby cleared his throat. "Looks like we have some time. I'll take questions."

The room remained silent.

"Okay, well, thank you all for coming."

Pierce heard Ponsonby storm off the stage, swearing under his breath.

Unmoving in his sniper position, Pierce slowed his breathing and calmed his mind. His eye tracked the CTICC entrance through his scope. His plan was to shoot Ponsonby from a distance, allowing Pierce sufficient time to escape afterwards, rather than shooting him inside the conference centre, where it would be more difficult to get away, and this meant Pierce could only shoot when the CEO exited the building.

With the lecture ended, Ponsonby might step outside now. If he did, Pierce would take his shot.

32

London, United Kingdom

Rachel Zang spent her morning in a café overlooking a typical London business complex. It was all modern buildings with rendered concrete facades stained white, and floor-to-ceiling glass windows. A courtyard wedged between the multi-storey offices included garden beds and arranged trees, the latter absent of leaves because it was winter. Despite the cold, the sun provided an unusual brightness for the season.

The particular business complex she watched housed the offices of the Greene Strategic Group, a consulting firm that advised governments and corporations on geopolitical risks present in various troubled countries, from North Korea and Ukraine to Venezuela and South Sudan, and every failed state in between. GSG employees operated as corporate intelligence analysts but used only open-source data. Zang mused, when the CIA disavows you, a high-paying role in a firm like GSG was preferable to the many alternatives. Zang would never be so lucky.

At lunchtime, Mackenzie Summerfield stepped from her office. She'd changed her appearance since Zang had last seen her. Gone was the dark pixie-style cut; the woman had grown out her hair and dyed it dark red. Missing too were the jeans and tight-fitting shirt, replaced by a conservative grey pants suit.

Summerfield walked to a Vietnamese roll shop and purchased an apple juice and a baguette with chicken and Asian vegetables. As she turned to leave, she spotted Zang waiting in the doorway.

"Remember me?" Zang said.

A moment passed before recognition reached Summerfield's stare. "If this is another job offer, I'm not interested."

"Not a job offer. Just want to walk and talk?"

Summerfield nodded and followed Zang outside. "We're near the Thames Barrier. I can talk long enough to walk there and back." She placed the food and drink in her handbag. "I'll eat at my desk."

Zang nodded, and they set off. She was a head taller than Summerfield, but then Zang was taller than most women and a good number of men. After they covered half a block and no one was in hearing distance, she said, "I take it you know who I am?" When Mackenzie said nothing, Zang said, "My name is Rachel Zang. I'm a CIA paramilitary operations officer."

"I remember. I believe the CIA considered you for a position in Gao, Mali."

"That never happened."

"I know. It was me who assessed you. I advised you lacked the required experience."

Zang could have taken that as a slight against her character, but chose not to.

Mackenzie turned to Zang and forced a smile. "I hear you did well regardless of my opinion."

"At the risk of failing a Bechdel-Wallace test, I'm here to talk about Mark Pierce."

Summerfield stopped dead, recovered, then kept walking. "Of course you are."

"It's not what you think."

"Oh yeah. What am I supposed to think?"

"I was with Pierce. Three days ago."

Summerfield's eyes were like ice as she locked stares with Zang. "Walsh sent you, didn't he? Bet he didn't bother telling you his mind games no longer work on me?"

"He didn't send me." Zang tucked a strand of her dark hair behind an ear. "I'm not here under false pretences, Summerfield. Can we talk, please? There are things you need to hear about Pierce, and things I need to hear from you, to understand what kind of man he really is."

"Really is?" Summerfield snorted. "I'm sure Walsh briefed you. Pierce and I were co-conspirators. We stole eleven million dollars from the CIA. That was until Pierce disappeared with the money and sold me out to the CIA. Is he still off enjoying the spoils while I'm left facing charges of treason?"

"And yet you are here. Free, in England."

They reached the end of the road and the boardwalk facing the Thames River. Ahead was the Thames Barrier, a series of ten ring-sector gates similar in architectural appearance to the Sydney Opera House's "sails" but much smaller. The gates featured rotating cylinders that prevented London from flooding during high tides and storm surges moving up from the North Sea. A walkway led out to the first three barriers, but they were closed to public access. Summerfield leaned against a railing and looked west towards the Millennium Dome, an architectural wonder that reminded Zang of some monstrous-sized World War Two sea mine.

"Walsh couldn't make anything stick," Summerfield said. "And his superiors knew I was innocent. Weeks of intense interrogation proved that."

"I'm sorry to hear that."

"Are you? You'd be the first person who was."

Zang leaned against the railing and touched her index fingers and thumbs together, forming a diamond shape between her hands, and stared down through it to the pavement. "What I'm about to tell you, I shouldn't."

"Is that what you expect in return, that I too divulge information I shouldn't, about Pierce?"

Zang took a deep breath, then exhaled, noticing the steam of her breath. Despite the sunshine, a chill permeated the air. "I work for Walsh, I won't lie about that, but I do so in a convoluted way. My superior reassigned me to his team shortly after the Trigger Man went rogue, for reasons I won't go into, but are pertinent to this conversation. Is that good enough information regarding my situation for now?"

Summerfield took a moment before nodding. "Why don't you tell me about Mark first?"

"Very well. In the last seven months, we've tracked Pierce across North Africa, Europe, and Asia. He used that eleven million to purchase nuclear materials and other associated materials, which we suspect he'll use to build a dirty bomb. Pierce left a high body count wherever he travelled and didn't seem to care who got hurt so long as he got what he wanted. Civilians and children included."

Summerfield growled. "But you don't believe any of it, do you, Zang? Not now, after you've met him?"

Zang nodded. "I was with the kill team tracking Pierce in Kazakhstan. We were ready to make our move when Kazakh criminals ambushed us, who knew exactly where to find us and how to exploit weaknesses in our defences. They murdered my colleagues, but took me prisoner. They stripped me... I think..." She struggled to express the terror she had almost faced.

Summerfield nodded. "I'm sorry."

"Anyway." Zang cleared her throat and refocused on why she was here. "I believed Pierce had masterminded the hit. But then he killed the Kazakhs. Executed them. Four armed and dangerous men. Pierce terrified me in that moment just by how efficiently he'd dispatched those men from a suboptimal starting position."

"I've seen your file, Zang. I didn't mean what I said before. I was just angry when I saw you, and you were an easy target to unleash my frustrations upon. You are as competent and as efficient as Pierce. Don't underestimate yourself."

Zang looked away. "Regardless, when Pierce found me, I convinced him I was a prostitute."

"Did he believe you?"

Zang shrugged. "He was suspicious, but he didn't kill me like I expected him to. I kept thinking, if the Kazakh criminals were his co-conspirators, he would have known I was lying from the onset. He..."

"Seemed concerned for your well-being?"

Zang nodded, relieved that Summerfield drew the same conclusions she had. "Yes. He didn't force himself upon me, and I don't believe the Kazakhs had while I was unconscious, but I'll never know..." She wiped tears from her eyes, then shook her head and stood taller. "Police pursued us across the country. Again, Pierce overpowered them, but didn't kill them when it would have been easier for him to do so. He did clinically eliminate a team of Kazakh soldiers connected to who he claimed were the real buyers of illegal nuclear material. Then, during the few nights we spent together, he experienced intense nightmares."

Summerfield frowned. "How did that happen?"

"Not like that." Then Zang couldn't speak and found herself not detesting the man, but imagined being intimate with Pierce for a moment. She put the thought out of her mind. "I never felt under threat that way from him. But as I was saying, during his sleep, he often had nightmares of intense torture. Later, when I pressed him, he mentioned his incarceration in an African paramilitary camp, but wasn't any more specific than that. But there was one name he blurted in his sleep that concerned me more than anything else he'd said so far."

"What name was that?"

"Idris Walsh. Pierce believed Walsh was his torturer."

Summerfield nodded and hugged her suit close against the chill. She wiped tears from her eyes.

"Did I say something wrong?"

Summerfield shook her head. "I always knew... Mark was innocent. I was stupid because I let everyone around me convince me he wasn't."

"Others? You mean Idris Walsh?"

The disgraced former CIA analyst nodded. "Him and his network of colleagues. A boys' club, all seeking power in the upper ranks of the CIA. You know the type."

Zang nodded and reflected on how those same men

considered Aaron Stone to be a better operative than she was. "I guess that's why I'm here, Mackenzie, to understand. Does any of what I said sound like the real Mark Pierce? Who he was before you thought he betrayed you? Because he was nothing like the man Walsh made me believe he was when he sent me to kill him."

Summerfield was about to answer when a gunshot sounded loud in Zang's ears.

A crimson stain suddenly blossomed on Summerfield's shoulder.

33

Zang spun around and immediately identified the approaching assailant. A man, four metres from them, standing near the fence overlooking the Thames, approached with speed. Tight jeans and black boots laced to his ankles revealed his thin frame, yet his face remained hidden by a hooded jacket. His right hand held a smoking .38 revolver. The man fired again. Zang ducked, knowing she was already too late to avoid a bullet, but the shooter had missed. Then the shooter rushed towards them.

Without conscious thought, Zang's training took over, and she too rushed the assailant. Her hand shot up, blocking his firing arm, which sent another bullet into the sky. Her opposite fist sped through the shortest distance and struck the assailant in the throat. He staggered back, stumbled against the railing.

Zang threw her body against him, lifted him around the waist and flipped him over the wooden guard.

He somersaulted, fell a dozen feet before he hit the frigid Thames water.

She watched him go under, then saw his head bob to the surface. He was struggling to breathe from the throat punch, and the current took him away. If he didn't get out of the flowing river soon, he'd freeze to death.

Zang didn't care. She scooped up the fallen .38 and pocketed it.

Behind her, Summerfield had struggled to her feet, a bloody hand gripping her right shoulder where the bullet had struck.

"Are you okay?" Two young joggers rushed to their aid. "We saw it all! We'll call the police and an ambulance!" One of them hurriedly went for his smartphone.

Zang reached into her pocket and activated a jamming device she'd brought with her, rendering the cell phone useless.

"No reception! Even triple nine."

Ignoring the runner, Zang moved next to Summerfield and held her steady. "How bad?"

The wounded woman gritted her teeth. The colour had drained from her face, and her pupils were dilated. "I think it's through and through."

"Can you clench your fist?"

Summerfield did so, tensing against the pain.

"Spread your fingers?"

She did so.

Zang tore off her scarf and used it to press down on the entry wound. She looked to the two joggers. They held each other, staring at their phones and not at her.

Zang said, "I'll drive her to the hospital. My car's just there."

"We'll come with you?"

"No!" Zang said. "The police will be here soon, with the

sound of the gunshot, so someone else will have already reported it. Tell them what you saw. Newham University Hospital is not far. Tell the police to interview us there." Zang didn't wait for a response as she led Mackenzie to her nearby car. After determining that the bullet had gone through the flesh, neither shattering bones nor rupturing major arteries, Zang tied a tourniquet around the wound and laid Mackenzie across the back seat. Then she drove.

After close to twenty minutes of frantic driving, they were on the A13 and headed east.

"You're... not taking me to the hospital?" Summerfield panted.

Through the rear-view mirror, Zang saw the sweat covering Summerfield's face. "That was a rushed hit. Someone targeted one or both of us."

"I... guessed."

"The only person I know who could have guessed we were about to meet has to be my boss — and your former boss — Idris Walsh. If he can orchestrate a hit in London, he won't fail a second time in a hospital. Do you have an off-the-books doctor we can use?"

Summerfield nodded. Her breathing became both faster and shallower.

Zang glanced back and saw the blood running down her arm. The wound was worse than Zang had initially assessed. "Don't you pass out on me, Summerfield. The doctor's address, please?"

Summerfield recited a location in Brentwood, a London suburb to the northeast of their current position. A half-hour drive. Zang used her encrypted cell phone to direct her rather than the car's satellite navigation system, in case the two joggers had memorised her plate number and reported it to the police.

"Call them, Summerfield! Make sure this doctor is ready for us."

The wounded woman nodded, keyed the number into her phone, then dropped it as she slipped into unconsciousness.

Zang pulled off the freeway, drove into a narrow street with no visible surveillance cameras, and parked. Then she checked on the wounded woman. Though unconscious, she was still breathing. Blood wasn't gushing from the wound, so Rachel knew she wouldn't die soon.

She found Summerfield's phone on the floor and dialled the number already keyed in.

A woman answered. "Hello?"

"I'm a friend of Mackenzie Summerfield. She's wounded. Bullet through and through in the right shoulder—"

"What?"

"Listen to me. She's still bleeding even though I've bandaged the wound. I'll be at your place in Brentwood in fifteen minutes. Can you perform field surgery from your home?"

"Yes... but—"

"Good, because I'm counting on you. I presume you are aware this is an off-the-book surgical protocol for field operatives?" Zang took a risk expressing herself openly to an asset she didn't know, but she had to trust that Summerfield knew her tradecraft and had cultivated competent and discreet contacts.

"I do. Who am I talking to?"

"Answers later. Be ready. Mackenzie has lost a lot of blood, and I'm a universal donor, so use that."

"Okay, but—"

Zang ended the call. She'd memorised the address and directions to get there, so removed the battery and SIM card from Mackenzie's phone. She took magnetic false number plates from her travel bag, gained from a field kit she'd prepared in the United Kingdom from a previous mission, and slapped them over the car's legal registration numbers. Then Zang drove again.

She reached the house in twenty minutes, parked in a garage and met the young British-Indian doctor, who introduced herself as Jaya. Zang carried Summerfield onto the kitchen table inside the small but modern apartment, and together they got down to the business of saving Mackenzie Summerfield's life.

34

Cape Town, South Africa

As the minutes passed, without Pierce moving a millimetre or taking his eye off his telescopic sight, he remained ready for when Rupert Ponsonby stepped out of the CTICC, to take his shot. In the meantime, he listened through his headpiece as the Englishman received a call.

"It's me."

The caller was unmistakably Idris Walsh, and at the sound of the spymaster's voice, Pierce involuntarily clamped down on his teeth and tensed every muscle in his body, affecting his aim. Not a good reaction for an operator about to perform a precise and calculated sniper shot. But telling in how close this man had come to destroying Pierce emotionally and physically.

"You encrypted?"

Ponsonby answered with his posh English accent. "Yes, of course, I'm running that software you installed right now."

"Good!"

"Wasn't expecting a call from you so soon. And by the way, I did it, Walsh! I murdered father with that undetectable poison you lifted from the CIA labs. And with that last will and testament you fabricated from my father, well, I'm now the majority shareholder at Polytope, as you promised. You should have seen the look on my sister's face when I broke the news to her that she was no longer in charge! I would have paid good money to see her soured puckered face like that, but I didn't have to, thanks to—"

Walsh growled. "I'm not here to talk about any of that. And don't use my name over what might be a compromised line!"

"What do you mean?"

Walsh drew in a deep breath and held it for a few seconds before deeming to answer. "Our Australian foot soldiers tell me our 'problem' has—"

"'Problem', as in the man we sent to Kazakhstan to die? You mean him?"

"Yes, him. It seems he's somehow managed to hire a professional assassin, but hell knows where he got the money to do that. And me and our foot soldiers all agree you are likely his target."

Pierce heard Ponsonby swallow, then snort loudly. "Fuck! Walsh! How the hell do you know that?"

"For fuck's sake, you idiot. Don't use my name! Who knows who could be listening."

Pierce nodded at Walsh's astute observation. Powerful supercomputers within America's NSA, National Security Agency, or England's GCHQ, Government Communications Headquarters, were amongst many signal intelligence or SIGINT groups that continuously monitored all the world's communications. Sophisticated programs relentlessly searched for keywords and phrases and the names of intelligence operatives, terrorists, mercenaries, special forces soldiers, assets and targets that when spoken out loud rang alarm bells somewhere in the walls of the various global spy organisations. This was especially true if two or more names appeared in the same conversation, as tracing programs were better able to correlate connections between multiple keywords. Walsh and Ponsonby had only used Walsh's surname, so unless they made another slip, the conversation wasn't likely to be flagged.

"I've just left Baku, Azerbaijan, where our 'problem' was seen. It's a strong possibility he's acquired state-of-the-art surveillance equipment, and he might already know more about us than we suspected. And you're not great at keeping your movements secret, for a five-second search on the internet tells me exactly where you are. Just finished presenting at the diamond conference, held at the CTICC on Long Street, have you?"

"Yes? So what?"

"Don't you understand, you fool? If Pierce is anywhere, he'll be there. You could already be in his trigger hairs!"

Ponsonby raised his voice. "Then fix it? Killing people is not my area. It's yours."

"Don't worry, I'm on it. Lie low; our foot soldiers and the scientist have just secured the second drum in the South African location. That means they are close to you and on their way to you now, to protect your fucking useless ass!"

Pierce smiled, enjoying the anger and frustration both men were expressing and slinging at each other, which lifted his mood. It seemed Pierce's schemes were having the desired effect of rattling his torturers, but there had been no mention yet of the missing millions, which suggested that Trager and Terzic had not shared this piece of information with Walsh yet. The threads of their conspiracy were starting to fray.

Walsh said, "Where are you? Don't go outside, and don't go near any windows."

Ponsonby huffed. "Too late. I'm at the entrance, getting ready to get the fuck out of here."

Then Pierce identified Ponsonby through his scope. Without a second thought, he fired the weapon. The first bullet grazed the flesh in the Englishman's right arm. And Pierce's next four bullets buried into the taxi pulling up next to Ponsonby, hitting the empty back seat and trunk, ensuring no harm to the driver.

As was inevitable with a shooter, suddenly there was a commotion as nearby civilians screamed and fled from the CTICC entrance. A mother shielded her child. A businessman clutched his laptop bag to his chest.

With his eyes still in the telescopic sight, Pierce watched as Khawuta wrestled Ponsonby to the ground, shielding him.

Pierce's aim had been true. His shots were close enough to scare Rupert Ponsonby and superficially wound him, but they also sent the message. Ponsonby was marked for death.

His work done, it was time to vanish.

Pierce dismantled the HK PSG-1, rolled it and the spent shells into the tarpaulin, then placed the inert weapon inside the sports bag. He wrapped the bag in blue plastic with asbestos hazard stickers marked across it.

He had minutes to make his escape. Police would already be on the way, and their first objective would be to find and identify the shooter. He guessed it would take them only minutes upon their arrival on the scene to identify this building as where the shooter had fired from.

Pierce doubted anyone had seen him yet, or that any civilians on the street had identified where the shots had originated, but he wasn't one to take a chance, so operated as if he were being pursued even when he wasn't. He took the stairs three steps at a time until he reached the twelfth floor, slipped his sunglasses and cap back on, then exited onto the roof.

The midday sun shone brightly overhead. Pierce saw that he was alone. He marched to the far side of this tower building, away from the CTICC, then glanced over the four-metre gap between this tower block and the next. The walls of both buildings on this side were windowless, ensuring his anonymity during this next phase of his escape.

He took the grappling hook and threw it up onto the roof of the second building, two storeys higher than this one. The hook caught the first time, so Pierce slung the loop of the sports bag over his shoulder, then took a deep breath, preparing himself.

Then he swung across the gap, braced against the impact as he hit the second building.

He collided harder than he expected, with his right shoulder and chest taking the brunt of the impact.

The air knocked out of him, his eyes watered, and spots formed across his vision. Tendons and muscles in his arm strained like they surged with fire.

His gloved hands slipped...

Pierce slid three metres before his grip on the rope tensed again. Another few metres and he'd have nothing to hold on to.

Now he hung suspended fifty metres above the streets.

He looked down at the narrow alley below. A few people walked the pavements, but no one looked up. Police vehicles pulled up on the main street at the end of the alley beneath him. All it would take was for one cop to look his way, and he would be an easy target.

Pierce tried to climb the rope, but his body refused.

His legs shook.

So did his hands.

He felt his grip slip again.

The street seemed to recede from him as vertigo almost overcame him.

The infliction, the shakes that had troubled him for too long, had returned to haunt him at the worst moment.

He needed his legs to walk himself up the wall.

He needed his hands to pull himself up the rope.

But each time he tried to use either, the shaking worsened.

The plan had been to swing from one building to the next. The commercial tower block he hung from was beyond the line of sight of the CTICC. No police officer would bother to check this building for a sniper trying to escape. Once in the second building, he could walk outside and disappear with the crowds. No one should have ever known he was here.

But now he was about to fall to his death, with the sniper weapon in his clutches.

The more he contemplated his predicament, the more effort he expelled trying to climb the rope, the worse his shakes became.

So he surrendered to his predicament, hung motionless for a moment, closed his eyes and focused.

He tried to still his mind, not focus on the fact that police would soon enter the building he had leaped from, and could soon reach the roof to discover him hanging here in plain sight. Or someone in the street below might look up and see him and call the police, resulting in the same outcome.

He opened his eyes and tried not to think. The trembling had lessened, but the ache in his arms from holding his own weight now burned his muscles.

Suppressing all feelings, he swung until he faced the blank wall, planted his feet against the concrete and dragged himself up, his leather gloves providing the grip he needed. Eight metres. Six. Three.

"There he is!" Pierce heard a man behind him yell.

He looked over his shoulder. At least two opponents had emerged on the roof from which he had jumped.

In desperation, he climbed fast, almost ran up the side of the wall.

As he somersaulted over the lip of the building, concrete chunks chipped around him. He registered the sounds of suppressed gunfire. The bullets had missed, and now he was behind cover and with the advantage of height.

"Pierce!" a man yelled across the distance. "You fucker!"

Pierce snuck a look over the roof's edge. He recognised the men. Alex Trager and Javor Terzic.

Terzic spotted Pierce and took a second shot.

Ducking back behind cover, Pierce pulled up the rope of his grappling hook and tucked it into the asbestos bag. "Don't tell me you want to talk now, Trager?"

No response.

"Sergeant Alex Trager, ex-SASR, and his *mate*, Corporal Javor Terzic."

"I'll fucking kill you, Pierce."

"We both fucking will!" said Terzic.

"Will you?" Pierce resisted the urge to leap up and shoot from his elevation. "The sniper fired from *your* building. The police are coming for *you!*"

"Not fucking likely—"

Pierce's intention had been to dump the sniper rifle in an asbestos collection bin on a nearby demolition site he'd scouted out earlier. Asbestos fibres were toxic, and no one would think to look in a bag wrapped as hazardous material mixed in with many more identically marked bags. Now Pierce had a better idea.

He held the package up high so they could see it over the building's edge.

More suppressed gunshots erupted. His foes remained on their rooftop.

He pulled the sniper rifle from the bag, reassembled it except for the magazine, then tossed the weapon across the gap between the buildings. He heard a thud as it landed on the roof between the two Australians.

"What the—!"

Pierce was up and fired his Glock, his aim towards the building, causing the two men to scatter. He didn't hit either, but his actions had the desired effect. Without a suppressor fitted to his Glock 22 pistol, the noise of the gunshots carried across many city blocks. He glanced down to the street and saw several police officers enter the building Pierce had leaped from.

With any luck, Trager and Terzic would soon find themselves cornered with the sniper rifle in their possession.

35

Pierce didn't stick around to see what happened next, and took the stairs down from the roof, sprinting to the street below.

Ninety seconds later Pierce was through the lobby and out on the streets. He walked with purpose away from the CTICC. Stripping off his blue shirt, he dropped it in a bin, lost the cap and walked onwards with the grey T-shirt he'd worn underneath the blue shirt. Pierce crossed Riebeck Street into Cape Town's central business district and into Greenmarket Square.

Police cars, blasting their sirens and flashing their lights, sped past in all directions. He heard further sporadic gunfire on the streets behind. Trager and Terzic must have shot their way out.

He waited in Greenmarket Square, pretending to examine South African Rugby Springbok T-shirts and prints of Zulu art. His eyes instead focused on the crowds to see if anyone had followed him, or if the police had somehow picked up his trail.

Then he spotted Terzic, perhaps twenty metres from Pierce.

The dark-haired Australian flitted through the crowds, with his head turned more often to who might follow him than what lay ahead.

Pierce quickly purchased a Panama hat and slipped it on. The Glock 22 tucked into his jeans and pressed against the small of his back comforted him. It was close should he need a weapon, but with the crowds on the streets, he wouldn't risk shooting unless Terzic got close enough so he wouldn't miss.

Then he spotted Trager also moving through the crowds at speed, but much further away. The man looked harried, but he had just fought his way past a blockade of armed response officers. His eyes also searched the crowds.

Pierce walked away fast and checked his hands.

They were still shaking, so he couldn't be certain of his aim should they engage in a shoot-out.

He felt the air compress next to his head as a bullet narrowly missed him. The window in the café he now passed shattered, and Pierce realised he had nearly had his head blown off. One of the Australians must have spotted him and taken a shot.

Soon pedestrians screamed and ducked for cover.

Pierce took off, sprinted through the mall crowds and lost the hat now that it marked him. Luckily, no glass had cut him.

He glanced back and saw Trager and Terzic in pursuit of him.

Pierce fled into a park opposite the old Parliament Building of South Africa. People still scattered or froze because of the earlier shooting, and this caused chaos in the streets. Police sirens wailed as several patrol cars closed off potential escape routes. The park Pierce traversed resembled a botanical garden, with neat lawns and palms and Morten Bay fig providing sufficient cover.

More bullets cracked in the hot air.

He ducked behind a Morten Bay fig, turned and readied himself for engagement with the enemy.

He spotted Javor Terzic at the same time the Australian locked eyes on Pierce. Terzic raised his pistol and aimed for a clean shot.

But Pierce couldn't return fire because of his shaking hands. The risk of hitting a pedestrian was too great. Instead, he hid behind the fig tree and let the trunk take all the damage.

During a lull in the shooting, he heard Terzic approach. When the man was close enough so Pierce wouldn't miss, even with his tremors, he would turn and shoot.

He heard further gunfire, not suppressed this time. When it halted, Pierce snuck a glance back in Terzic's direction. The Australian soldier was now on his knees, blood leaking from the many holes in his chest and throat. He fell forward, landed flat on his face on the pavement, and didn't move again.

Pierce tucked the Glock back against his belt and sprinted on. He wasn't the only person fleeing for their life, so his actions wouldn't look unusual.

He ducked down a side street away from the shooting. A blue Toyota hatchback pulled up, and a young man climbed out. Moving fast, Pierce stepped up behind him to press the muzzle of the Glock into the back of the man's head. "Keys, please. And don't look at me."

The shaking man offered the keys without question.

"On the ground. Face down until I'm gone."

He obeyed.

Once in the car, Pierce drove fast from the city, knowing that the GPS in the car would soon track his movements, informing the police of his exact location. When he reached a Greyhound bus terminal, he drove on two more blocks, then jumped from the car, leaving the door open and the engine running. Almost immediately, he watched as another man stole it, and the vehicle disappeared down a freeway.

Jogging to the bus station, Pierce purchased two tickets, one for Pretoria via Johannesburg, the other for Port Elizabeth on the coast. If the police later checked, they would have two trails to follow, tying up their resources. The Joburg-Pretoria bus was the first to depart, in just under twenty minutes, so he would take that route. An overnight journey, but that suited him.

After purchasing a cap at a street stall, Pierce found a bar next to the bus station, where he ordered a beer. On the television hung above the caged street-facing window, a SABC News report from the South African Broadcasting Corporation played on today's shooting. Nine dead, including seven officers killed during police efforts to apprehend two white men responsible for an assassination attempt at the CTICC. A fake-smiling Rupert Ponsonby flashed up on the screen with words denoting him as the victim of the failed assassination attempt. The police had killed one assassin during the ordeal. The other had escaped and was described as muscular, Caucasian, with ginger hair and a matching beard. Alex Trager. There was no mention of anyone matching Pierce's description in the report.

Pierce felt conflicted. On the one hand, he had caused chaos for Trager's and Walsh's conspiracy, but his activities had led to the death of innocent people. He'd not known that Trager and Terzic were in Cape Town hunting him until he had overheard Walsh and Ponsonby's conversation at the last possible moment to act. If he'd had time, he would have implemented a different strategy.

Pierce sipped his beer and silently honoured the dead. Then he stepped onto the bus just before it pulled out of the terminal and drove east.

He sat towards the back and pulled down his new cap.

He wondered again if his path of revenge was worth it, considering the carnage he had caused...

Pierce shook that thought from his mind. Innocents had died, but he hadn't pulled the trigger on those deaths. That blood and the violence of their actions were on Trager's and Terzic's hands. Not his.

Pierce finished his beer. It was the only taste in his mouth that he savoured.

36

Western Cape, South Africa

It was four hours into his bus journey along the N1 Highway before Mark Pierce finally relaxed. If the police hadn't stopped and searched the bus by now, they never would. Perhaps this was because the South African authorities had never pursued him, never suspecting his involvement in the killings.

He again studied the cabin of the modern coach. It featured an onboard toilet, comfortable seats and air-conditioning for the passengers who could afford this level of comfort in their travels, who were a mixture of locals and tourists of many ethnicities. The young man next to him snored lightly, his head resting on his jacket pressed up against the glass window. They hadn't talked during the long drive to Johannesburg, which suited Pierce. Everything about this setting was perfect because Pierce didn't stand out.

He wore his headphones so no one would talk to him,

and kept his cap low, then locked his phone, leaned back in his seat and tried to sleep.

He couldn't.

He checked his hands. They weren't shaking now when it wouldn't have mattered if they did. The randomness of the tremors coming and going infuriated him.

Pierce had experienced mild tremors for many years now, but after a grenade blast in Yemen during a mission behind enemy lines, his shakes had worsened. Too much alcohol and a lack of sleep aggravated his condition, so he avoided both as much as possible — no easy accomplishment in his "profession". The only means by which he could control his tremors was by stilling his mind, through meditation and clearing his head of all thought. A technique that wasn't always practical and didn't always produce results, like today hanging by a rope off the edge of a skyscraper. The tremors had almost killed him in Cape Town. They might kill him in the future.

He clenched his hand into a fist and stared out the window. The landscape was rolling hills with flat scrub grass and cloudless horizons. Behind the bus, the setting sun turned the sky and landscapes into hues of reds, oranges, purples and blues.

His cell phone pinged. A conversation had recorded on Rupert Ponsonby's phone and was ready for listening.

Pierce pressed play.

"Fucking hell! You took your time calling back!" Ponsonby yelled down the phone line. "I almost fucking died today!"

"It's only been nine minutes since I got your message. Get a grip."

Hearing Idris Walsh's voice again, his body broke out in a sweat as every muscle tensed.

He imagined pressing a pistol against Walsh's forehead and squeezing the trigger...

He imagined Walsh begging for his life, and Pierce denying the spymaster his wish...

He imagined... much more...

Shaking his head to clear away his self-destructive thoughts, Pierce checked to ensure he'd backed up the conversation on a cloud computing account he had established earlier, which he had not done with the last conversation while distracted with the sniper rifle in his hand. With this conversation backed up, he continued listening.

"No, you get a grip! First someone tries to assassinate me! Then Angola's Minister of Natural Resources, Odel Nunes, visits me in hospital, where he fucking threatens me if I don't pay him his regular five-million monthly pay cheque. I tell him I will, and then he has the gall to break my fucking finger!"

Back in his days with the CIA, Pierce had studied Minister Nunes's file, and recalled several facts on the corrupt politician. Since taking on his ministerial role three years ago, the kleptomaniac had already squandered over half a billion dollars from the Angolan Treasury and transferred the money into several private bank accounts in Europe and the Caribbean, and he had done so without the president knowing about it. Arguing with Ponsonby over a five-million-dollar payment plan seemed trivial compared to the wealth and power Nunes controlled, but that was always the way with greedy people. No amount of money was ever enough.

It was a comforting thought, however, that Pierce wasn't the only individual currently complicating Ponsonby's life.

He listened as Ponsonby rattled on in his high-pitched whine. "I'm supposed to be in partnership with Nunes on the diamond marine mining operation I run in his country, not cowering to him!"

Walsh sighed. "You're hyperventilating. Calm yourself, or you'll pass out."

"I'm fucking calm, okay! Just fucking tell me what's going on? And how did your foot soldiers fail to protect me? You should see my arm. The big fucking 'problem' almost killed me."

"No, he didn't."

"Didn't what?"

"If he wanted you dead, he wouldn't have missed," Walsh growled. "His ploy was to scare you."

"Scare me? How the hell does he even know about my involvement?"

Walsh sighed. "The more pressing problem is our Aussie friends. The corporal is dead. Shot in the streets while evading Cape Town first-response officers, which means they have a body that they can identify. They'll soon know he is a close associate of our sergeant, and with a bit of smart intelligence work, it will all link back to us."

"Can't you clean it up?"

"No, I fucking can't just clean it up."

"Fuck!"

"Yes. Fuck!" Walsh cleared his throat. "However, the sergeant escaped. But it seems our 'problem' cleverly framed him as your assassin, forcing him to flee South Africa and compromising our operation further."

"Fuck, again!" Ponsonby's breaths were fast and shallow.

"But we did get the second nuclear device placed in the South African location."

"Yes, at least we did that."

"Good! But you need to deal with this bloody fall guy that he was supposed to be, once and for all. If he found me in Cape Town, God knows what else he knows."

"I agree. Get yourself to Bayanga. I'll send word to the others. This scheme of making the world believe he's the real nuclear terrorist is at risk of falling apart. We can't risk any further discussions that aren't face to face, because the 'problem' may have tapped into us."

"Tapped? You mean he's spying on us?"

"It's a possibility." Walsh sounded as if he now ground his teeth together. "He must have outside help. I tracked him to two of his assets aiding him in Azerbaijan, who killed themselves before I got to them, but there could be others. And another thing. I saw your presentation, when it was uploaded on the diamond conference's website."

Ponsonby's voice suddenly became lighter. "Oh, did you like it?"

"I don't fucking care about it, but you spent too much time on tailings dams. I mean way too much time."

"So what?"

"Because it's the key to the success of our operations, that's why. Shut the fuck up about them from now on."

"Oh, shit!"

"What now?"

"There's one more thing I should have mentioned..."

"*What?*" Annoyance grew in Walsh's voice.

Ponsonby mumbled, "I..."

"What are you not telling me?"

"It's probably nothing, but I misplaced my cell phone at the diamond conference for perhaps ten minutes."

"*WHAT?*"

"Don't worry, I got it back."

"Don't you ever fucking listen to me about safe operating protocols? Get rid of it, now!"

"But it's a Galaxy Note10. Platinum plated—"

"I don't fucking care. It's compromised. Everything you've just said to me, someone's just heard it. That someone was probably the man who took a shot at you earlier today. Don't contact me again until you are in the CAR."

The line went dead.

Pierce checked his app. The signal on Ponsonby's phone was no longer active. Pierce would receive no further intelligence from this source, but he had everything he needed now. The conversation had provided Pierce with a telling piece of intelligence that Ponsonby and Walsh weren't as cashed up as Pierce had first suspected. Financial woes must strain their relationship, and the three and a half million Pierce had taken from them would fuel that tension further.

He also had a rough timetable for when all the players who had wronged him would converge in the same location.

But Walsh would also guess that Pierce would come for him there and lay a trap.

That wouldn't stop Pierce though, just make him more careful.

He felt sad to hear the news that Valeriya and Yebin were dead, they were good people, but they had, like Pierce, chosen to play in this dangerous world of global espionage, so they knew the risks like Pierce did. He would drink a toast to them when this was all over and honour their memories.

It seemed fitting now that he should release the intel

package Valeriya and Yebin had prepared for him in Baku. With a few quick commands, he sent the data pack to thirty reputable news organisations across the globe, via an anonymous email account that, if scrutinised, would lead back to the US Department of Justice.

It was time for his own brand of covert reckoning.

He closed his eyes and finally slept, allowing his subconscious dreaming-self to plan out his next moves and ask himself how Rachel Zang factored into this conspiracy.

He hoped in a good way.

37

London, United Kingdom

Idris Walsh nursed his lemonade in the tiny booth towards the back of the busy pub. The décor was modern but tired, and the patrons were a mixture of twenty-something professionals out after work with colleagues, or retirees out for a cheap meal and a glass of house wine.

A muscular but weathered man approached, carrying two pints of lager. He sat diagonally to Walsh so he too could watch the patrons, pushed one pint over to Walsh and raised the other in a toast. "Cheers, my friend."

Walsh looked the man up and down. His thick South African accent was noticeable even with only a few words spoken.

When Walsh didn't drink, the man consumed a mouthful of his amber liquid, then licked his lips. "Ah, been a while since I've enjoyed a good old-fashioned English beer with a friend from the old days."

Walsh raised his glass and clinked the South African's drink, then put his glass down again. "Cheers."

"You're not drinking?"

"No. Bullet wound, which ended with a liver transplant. Can't ever fucking drink again." Walsh was not a man prone to letting his emotions control him, but with Mark Pierce, he could no longer hold the rage in check that ate at him constantly. He imagined throttling the Trigger Man's throat until oxygen starvation killed him.

"Well, in that case..." The South African reached over, took Walsh's glass and drank from it. "I won't let this one go to waste."

"Thanks for coming, Kurt."

The fifty-something soldier Walsh had called to this impromptu meeting went by the name Kurt Krige. He sported a close-cropped beard, while the sandy hair he'd grown out was thinning, a sight Walsh had never expected to see. A former Recces special forces soldier, Krige had turned private contractor many decades ago, and the hard life he had led showed in the creases and leathery texture of his skin. Walsh and Krige had a history that went back to those distant contracting days. They had killed men together, operated for weeks as a team behind enemy lines, and saved each other's lives more often than either had bothered to count. Nobody knew Walsh better than Krige did, but the reverse was also true. Walsh trusted no one in the world, but if forced to choose a single individual to trust, it would be Kurt Krige.

"It's been a while, Idris. Surprised me when you called wanting a hit taken out on two beautiful women."

"Your man failed."

"And drowned in the Thames for his troubles. I told you I couldn't organise a quality kill in that short a time."

Walsh nodded and stared into his lemonade. "It sent a message."

"So even after that botched operation, you still wanted to meet?" When Walsh didn't answer, Krige said, "You still with the CIA?"

Walsh watched the crowds to see if anyone showed any interest in their conversation. Nobody did. "Not for much longer."

Krige chuckled. "I can't believe you actually scored a high-ranking position with them after all those fucked-up years together killing rebels in the Congo jungles as mercenaries."

Walsh shrugged and said nothing.

"Finally saved up enough money to properly support your sister. How's she doing, by the way?"

Walsh cringed as images of a staircase came to mind. "Nothing changes there, Kurt."

"I'm sorry to hear that." Krige drank more beer while he rubbed an itch at the back of his neck. "So, you can't drink to drown your sorrows. Idris, you are one unlucky bastard."

The crease-lines around Walsh's eyes grew darker as he squinted. "Actually, Kurt, I'm on the verge of securing the mother lode of fucking money."

Krige sat straighter. His eyes stopped watching the crowds and focused only on Walsh. "Why are you telling me this? You're not one prone to sharing! And truth be told, neither am I." Then realisation spread across his face. "But you'll only secure this mother lode of money through my help?"

Walsh resisted the urge to nod, for Krige had guessed

correctly. "The people I'm working with, they're about to fuck up my scheme spectacularly. I need your help with a few jobs to get that scheme, and my people, back on track."

"I'm listening."

"Enjoying life in rainy, miserable England?"

Krige shrugged. "Not much to do here for a man with my skills. Africa, the Middle East and Central America is where I operate best. But until the money runs out, England suits me fine for a vacation. I gamble and enjoy whores to pass the time. The whores I know in Soho, in particular, keep me content."

"How about returning to Africa?"

Krige shrugged. "Depends on the scenario and the pay cheque."

Walsh grinned. "I'm talking protection duty."

"Protection duty? That doesn't sound like you."

"It's what I'm offering."

"You going to elaborate?"

"Let's say it involves a diamond mining ship."

His face flushed, Krige took a long sip of his beer and didn't stop until he finished the first glass.

"It will be like the old days, Kurt. If my scheme goes south, I need an exit plan. That exit plan involves you, me, and the old team being on that ship. But don't worry, if the scheme fails, I have a contingency in place to ensure you and I get rich, at least."

"And if your scheme doesn't go south?"

Walsh drank from his, until now, untouched glass of lemonade, and decided it wasn't too bad a substitute for a proper drink. "I'll make you an investor in my original scheme. We'll make so much money, the exit plan payout will look like small change."

Krige leaned back and rested his arm on the chair next to his. "Sounds too good to be true. What is it you're not telling me?"

"Lots. Actually. But nothing changes there. Are you in or not?"

38

After a night of frantic activity, Zang returned to Jaya's home just before dawn, exhausted and buzzed on too much coffee. She couldn't rest yet. There was still much to do. Before she stepped inside, however, she made a quick call on the burner phone she had secured earlier, reported in, then erased the call.

Yesterday's battle had been to save Mackenzie Summerfield's life. The bullet had nicked a major artery in the former analyst's arm, which had caused her to lose a lot of blood. Being a universal donor, Zang had transfused a significant quantity of her own blood into Summerfield's veins, saving her life.

Many hours later, when Summerfield had been stabilised and Zang could give no more blood, she disappeared, saying she needed to clean up a few loose ends, and would return within twenty-four hours. Jaya had looked less than impressed, knowing that she might soon have a dead body on her hands and no means to dispose of it if Zang didn't return. But Zang had returned, and Mackenzie Summerfield had survived.

"Where did you go?" Jaya stood in the hallway, her eyes sunken and bloodshot. Her tone accusatory.

Zang shrugged. "Like I said, loose ends."

"You won't tell me?"

"It's better you don't know."

Jaya stood motionless for a moment, used the wall to hold herself upright. "You would say that. Why should I have expected more?" She motioned down the hall. "Mackenzie's sleeping. Earlier she was responsive. She's lucky she survived."

"That's good."

Jaya shook her head. "A 'thank you' would be nice."

Zang smiled. "Sorry. I forgot my manners. Thank you, Jaya."

The surgeon returned a faint smile. "I've just boiled the kettle. You want a coffee?"

"How about a tea?"

"I can do that."

Five minutes later they sat together on the kitchen bench. Zang had worried that upon her return she would discover police or a surveillance team watching the house, but a thorough check of the street and surrounding buildings showed no sign that anyone had tracked them here.

With hot steaming mugs in their hands, Jaya and Zang sipped their beverages and stared at nothing, both too exhausted to talk. Zang soon had a headache, and if she wasn't careful, it would turn into a migraine. She'd already drunk too much caffeine in the last twelve hours, which would only aggravate the dull but concentrated pain in her head. Sleep would help, but she needed to stay awake a little longer.

Jaya opened the refrigerator and poured two large glasses of orange juice. She passed one to Zang and drank the other. "Your blood sugar will be low. Drink up."

Zang obeyed.

The surgeon laughed without humour. "You make one mistake, that will cost you your career if it ever comes out, and then people like you abuse it, again and again."

"What did you do?"

Jaya laughed louder than before. "If you don't know, I'm not telling. Enough people in your business, whatever it is, already abuse that knowledge. I don't need more of your kind holding my dirty secret over me like some kind of threat." She finished her orange juice. "Another day I've had to call in sick at the hospital. One day, my superiors will question all my absences."

"You do this a lot? Save people from bullet wounds?"

She nodded. "More than I thought possible in a safe town like London."

Zang finished her orange juice and stood. The sugar had helped lessen her headache, a trick to remember for the future. "Thank you for your help, Jaya. It's not a lie when I say I appreciate it."

"You're leaving already?"

Zang nodded.

"Mackenzie isn't well enough to travel."

"That doesn't matter. The longer we stay here, the greater the risk we put you in, and her. Bad people are looking for both of us. We need to be away from here, and soon."

Jaya paled at the realisation she herself might be in mortal danger. "Where will you take her?"

"Better you don't know."

Jaya didn't argue and just nodded again.

Zang headed down the hall. Jaya followed her. Splashes of blood stained the floors and walls. "You must clean that, and soon."

In the bedroom, a listless Summerfield lay on the double bed, but stirred as Zang and Jaya entered. Then she winced as a fresh surge of pain erupted through her.

"A man shot you," Zang explained. "Jaya saved your life, but now we must leave."

Without protest, Summerfield climbed out of the bed while Zang helped her to get dressed. Ten minutes later, they were on the road in the silver Ford Fiesta Zang had stolen the previous night from a long-term car park, where its absence wouldn't be immediately noticed.

"Mackenzie, do you have an off-the-books place we can stay?"

"Yes. A cottage in Nottingham."

They took the back roads, avoiding built-up areas, where surveillance cameras were unlikely. The countryside was green and covered with a constant drizzle. Summerfield remained pale and unresponsive to the outside world, but she kept herself awake.

"I was thinking." Zang broke the silence, knowing there was much to talk about, and now was as good a time as any. "My team in Kazakhstan. Everyone on it were the most vocal against Idris Walsh's methods..." She let the statement hang as she zipped past several cyclists in their bright, body-hugging jerseys who didn't seem to care about the miserable weather.

Summerfield didn't answer straight away. When she did,

it was a hoarse whisper. "You want to know if I think it was Walsh who tried to have me and you killed?"

"The thought had crossed my mind."

"It's possible. Walsh and I only worked together for a week. But long enough for me to understand what kind of psychopath he was. Still is."

"I'll call Walsh soon. Fabricate a story and see how he responds. Don't worry, I'll set it up so he can't find us, but I need to do this to know what kind of man he really is."

Summerfield tensed as she readjusted her position in the passenger seat.

"Hurts like hell?"

Summerfield nodded as she gritted her teeth.

"First time you've taken a bullet?"

"Yes. But I've suffered far worse wounds."

Zang didn't ask. She wasn't here to learn Summerfield's every secret, just enough to understand what kind of mess she was in. What kind of mess they were both in.

Summerfield cleared her throat. "Mark Pierce is a good man. Don't get me wrong, he's a killer, and a proficient one at that. Despite few of his CIA peers liking or respecting him, he's a hyper-efficient field operative, but also able to express the deepest sympathy and compassion. I've met no one like him. He also holds back much information about himself. Even when we worked together for so long and came to trust each other, there was much he didn't tell me. If what Walsh is saying is true, that Pierce is stealing nuclear waste to make a dirty bomb, then Pierce has a good reason to that has nothing to do with terrorism or profiteering."

"You still trust him?"

"Yes... I did... Once."

"What stopped you?"

"Mark betrayed me in Morocco."

"Could he have been protecting you?"

Summerfield didn't answer. She instead stared ahead at the road and the light traffic as they fled north across England. The drizzle turned into rain, and soon the windscreen wipers operated on full speed. Minutes later she said, "You're like Pierce in many ways."

Zang said, "As in no one in the CIA respects me?"

"No, as in you are as competent as he is. You're a field assassin, just like him. Probably just as hyper-efficient."

Zang sighed through clenched teeth and stared through the windscreen wipers. "It's all academic, Mackenzie, what you and I think. I'll call Walsh shortly and provoke him. His actions after that will prove who the liar is. Walsh or Pierce."

39

Heathrow Airport, United Kingdom

Idris Walsh drummed his fingers on the leather armchair as he reflected on his plan to control the world's diamond market. He might have been too ambitious.

Too many elements had unravelled. Too many participants had failed to perform. Willpower had eroded.

The view beyond the floor-to-ceiling window of the premium lounge showed a dozen airplanes ready to take flight from Heathrow Airport to all corners of the earth. New York. Frankfurt. Dubai. Sydney. Moscow. Beijing. All cities he knew well, where he had killed men who had stood in his way, and where he had betrayed others. Drizzle flowed down the window, and rain fell on the taxiways and runways, washing away into puddles of nothingness like all those individuals who had impeded him in the past. It would be so easy to step onto one of those flights and disappear from this mess. Instead, he'd met Aaron Stone here and sent him on a mission into Central Africa to assassinate Pierce, knowing that was where his nemesis was likely to head next.

He was about to leave when his cell phone rang, and he realised he knew the number. A cell phone assigned to Rachel Zang. This, he mused, would be an interesting conversation.

"Sir?" Zang was out of breath.

"Aren't you supposed to be in Langley?"

"Yes. Sorry about that."

Walsh switched to his headpiece, then activated the call-tracing app on Zang's phone. The tracker soon positioned her just outside the university town of Cambridge, about seventy miles north of Heathrow Airport. "What's going on, Zang? I haven't heard from you since you got back."

"Why I'm calling, sir. I presume Stone filled you in on my five days with Pierce?"

"He did."

"Well, I got thinking about Mackenzie Summerfield and how she could help me understand Pierce's actions a little better."

"I told you not to go near her."

"I know, sir, and I'm sorry. It was a mistake. Pierce had her killed. You... saw the news?"

"Yes."

"I tried to save Summerfield, but she bled out."

"I'm disappointed. You led Pierce straight to her!"

"I did... I know, and I'm sorry."

Walsh studied the people seated near him, ensured none were in earshot. "What did you do with her... body?"

"Don't worry. No one will ever find it. But I have another problem..."

"Go on."

"I've gone to ground. If I show my face anywhere public, Pierce could take me out too. I need an emergency exfil."

Walsh drew a silent breath. This was the opportunity he was waiting for, and a plan formed in his mind. "I can help with that. Where are you now?"

"The CIA's Birmingham safe house." He knew this was a lie because the app placed her in Cambridge. "It's just me. What do you want me to do?"

"Stay there. I'll come to you. Just need a few hours to get your exfil sorted."

"You're here? In England."

"Yes. Stay where you are, Zang. Go dark. Don't contact anyone, and don't share any intel until I can talk to you face to face."

"Okay. Why face to face? Isn't that a risk for you? I might lead Pierce to you as well?"

"There are developments..."

"What kind?"

"Not over a line that might be compromised."

"But we're encrypted?"

"Trust me, Zang. I need to tell you this to your face."

Several seconds passed in silence. Then she said, "Okay. I'll see you soon. Thank you, sir."

The call ended. Walsh kept his app locked in on her cell phone signal, which was motionless for the moment. Eight minutes passed before it moved, at a speed of forty miles per hour, headed west towards Birmingham.

Zang should have died in Kazakhstan. The criminals Trager had hired should have killed the four CIA operators and field support officers and left Pierce's corpse as the culprit. Four CIA employees who for too long had questioned Walsh's methods and motives for going after the

Trigger Man. When Pierce had saved Zang's life, fuck knew what he had told her in those five days they spent together, and what she had told him. Zang's meeting with Mackenzie Summerfield would have been to confirm whatever it was they had discussed, which would be nothing that supported the fake narrative Walsh had spent months preparing and pushing out into the world.

Like Pierce, Zang had to die. There was no other path for her now. He'd perform the messy task himself if he had to.

But the CIA operator was no fool, and a highly trained and efficient field operative. He'd have to be careful with her.

He suspected she knew that he knew she'd turned traitor, and would wait to trap him. But Walsh hadn't survived this long with the CIA through luck alone. He would find her first, and he would eliminate her, and then he would hide her body so no one ever found it again, just like she had claimed to have done with Mackenzie Summerfield. The bitch was full of lies.

Walsh paid for the drinks, found his BMW Series 8 Coupé in the long-term car park, then drove with speed towards Birmingham and his forced date with the problematic woman whose life expectancy was long overdue.

40

Gaborone, Botswana

Pierce stepped off the goods truck, thanked the
driver for the lift, then stood for a moment on the
streets of Gaborone as he gathered his bearings.
Botswana's capital was a mixture of British Colonial and
modern buildings. The sun shone overhead in a clear sky,
and the weather was a perfect thirty plus degrees, or about
eighty-five degrees in the old system. People in their well-cut
clothes smiled at each other and didn't pick up their pace
when they thought someone was about to mug them.
Thanks to a bountiful diamond industry, low levels of
corruption and a progressive government, Botswana was one
of Africa's success stories, and that was obvious in the
serenity before him.

He found a modern bar, the Zenyatta Mondatta, and
stepped inside. Being early morning, the few patrons drank
non-alcoholic beverages of coffee, tea, and fruit juices. Pierce
ordered a coffee, a beef burger and chips. He hadn't eaten a

meal like it in more than half a year, and his mouth soon salivated thinking about its taste.

A wall-mounted wide-screen television played a clip from the BBC World News channel. An image of Rupert Ponsonby drew Pierce to the screen, a public relations photo of the Englishman flashing a smug grin. A reporter appeared and proclaimed that the police still hunted for the second of two Australian suspects in the assassination attempt on the Polytope chief executive officer. The first had died during a dramatic shoot-out with Cape Town police. A sketch of the surviving man flashed up with a passing resemblance to Alex Trager.

"Crazy South Africans," said a bar worker when he brought Pierce his food. The young man wore a brightly patterned shirt, stoplight red jeans and yellow canvas shoes. "Highest murder rate in the world, South Africa has, and they make a fuss about one rich white guy who survived a single attack."

Pierce nodded and thanked him for the food.

"Where you from?" the man asked.

"America. The United States."

"You're a long way from home."

"Quit my job two months ago. Thought I'd challenge myself to an African overland adventure."

"On your own?"

Pierce nodded again. "More people should come to Africa. It's a beautiful continent and not anywhere as bad as the Western media likes to make it out to be."

"That's for sure. Let me know if you want a refill on the coffee. Complimentary second cup before eleven."

"Thank you, I will."

The man returned to the bar, and Pierce ate. In between

watching the room for any potential threats, his eyes often returned to the television. The BBC had come into information that Rupert Ponsonby maintained a financial relationship with the Central African Republic warlord Captain Daniel Eloko, also described as an evangelistic and fanatical Christian terrorist. The Hague wanted Eloko to stand trial for many international crimes, including genocide in the Seleka-Anti-Balaka conflict, and a host of other crimes Pierce already knew about.

As the report continued, Pierce couldn't help but smile as the reporter laid out the details as he had provided them, one fact after the other.

Recent documents provided by an anonymous governmental source, said the reporter, revealed how Polytope Diamonds frequently paid off Eloko through various front companies, which the reporter then listed. Highlighted sections of correspondence between the two individuals detailed how Ponsonby planned to construct a full production mine in Eloko's territory, with twenty per cent of the profits going to Eloko when the mine was operational.

The BBC and likely other networks across the globe had run with the same intel package Valeriya and Yebin had provided to Pierce. There was no mention of the former Australian SASR soldiers Alex Trager or Javor Terzic, but at least Polytope's links to an African warlord and conflict diamonds were now in the public domain.

Pierce grinned. Twice now he had struck at Walsh and his co-conspirators. They would wonder how and when he would strike again.

When he finished his meal, he paid at the counter, then took a taxi to the airport. Walsh, Trager, Ponsonby and Eloko would soon congregate in Bayanga, and that was where Pierce would seek his final retribution.

During the drive past avenues of lush trees, his thoughts turned to the CIA operator Rachel Zang.

Despite his tormented state of mind during their time together, he had enjoyed her company — particularly when he believed she might be a Russian prostitute called Irina. Pierce again wondered how much of that personality was genuine, and how much she had faked so Pierce would only see her as Zang had wanted him to see her?

He also considered the possibility that she worked for Idris Walsh and was hunting him even now. That she was as dangerous an enemy as the rest of them.

Pierce pushed the thought from his mind. The next stages of his plan required careful execution, which started with a visit to another location from his pre-CIA past.

And then it involved smuggling himself into Central Africa via its neighbour Cameroon.

41

Birmingham, United Kingdom

Athunderstorm erupted late into the night as Idris Walsh entered Birmingham, yet the overcast weather suited him. Rain kept most people inside, or if they were outside, they hid behind hats, coats and underneath umbrellas. No one would see or remember him coming or leaving.

Zang's cell phone had deactivated as soon as she had entered the outskirts of the city. But he expected that. The operator was merely applying tradecraft as taught to her by the CIA.

The safe house's location was in a middle-class suburb of brown, two-storey houses packed close together with lush green garden frontages. Bars protected the safe house's windows, and all curtains were closed. Walsh knew from CIA manuals the glass was bulletproof and the wooden doors hid steel-lined armour.

He parked at the end of a cul-de-sac and planned his next move.

Walsh's BMW Series 8 Coupé's suite of weapons included a Heckler and Koch SA80 A2 assault rifle with NATO standard 5.56x45mm rounds, two Glock 17 Gen 4 pistols with 9mm rounds, a 12-gauge ARGO or auto-regulating gas-operated system shotgun, several Fairbairn-Sykes fighting knives, and flashbang and fragmentation grenades. Weapons curtsy of Walsh's contacts within the British Army.

Behind the house was a forested park with a lake in the middle. Walsh would arm himself and approach from that direction.

Out of the car, he opened the trunk. While the rain drenched his clothes and hair, Walsh slipped on body armour, then a trench coat. He fitted a suppressor to one of the Glocks and slipped it into the coat's pocket. The fighting knife he strapped to his forearm. He looked down the street, glad that overhanging trees provided cover and cast him in shadow. Then the combat shotgun came out, and he slipped it under his coat.

Walsh took off across the forested park and approached the safe house from the rear. There was no one in the park because of the heavy rain and late hour.

At the back door, after twinging because of a short but sharp pain emanating from his gut, distracting him momentarily, Walsh keyed in the PIN that would let him in and disable the alarm. He keyed in a second code known only by senior officers that would permanently delete all audiovisual recordings of his time inside and ten minutes before and after he left.

He closed the door behind him and took a long, centring breath. CIA safe houses included soundproofing in case captured hostiles required "interrogation", and neighbours didn't need to hear their screams. If he fired the shotgun now, to outsiders the noise would sound like nothing more than a stifled cough.

With a smirk on his face, Walsh progressed through the building and cleared each room, noting signs of recent habitation but not sensing any living person within its walls. He expected Zang was aware of his presence and would now stalk him as he stalked her. It was a risk, this meeting, but it could end in only one of two outcomes. Either she died, or he did. Either outcome solved his problems.

Lightning flashed outside.

Convinced that Zang wasn't downstairs, he tensed against disturbing teenage memories and headed upstairs.

Keeping the lights off, he snuck into the bedroom.

He heard a whirling noise of a motor. A shape moved under the bedcovers.

More lightning.

Walsh fired the shotgun twice, disintegrating the shape and the mattress beneath.

With the stench of cordite thick in the air, he pulled back the cover.

The 12-gauge ARGO had pulverised a desk fan. It had started up as soon as he'd entered the bedroom. The fan had blown air through a sheet over an arrangement of pillows, so the configuration resembled a human moving under the bedcovers.

He checked the power cord. A digitally activated on-off switch lay between the cord and the power socket.

Walsh checked the room, discovering the digital camera that had recorded him enter, then shoot the shape under the bedcovers. No doubt the video file was already on its way to Zang's laptop.

For a moment, Walsh asked himself what the purpose of this ruse was.

Then he understood. This was a test to determine Walsh's allegiances. Zang now knew his loyalties were never with her, and that his intention was to kill her. She'd gathered actionable intelligence in this moment, and he had not.

He bit down on his teeth and pressed his tongue against the roof of his mouth so he wouldn't bellow his anger while she was watching.

Before Zang could learn more, Walsh blew apart the camera with a third blast of the shotgun, then disappeared outside again into the rain, thunder and lightning, where no one would dare come look for him.

42

Nottingham, United Kingdom

The video recording of Walsh played out as Zang expected, but not how she had hoped. She wanted him to be on her side, but if there was any doubt of Walsh's loyalties towards her, that thought vanished like it had never existed. He'd journeyed to Birmingham with the sole purpose of killing her.

Zang had considered confronting Walsh, but didn't trust that in her hesitation to determine if Walsh was one of the good people or not, he wouldn't shoot her. Now she knew that he would have.

A pale and listless Summerfield stood next to her, unblinking as she watched the video feed of Walsh firing his shotgun into the camera. The wounded woman looked in need of at least three more cups of coffee if she were to keep herself awake much longer. Her skin was paler than alabaster, her wounded arm hung limp in its sling, and the dark circles around bloodshot eyes expressed the pain she'd endured. Zang watched as she sat down before she fell down. "Everything I believed, Zang... Everything the CIA told me... was a lie."

"I'm sorry." Zang clenched her fists, furious that Idris Walsh had used them both in an operation that benefitted not America and her people, but a personal agenda. If Pierce hadn't stolen the nuclear waste, that suggested Walsh had, but for what purpose? Perhaps Mackenzie Summerfield could help her understand.

"Walsh can't find us here," Summerfield said, filling the silence that had stretched out in that moment. "The monthly payments for this place, the lease records, the ghosting of my internet protocols, none are traceable back to me."

"That's good to know. Thank you." Zang looked to the kitchen. "You want a coffee? I need one."

Summerfield nodded.

Zang boiled the kettle and poured them both long blacks. Summerfield added milk and sugar to hers.

They sat opposite each other at the quaint cottage's kitchen table. The patter of rain falling on the roof was soothing in its regular rhythm.

Zang said, "How is the shoulder?"

Summerfield winced. "Hurts like hell. I can move it all right, so no lasting damage."

"You lost a lot of blood. In a few days you should feel much better."

"Have you ever taken a bullet?"

Zang nodded, lowered her pants line to show the scar above her left hip. "I know it doesn't look like a bullet wound, but it is. Indescribable pain. I vowed never to get shot again, but you know... In our business it's a hazard we face every day."

"A first for me."

"Sorry to be a bore, but can we return to our current predicament?"

Summerfield nodded. "I guess we should."

"Seven months ago, Idris Walsh framed you and Pierce for stealing eleven million in CIA funds. The CIA forcibly returned you from the field to the States, investigated your recent activities, and found that Pierce used you unwittingly to steal that money. You received no criminal charges, but the CIA fired you for incompetence. Sometime later, you accepted a position in London with Greene Strategic Group, where you've been ever since. Civilian life treated you fairly, and in that time, you never once heard from Pierce or Walsh?"

Summerfield held her cup in both hands to warm them, then sipped it. "Yes, that's about it."

"From my perspective, our team spotted Pierce in several locations across North Africa, Europe and Asia in those same seven months. Soon a pattern emerged. He was trying to buy components to build a dirty nuclear bomb while seeking buyers for radioactive isotopes. The CIA quickly branded Pierce as a terrorist, and somehow Idris Walsh ended up as the guy running the operation to take him down. Walsh recruited me as one of his operators tasked to capture or kill Pierce, but somehow, Pierce always avoided us. Then he was in Kazakhstan, planning to purchase six canisters of radioactive waste from corrupt elements of the Kazakh military."

Zang sipped at her coffee, enjoying the buzz it provided. She hadn't told Mackenzie who she really worked for inside the CIA, and had no intention of doing so, but everything else she had said was the truth from her perspective. "Two weeks ago, Kazakh criminals murdered three of my CIA peers, kidnapped me, and a short time later I ended up in Pierce's custody. We went on the run together, and he let it slip that he's not a nuclear terrorist. He also let it slip that someone had held him captive in a secret African paramilitary prison during a period just before we met, and tortured him there. That 'someone' I now know was Walsh."

"Of the two stories, Zang, I'm inclined to believe Pierce, particularly after what we just saw."

Zang nodded. "The implication then is that Walsh used Pierce to fabricate a false trail of Pierce sightings across various countries, using the man's fingerprints and blood with his DNA markers. During my time with Pierce in Central Asia, all I saw was a man who — while wounded and angry — held compassion for others, myself included. Not the behaviour of an individual seeking to unleash a dirty bomb on the world."

"And all this time, I hated Mark, because I thought he had betrayed me. Walsh made me believe that."

"Indeed."

They sat for a moment, not speaking or drinking as their respective understandings of the situation merged in their minds.

Zang, after her earlier conversation with Walsh, had left her CIA-issued cell phone in a mail package with the battery almost flat, and hired a courier to drive it to an innocuous address in Birmingham near to the safe house, knowing that Walsh would track it there.

Summerfield shuddered. "Stealing nuclear material is a serious crime. It puts you at the top of the most wanted lists for all the federal intelligence and law enforcement agencies. There's nowhere you can hide where the US won't hunt you down. Walsh must desperately want nuclear waste for his own purposes to take a risk like that. The scheme to blame Mark would be brilliant... if it weren't so horrific."

"And yet, other intelligence and law enforcement agencies were never told of Pierce's rogue status. Even the FBI wasn't told. Why is that?"

The wounded woman raised an eyebrow. "Pierce was on some big, protracted secret op before he joined the CIA. I guess someone high up feels they owe him for his past service to his country, or they have suspicions about Walsh."

Zang tensed, for there was much truth to Summerfield's last statement. "Or both. What was the big op?"

Summerfield shook her head. "No one knows."

"He never told you, Summerfield?"

"No, and I never asked. If I've met anyone other than Mark who knows, they're not telling."

"But why a dirty bomb, or bombs?" Zang asked, returning the conversation to their current predicament, for she already knew higher authorities had locked down Pierce's past tighter than a Swiss bank vault. "What does Walsh want with radioactive waste? How do dirty bombs benefit him?"

Summerfield smiled. "Initially, I would say extortion. But I might have a different answer there." She took her laptop from its bag and fired it up. After checking all the encryption programs, IP masking applications and firewalls were in place, she pulled up a news article on Rupert Ponsonby, CEO of Polytope Diamonds, linking him to the Central African Republic's warlord, Daniel Eloko. The article implied the two profited from conflict diamond mining in the country's south-east.

Zang grinned. "Polytope's shares will have taken a hit with news like that, but how is it relevant?"

Summerfield returned the grin. "I still have contacts in the intelligence services. Yesterday, South Africa's State Security Agency, who owes me, spotted Pierce in Cape Town, although not knowing he's on a CIA wanted list, they made no moves against him. The same time someone made a failed assassination attempt on Rupert Ponsonby."

The grin on Zang's face soon grew into an enormous smile. "That makes sense. The secret paramilitary camp he mentioned was somewhere in Africa. The CAR is a perfect location for an off-the-books CIA black prison."

"I don't think it is CIA controlled though, Zang. My guess, it's barely a prison at all, but a makeshift torture chamber that belongs to Captain Eloko. He controls much of the CAR region known as Bayanga, rulership enforced by his army of evangelical Christian insurgents who also control all the local diamond mines. I would say that was where Eloko and Walsh imprisoned Pierce, and where we will find him now. Because if Pierce is the same man I remember, he'll now hunt down the people who tortured and imprisoned him. Even if it means returning to where he escaped from."

Zang stood, walked to the sink and poured herself a glass of water. She motioned to Summerfield if she wanted water too, and the woman nodded. Zang returned to the table with two full glasses. "Walsh has made enemies of us all. I know he's muddied your and Pierce's names within the CIA and is likely doing the same with me right now. So now I'm determined to bring Walsh to justice. Will you help?"

Summerfield looked to her wounded arm. "I'll do what I can."

"Thank you. The first step is to find Pierce again and

learn what he knows."

"Agreed."

"If he was the assassin in Cape Town, I doubt he would have missed."

"Unless his intention was to shake up things." Summerfield loaded a second file on her laptop. A first-class ticket from Cape Town to the Central African Republic's capital, Bangui, on a Kenya Airways flight via Nairobi. The name on the ticket was Rupert Ponsonby. "An assassination attempt might have been to force the conspirators to regroup. Walsh is skilled in masking his movements, so no flight details for him, but my bet is they'll all be meeting in Bayanga soon. Mark won't be far behind."

"Well then. I need to reach Pierce before Walsh does."

"You?" Summerfield frowned. "But I'm coming with you."

Zang shrugged. "We are a team, yes, but you're wounded, and I need a functional operations officer and intelligence analyst. Look at how quickly you sourced all that intel on the CAR. I can't do that, not with your speed, efficiency and insight. I need someone hidden away who can. That's you, Summerfield."

"Mark won't trust you if you turn up alone, especially after your time together in Kazakhstan and Azerbaijan under false pretences."

"I'll call you, Mackenzie, once I find Pierce. You can explain our working relationship to him."

Summerfield raised an eyebrow. "Make introductions, you mean? That might work." She adjusted her weight on her chair, only to cause an intense jolt of pain in her shoulder. "Okay, you're right. I'm not up to travel in war-ravaged Central Africa."

Zang drank more of her water and grinned.

"It will be dangerous," Summerfield said.

"I know. But I'm experienced in these kinds of operations, and I have you backing me up. No one knows Mark Pierce better than you do. So that begs the question, if you were him, how would you get yourself into Bayanga?"

"Cameroon," the wounded woman said without hesitation. "He can't fly into the CAR, not directly, as Walsh and Eloko will have people closely watching all the airports. A boat trip up the Congo and Ubangi River from Kinshasa would be the simplest route, but he won't do that."

"Why not?"

"Because it is the simplest route, and Pierce knows Walsh will know this. Cameroon is viable but complex. The roads are poor, especially in eastern Cameroon, and once he's in CAR, the transportation situation deteriorates further. But Bayanga is near the border, so easy for Pierce to reach." She turned to her laptop. "I'll arrange flights into Cameroon's capital, Yaounde, with a transfer flight to nearby Berberati in the CAR if you need it. What languages do you speak?"

"English, Russian and Mandarin."

"All fluently?"

Zang nodded.

"I was hoping you spoke French, so let's stick with English." Summerfield smiled. "I can fabricate a British passport easily enough, an engineer with a prospecting mining company. It involves reaching out to a contact I know, but she's discreet. Factoring in the time it would take to prepare the passport and arrange flights, I could get you into CAR in three days, maybe two."

"Excellent!" Zang smirked. "Feels like I'm on a real mission again rather than pandering to Walsh's perpetual bullshit."

PART III

BULLETPROOF

43

Kenzou, Cameroon

Pierce parked his Toyota Land Cruiser at a gas station overlooked by a rusted logo of a prominent petrochemical corporation. A hand-painted sign proclaimed this to be the last gas stop before entering Central Africa, less than ten kilometres distant. He decided he might as well heed that warning.

Stopping the Land Cruiser by the bowser, Pierce switched off the engine, stepped out and locked the vehicle with his fob. He didn't want anyone stealing it, because under the tarpaulin in the back lay enough weapons to outfit a sizable mercenary force. The HK45CT pistol taken from that cache he kept secure in his belt covered by his jungle-green shirt. A Ka-Bar fighting knife strapped to his leg was hidden under his khaki pants. Every other weapon inside the vehicle would be useful later.

A light rain fell. Mist swirled around the tops of jungle trees, their trunks entwined in strangler vines, while sweat

clung to his skin because it couldn't evaporate in the saturated air. The air temperature was a warm thirty degrees
Celsius, not overbearing but enough to drain his energy fast
if he exerted himself for long periods, which he would have
to do at some point. The town of Kenzou itself was typically
backwater African, with muddy orange roads, trash everywhere, and houses of mud and concrete brick construction
with tinned roofs. People were thin and dressed in bright
clothes. Chickens and pigs ran wild, but their fate would
always be as somebody's future dinner.

Inside the shop, Pierce negotiated a price for gas,
knowing that the gauge wouldn't work, and there were no
CFA francs-per-litre signs listed anywhere. The proprietor
asked for the equivalent of fifty US dollars for a full tank.
Pierce didn't argue and paid in cash.

"I'm off to the Central African Republic," Pierce said in
his barely passable French. He'd learned fragments of the
language for eleven months during his recent tour of duty in
West Africa. As a child, languages had come easily to him.
His parents had moved often, and before he was sixteen,
Pierce had mastered Russian, Arabic, Spanish and Mandarin
through exposure to local cultures and people. As an adult,
however, he'd discovered his ability to pick up new tongues
had severely diminished. His French identified him as a
foreigner; he had to speak it slowly and wasted seconds as he
translated in his head. He doubted he knew even a thousand
words. "Can you tell me what to expect over there?"

The proprietor shrugged. "You don't want to go to the
CAR."

"Why not?"

The man laughed as he placed the cash in his wallet
rather than the cash register. "It's a war, man. The CAR is

eating itself alive. Muslim versus Christian. Christian versus Muslim. Refugees turn up here every day, have done so since 2014, escaping the violence. They swamp the NGOs in this town with almost twenty thousand displaced persons now. You'll see refugees if you head to the CAR, walking the road but all coming the other way."

"Violence?" Pierce asked, playing the innocent. "I thought the CAR situation had settled down?"

The man's laughter became like a roar. "Not with Daniel Eloko and his terrorists. He thinks he's the next Joseph Kony. He thinks his soldiers are the next Lord Resistance Army. They find you, they will rob and kill you. They'll use machetes to hack you to pieces. Don't go to the CAR."

Pierce nodded. From what he had read on Daniel Eloko, the warlord was very much like the terrorist Kony, controlling paramilitary organisations that raped and murdered their way across large tracts of Africa, smuggled diamonds, gold and ivory to fund their operations and purchase weapons, and promoted child prostitution and child soldiers. Ironically, Eloko had started out as a child soldier himself, so knew no better life to strive for. "Thanks for the advice. I'll be careful."

Outside at the bowser, a rusted 1980s model Jeep had parked next to Pierce's Land Cruiser. A tall thin man in an orange shirt and sky-blue cargo pants several sizes too large peered into the vehicle's windshield.

"Can I help you?" Pierce asked, his hand resting on the HK45CT pressed up against the small of his back.

The man looked up, startled. When he saw Pierce, he relaxed his stance and said, "Sorry. Are you Dr Mendez?"

"No."

"Oh." The hope drained from his face. "Are you a doctor? A medical professional?"

"No," Pierce said again. "I'm a journalist. Danny Hunter." He used the second of the two legends Valeriya and Yebin had prepared for him.

The man nodded. "A journalist, hey? Print?"

Pierce nodded. "Well, all the broadsheets are online now as well."

"Which paper?"

"All of them. I'm freelance."

"Okay. Well, maybe you could write a story about the refugee situation here. I'm happy to have our story published anywhere. The UN is moving in, again, because of Eloko and his forces. Refugee numbers are on the rise, and these people need doctors. We all need doctors." He handed Pierce a business card, with the blue-on-white globe of the United Nations imprinted in the corner. It said his name was David Nogambi, an Aid Worker with the United Nations Refugee Agency. The address was Cameroon's capital, Yaoundé.

"Sorry," Pierce said as he took the gas pump and fuelled his Land Cruiser. "I only write travel articles. I'm here for the Dzanga-Sangha Special Reserve. You know, African forest elephants, western lowland gorillas, and bongo antelopes."

"You are crazy. People don't need to read about reserves they'll never visit. Eloko's bandits, they are there. You should stay here to write your story about him. Otherwise, he finds you, kills you, and takes your money and equipment. The UN gets nothing."

"The reserve, you're saying it's dangerous?"

Nogambi laughed.

"Okay. I'll be careful." Pierce made a deliberate gesture to scratch his head as the tank filled, and he returned the pump to the bowser. "I have expensive cameras and audio equipment, laptops, satellite phones and... David, can you tell me how to secure it across the border?"

The UN worker looked bored now that he had figured there was nothing Pierce could do for him. "The border guards aren't your problem. Pay them fifty euros each and you'll cross, no problem. Other than the bandits, the deteriorated roads are problematic, from here all the way to Rwanda. This is the wet season, so sometimes the rivers are too high to cross. Also, the Anti-Balaka and Eloko's thugs, they like to dig trenches through roads to make them impassable. Like I said, you are crazy to go. But I see you will go anyway. And I need to find my doctor."

He climbed into his Jeep and drove off.

Pierce took his Land Cruiser through the town until he found a house with thick wooden planks scattered in its yard. He offered ten euros for four lengths of timber, which the owner accepted, strapped them to the rack of his Land Cruiser, and drove east into the mud, the rain, the mist and the dense, imposing jungle.

44

Bayanga, Central African Republic

After the Cessna taxied and came to a halt in Polytope's poor excuse for a mining camp, Walsh stepped out and immediately smelled the stench of a rotting jungle. Then he heard screeching monkeys scrambling in the tall jungle trees growing to the edge of the runway. The army of primates had discovered a flowering tree ripe with fruit ready for the eating. They fought each other for the easy pickings and hissed often, warning other hungry animals and birds away. They reminded Walsh of the team he had picked for this failing mission.

He checked the straps were tight on his ballistic vest and that the holstered M9 Beretta semi-automatic pistol on his hip was within easy reach. He could do nothing about the constant stabbing pain in his gut.

"Sergeant. Molly," he said with a nod as Alex Trager and the Scottish nuclear scientist approached him, both with red eyes and glum faces. "I'm sorry to hear about Javor. He was a good man."

Trager's lips tightened. "Pierce killed him."

"Not directly, but that is why we are here, to deal with him. Pierce is coming to us, so we'll be ready."

Trager raised a questioning eyebrow to this revelation, but made no comment.

They took Trager's Jeep and drove to the camp. Trager behind the wheel, Walsh next to him and Molly in the back. The roads were more mud than anything else, and the jungle grew close enough for the leaves to hit them through the open windows. Litter of every kind polluted the road.

"You two aren't saying much?" Walsh said after some time.

"Lots of people are dying, Idris," Molly said without looking at either of them. Walsh could tell because he regularly checked on her through the rear-view mirror.

"And lots more will. You're not losing your nerve, are you, Molly? You're not starting to think you had a better deal with Hezbollah?"

No one said a word. Walsh again reminded them of the hellholes he had saved them from, and how he could make their lives miserable once more if they didn't cooperate. He needed them focused and afraid, just long enough so he could extract himself from this mess should he need to.

Molly said, "Idris, don't you care that thousands of people will die of radiation poisoning? Do you know how horrible that kind of death is? Your body erupts with sores. Your gums bleed, and the constant nausea stops you from eating. Hair falls out as your organs fail. If you're lucky, you die before you go blind."

Walsh tensed, then grimaced. "Stop the car!"

Trager slowed, then halted the Jeep.

Walsh turned to Molly and stared her down. "I'll give you one chance, Molly McEwan. You can get out of the car now and walk away from all this. I won't stop you. I'll make sure no one stops you. You are free to go, to live your life however you want to live it." He stepped out, opened her door and gestured for her to get out.

She didn't move, and she wouldn't look at him.

"Last chance."

She crossed her arms and sank into the back seat.

"I thought so. If I hear you complain or question me again, or moan about the unfairness of our conspiracy, then it's all over for you. You understand me? I'll hand you over to Eloko and his men, and we all know that won't end well. Your torments will become so horrible you will beg for death long before your end."

After many seconds passed, while Molly refused to look at Walsh or speak to him, he noticed Trager fidgeting out of the corner of his eye. Closing the door again and returning to his seat, Walsh quickly spied Trager slipping his SIG Sauer P226 semi-automatic pistol behind his leg and out of Walsh's sight. He looked guilty, but also terrified. Walsh decided it was best just to pretend he hadn't seen the gun. He still needed these two weak-assed individuals, so he'd pander to their emotions just a little longer.

"Neither of you have anything to say?"

Trager cleared his throat. "No. I'm good." He looked to Molly. "We're both good."

"Good! Now that's sorted, shut the fuck up, Molly." Walsh turned to Trager. "Drive, Sergeant. We have an important meeting to attend."

They arrived at Eloko's headquarters a few minutes later.

Many quasi-soldiers in their green military uniforms and with outdated assault rifles wandered the base on supposed guard duty, cigarettes or marijuana spliffs hanging from their mouths. The base too was a disgrace and lacked the military discipline Trager had grown to expect during his career. Rubbish piles had a sickly-sweet smell that would have left Walsh gagging if he hadn't already grown used to their stench from his many previous visits. The huts were rotten wood and falling apart. Rusting military vehicles and armoured personnel carriers were older models from the Cold War era that spewed thick diesel fumes from their exhausts. Loud thrash-metal music played from whining speakers. Under a thatched hut roof, a soldier fucked a prostitute, his ass gyrating in the air for everyone to see. Further down the road, the naked corpse of a supposed Seleka spy hung upside down from the branch of a high jungle tree. Eloko's men had cut him in many places so he had bled out, and now the flies circled him night and day.

Fuck, he hated this hellhole.

When they stepped from the Jeep, the three entered the one decent transportable hut, propped up on concrete blocks so the wet wouldn't rot the shaky floorboards.

Inside, Ponsonby and Eloko sat next to each other at the table. For the first time in months, all the key conspirators had congregated in one location.

Seated in the middle of the room was Rupert Ponsonby, with his ironed and expensive shirt, designer jeans, aviator sunglasses and buffed-up hair to hide his thinning scalp. The only aspect of him that was cheap was the gumboots worn to protect his feet from mud. His left hand hid under a bandage, healing a broken finger. Another bandage under his shirt covered his recent bullet wound. Yet Ponsonby looked elated, like he had just won big on the races or completed a business deal that would make him another easy million dollars. Almost dying from an assassin's bullet didn't seem to bother him in the slightest.

At the worktable next to Ponsonby, Captain Daniel Eloko sat in meditation, yet projected the typical arrogance expected of African warlords. His uniform, while thread-bare, was clean, and his burgundy beret projected an unspoken image of authority. He sat with his hands clasped in prayer around a gold cross that hung around his throat, and mumbled a sermon to his god. The captain asked the "all mighty" for the strength to destroy his enemies and bring peace to the Christian paradise he had created inside the Central African Republic. He prayed for several minutes, ignoring everyone in the room.

Clasping his hands together, Walsh looked at them all one by one and said, "Good. You are all here. It's time to slaughter Mark Pierce and bring our conspiracy to a close."

45

Eloko called a boy soldier into the hut, then told him to bring beers for his guests. Because of his liver, Walsh insisted on a non-alcoholic beverage and requested a Coke. The boy nodded and exited, while the stock of his AK-47 slung over his back dragged on the floor.

The warlord gestured for everyone to take a seat, to remind everyone he was in charge. But everyone knew the actual power of their group lay with Idris Walsh. The American spymaster, however, didn't care for other people's pretences, only for results, so didn't correct Eloko.

Once seated, they waited in silence until the drinks came. When the boy returned, he still carried his AK-47 while he balanced the drinks in his tiny hands, the weapon weighing him down and exaggerating his already small stature.

Walsh took the Coke the young boy offered him. The humidity was worse inside the hut, where there was no breeze, and the spymaster was soon sweating more than anyone else. He took a tablet from a prescription bottle and washed it down with the sugary caffeinated drink. He touched his gut as it spasmed painfully. When the pain passed, he said, "Pierce is on his way to us. I have an asset in play who just reported he's tracked our enemy to Cameroon. This asset should soon eliminate Pierce once and for all. But if my man fails and Pierce reaches us, Captain, you will need to have your men ready."

"Do not be afraid. Captain Eloko's Ghost Men of Africa will not fail me. They have God's strength and my magic to protect them. Each volunteer carries the bullet I have divined will be the bullet that kills them, so as long as they carry their bullets on their person, no other bullet can harm them. Even if fired from a weapon used by Mark Pierce."

Walsh snorted out a fake laugh. "Bulletproof, hey?"

"Exactly!"

"More importantly, they have my training," said Trager.

Eloko gave the Australian an icy stare.

Trager drank his beer and looked away. Walsh noted that the special forces veteran was falling apart. Or perhaps, instead, he was detecting the signs of guilt. What was Trager hiding from Idris Walsh?

Trager eventually stared back, and Walsh found his confidence again, and Trager said, "Well, what intel do you have?"

Walsh threw two files on the table with prominent photographs of two women pinned to their front covers. Both were attractive, the first Asian with long dark hair, the other a fair-skinned Caucasian with a dark pixie-style hair-cut. "Rachel Zang and Mackenzie Summerfield. Two disgraced CIA operatives who turned against me and have allied with Pierce. Both are dangerous in their own ways. Zang because she is a skilled paramilitary operator, as dangerous as Pierce and just as effective. Summerfield because she is one of the best intelligence analysts and mission planners I've ever come across. Captain, you need to watch the airports and borders for these women too, and you need to kill them on sight. Pierce alone will be dangerous enough, but if he teams up with these two..."

"May I?" Trager gestured to the files. Walsh nodded, so Trager gathered them up. He perused them for a long minute, then threw the files back on the table. "I'll deal with them both."

Eloko and Trager both hunting Pierce, Zang and Summerfield with separate teams. This concept appealed to Walsh because of the chaos and confusion it would cause, so said, "Well then, we are all agreed. The three enemies must die. No capture. No intimidation. Two teams to take him out, delivering just simple death?"

Ponsonby picked at a nail. "I want to see the bodies." When all eyes fell upon the Englishman, his voice rose an octave. "The cad shot me. I could have died. I need to know Pierce won't come after me again."

Walsh's nod was slight.

No one else spoke a word.

Then Walsh threw another file on the table. "You should also know that this morning, Pierce secured a secret US Navy SEAL weapon and supply cache in Cameroon. That's how my man knows he's there, because the cache triggered a coded message back to SEAL headquarters, and a camera inside filmed Pierce opening it."

Trager said, "Your man is ex-SEAL?"

Walsh nodded. "That's the inventory list Pierce stole."

Trager grabbed it without asking for permission and scanned the contents. "Modern assault rifles, pistols, sniper rifles, even a fucking Switchblade drone-missile combo. This just gets better and better."

"I'm not the one who allowed Pierce to frame me as an assassin." Walsh spoke through gritted teeth.

Trager tensed, then slowed his breathing and seemed to focus on what all this intel Walsh was throwing at them meant. "What about Pierce's past, before he joined the CIA? Walsh, do you have clearance to know what that was? Because if Pierce knows secret SEAL in-country supply drop locations, he's got to be ex-SEAL. Intel like that could be the difference between us surviving this, or all of us dying in a muddy jungle cesspit in a few days from now."

"You overestimate Pierce," said Eloko, his hands again in prayer. "The man is a non-believer. I've already divined his future. He will die, in two days from now, at my hands. I will shoot him in the gut, just outside this hut after I have tortured him, and he will bleed out. You need not fear this man."

"This is bullshit!" Trager exploded. "This operation is a fucking mess, and none of you seem to see it. Javor's dead. Pierce is free and now has allies. The assassination attempt against you, Ponsonby, has exposed us and drawn public links between us all except Walsh." He pointed to Ponsonby and Eloko. "And worst of all, we've got two volatile dirty bombs in play that anyone could discover before we get the other four into place."

"We are all aware of the situation, Trager," said Ponsonby, looking down his nose at him.

Trager squeezed his fists together, and the muscles in his arms tightened like coiled ropes. Then a mosquito buzzed near Trager's ear, distracting him, so he waved his hand close to warn it away, ruining the macho display of his raw power.

"Are you done?" said Walsh.

Trager nodded, realising that he had overreacted to the mosquito.

"Then we are in agreement." Walsh spoke before any of the other conspirators could. "Three targets, marked for death."

Eloko, Ponsonby and Trager nodded their heads. Molly leaned back in her chair, folded her arms and said nothing.

"Good. But onto other matters, as the sergeant rightly points out, our original plan. Only two of the six radioactive drums are in play. We need to step up on the original program and get the other four into place as soon as possible."

Ponsonby cleared his throat, then tested his hair to ensure it still carried its bounce. "Angola's Minister Odel Nunes is still causing me trouble."

"Then pay him," Trager snarled.

"I don't expect you to understand, Sergeant, with your pedestrian education, but the situation is far more complicated than just handing over cash."

Walsh said, "Then explain yourself, Ponsonby, so we can all enjoy your level of financial enlightenment."

Ponsonby frowned. "It's a cash-flow situation, Walsh. There isn't enough in my reserve funds to pay Nunes. I can secure bonds, loans, advances, but that results in the banks auditing Polytope's accounts, a complication we don't need right now."

Walsh leaned across the table. "You told me the construction contracts are in place, and we have commitments from investors. Use that money. We can pay it back later."

Ponsonby pouted. "You know as I do, Walsh, there are

investor commitments and there are investor commitments. That money is not in our accounts. It will only be transferred once the market value of diamonds goes up."

"Up? By how much?"

Ponsonby told them.

"That's a lot," said Eloko. "What we were hoping for once the dirty bombs go off."

Ponsonby cleared his throat. "And some more. When the diamond price is high, investor money will flow in. They'll fall over each other trying to give us their cash."

"Then we need to detonate those dirty bombs soon," said Eloko.

Walsh scratched his chin, then turned to Trager. "Why are we arguing over this? Trager, your operational funds are available. Take half a million—"

"One million," Ponsonby interrupted. When everyone in the room stared at him, he said, "Nunes is greedy. He upped his fee."

"One million, then," Walsh answered. "That won't be a problem, will it, Trager?"

The former special forces soldier coughed and looked away. Now he really did look guilty, and Walsh wondered why. He would have to confront the sergeant about this further later, when current matters such as Pierce weren't so important to deal with.

"No, Walsh. It's there. I'll make it happen."

"Good." Walsh stood. "Trager, Captain, prepare for engagement with Pierce, Zang and Summerfield; if my man fails and they show up, then kill them."

"Yes, sir."

Eloko said, "Kiambi, the doctor, treated Pierce several times when the American got sick in our camp. They became friends, and the doctor pathetically tried to help Pierce escape the camp once. He learned his lesson and fears my sorcery now. I'll send Kiambi into the town of Berberati, just north of here, where Pierce must pass through before heading here. By leveraging supernatural threats upon the good doctor's family, Kiambi can be persuaded to contact us should Pierce contact him there."

Walsh bit his lower lip. "That's a good plan. Do it. Ponsonby?"

"Yes, my friend?" The Englishman picked at his long, effeminate fingernails.

"I want you on the *Cancri,* watching over our diamond production in Angola. You handle Nunes until we resolve the Pierce situation, however you can."

"*Our* diamond production ship? Last time I checked, Walsh, *I* owned it."

Walsh chuckled. "We all profit from this, Ponsonby, unless I need to fabricate another false will, leaving all of your Polytope shares to me and Eloko?"

Ponsonby looked away and shook his head.

Molly, who'd been standing behind Trager and not speaking, now stood and brushed her fiery red hair from her sullen, grey eyes. "And what about you, our fearless leader? Where will you be hiding while the rest of us do your dirty work?"

Walsh crushed the Coke can in his hand as his face reddened. "Back at the CIA, McEwan. They still believe I work for them, and I need their intelligence resources. And I warned you, don't question me again with this unattractive attitude you've suddenly adopted."

"Or what?" Trager blurted, finally finding his courage to stand up for the woman he loved, after all these months of just allowing Walsh to treat her however he wanted. Perhaps that was what all the guilt was about, how weak he felt around the woman he fucked every night when Walsh was around, and wanted to be a stronger man than he was. Walsh wanted to admire Trager in that moment for finally taking a stance, but just couldn't find it in himself to do so.

Instead, Walsh just looked at them both without blinking, then shook his head. "Just get it fucking done. Obey orders, like good fucking foot soldiers do, and kill Mark Pierce."

46

Dr Derek Kiambi was awakened suddenly by two burly soldiers, who dragged him from his bed of palm leaves and marched him outside.

He struggled against the bright sunlight until his eyes adjusted. Kiambi had worked all night, trying to save the life of a soldier who'd taken off the top of his foot with a machete while cutting jungle growth back from the roads. With insufficient medical supplies, no bandages, and no means to secure boiled, sterilised and soapy water, the man had bled out. Eloko hadn't been happy, and Kiambi had spent another hour that night explaining he had done everything he could to save the man. Eloko didn't believe a man could die from an amputation, but this was the jungle and one of the world's most inhospitable environments. Humans were not welcome here, and the jungle had proved it again by claiming another victim.

With no patients to attend to this morning, Kiambi caught up on his sleep. He held no hope that he might one day escape or receive his pardon and be sent on his way. Eloko would use Kiambi's skills until the doctor died, however long that took.

The forcefulness of the soldiers this morning, however, surprised him. Normally they just told him where to be and when, and Kiambi complied. Today they acted as if he might flee if he knew where they were taking him, and so kept close to him.

Confirmation of Kiambi's fears came when they marched him to the torture house.

The same windowless structure where they had beaten and electrocuted the American spy, Mark Pierce.

Now Kiambi resisted, but the soldiers' grips were too powerful. A punch to his head stunned Kiambi, and he gave up all pretence of defiance.

Inside were three chairs lined up against a long table. Two prisoners with their hands bound behind them sat in two seats. Muslim workers from the diamond mines, both of whom Kiambi had treated for minor ailments in the past. Wide-open eyes and sweaty foreheads told of the same fear Kiambi felt.

He heard mosquitos, angry in the air, buzz around his sweating ears. The stench of urine, sweat and rotten meat permeating the room caused him to gag. The hooks in the supporting beam made him shrink backwards.

Then he noticed a body hung from meat hooks, covered in a bloody sheet. He wondered who had been tortured because they had displeased Captain Eloko too much. And was the corpse here as a message to Kiambi and the others to cooperate or face a similar fate?

Eloko's soldiers ignored his silent protests and bound him to the last chair.

Overcome with both dread and relief, Kiambi believed these would be his last moments on Earth. God would take him into his embrace, and he would finally know peace at the gates of Heaven.

But he had to first endure the pain that would soon be upon him.

Minutes passed as the soldiers stood behind the three silent prisoners, their heads hung low as each prisoner contemplated their fates.

Then Captain Eloko entered and sat on the single chair on the other side of the table and placed four wooden cups on its surface.

The warlord leaned forward and looked at each man, waited until they dared to catch his stare. When he had their attention, he leaned in and whispered, "The African jungle, my brothers, is the oldest jungle on the planet. Older than even the Amazon. You know why it has survived through the eons?"

He looked to each of them, willing them to answer, but no one spoke a word.

"Chemical warfare is why. Plant versus plant. Plant versus animal. Animal versus animal. Over millions of years, the ecosystem has been at war with itself, each species fighting for dominance, with the fit surviving and the weak falling into extinction. Trees battle to reach the sunlight in the canopy. Strangler figs and lianas take those same trees hostage, leveraging their branches in a race to the top. Monkeys and chimpanzees battle each other for fruit when it ripens. Leopards kill bongos and other antelopes for their fresh meat. But the most successful combatant in the jungle is poison."

He took a small bottle from a pocket and poured four

equal measures of its liquid into each cup. "This is one of the jungle's many poisons, and a potent one at that. I conversed with the many spirits, ghosts, and demons of the darkest recesses of the canopy, and they led me to its source, this black poison of truth... or death."

Eloko nodded to his men, who then cut the bindings off each man.

From the corner of his eye, Kiambi noticed that the soldiers now held automatic pistols, ready to use.

"This is a simple test, because I need one, and only one, of you to perform a simple task. But that man must be loyal. Which one of you is loyal to me?"

No one spoke a word.

"*ANSWER ME!*" Eloko burst from his chair as he screamed; the spit from his mouth showered them with its thick droplets.

"I am!" one man answered.

Kiambi burst into tears because he knew he was not a loyal man. Every waking moment, he dreamed of his freedom or a quick death for Eloko and his men, or to flee without fear of being hunted. But that dream was now over.

Meanwhile, Eloko had regained his composure.

"Good." Eloko spoke in his deep, commanding voice. "Time to drink!"

Eloko took his cup and drank.

Kiambi and the Muslim men followed his lead.

The liquid was thick and foul-tasting, with repulsive flavours Kiambi could not describe, nor did he wish to. Yet he forced himself to finish his cup, then dropped the empty vessel back onto the table and bit down on the vomit rising in his throat.

"Very good," said Eloko with a smug grin. "Very good. Now we see who is loyal and who is not. If you are my enemy, the poison will soon have its effect. Your temperature will spike. Your windpipe will swell and compress. Soon you won't be able to breathe."

No sooner had he spoken, the Muslim men grabbed their throats and choked for air as their faces turned red. Eyes bulged in their sockets. Bloated tongues popped from their mouths. They fell to the mud-strewn wooden floor, convulsed for a few minutes, then stopped moving altogether.

Kiambi felt no pain. Had no difficulty breathing.

Eloko kept his eyes on Kiambi through the whole gory incident. "It seems, Dr Kiambi, you and I are the only loyal men in this room."

The doctor forced a nod.

A breeze blew around the corpse hung in the room, but the sheet didn't lift high enough to see who was behind it.

"I'm glad, because I have an important mission for you, my loyal subject."

"Yes." Kiambi struggled to speak. As a man of science, he knew this had to be a trick, a sleight of hand. But as a religious man and a firm believer in the power of Christ, Kiambi had to ask himself if he had just witnessed real magic. "What do you want me to do?"

"I want you to be with your family again, in Berberati."

"What? You're releasing me from servitude?"

Eloko's smile grew in size. "I am, but it is conditional."

"How so?"

He cut Kiambi's bindings and helped him to his feet. "You were once friends with Mark Pierce."

"I guess I was. He has returned?" Kiambi didn't believe it, and wondered what trickery was involved here.

"Yes, and his scheme is to kill us all. But first he will seek you out, and when he does, you will contact me and tell me where to find him."

"Thank you, sir, I will." The doctor bowed because he thought it was the right thing to do to appease this megalomaniac.

"Oh, and there is one more thing to remember before you go." He looked to the hanging corpse, covered by the saturated sheet, and smiled with a display of all his teeth.

Kiambi felt sick at the sight of it now that Eloko had drawn his attention to it. He didn't want to know who it was or how they had died. "I understand. I know what has to be done."

"Go on," said Eloko with a smirk. "Pull down the sheet."

Kiambi felt dizzy, then nauseous like he was about to throw up.

"*DO IT!*" Eloko screamed, his face puffing and sweating.

Before the doctor thought too hard on what he was doing, he ripped the sticky wet sheet off the corpse.

Wearing only a T-shirt and covered with multiple deep and fatal machete cuts, hung Molly McEwan, bound by her hands to a hook in the rafters. Her dead eyes expressed a horror that the doctor feared to know, and he already thought he knew the worst of anything that was ever possible.

Suddenly he was vomiting the thick and foul-tasting liquid, much worse on the way out than on the way in.

"She wasn't loyal, so she had to pay the price. You understand this, Doctor? I really hope that you do."

Kiambi nodded and wondered if Trager yet knew that his

lover had died under such horrific circumstances, and how would he react when he found out?

Then gagging, Kiambi fled from the torture room. His eyes watered, and he wanted to sob, but he was even too afraid to do that.

47

Gamboula to Berberati Road, Central African Republic

Mark Pierce pushed on through the mud and rain, slow going on a road that was more a stream than a transportation route. The thick leafy jungle clumped close to the edges, and often the canopy covered his passage, creating tunnels of thick-trunked trees, palms, stranglers, and vines.

Frequently he passed hordes of men, women and children. Refugees marching east with baskets balanced on their heads to hold their life's possessions, or dragging suitcases through the mud. All looked exhausted and underfed. War did that to people, and Pierce had seen similar refugees in Mali, Niger and Yemen. He could do little to help them individually, but if he could eradicate Eloko's army, fewer Central Africans might feel the need to flee their homelands.

The border crossing at both the Cameroon and Central African Republic checkpoints had been little more than a formality and a series of bribes that had cost him two hundred and fifty euros, but saved him from awkward questions had the guards investigating his Land Cruiser discovered his many weapons.

Once inside the CAR, the roads deteriorated further, so Pierce dropped his speed.

Unearthing the Navy SEAL cache had come with a risk, because Pierce only knew its location through intel he had acquired *before* he had officially joined the CIA. That was two instances now where Pierce had gone back on his word to himself and connected his current cover identity to one that must remain buried and forgotten. But he needed weapons, lots of them, to have any chance of taking out Walsh, Trager, Eloko and Ponsonby and stopping whatever scheme they were cooking up with the nuclear waste.

Yet Pierce felt confident that Walsh had not been cleared to access his past operations. Very few people knew what he had achieved during that time, and he could count those people on one hand. If Walsh knew, it would have come up during his seven months of torture and interrogation. It hadn't, so Pierce felt he still had friends in the CIA.

His thoughts drifted again to Rachel Zang. Was she an ally or an enemy?

He had liked her. He missed her since her disappearance in Baku. She might be one of Idris Walsh's inner circle. Either an honest but duped patriot serving her country as a Central Intelligence Agency officer or in on his scheme. Pierce hoped for the former. He imagined what it would be like to go on a date with her, like normal people did.

Then his thoughts turned to Mackenzie Summerfield, his one genuine friend, and a pang of guilt struck him. He had abandoned her in Morocco, left her to face disciplinary action with their CIA masters, but he had done so to protect her from Walsh. Otherwise, it would have been not just him tortured in the filthy African cell, but both of them. She might not have survived the physical and mental torments he had, and Pierce would have never held out as long if Walsh and Trager had threatened Mackenzie with harm or death.

But where was she now? Was she still with the CIA but in a diminished role? In a US prison? Out in the private sector? Or on the run and hiding like he was? This was the problem with trying to second-guess the CIA, for there were many potential outcomes to her fate, and much of it came down to how much influence Idris Walsh commanded within America's premier overseas intelligence agency.

Pierce had a means to contact Mackenzie, but only if she had her freedom. He'd had opportunities to do so since his escape, but he'd always held back. She might no longer trust him, or he might get her killed by dragging her into this vendetta he had set into motion against his newest enemies. But what stopped him more was the thought she might already be dead, and he wasn't ready to hear that news if it was true.

He told himself he would find Mackenzie Summerfield when this was over, if he survived the threat he now faced.

The road took a sharp turn and came upon a fast-flowing river washing over where the track ahead had once been. The river was perhaps thirty metres wide. Pierce suspected the water was shallow, and he could see the road continue on across the opposite side. But nothing made for a simple crossing.

A black Jeep Wrangler appeared in his rear-view mirror.

The driver slammed on the brakes before he hit the water. Pierce saw a white man behind the wheel. He wore a baseball cap and dark sunglasses.

Pierce didn't know how, but he knew this man was here to kill him.

Confirming Pierce's supposition, the man pulled an M4 carbine and leaned out of the window.

Pierce ducked low and sped through the fast-flowing water, the tyres slipping in the wet mud.

Gunfire sounded loud, and he felt the thuds as bullets embedded into the chassis. He tensed, worried that a bullet might hit a grenade, and then it would all be over in seconds, but nothing exploded. Soon Pierce was across the opposite side and raced along the muddy road.

The Wrangler sped through the river crossing and took pursuit.

Leaves and branches from the thick jungle smashed against the sides of his vehicle as Pierce increased his speed. There was nowhere to turn off the road because the foliage was too thick, and the ground was an obstacle course with its buttress roots, tree trunks and thick plants. Pierce could only try to outrun his foe, but the conditions of the already deteriorated road varied, so fallen branches and potholes ahead would eventually force him to slow. He'd deal with each as he encountered them.

He heard gunshots.

The rear window shattered as two frosted bullet holes appeared in the front passenger-side windshield. Pierce revved the engine. The wheels spun, churning up a spray of thick orange mud behind him. He dovetailed as he drove so his would-be assassin could not get a bead on him.

With one hand on the steering wheel, Pierce ejected the

fragmentation grenade from the MK 17, charged it and flung it behind him through his side window.

Through his side mirror, he saw the Wrangler brake and drift in the mud. The explosion was sudden and loud, throwing mud, roots, branches and leaves in every direction.

Pierce turned a corner and maintained his speed.

He heard the Wrangler creeping up behind him. The grenade had fallen between them, so hadn't incapacitated his foe. The blast, however, had destroyed the opponent's windshield, and now mud and small debris sprayed the driver, obscuring his vision. Pierce lifted his pistol and fired. The driver's side mirror shattered in a cloud of tiny glass and plastic fragments.

Ahead, a long branch as thick as his arm had fallen across the road.

Alone, he would have stopped and removed it, but while the foe pursued him, Pierce drove straight through it. He barely slowed as he went over and heard the wood break, making the same nerve-racking noise a human bone made when it snapped. He waited for the telltale pull on the steering wheel from a punctured tyre, but again, his luck held out, and the damage to his Land Cruiser remained superficial.

He turned another corner and didn't stop in time as he sped across another fast-flowing, but shallow river, this one fifty metres wide.

The Wrangler's engine screamed as it too ploughed into the fast-flowing current and smashed hard into the Land Cruiser's rear. Both vehicles came to a sudden halt. Pierce's seat belt was all that saved him from being flung through the windshield.

Pierce noticed they were drifting, and soon both vehicles dropped into deep, faster flowing water. The current took them, and both four-wheel drives soon drifted downstream.

48

Pierce grabbed the Mk 17 and released a volley of twenty 7.62mm rounds into his foe's vehicle. The noise in the confines of the cabin was like hammers beating at his eardrums. As the bullets drilled into the Wrangler, headlights shattered, and the radiator grille bent and buckled. What remained of the windshield had vanished as vaporised glass. And yet, Pierce sensed he had missed his assailant completely.

He couldn't see the man anywhere.

Pierce reached back to the steering wheel of the Land Cruiser, discovering the engine still turned over.

He shifted down to first and drove, bounced as submerged wheels gripped on loose pebbles. He spotted a sand embankment and made for that. Miraculously, the battered four-by-four took him out of the water and onto a flat, open grassland about two hundred metres wide, with swampy patches encircled by the vast jungle.

A troop of chimpanzees had gathered in the grass. Several stripped twigs off larger sticks and gnawed on the ends to sharpen them into hunting spears. When Pierce's vehicle appeared, the primates dropped their weapons and disappeared into the thick jungle. Chimps had learned long ago that despite their physical strength being superior to any human's, they were no match for men with guns.

Once on solid ground, Pierce spun his Land Cruiser in a circle until he found the Wrangler caught in the fast-flowing water and tipped at an angle. Of the driver, there was no sign.

Then Pierce spotted movement in the treeline. It was the foe, who must have scrambled to shore out of sight. He fired his pistol at Pierce. Bullets buried into the chassis and sped past only centimetres from his head.

Pierce rolled, dropped out onto the opposite side of the Land Cruiser where he had cover.

More bullets cracked in the damp air as they penetrated the vehicle.

Then Pierce heard the unmistakable sound of a gun locking, signalling an empty magazine.

Pierce raised his Mk 17 and fired in sweeping arcs, forcing the assassin to seek cover. Then he looked over the Land Cruiser and searched for his target.

His foe had vanished.

Then he appeared, closer. He had snuck up towards Pierce, using the Land Cruiser as cover. He fired again, causing Pierce to duck. Then he catapulted over the Land Cruiser roof and landed on Pierce, knocking the Mk 17 from Pierce's hands.

Pierce struggled to his feet.

The assassin advanced with fists, kicks, and elbows aimed at Pierce, coming from multiple directions. Pierce blocked and parried but had trouble guessing his attacker's moves. They wrestled for a moment, tripped and fell into the black, swampy water.

As both men clambered to their feet, they came at each other again.

Pierce went for his pistol, then fighting knife, but he'd lost both in the melee.

The foe's aggression was relentless. He too went for a knife, but he too was without a weapon. He came at Pierce with his fists. Each strike was a different fighting style, ranging from karate to judo, to Krav Maga taught in the Israel Defence Forces.

Pierce blocked and deflected, searched for an advantage. They were the same height, but the foe carried ten kilograms more muscle than Pierce did, and pressed that advantage with the power projected through his fists.

Soon the assailant found a gap in Pierce's defences and kidney punched him with such force that Pierce's eyes watered, and he staggered back.

Knee-deep in the black mud, their feet were now getting caught in the suction of the wet ground. Neither man could move fast, so when Pierce stepped back awkwardly, the foe didn't immediately come for him.

With a distance of a few metres between them now, Pierce took a moment to catch his breath. He glanced around again for his fallen pistol in the swampy patch they stood in.

"You dropped it, remember?" said the assailant. His accent was American.

Pierce nodded. "I guess you lost yours too."

That brought a smile to the man's lips. "Wouldn't have rushed you like I had if my pistol hadn't locked up."

"Tough break, hey?" Pierce had manoeuvred onto a log

under the water, so the mud could no longer suck him down. He made to move, but it seemed his foe had also found sturdier ground. He came at Pierce again, further fast strike attacks directed at Pierce's body.

There was one style of fighting the assassin had not adopted. Kung fu. A fluid and nimble style Pierce had first learned in Beijing, and his favourite fighting technique. He used it now, sending his attacker's strikes towards nothing but air. The Chinese martial arts used an opponent's strength against them, didn't block force with force, but deflected its direction. Many times, a death-delivering blow hit nothing but air.

Now it was the assailant who was tiring.

And yet, Pierce could not get an effective strike past the assassin's defences.

He came at Pierce again, aggression fuelling his technique, and suddenly the man's strikes were also kung fu.

Soon both men slipped and diverted opposing blows around each other. Pierce tried for a kick, but he lost his footing off the submerged log, and the water soaked into his trousers, and the mud underfoot again suctioned him down.

The assassin found another gap in Pierce's parries and punched him hard in the chest, right above the heart.

Pierce staggered backward, fell into the mud as he struggled to breathe.

Down, his foe had the advantage.

Then, without expecting to, Pierce felt another stick where his hand had dropped into the water to steady himself.

The assassin rushed him.

Pierce turned the stick fast and aim the gnawed, sharpened end at the advancing assassin.

The chimpanzee's spear penetrated the attacker's guts and went right through him.

Surprise was sudden on his foe's face, then pain, and he dropped to his knees until he was waist-deep in the swampy water with Pierce.

Pierce stepped up and backwards. He spotted his fallen HK45CT on the muddy ground with the .45 ACP rounds, lifted it and aimed it at the impaled man.

Holding himself upright, breaths came fast and shallow from the fatally wounded man as sweat poured off his face. He gripped his stomach as blood flowed fast from the gut wound. He was good-looking, about Pierce's age, with the same toned muscle definition that revealed his specialised military training.

The dying man looked up at Pierce, defeat in his eyes. "Fuck!"

"Sorry, I just got lucky."

The man nodded, then tried to laugh but only brought up blood from his mouth.

Pierce kept his distance. The HK45CT he kept pointed at the American operative's head. "Who are you?"

"I'm... the same... as you."

"Special Activities Group?" Pierce asked, referring to the same CIA group he had once served with. "Ground Branch?"

The dying man nodded.

"But specialised in independent action?"

He nodded again.

"You have a name?"

"I know... yours. Mark Pierce... Code name... Trigger Man."

Pierce laughed. "Got to love those code names. What's yours?"

"Night Viper."

Pierce had never heard of him, but this was no surprise. Handlers kept independent operatives separate from others of their kind. "Compartmentalised" was the word the CIA liked to use.

"Aaron... Stone... That's... my actual name."

"Idris Walsh sent you?"

With an effort, Stone held Pierce's stare. But he didn't answer.

A thought struck Pierce. "You believe Walsh works for the CIA, don't you?"

That comment caused Stone to pause.

Without taking his eyes off Stone, Pierce held his pistol in one hand and removed his waterproof satellite phone in the other, then played the message he'd recorded between Walsh and Ponsonby in Cape Town.

"—I agree. Get yourself to Bayanga. I'll send word to the others. This scheme of making the world believe he's the real nuclear terrorist is at risk of falling apart. We can't risk any further discussions that aren't face to face, because the 'problem' may have tapped into us—"

Pierce paused the recording.

Stone's breathing slowed when he heard the voice. Nobody talked quite like Idris Walsh did. "Fuck!"

Catching his breath, Pierce said, "Walsh betrayed you too."

Stone held his stomach wound. "I knew... something was off." His palm came away soaked in blood. "I'm... about to die... because of a lie?"

Pierce lowered his weapon but kept his distance. "I'm afraid so, friend."

"Zang." Stone now spoke in a whisper. "She's... one of

the good guys... I know you know her... from Kazakhstan... She's... been... duped... too..."

Before he could say more, Stone's eyes rolled up into the back of his head, and he fell forward, face down in the mud.

Pierce approached in a slow, controlled motion. He didn't believe Stone was faking, but he'd been wrong before in similar situations. With the gun still pointed at Stone's head, he felt for a pulse in the neck. Nothing. He rolled Stone over and felt for breath. Still nothing.

Lying the former patriot on his back, removing the primate spear and then closing the dead man's eyes, Pierce snapped off a respectable salute. Suddenly, retribution didn't seem all that desirable a path to follow when the cost was the lives of good men.

"Sorry, friend."

It took Pierce the rest of the afternoon to hack a path through the jungle back to the road, then drive out on the planks of wood he'd secured in Kenzou to cross the worst of the mud.

On the road again and driving in the dark, Pierce recognised that he had finally confirmed two aspects of his enemy's operations that until now he had only suspected.

First, Walsh still operated through the CIA.

Second, Zang seemed to be an ally he could trust.

When he hit the outskirts of Berberati, he stopped his four-by-four, then emailed links of the audio file of Walsh and Ponsonby's conversation to various high-ranking officers of the Central intelligence Agency, packaged up with the GPS location of Stone's body.

Now it was Walsh's turn to run for his life.

49

Berberati Airport, Central African Republic

Berberati didn't seem real, or at least not as a proper city as maps suggested, but a squalor of human existence.

The metropolis lay some two hundred miles west of the capital Bangui, nestled within a subtropical forest on the edge of the vast Congo rainforest. By population it was the third-largest city in the war-torn country, but didn't look large enough. From the air, Rachel Zang saw only shanty towns and decrepit single-storey houses intersected by muddy roads, wood piles and mounds of trash. From the ground, the same habitats seemed grimmer and in an even greater state of disrepair. Even the airport, while functional, would have been condemned for demolition anywhere else in the world.

Earlier in the morning, Zang had passed through Bangui customs without complication. She travelled under the cover identity of Erin Watts, an engineer employed by the multinational mining company BHP, and had hoped but didn't presume her arrival had gone unnoticed by Eloko and Walsh. To look the part, she dressed in cargo pants, a fitted shirt and sturdy hiking boots, perfect for the tropical heat. She'd tied her hair back in a ponytail and hid her eyes behind dark sunglasses. Mackenzie Summerfield had done well to produce a legend with a matching passport and identity papers that had secured her entrance into this failed nation, but now Zang had reached her destination, she suspected the straightforward part of her journey was behind her.

As the terminal quickly cleared, for it was not a busy airport, Zang grabbed food and a drink at the airport's only café. Her already alerted senses soon identified two men standing outside who watched each departing traveller. When their eyes found her, they checked a photograph held in the first man's hand, then kept their gazes locked on her. Zang was easy to spot. An Asian face in a country where everyone was black.

The second man made a call on his cell phone. He spoke, nodded a few times, then hung up. His eyes never left her.

It seemed prudent to presume their goal was to kill or kidnap her.

Zang had different plans.

She approached, pretended to notice the two men for the first time, then smiled and waved at them.

They hesitated for several seconds, then waved back.

Securing her backpack over her shoulders, freeing up her hands and offering improved mobility, she stepped close to the men. In their twenties, they were each muscular and dressed in clean clothes and better brands than what the average citizen wore. She noticed the concealed pistols in their belts, but they didn't reach for them.

"Hi." Zang gave a smile, speaking English because her French was near to non-existent. "Are you my drivers?"

The second man caught on faster than his friend and said with a toothy grin in the same language, "Yes, lady, we are. Would you like me to take your pack?"

"I'm good. But I'm dead tired and keen to get to my hotel?"

"Of course."

They walked one on each side of her as they exited the terminal and headed towards the car park. The heat outside was as oppressive as it had been in the airport. Soon sweat glistened off her skin.

At one point she halted as if she had forgotten something, and they stumbled past. Zang glanced towards where the second man now looked, at two other men waiting outside the gates with AK-47s slung over their shoulders.

She scanned the car park, but saw no one else interested in her. She bit her lip and planned her next steps.

Through the airport's cyclone fence, she noticed palms and thick vegetation close to the roads. Like most roads in tropical Africa, they were compacted orange dirt without dividing lines. A delivery truck had parked adjacent to the cyclone fence, and it was of the same height as the barrier, which gave her an idea. Many trucks and cars ploughed on through the streets overloaded with people, thirty or more seated on roofs, bonnets and trunks, or holding on to the sides. The weight on each car so great the suspension had no more give.

Dozens of local men and women waited outside the airport, offering taxi fares, sweets, fruit and vegetable snacks, and tour guide services. They spoke first in French, then German and English until she responded. The men with her warned them away, showing their pistols, and they complied.

She waited until they were close to a van, providing cover, before she said, "Eloko's not here?"

"No," said the second man, realising too late that she had called them out.

Zang was already moving. A sharp punch in the throat sent the first man down on his knees, gasping for air.

Spotting that the two men with the Russian assault rifles were close behind, she grabbed the second man, pinned his arm in a nerve-firing grip and spun him as a human shield. Bullets peppered his body, killing him instantly.

The crowds panicked from the noise of gunfire, sprinting away and/or dropping to the ground.

She pulled the ancient Walther PPK from the dead man's waistband and fired back at the two remaining men.

The two armed assailants sought cover behind a grey sedan.

After two more shots from the Walther, Zang turned and sprinted while keeping the van between her and her enemies. In ten seconds, she'd reached the cyclone fence encircling the airport.

On the other side lay a shanty town of thatch-roofed huts.

Zang ran straight for the truck parked by the cyclone fence, leaped high and swung her body up onto its roof. Bouncing to her feet, she sprinted to the edge of the truck and flung her body over the barbwire, landed after a ten-foot drop into the mud, and rolled with the impact. Pain shot through her left leg as she landed roughly, and when she tried to put weight on it, Zang found she couldn't.

Ignoring her injury for the moment, Zang turned with her Walther raised.

The assault rifle-carrying soldiers were running to the fence.

She fired at them, one went down as she hit him in the leg, the other ducked behind the truck.

The slide clicked open on the Walther, denoting the weapon's lack of ammunition.

Dropping it, Zang hobbled further away from the fence into the shanty town, pulling down a wooden pole holding up a makeshift tent to use as a crutch.

She heard windows smashing behind her, and looking back, she saw her last opponent had broken into the truck and fired up the engine. Zang knew what he would do, and started to move as fast as she could through the crowds of refugees who hadn't yet fled, every one of them staring at her like she was an invader from another planet.

Zang covered thirty feet before the truck reversed into the fence and tore it and several dwellings down.

Then several more men in quasi-military uniforms whom she didn't recognise appeared on her side of the fence, moving rapidly through the slums. She recognised that their focus was on her, and that they were armed with various assault rifles. The leader then appeared in her line of vision, a white Caucasian man in his thirties with ginger hair and a beard. Judging by how he moved, she knew he was a professional soldier. He soon spotted her, then ordered his mercenaries to take her down.

Dropping the stick, Zang started to sprint and ignored the pain that shot through her leg like an electric current every time her boot impacted with the muck. Pain was always preferable to death.

She crossed the shanty town in minutes and reached a road on the other side, of compacted earth with only a few cars and motorcycles traversing it. On the other side all she saw was wide-open grass. No cover anywhere.

She heard the mercenaries pounding the same track through the slum she had followed. She knew they would be upon her in seconds.

Then a white Land Cruiser appeared, turning from a side road fifty feet to her left. It was caked in mud and dust and covered in scratches and dents. Within seconds it came to a screeching halt next to her.

The door flung open.

The man behind the wheel beckoned her in.

"If you don't mess with me, Zang," said Mark Pierce, "we can escape together."

50

S
econds later they were away.

Eloko's soldiers shot at them from afar, but Pierce was a nimble driver and spirited them beyond their effective firing range in seconds, then disappeared into the traffic along a major road and drove towards the centre of town.

Zang turned to Pierce and said, "How did you find me?"

"All the shooting. Could hear it from kilometres off and figured there was a good chance you were part of it. Keep your hands on the dashboard, by the way."

Zang eyed Pierce suspiciously. He had his HK45CT pistol out now, aimed her way while his other hand controlled the steering wheel and his furious driving.

She placed her hands where he asked, fingers spread out like fans. Her leg throbbed, but without her weight pressing down on it, the intensity was bearable. She felt the tension build in the back of her skull, the first sign of an oncoming migraine.

"Pierce, we're on the same side."

"Maybe." He glanced in the rear-view mirror. His eyes were dark and his stare unblinking. The red in his eyes suggested exhaustion and a lack of sleep, but otherwise he was the same man she had known during their week together in Central Asia.

He turned down a side street lined with houses and tall trees, then pulled over near a rusting truck to provide some cover. Zang hadn't noticed anyone following them, and she guessed Pierce had reached the same conclusion. With the handbrake engaged, he focused on her, and so did the dangerous end of his pistol.

"I'm telling the truth."

He passed her cable ties. Three of them.

"You know I know how to escape those in seconds?"

"That's why you need three."

She frowned but obeyed. The first two she tightened using her teeth around her own wrists while the pistol never drifted from her chest. The third Pierce tied between her binding and the safety handle on the passenger side, leaving her arms up high and vulnerable.

"I'm going to pat you down. Okay?"

She nodded. His hands didn't linger anywhere inappropriate, and she reminded herself this was what she would also have done if Pierce were her prisoner. He then searched through her backpack, finding nothing out of the ordinary that a normal traveller wouldn't have on them apart from a satellite phone. The phone had its PIN lock activated, and he didn't insist she unlock it. When Pierce felt satisfied that she was unarmed, he drove again, finding a road leading to the outskirts of Berberati.

"So you've worked out I'm Rachel Zang. I'm guessing you've also figured I'm a CIA operator, like you."

"Yes. I know. Except I'm no longer with the CIA."

Zang bit her lip and strategised. She could reveal that Mackenzie and she were a team, but she wanted Pierce to be more relaxed than he was now before she brought that subject up. For now, she would play the emotional card, make him like her. "When I was naked, when we first met... it terrified me, what you might do to me... You left me standing there... vulnerable for so long."

He nodded, cast his eyes downwards for the first time. "I know. I'm sorry you had to go through that."

"I feared what you would do to me. The same as what those criminals planned to do. But if you thought I was a spy... I was more fearful you would execute me, so I pretended to be Irina."

Pierce glanced at her. His muscles tensed. "I would never have hurt you like that, Zang. Everything Walsh told you about me was a lie."

She forced a smile, but inside, she felt numb and shaky. She recognised her emotion as fear. "I know that now. I know because Walsh tried to kill me too."

"He did?"

His surprise seemed genuine.

"Yes."

Pierce massaged his forehead.

She said, "Walsh murdered three of my team in Kazakhstan, got those criminals who held you hostage to do his dirty work, and tasked them with killing me too. When they failed, Walsh tried to kill me again in England."

"England? What were you doing there?"

Zang swallowed. The cable tie cuffs cut into her hands, and her fingers felt numb. She could escape the bonds if she wanted to, but not fast enough to stop Pierce from killing her, if that was his intention. The tension in the back of her head spread. White lights appeared in her eyes. Conversely, the pain in her leg had subsided and didn't seem lasting. "I was in England to find Mackenzie Summerfield."

Pierce sat motionless for a moment, stared out at the road ahead.

As she watched him, Zang noticed Pierce's hands. They carried a slight tremor, and she could see he was fighting to control them.

She saw in his eyes he didn't want her to know of this infliction, but then he seemed to remember that she'd known about his tremors since their time together in Kazakhstan and Azerbaijan, so gave up all pretence that he was unaffected, and smiled weakly.

The stabbing pain in the back of her head intensified. Manageable for the moment, but that could change quickly.

He said, "Did you...?"

"Find her? Yes. And before you worry, Pierce, she's fine. Well, an assassin shot her, but she's okay now."

"An assassin?" He gritted his teeth.

Zang had not felt this vulnerable since she'd stood naked before him in the Aral Sea. The same fear of what he might do to her then gripped her now. Then she asked herself, why was she scared of the Trigger Man when she'd handled so many other men she had encountered in the past easily, both in physical combat and in mental battles of wits? Was it because she'd witnessed how efficiently the Trigger Man could take out enemy operatives? Then she realised, with Mark Pierce, she *wanted* to be vulnerable in his presence.

"Pierce, Walsh tried to kill Mackenzie too."

"Where is she now?"

"In a safe house in England. We can call her."

Pierce nodded and licked his lips. "That sounds like a good idea."

51

Pierce drove until he found a road leading out of Berberati. The jungle wasn't as thick here, and in parts it resembled a subtropical forest or green savanna landscape with occasional acacia and palm trees. Unlike many parts of Africa where Pierce had operated in the past, there weren't many power lines or satellite dishes. This city was truly cut off from the essential services most of the world took for granted.

When he found a secluded side road, Pierce parked, climbed out and walked around to Rachel still constrained in the passenger seat. Sweat was pouring off both of them because of the humidity, so much so that Zang looked like she had just stepped out of a swimming pool. He was almost convinced they were allies, but he'd been duped before in the past. He had to be certain.

"You probably think I'm being unfair," he said.

"Did anyone come for you in Kazakhstan after we separated?"

Pierce shook his head, conceding her point. "This won't take long."

"Wait!"

"What is it?"

"In my backpack, front pocket, are migraine pills. Can you give me two?"

Pierce nodded and followed her instructions, but not before checking for traps that would snap around his finger or jab him with a poison dart. True to her word, he found the pill bottle.

"That's them."

He popped two in her mouth, then helped her drink water from a canteen to wash them down. "Anything else?"

She shook her head. "Thank you."

He nodded, then walked five metres from her, but always watching her. He couldn't forget for a moment that she was as well trained and experienced as he was. Her mission might still be to kill him, even if she wasn't working for Walsh.

He dialled the number Zang had provided, but not before ensuring the encryption on his phone was secure. He'd have to use real names in this conversation, but that was a risk he was willing to take. After sending the audio files of Walsh's and Ponsonby's dialogue to Langley, Pierce felt certain that powers inside the CIA had already guessed much of what Mackenzie and he would now discuss. Presuming it was her and not a tracing program that he'd called, bringing in a team of US Rangers to kill or capture him.

The line answered, but no one spoke.

"It's me," he said, feeling himself choke up.

"Mark?"

The voice he thought he would never hear again. Mackenzie Summerfield.

"Mackenzie, I'm so sorry."

"Sorry? I'm sorry." He heard a sob.

"It's okay. I'm okay. No lasting damage. Like a sturdy cactus." The last phrase was an old, pre-planned code between them, to say the previous statements were the truth, and he was not being forced to lie. "I'm with your friend Rachel Zang."

There was a pause. "I'm okay too. Took a bullet in the arm, but Zang saved me. It was Walsh who hired the assassin, and I witnessed direct evidence that Walsh wants Zang dead too. I'm no crumbling cliff edge." That last phrase too was a statement of truth and freedom from duress.

Pierce took a deep breath and felt himself relax. "Do you trust Zang?"

"Like snowfall in summer." A contradictory statement, but again a pre-planned code. Zang had given Mackenzie every indication that she was on their side, but that Mackenzie couldn't know for certain.

"Thanks, Mackenzie. I feel the same way."

"You're alive, Mark." She sobbed again. "I was worried that..."

"I was worried about you too."

"But I also hated you. Then I feared for your safety. I shouldn't have believed all those lies Idris Walsh said about you."

"Yes, well, talking of Walsh..."

They spoke for a while longer. Told their stories and exchanged their suspicions on what Walsh schemed, whom he was aligned with, and what his team of conspirators might do next.

"Why does Walsh need nuclear waste?" Mackenzie asked.

Pierce thought about this. "My guess is he plans to pollute competitor diamond mines. It would drive up the market value of precious gems and produce investor funding for the Polytope operations in the CAR."

"Oh hell, you're right! How would he do it?"

"When I listened in on Ponsonby's talk at the diamond mining conference, he kept talking about tailings dams. You know what they are?"

"I do, actually. They are like normal earthen dams, but with ponds of toxic chemicals mixed with water that are used in the chemical processes of extracting precious metals from ore."

"Yes, Mackenzie, that's about right." Pierce recalled what he had read up on tailings dams during his flight to Cameroon. "I'm guessing, since Trager is a qualified plumber, he could masquerade as a contractor to the various diamond mines they want to infiltrate, to 'repair' pumps operating at the various tailings dams while securing the radioactive drums on site at the same time. Rig them with explosives charged so the dam walls break in the process, it would be an easy process to flood each mine with not only toxic tailings sludge, but radioactive tailings sludge as well. It would all leak into the earth, and..."

"Irradiate each mine, making them no longer viable. Do you know which mines?"

Pierce remembered back to the presentation. "Ponsonby mentioned six diamond mines as being the world's most productive. I'd say they are the targets. With those mines irradiated, the price of diamonds will skyrocket around the world."

"Of course they will. Walsh's scheme is pure evil. Thousands will become very sick and die from this, just to make some quick cash."

"Yes. My thoughts exactly."

"And Walsh frames you for the theft of six radioactive waste canisters in Kazakhstan so no one comes looking for him afterwards."

Pierce glanced back at Zang. She shot him an intense stare, but otherwise had made no effort to escape. He said, "Then the goal now is to recover the six canisters, get them to the US government."

"Not go after Walsh?"

"Oh, I'm going after Walsh. And Ponsonby and Trager and Captain Eloko. This ends here and now."

"I'm set up here, Mark. I can be your operations centre."

"That's great, Mackenzie. Also, there is a bank account I've left for you, on the February site." Another code leading Mackenzie to a website they had both used in the past to communicate information during Pierce's past missions in Yemen and Mali. "It has about one million in funds. I stole it from Walsh. Use it however you need to, particularly if you need to go dark again."

"Thank you." Then for several seconds she was silent. "Mark..."

"Yes?"

"I'm glad you're back. I'm glad we are a team again."

He smiled. For the first time in more than half a year, he felt warmth inside him again. "Me too, Mackenzie."

With the call ended, he returned to Zang. She struggled as he pulled his Ka-Bar fighting knife, used it only to cut her free from her bonds.

Zang dropped her arms and rubbed her wrists. "You

trust me now? Mackenzie gave you the right codes and told you I'm the real deal?"

"More or less."

Zang pouted as she climbed out of the Land Cruiser to stretch her limbs as she massaged the back of her head. "What do you mean by that?"

"I have some bad news about your friend. Aaron Stone." He described their encounter in the jungle and the fight to the death. She accepted his story without question, became withdrawn as she contemplated Stone's passing. "His last words, he vouched for you too, Zang. I thought you'd want to know."

"He was a good man." She scanned their surroundings as Pierce did, looking for threats. "I don't blame you, Pierce. Everything that's wrong about our situation comes back to one asshole. Idris Walsh."

"I agree."

They shared stories, recounted what had happened to them both these last seven months. Pierce couldn't help but think how stunning she was. Tall and slim, with toned muscles and a perfectly proportioned face, and emerald eyes he couldn't look away from. Secretly, he was glad they weren't enemies.

"What was your plan?" Pierce asked.

"Find you, and team up. What was yours?"

"Find Eloko's camp and take them all out." He nodded to the four-wheel drive. "I have enough weapons to start a small war in there. Including a Switchblade drone-missile combo."

"Wow! How did you get hold of that?"

"A SEAL Team Six hidden cache of weaponry they didn't know I knew about. Mk 17 SCAR assault combo sniper rifles, an M2 .50-calibre heavy machine gun, HK45CT handguns, Javelin missiles, and fragmentation, smoke, and flashbang grenades."

"Snatching that arsenal would have pissed someone off."

"I hope so."

Zang stretched her arms out in front. "But how do we find Eloko's camp? Do you know where it is?"

"Kind of. I have rough latitude and longitude coordinates. Never gathered enough intel to know its exact location while I was held here. But I spotted someone this morning while I was driving around, here in Berberati, who will."

52

Maryland, United States

Idris Walsh didn't slow as he drove past his townhouse in South Kensington.

Several black sedans with tinted windows and Washington, DC, government plates waited in a street around the corner where they thought he wouldn't see them. The woman walking with a pram wouldn't have nursed a real baby, but it would conceal a pistol. The man trimming a neighbour's hedges would know how to use his shears as a weapon. With his conspiracy exposed, the CIA was now coming for Walsh.

He had taken the extra precaution of leaving and returning to the United States under a passport the CIA didn't know about, then travelling with his cell phones switched off and batteries and SIM cards disabled; otherwise the NSA and CIA would have already tracked his movements, and they would have him in custody already.

Walsh drove several blocks to a garage he rented off the

books, switched cars to a Lexus registered to an advertising executive who worked in Washington, DC, and drove north.

Once he hit a forested road near Gettysburg, he turned down a dirt track and parked out of sight. Twenty minutes later he'd excavated a field kit prepared for an event like this. The kit contained another false passport, Canadian this time under a false name with a home address in Toronto, various credit cards and bank accounts with over fifty thousand Canadian dollars. Walsh buried his legitimate passport, identity papers and cell phones in the field kit, covered over the hole with forest debris, disguising that there had ever been a hole, and was on his way. The passport he had used to get into and out of the Central African Republic he had already destroyed because he felt the risk of using it and getting caught with it was too great with everything that had gone down already.

Within twelve hours Walsh would be outside the United States. Within twenty-four he would be in Europe, where he would disappear again.

In Harrisburg, Pennsylvania, Walsh purchased a prepaid cell phone, downloaded state-of-the-art encryption software, then called Kurt Krige.

"Yes?" answered the South African.

"It's me. Seven-eight, three-seven."

"Four-nine, eight-zero."

Their respective codes confirmed, Walsh felt a sudden sharp and stabbing pain erupt in his gut where his new liver lived. It wasn't the first time these bursts of intense pain had crippled him. He waited until the pain subsided, but never fully went away, then said, "I'm blown. The CIA knows everything, so get to Angola and secure the mining ship, as we discussed. Once I'm there, we'll move to the contingency plan."

"Roger that. Want me to eliminate your troublesome CEO or just babysit him?"

"Babysit. We move on him only when I'm there."

"It's your operation."

"Damn right it is. We need the codes to access his ship's safe with the diamonds. I can get it out of him. So sit tight, and I'll see you in Angola."

With the call ended, Walsh drove again until he crossed into Canada. Thirty miles north of the US border, he called Rupert Ponsonby with the hands-free option activated. While he waited for an answer, he popped two pills, one was his anti-rejection medication for the transplanted liver, and the other for the pain in his abdominal area. Even with the drugs, today the stabbing pain had lingered longer than it ever had before.

"Hello?"

"Where are you?" Walsh asked.

To his credit, Ponsonby bypassed greeting norms and said, "Angola. On the mining ship, as you suggested."

"Good. Stay there. I'm sending a mercenary outfit to you. Headed up by a South African named Krige."

"What? Why? Our 'problem' can't reach me here."

Walsh gritted his teeth. "Don't be so sure. Has the Angolan minister bothered you yet?"

"No. Why?"

Walsh thought through his next moves. The scheme to get nuclear waste into various mines and spread their waste far and wide had failed. Too many powerful groups knew of their conspiracy now, and with the CIA closing in on him, there was no point progressing the plan further. Walsh had sufficient funds to hide away, but not enough to flee from the CIA forever. He needed a little more, and that was where Krige and his mercenaries came in. Once he and Krige had stolen the *Cancri*'s diamond stock and turned Ponsonby into fish food, he would go into hiding in a luxurious Mediterranean getaway, as he'd always planned. Krige too would disappear with his sizable pay cheque. He'd keep the man alive because the mercenary could always prove useful in the future.

Walsh said, "The diamonds that you dredge up from the ocean floor, when was the last time you flew them out?"

"The helicopter comes every day. Takes them to a secure location in Luanda," he said, referring to the country's capital city, "where half the diamonds go to the Angolan president. From there, the rest I fly to my sorting house in London."

"Don't fly out any more, at least not until we meet up. Our associate has compromised your route. Keep the diamonds locked up on the *Cancri* until I get there; then we'll work out a different strategy for getting them out."

He heard Ponsonby's breathing now. Walsh had caused the Englishman's heart rate to speed up. "That's a lot of raw diamonds to leave on the ship."

"I know. That's why I'm sending the mercenaries. We can trust them."

"Maybe you can. I don't like this."

"You don't have to fucking like it! Just do it! Our 'problem' is fucking everything up, and until he's under control, you do everything I fucking say! Got it?"

"Y-yes," Ponsonby stuttered.

"Keep your wits about you. I do, and so can you."

"I have a lot riding on this—"

"And so the fuck do I! Don't fuck with me, Rupert. We'll all get rich, but only if you follow my every instruction." Walsh ended the call before Ponsonby could respond.

He returned his full attention to the forested roads ahead. The pills helped with the pain, dulled rather than dismissed it.

Pierce, Zang, and Summerfield would pay for this fuck-up. When he was ready, when he had the diamonds, then disappeared and established himself with a new identity and lifestyle, he would come for them all, one by one, and end their lives through the most painful and protracted methods he could conceive.

That wouldn't be difficult, because he had already perfected many ways to kill a man, or a woman, during his long and duplicitous career with the C-I-fucking-A.

53

Berberati, Central African Republic

Now that Derek Kiambi had freedom again, it terrified him.

He had to think for himself, but every decision almost paralysed him. If he acted as he should not, he feared Anti-Balaka would again snatch his freedom from him. Yesterday he'd done nothing but wander the streets of Berberati, which had not changed since Eloko's men kidnapped him seven months ago. He slept the night inside a rusted shell of a car. A torrential downpour in the early morning soaked him because of the rust holes, and thousands of mosquitoes bit at his skin. This was no different to imprisonment with the Anti-Balaka.

The next morning, Kiambi walked to his home. It was a nicer dwelling than most, with a roof that didn't leak, concrete brickwork that kept the rats out, and doors and windows that locked. He watched his house for hours, hidden behind the burned-out ruins of another house across the road, torched during the religious fighting many years back.

In time, he spied his daughters Alzina, Edmee and Saforah. They crowded around an older model iphone with a cracked screen, arguing over whose turn it was to play a colourful puzzle game.

They were alive and safe.

Kiambi cried.

Later, he watched a man exit the house. Tall and muscular, he wore a mismatched military uniform and slung an AK-47 across his back, and his boots were sturdy and without holes. Kiambi quickly recognised him as Mamadou, the soldier whose brother Kiambi had recently failed to save on his operating table. Kiambi had also once treated this man for a sexually transmitted disease, but now he felt the urge to throttle the life out of him with his bare hands.

An army truck pulled up with several of Eloko's soldiers in the tray and a heavy machine gun mounted over the cabin. Mamadou laughed and joined the other soldiers, shook hands with each man, then shared a clicking of the fingers moment that was a common greeting in his country.

Then Kiambi spotted Sergeant Trager in the driver's seat. Kiambi considered that Trager didn't looked upset, and wondered again if he yet knew Molly's terrible fate.

When the Australian soldier scanned the streets, Kiambi shrank into the shadows of the ruined house, until Trager, Mamadou and the others decided they had lingered long enough, and drove off.

If Trager was in town, it meant Mark Pierce was too, and the Australian was here to kill the American spy.

Five minutes passed before Kiambi walked out onto the street. His children played only twenty metres from him, and even when they looked his way, they didn't seem to recognise him.

He wiped the tears from his eyes and, with trembling hands, knocked on his front door.

Lifeway Kiambi answered, her skin as silky as he remembered, her lips full and eyes large and expressive. She wore a floral skirt, a tan singlet top, and her hair was wrapped in a lemon-coloured scarf. Lifeway had lost weight since he had last seen her.

"Who are you?" she asked as her body tensed.

"Lifeway." He stepped forward, arms out, ready to embrace her. "It's me. Derek, your husband."

"Derek?" She squinted as she looked at him again.

He remembered his own appearance, dirty and thin from stress and lack of food. His face had sunken in the last seven months, and his eyes had grown darker. It was no surprise she did not recognise him.

"You are not my husband."

Kiambi felt as if someone had thrust a knife into his heart.

"My husband is dead. The Seleka butchered him. I have a new husband now."

"No!" Even to his own ears, Kiambi's words sounded like the cry of a wild dog caught in a trap. "No. I am not dead."

"Then you are a ghost. One of Captain Eloko's malevolent spirits."

Kiambi fell to his knees and clasped his hands together. "Please, Lifeway. It is me. I am no trickery. Eloko held me hostage. Kept me away from you and the children."

Lifeway disappeared inside, then returned with a broom. She hit him across the head, then repeatedly on his back.

"Get away! You devil! You endanger my children and endanger me. Get away!"

For a time, Kiambi let her beat him. When the pain became too unbearable, he stood and stepped back. She chased him, swung the broom to scare him off. "I'm protected!" she screamed. "Don't you come round here again, frightening me and my children." With an ugly-shaped mouth, she called for their children to return to the house. "Go now!" she hissed. "Or my husband will slit your throat."

Kiambi stepped back, then stumbled. His face became numb, and he couldn't talk. The world seemed to shrink from him. He let Lifeway herd his children inside and slam the door.

A white, battered four-wheel drive pulled up next to him. He turned and saw the door open. Kiambi recognised the man behind the wheel in an instant.

Mark Pierce.

"Get in," said the American.

In a daze, Kiambi obeyed. "How did you know I was here?"

"You told me where you lived, once. I remembered, and when I spotted you in the streets yesterday from afar, I knew I'd eventually find you here."

Soon they were moving again, and Kiambi recognised a third occupant in the back. She was tall, slim, and muscular with an Asian cast to her features. When he glimpsed the pistol in her grip, he knew to be wary of her.

"Don't worry about Zang," Pierce said, his eyes focused on the road as he zipped around pedestrians walking in the middle of the street, and sent a flock of chickens fluttering for cover. "She thinks you might be one of Eloko's spies."

"I am a spy." His words sounded like they didn't belong to

him, but to another man who had borrowed his body for the day. He felt like he was disappearing from his body, becoming the ghost Lifeway already thought he was.

"Eloko sent you here, didn't he?"

"Yes. I'm sorry. Captain Eloko said if I told them where you were, he'd give me my freedom."

"You believe him?" said Zang.

Kiambi shook his head.

Pierce said, "Relax, Derek. Your wife has lived with her own fear these last seven months, just as you have. She'll come round when Zang and I deal with Eloko, Trager and the others. Once and for all."

"You've returned to kill them?"

"Yes," Pierce answered without hesitation or any sign of doubt in his abilities to perform as he suggested. "I promised you, Doctor, long ago, if I could help you and your family, I would. Now I can, and this is how I will do it."

"But the problem is" — Zang's voice had softened — "we don't exactly know where Eloko's camp is."

Kiambi nodded, understanding now. "You want me to take you there?"

"Or at least tell us how to find it," said Pierce.

Kiambi felt the warmth and control return to his body. He had never expected to see Mark Pierce again, but he was here, and that told him many truths he hadn't believed possible in this world for some time. That some people cared and kept their word. "I'll take you and tell you everything I know, but I'll ask for something in return."

"What's that?" Zang asked.

"Mr. Pierce already knows this. Eloko holds many children hostage in his camp, forces them into prostitution and soldiering. I want you to help me help them escape, as many as we can bring with us."

Pierce and Zang exchanged a glance.

"I wouldn't have it any other way," Pierce answered for both of them. "And also, recover any nuclear waste Walsh and the others have hidden in the camp."

"Nuclear waste?" Kiambi asked, shuddering. He remembered his conversation with Trager and Molly, concerning his fear that Trager might have radiation poisoning, and the canisters containing the nuclear waste.

"Six metal drums, about a metre high," Zang explained. "They'll keep them in water to stop them overheating."

"Yes. I know where they are. But there is a problem."

"What is that?" asked Pierce.

"Only four canisters remain. Two are missing."

54

Berberati barely resembled a town, with puddle-strewn roads, large but neglected churches with stained-glass windows, burned husks of mosques, corner stores with faded Coca-Cola branding from the 1980s, and buildings that looked as if only the daily prayer kept them standing. People were mostly young, and many were children. Women wearing turbans carried pots and crates on their heads. Piles of compacted trash built up on street corners and in the alleyways between town houses. Dirty puddles reflected the bright sun.

Zang had operated in Africa in the past, but never had she seen a city this desperate. Everywhere were bullet holes in the concrete, burned thatched roofing, and crumbled walls where presumably armoured personnel carriers had knocked into them. Many citizens carried old scars from horrific burns or missing limbs. This was a country at war, which the West had not forgotten about because they'd never known about it. Zang, Pierce and Kiambi were about to go to war here again.

She looked from the streets to her companions. The Navy SEAL cache Pierce had told her about and carried in the back of the Land Cruiser provided them with every type of weapon they would need. In an out-of-the-way street with extensive tree cover, they planned their exfil from the city. Trager and his men would watch all routes out of Berberati, for there weren't many, and would have armed teams waiting for them at each choke point.

"The problem is Bayanga," Pierce explained. "As Kiambi said, the Kadei River is the only route we can take to get there, and the only nearby port that connects us with it is Nola, about a hundred klicks' drive south of here. Bayanga is home to Baku Pygmies, or was until Eloko and Polytope Diamonds moved in and forced them out. It's also well within the Dzanga-Sangha Special Reserve, comprising mostly jungles, swamps and fast-flowing waterways all leading to the Congo Basin in the south. A horrible environment to fight in, and no easy exfil routes once we're in the middle of it."

Zang watched with interest as Pierce laid out their situation. A plan soon came together in her head. "The best solution I see is sniper positions. We commandeer a boat and take it downstream. It will be dark in a couple of hours, so we can travel at night, and your SEAL kit includes night optical devices and light-intensifier scopes, so we can travel without illumination and remain invisible. We reach a position about half a klick from the camp, then move inland through the jungle. We establish two sniper points. One for each of us and then wait. When Eloko, Walsh and Trager are all out and about, we take them out in a coordinated strike. Leaderless, we should soon cause chaos in the camp."

Kiambi scratched his head. "There is a problem with your plan. Mr Walsh and Mr Ponsonby flew out yesterday."

Zang's stomach knotted. "That's unfortunate."

So much for confronting Walsh here in the jungle, where killing him would go unnoticed and remain deniable. But from a positive perspective, if she and Pierce could take down Eloko's paramilitary force, doing so would hinder Walsh's schemes of nuclear terrorism, particularly if they could secure the four remaining nuclear waste drums.

Kiambi said, "I'm not sure if you know, Ms Zang, but Sergeant Trager's friend, Corporal Terzic, didn't come back either. Apparently, he died in South Africa."

"Yes," Pierce said. "I knew that already."

"And Sergeant Trager's girlfriend. She's... dead too. I saw..."

Zang watched as Kiambi grew pale and his eyes lost their focus, suggesting this woman had not died well.

"Girlfriend?" Pierce and Zang asked at the same time.

"Yes, her name was Molly McEwan."

"The Scottish nuclear scientist?" Zang remembered a classified CIA file that had crossed her desk more than a year ago now.

Pierce raised an eyebrow. "You know her, Zang?"

"Know of her. She was once a respectable nuclear scientist. Worked at a British nuclear power plant. Three years ago, she sold out to Hezbollah and disappeared into Beirut. Motive was unclear. It might have been coercion, or it could have been ideological or for money. Either way, once in Lebanon, no one heard from her again. The CIA kept McEwan on their active list just in case she reappeared, but no one held out any hope she'd survive that long."

Pierce nodded. "Makes sense. Walsh would want a

nuclear specialist on his team. My guess is he bought her from Hezbollah, traded her like a slave for who knows what secrets he passed on to Hezbollah in return."

Kiambi shuddered. "Trager was her boyfriend. I don't think he knows yet."

Pierce nodded, and Zang could see he was mulling over how he could use this knowledge to his advantage.

The doctor spoke again. "Captain Eloko murdered her last night. Hacked her the death with a machete. On Walsh's orders, I'm certain."

Zang gritted her teeth and tightened her fists. No one deserved a horrific ending, and the more Zang learned about who the real Walsh was, the more she detested him. "Then I must be the one to take out Walsh."

Pierce nodded. "If the opportunity presents itself, sure. But remember, recovering the nuclear waste and freeing children are our priorities. The dead need nothing, unfortunately. Not even revenge."

The comment surprised Zang, and she frowned. "I thought you too wanted retribution against Walsh and the others, for what they did to you?"

Pierce nodded and looked away. "I did, at first. Sometimes I still think I do. But something Walsh said to me once, while I was his prisoner, has played on my mind since I gained my freedom. What is retribution? He told me what it meant to him, but I realised it's a hollow motivation that serves no purpose other than to propagate cycles of violence and tyranny. Seeking revenge on Walsh, Trager, Eloko and Ponsonby won't settle my inner demons, but doing good in the world instead, that will."

Zang's frown deepened. Walsh had betrayed her and sentenced her to death, and that was not a crime she would leave unpunished. "You just going to let them go? Forgive them?"

"No," Pierce said with a smile, the first she'd seen him give her since their initial encounter in Kazakhstan. "I will kill them, or you will, Zang. I don't care who does."

"I don't understand you."

"For me, it's a numbers game. If our four enemies remain alive, they will cause more suffering, pain and deaths for others across the world, because it's their nature to do so. Dead, they cannot propagate their habitual infliction of suffering."

"You've really thought this through."

Pierce grinned again. "I spent much time in dark cells with nothing else to do but think. Plus, my encounter with Aaron Stone gave me some additional perspective."

Zang nodded and studied Pierce. He was a tall and muscular man, and his eyes held an intensity in them, like they were a pathway into a world she could become lost in. Mysteries hid in there, the kind worth knowing. He was nothing like the ruthless terrorist Idris Walsh had painted him as these last seven months, and now his talk of moving beyond retribution cast him in a new, more attractive light.

Zang asked, "How many soldiers are in the camp?"

"About a hundred competent fighters," Kiambi answered. Pierce nodded in agreement. "Maybe two hundred if you count child soldiers. But they are all undisciplined. Without Eloko's sorcerous threats, I suspect the entire outfit would fall apart."

"Sorcery?" Zang asked.

Kiambi nodded. "Eloko comes from a long line of witch doctors, or so he claims. He professes he is a Christian, but he's not. I am a Christian, and I don't accept as truth any of the animistic beliefs he does. It's all tricks, anyway. His deception with the drink we all shared that kills two of us and leaves one of us unharmed, well, it was the cups and not the liquid that he'd poisoned. He also has this poison called the Blood of Ahtu. It's horrible stuff, which makes you hallucinate like crazy. He gives it to prisoners, and they scream and wail, and victims can only survive two, maybe three doses before it kills them."

Pierce said, "I never met Eloko while I was his prisoner."

Kiambi shrugged. "Mr Walsh and Sergeant Trager needed you alive. Eloko has the opposite effect on people."

Pierce and Zang laughed.

Kiambi crossed his arms and stepped back. "Did I say something wrong?"

"No." Zang tucked a loose strand of hair behind her ear and considered how different Pierce and she were when compared to the doctor. "You made a joke, that's all."

"Joke?" He looked back and forth between the two Americans.

She touched his arm. "It doesn't matter, Doctor. Eloko is a horrid individual who doesn't deserve to live. We both hear it in your voice, the despicable things he did to you. We understand his brutality, and he will pay for it."

Kiambi waved his arms about. "If you want to destroy his reputation and turn his men against him, you'll do so by destroying his Bottle Room."

"Bottle Room?" Pierce asked.

"A wooden building with hundreds and hundreds of glass bottles. Each with a name on it and a sample of that individual's blood."

Zang felt her facial muscles tighten. "Yikes. Sounds horrible."

"It is. Most of the camp believes those bottles contain their souls, and that Eloko can torment his people from afar by heating the bottles over a flame or mixing poisons with their captured blood, and that the effects will transfer to their physical bodies. Whenever someone falls ill in the camp, they believe it is because Eloko's sorcery has tormented their soul bottles. You blow up the Bottle House, and no one falls over and dies as a result, they'll realise Eloko holds no power over them."

Zang grinned. "Sounds like a plan. If we're done here, we can further develop our strategy once we recon the camp."

"Agreed." Pierce rubbed the sweat off his brow.

She saw the redness in his eyes. For a moment she glimpsed how run-down he was and reminded herself that the man had endured seven months of brutal torture and imprisonment. It was a wonder he still operated as effectively as he did.

He caught her staring and gave a smile. "Are you okay, Zang?"

"Me? I'm fine. Pierce, we should use the Switchblade for reconnaissance once we are at the camp, and then to—"

"What are you talking about?" Kiambi asked.

"A combo drone missile, Doctor. Carry it on a backpack and launch it like a mortar round. Operates like a drone, and it can provide aerial surveillance of the camp. Once we have the intel we need, it becomes a grenade-sized warhead we'll use to take out the Bottle House." He turned to Zang and raised an eyebrow. "You're the pilot. I think the honour should be yours."

A brief flash lit up in the distance, over the top of the nearby houses, followed a second later by a loud detonation. Zang looked east with the others, towards the city centre. A column of smoke soon climbed into the blue sky. Then they heard the distant clatter of machine-gun fire.

"Seleka rebels," Zang said. "If Trager and his killers are roaming the streets, he's likely provoked a Muslim uprising against them." She grabbed a pair of binoculars and climbed onto the roof of their four-wheel drive for a better look, but at this distance in the flat landscape and with too many trees and buildings between them and the epicentre of the battle, she saw nothing helpful. "Can't see anything."

"Worth a try." Pierce put out his hand to help her down, which she accepted. "But this gives us an opportunity, to escape Berberati."

In less than a minute they had all the equipment packed and were pounding the puddle-strewn roads again.

55

Navigating Berberati's streets proved more complicated than Pierce expected. Before they had covered three blocks, they ran into a barrier laid across the road. Civilians with ancient rifles had prepared a wall of concrete bricks, fallen branches and burning tyres. They waved Pierce and his Land Cruiser to a stop.

Pierce thought of reversing, until additional men with more guns closed in from behind.

Kiambi in the passenger seat next to Pierce gripped the dashboard and stared straight ahead, his every muscle rigid. Zang in the back had her Mk 17 SCAR-H in assault-rifle configuration, ready for killing, but down out of sight. Pierce held the HK45CT pistol in his firing hand now they were at a stop, ready to use in an instant. Each of them wore combat rigs and body armour, so there was no hiding their military expertise and funding.

A tall, plump man with a bandolier of bullets and a

dented AK-47 strapped across his back knocked on Pierce's window, then motioned he should wind it down.

Figuring glass wouldn't slow bullets, Pierce capitulated. "How much to pass through?" he asked in French.

"One thousand euros."

Pierce laughed. "I'll give you fifty."

"One hundred."

"Done," Pierce said before the man could change his bid. He showed the rebel the money. "You get it when you clear a path, please."

The man looked at Pierce for a long moment; then his eyes caught Zang's return stare before his throat tightened and his Adam's apple ran up and down his throat. Pierce guessed she must have him lined up in her sights, and he knew it. "One hundred it is." He turned to the other men in his posse, whistled and gave instructions in what was presumably Sango.

Pierce handed over the money once a path had been cleared. As he drove off, he glanced back through the rearview mirror to notice the leader speaking into a two-way radio while he looked their way. "They've tagged us."

"I saw it too," said Zang.

A man on the street no different to anyone else suddenly lobbed a bottle that shattered across the windscreen and exploded as glass fragments and fire.

The windscreen held as Pierce sped up and sent the wipers into frantic activity, clearing the flames. He turned a corner, inertia pulling them as men rushed onto the streets behind them and threw more Molotov cocktails. No more bullets hit their vehicle as they escaped.

"Why aren't you shooting back?" Kiambi said fast, in a raised voice.

"We will when we hit serious opposition," Zang said.

"That wasn't serious?"

"No," said Pierce, slamming down on the brake as several women crossed the road at that moment, not bothering about traffic. Mopeds sped past the women, but Pierce, in his larger vehicle, had nowhere to go. He turned and tried an alternative route only to find a street blocked by temporary market stalls, and soon people crowded around the Land Cruiser. Children offered overripe mangos, bananas, and cashews for sale. Pierce couldn't believe people were out and about when there was violence just down the road. He waved the children away, and as soon as a passage cleared, he drove again.

In the distance, but closer than before, more gunfire sounded.

"How far to the Nola road?"

Kiambi pointed. "Turn left here."

Pierce took the corner, churned mud and dodged around an oncoming truck and a decrepit ruin of a rusted bus with no wheels or windows. As soon as they were clear, Pierce spotted four men in paramilitary uniforms with M16 and AK-47 assault rifles on the street ahead.

"Twelve o'clock," Pierce reported. "Four hostiles."

The first man turned, tripped over a chicken running between his legs, and yelled in a shrill voice as he fired a volley of bullets in their direction.

Pierce pulled on the steering wheel in the same moment he ducked and pulled Kiambi down. The windshield fragmented into tiny pellets of glass.

Zang had kept her cool and lined up the Mk 17 through the open rear passenger window, then neutralised the shooter with a single bullet.

Her second and third bullets fired within seconds of the first, and two more targets fell as showers of blood erupted from their necks and backs.

The last target lowered his weapon and ran, seeking cover. Zang switched to automatic mode and peppered him with a dozen 7.62x51mm NATO rounds.

"Nice shooting." Pierce sped through a narrow alleyway, knocking both side mirrors off the Land Cruiser and scraping away most of the paint on the concrete walls that almost boxed them in. The ground was a series of deep ruts filled with dirty water, and they bounced up and down with the undulations until they were out on the other side.

"Thanks," Zang said with an enormous smile when he caught her staring through the rear-view mirror.

Pierce grinned with her, then noticed Kiambi sweating, his hands clasped in prayer. "How far now, Doctor?"

Kiambi cleared his throat and sat straighter in his chair. "Two, maybe three kilometres. Turn right here."

As they hit the next open road, the puddles were deep, and their tyres sprayed water everywhere as they passed through.

A streak of bright light flared past the windscreen, leaving temporary white lines in Pierce's vision. Pierce tensed as his fingers gripped the steering wheel tighter than necessary. The latest attack had seemingly come from nowhere, and he still didn't understand what the threat was.

Then a parked car next to them absorbed the impact of the projectile that had just missed them, exploded with a rush of hell-like flames as the chassis tore into several large pieces that were flung in all directions. They had just narrowly avoided being taken out by a rocket.

But the carnage was not yet concluded. The front of the

decimated car propelled forward and collided with the Land Cruiser. Every remaining window in their vehicle disintegrated, sprayed them with glass fragments, and cut them in multiple locations. Pierce closed his eyes only just fast enough and threw his hands up to avoid blinding injuries. The Land Cruiser shuddered and wobbled on its tyres for a moment, then settled again.

Pierce opened his eyes, spotted an armoured personnel carrier with a mounted rocket weapon no less than fifty metres behind them that had fired the rocket...

Every muscle in Pierce's body tensed at what he saw, but he didn't let his fear take control of his actions, and sped behind an overcrowded bus coming the other way. The armoured personnel carrier would be equipped with many more rockets.

The driver of the bus turned too fast, perhaps panicked by the carnage he had unexpectedly driven into, and crushed several parked mopeds and demolished the wall of a thatch-roofed house.

A second explosive shell arced through the air, hit the house damaged by the bus. It too disintegrated in a sudden fireball that soon spewed black smoke into the air. Anyone inside would have died instantly.

Too close to the explosion, the bus shuddered, then tipped sideways as the damaged wheels on the blast side gave out. As Pierce sped down a narrow street, passengers scrambled out from the now burning husk.

Behind him, Zang returned short bursts from her assault rifle, pinning down any soldiers on the street who might chance a shot at them.

Pierce turned another corner, and they were soon out of sight of their dangerous foes again.

"That was a South African Ratel 80 IFV," Zang reported as she switched out her spent magazine with a fresh one.

Pierce nodded, pulled a shard of glass from his forearm and threw it through the gap where the side window had been. IFV. Infantry fighting vehicle. The model he had witnessed shooting at them was a cross between a tank and an armoured personnel carrier, and painted tan to blend in with bush terrain. "Armaments?"

"90mm GT-2 Cannon with 60mm K1 mortar rounds. A 7.62mm Browning M1919 machine gun with two-hundred-and-fifty-round belts."

"Fuck! I thought the CAR Armed Forces didn't have any working models."

"They probably don't," Zang said. "Eloko probably 'acquired' it and fixed it for his own purposes."

Pierce sped through several roads and soon discovered what he feared. There was no road out of this maze except the one they could now hear the Ratel 90 pounding down, gaining on them. They had not lost their foe after all.

Pierce parked the Land Cruiser, ensured several fragmentation grenades hung from his combat vest, and climbed out. Zang followed him with a Javelin missile. They needed to be on the ground to fight back. They could hear it gaining on them fast.

No more words were possible as the Ratel 90 smashed through a nearby house, destroying it, sending bricks flying all around. When the machine gunner in the turret spotted them, he fired a wide volley of high-velocity projectiles over Zang's and Pierce's heads as the infantry fighting vehicle raced towards them.

To escape the rain of bullets, Zang dropped the Javelin

and sprinted in one direction as Pierce turned and fled in the other.

The Ratel 90 powered right past their Land Cruiser; its large solid-rubber tyres drove over the Javelin, rendering it useless. The driver wasn't an expert at handling the beast of a machine; otherwise Pierce felt certain he would have driven over Zang, him or their vehicle.

Now the Ratel 90 braked hard. The gunner in his turret pivoted his belt-feed .50 Browning machine gun in Pierce's direction.

Pierce, in his frantic sprint to escape his foe, rolled over the top of an old car and ducked down behind it just before a hundred bullets tore off its roof and shattered all its windows.

56

From his temporary position of cover, and his eyes stinging from the acrid smoke now lingering in the air, Pierce assessed his position. Three fragmentation grenades and the .45 semi-automatic pistol were his only weapons, nothing that could seriously damage the Ratel 90. But there was the Switchblade, and if he could distract the infantry fighting vehicle, he might present Zang with a better chance to arm herself.

When there came a lull in the machine-gun fire from the Ratel 90, Pierce lobbed a grenade. It landed on the Ratel 90's roof, then tipped off and fell to the side before detonating. The blast was loud and bright, but when the smoke cleared, Pierce saw it had done nothing to slow the deadly vehicle nor incapacitate the soldier arming the machine gun.

Now that gunner tried to swing the Browning around and line up Pierce in his sights, but the weapon was caught on something Pierce couldn't see from his lowered position. Perhaps the grenade blast had not been completely useless and had damaged the swivel mechanism.

When the soldier again fought to dislodge his weapon, Pierce decided this was his chance to escape, and sprinted down a narrow side street, wet with puddles and dirty with garbage underfoot, but with solid brick walls offering concealment if not solid enough protection from the .50-calibre bullets he had been enduring. His lungs burning and his feet pounding, as Pierce reached the street ready to turn a corner, a new volley of machine-gun fire tore apart the side of the building to his left. The gunner had obviously unjammed the weapon, and how he had, Pierce did not know, but he now used that opportunity to take Pierce out again. The gunner failed, because Pierce had sprinted down another street and was soon well beyond the gunner's line of sight.

Then Pierce realised this was the building Zang would have positioned herself on with the Javelin if their earlier plan had worked.

He jumped up onto a broken outdoor refrigerator and used it to climb up onto the roof. From his higher vantage point, he spotted the gunner in the turret, looking down and not up for his target.

Pierce steadied his grip on the HK45CT semi-automatic pistol and fired off three closely grouped .45 ACP rounds, hitting the gunner with nearly five hundred megapascals of pressure on his face and neck, effectively disintegrating his head and spraying the metal with wet redness and brain fluid.

He ran fast off the roof and landed on the Ratel 90, then pulled the pin on a single fragmentation grenade and dropped it down past the dead gunner's legs into the cabin. Pierce jumped onto the street and rolled as the grenade detonated within. The armour-plating constrained the blast. Everyone inside would have died instantly.

Pierce climbed to his feet and jogged back down the narrow streets towards where he had lost Zang.

Two soldiers armed with AK-47s sprinted around the corner behind him. Their surprise lasted long enough for Pierce to turn sharply and put two bullets into each man's chest. Squirming in the mud, one man twisted in pain. Pierce fired a single shot into his head, ending his misery. He collected one AK-47 and all the spare banana-shaped magazines the two men carried, then marched on again in search of Zang.

When a minute had passed without anyone attempting to shoot him, Pierce noticed that the streets had emptied. Acrid smoke hung in the air while a nearby palm tree burned like some kind of pagan effigy. A wall tilted, then fell to the ground with a loud crash.

Pierce checked his hands and immediately regretted doing so. They were shaking, badly. It was like they had forgotten to until Pierce reminded them that they had neglected him lately.

He was also covered in his own blood from multiple minor cuts and abrasions.

He looked up and was about to take another street back the way he had come, when he recognised that he had lost his bearings.

A shot rang out behind him.

Without immediately trying to identify where the shooter had come from, Pierce sprinted, seeking cover, as he felt a burning in his left arm. Ahead, he spotted a rusted warehouse, and decided it suited his purposes.

He crossed a street in a rush, leaping over several civilian corpses, and disappeared inside the warehouse.

Ducking further inside to avoid further bullet fire, he looked around. The warehouse floor was home to several old cars in various states of mechanical repair. Three men and a woman, all in overalls and smeared with grease, hid behind a Land Rover without wheels or doors.

Pierce's presence placed the mechanics in the crossfire. He waved a hand in a friendly gesture to say he wouldn't hurt them. One man's stare lingered on Pierce's shoulder. Pierce looked down and noticed where a bullet had torn through his flesh, leaving a bloody, but otherwise superficial, wound. He'd patch it later. Right now, he needed to understand who was shooting at him and where they were positioned.

He heard men moving around the warehouse, with only the metal wall sheets separating Pierce and the mechanics from the soldiers who had tracked him here. Then he heard a familiar voice shout at him, perhaps from a distance of fifty metres just outside and beyond the line of sight of the open roller doors Pierce had entered by.

"You're surrounded, Pierce."

He recognised the Aussie accent immediately. "Hemsworth."

"Hilarious, Pierce. I'll give you five seconds before my dozen men storm the workshop and kill you all. Yes, that's right, I know there are civilians in there. I know how much you will try to ensure no harm comes to any of them."

Pierce raised his AK-47 and stared down the sight onto the street visible through the large, open roller doors, too far from him now to try to attempt to close them, where a sniper might easily target him. Hearing only their footfalls and grunts, he could only guess at their numbers and how close they were.

"I'll count to five, Pierce; then it's all over for you. It doesn't have to be over for the others."

He spotted two soldiers who thought the cover of a mahogany tree protected them, but leaves didn't slow bullets.

"One!"

Pierce took aim and, with careful, single shots, blew off the heads of both men.

"Fuck, Pierce!"

Pierce yelled back, "You won't kill me, Trager. Not yet. I still have the money I stole from you, and you'll want it returned. You need me alive to do that. Therefore, I have time to take your men out, one by one."

There was no reply. A silence had descended on the scene. Pierce guessed Trager would still send his men in to surround him. He had to act now, or they would capture or kill him.

He thought about his tremors and again immediately regretted that he had. Straight away, as before, he felt his legs twitch unsteadily. His infliction was as confusing as it was frustrating.

"Surrender, Pierce, and I promise you, when we kill you, we'll make it quick."

An offer with no upsides, Pierce chose to ignore it.

Remaining in the workshop would get him and the civilians killed. With fumbling hands, Pierce switched a fresh magazine into his pistol and took the last grenade from his combat harness, tasks that took far longer than they should have. Then he sneaked close to the wide entrance. Through a rusted hole in the warehouse's corrugated iron shell, he saw boots moving past.

They were just outside.

Checking that the mechanics were on the opposite side of the warehouse and protected by the shell of a half-repaired car, Pierce pulled the pin on the grenade, held it for a few seconds and lobbed it through the hole, then sprinted through the exit.

He didn't look back as the frag grenade detonated, pulverising the men who probably hadn't seen the grenade at their feet. He felt the pressure wave at his back propel him forward. Pierce figured everyone would be too distracted by the blast to return fire. But he was wrong.

A burst of bullets tore up the dirt around him.

Pierce slid over the bonnet of a car parked ahead and ducked down behind it. More bullets ripped through the engine block.

It was then that Pierce sensed various weapons trained on his back.

He turned, discovering three soldiers hidden in the lush green foliage with their M16A1 assault rifles trained on him.

He was cornered.

Carefully, with shaking hands and legs surging with tremors, Pierce laid his HK45CT and AK-47 on the dirt and stood just as carefully with his arms raised. Trager had guessed Pierce might make a break for it in this direction, and had established an ambush point. Pierce had to admire the man's tactical skills.

Within ten seconds of his capture, Sergeant Alex Trager joined them, his FN-FAL assault rifle lined up, ready to blow Pierce's brains into tiny pieces. "My men aren't happy with you, Pierce. You killed a good number of their friends today."

"The same men who raped and murdered your girl-friend, Molly McEwan." Pierce watched as the colour drained from the Australian's face, and saw this was news to him. "That's right, butchered with a machete is what I heard. You keep odd friends, Sergeant."

Trager snarled, advanced with his weapon as his face turned red. "How the fuck do you know about her? And she's not dead!"

"Sure about that? She didn't believe what you were doing was right, did she?" Pierce was guessing now, but he could tell by his opponent's widening eyes and clenching teeth his speculation held much truth. His raised hands shook like they were waving.

"What the fuck is wrong with you?"

Pierce ignored the question. "Let me guess, you sourced dirty nuclear bombs to decimate competitor diamond mines."

"How the fuck do you know that?"

Pierce decided not to answer him, and instead said, "Molly couldn't handle the human cost. Eloko and Walsh didn't like that she had developed a conscience, so had her killed, brutally. To teach you a lesson so not to end up like her."

Trager's face became ugly as his muscles twisted in unnatural angles and his bared teeth clamped down. "Do it!" he ordered a man standing behind Pierce.

The former CIA operator turned just fast enough to see the stock of an M16 come down on his head, and the world faded from view.

57

Bayanga, Central African Republic

Pierce stood on a vast ice sheet.

A man threatened him with a pistol.

Nowhere to run, Pierce shot out the ice, dropped through the frozen shards and descended into its dark, cold abyss...

He came to.

The shock of water splashed on his face and upper torso woke him.

He tested his arms, then legs, bound with cord to a chair.

He was naked.

The room he found himself in was stifling and stank of sweat and urine, and the air buzzed with disease-carrying mosquitos. Someone had patched the bullet graze on his arm with a soaked bandage, but his other injuries were untreated. Pain stabbed at his forehead, as Pierce remembered the blow from the M16 that had rendered him unconscious.

"You've come so far, Pierce." Sergeant Alex Trager stepped from the shadows. "Only to find yourself exactly where you started. Back in hell."

Pierce studied the room. Unless someone else hid in the shadows, it was only the two of them.

"The only reason you are alive is because of the money you stole. Once I have it back, you will die."

Pierce tugged against the cords, but they were thick and expertly tied. Trager had similar special forces training as he did, so wasn't prone to amateur mistakes. "Not much incentive for me to talk."

Trager grinned. "Last time, we had to keep your body intact, for the CIA to discover it in top physical shape. Not anymore." Trager took out his radio and spoke into it without taking his eyes off Pierce. "He's awake... Yes, he's ready..."

"I won't return the money. You'll just have to kill me."

"Don't be so sure. You'll know all about Captain Eloko by now." He watched Pierce's eyes and smiled when he saw the expression he was looking for. "Of course you do. There was a reason Walsh and I wouldn't allow him anywhere near you during your long incarceration. He gets results; I've seen it myself. Unfortunately, everyone he tortures dies shortly afterwards. He can't help but be brutal beyond all normal human understanding."

Pierce felt himself sweat. His naked body felt feverish, and the humidity left his skin glistening. He tugged again at the cords, but to no effect. "So it was Eloko who murdered and butchered your lover. Makes perfect sense."

Trager snarled and raced at Pierce with a grip ready to strangle him.

"Not so fast, Sergeant!"

The door had burst open behind Pierce, distracting Trager from his murderous intent. Four men, including Eloko, marched around Pierce and stood before him. All were soldiers in paramilitary uniforms of dappled green with streaks of claw-like brown. The three underlings carried AK-47s slung ready to fire. On their belts, they holstered semi-automatic pistols, each a different make and model.

Captain Eloko slung a Beretta APX semi-automatic pistol in a leather belt holster. The man was average looking, but his eyes, Pierce recognised. Eyes that carried the stare of a psychopath, an individual who never felt remorse or pity for others, whose pathological confidence in their own capabilities was far removed from reality.

Eloko sat in the chair opposite and stared into Pierce's eyes. "Are you afraid?"

Pierce said nothing.

"It's okay if you are not. It doesn't matter what you believe or feel or think. Because in minutes, your mind won't belong to you, but to me."

Eloko's calmness unsettled Pierce more than anything he had witnessed since waking. Torture, for months on end, had broken him again and again, but somehow, he had held himself together, drew on hidden reserves of mental fortitude to propel him through his suffering. But now, gazing at Eloko staring back at him, he wondered if his mental strength was enough to resist this man.

The warlord took a small glass bottle from his pocket, thick with black liquid sloshing inside. He held it close to Pierce's eyes. "This is the Blood of Ahtu. The life force of a malevolent spirit that permeates these jungles. Its effects only last a few minutes, ten, maybe fifteen at the most, but to the drinker, those moments feel like a lifetime. You will see visions the likes of which you can't possibly imagine. Your mind will tear itself apart, trying to understand what you witness. You won't even know we are asking questions. Won't even know if you are answering them. But you will."

He unscrewed the lid.

The soldiers stepped back, and so did Trager. The Australian had regained some of his composure, as if he knew that whatever Eloko was about to do to Pierce would be far worse than anything the sergeant could achieve on his own.

Eloko grinned. "See, they are all afraid. Are you afraid now, Mr Pierce?"

Pierce tugged at his bindings, but he wasn't anywhere close to loosening them. The chair, however, felt flimsy. If he threw himself hard on the floor, the wood might shatter, and he could slip his bonds from between the broken sections. But he needed to time his ploy, act when everyone was distracted, and now was not the right time.

He turned to Trager. "This is the man who butchered Molly. You just going to stand there and not punish him."

Trager stiffened to restrain the quakes in his body, but Pierce's taunts were not enough to propel him into action. Did Trager fear Eloko?

The warlord snapped his fingers across Pierce's eyes. "It's just you and me and the invisible world, Pierce. No one else here matters."

Knowing that he was getting nowhere, he held Eloko's stare instead. "I'll tell you what, get Walsh in here, and I'll tell you whatever you want to know."

Eloko turned to Trager and belly laughed. Trager smiled but kept himself alert and ready for action. Pierce hadn't noticed until now, but the Australian held his SIG Sauer semi-automatic pistol ready to fire. But who would he shoot?

The warlord turned back to Pierce. "A powerful man can survive one dose, maybe two if he's lucky. Three will kill him. That's how many times you have to tell Sergeant Trager here what he needs to know."

Pierce had trained for torture and interrogation, and he'd experienced the real thing too many times in his past. Tortures that had pushed him to the brink of what he thought was possible to endure. One day, Pierce feared he might pass the point of no return when the trauma destroyed his mind and body, and that moment might be now. He had a plan to turn the tables, but it required one additional person to join them. "Get Walsh on the phone! Then I'll talk!"

Eloko's dark eyes seemed to shrink into his skull. "Oh, you will talk, Pierce. You will talk very much." He nodded to the soldier standing at the back, who grabbed Pierce's head and forced his mouth open. Eloko stood, opened his bottle, and let the foul-smelling liquid drop into Pierce's mouth.

One. Two.

Three drops...

58

P ierce gagged, tried to spit out the poison, but there
was so little liquid there was nothing to expel.
Then, as if suddenly from nowhere and everywhere, the world seemed to morph around him, as if reality
began to flow and bend and distort. Distances seemed to
recede and come closer in the same moment. He heard
voices, but they were muffled and indiscernible. His head
pounded, and his mouth felt parched.

Eloko, Trager, and other soldiers transformed into
corpses, with exposed skulls and blood pouring off their
skinless flesh as rivers of blood.

Pierce recoiled, but nothing changed.

Now he heard voices. Ethereal and distant.

"We are the Walking Dead Men of Africa."

"The Zombie Mercenaries of Fidelity."

"The Bullet Eaters of the Night."

Then the voices made no sense again.

Pierce felt his muscles thrashing, his mouth cracking,

and his eyes bleeding. He couldn't tell what was real and what was not. The undead men moved around him, shook him, yelled at him.

And then it ended as suddenly as it had started.

"Did you get what you wanted?"

"No. Only one fucking account and not even two hundred thousand in it."

"You should have been more specific."

"And you shouldn't have almost killed him."

Pierce felt himself coming round, but he kept his eyes closed and his head hung low. This was difficult because his mouth tasted of bile and blood, while a fever burned through his body, and the world still spun. He had no concept of how long he had suffered hallucinations. It could have been minutes, but it could have easily been hours too.

Then the tremors hit.

Unable to feign unconsciousness any longer, Pierce raised his head. His arms and legs shook as if surges of electricity fired through his muscles. Focus did nothing to gain any control over his spasms. Spit dribbled from his mouth.

Eloko and Trager, with normal faces and bodies again, looked on in amusement. The three other soldiers who stood in the background watched with silent interest.

The warlord said, "Pierce is a powerful man, it seems. He survived the wrath of Ahtu."

"He's shaking like a fucking epileptic!" said Trager.

Eloko shrugged. "That will pass."

Trager grabbed a bucket of water and threw it over Pierce.

Somehow that worked. The shock of distraction refocused Pierce's mind, and his tremors and head spins subsided. They didn't go away, but reduced to a mild shaking in his hands and legs.

"You're a fucking mess, Pierce." Trager snarled and looked down his nose at Pierce's bound body.

Pierce chuckled despite the fever gripping his body and the headache borne of dehydration. "Get what you wanted?"

Trager tensed but didn't answer.

The door behind Pierce flung open. A soldier raced in, holding a satellite phone for Trager to take. "It's Mr Walsh," he said in French. "He's been trying to reach you for the last hour."

At last, thought Pierce as his muscles relaxed.

Trager and Walsh conversed for a moment. Then Trager placed the phone on the chair in front of Pierce where Eloko had sat and set it to speaker mode.

"You're missing all the fun." Pierce laughed. He looked down, saw the blood and streaks of vomit on his chest. Disturbing, but nowhere near the quantities he had imagined during his drug-induced nightmare.

Walsh spoke from far away. "Why are you still alive, Pierce?"

This time Pierce's laugh came out as a snort. "Didn't Trager tell you?"

"Tell me what?"

Pierce turned to the former Special Air Service Regiment soldier. "Fuck you, Trager. We had a fucking deal, and you fucking reneged."

The stillness that gripped the torture room told Pierce he'd read his enemy's mood with precision.

"What are you talking about, Pierce?" Walsh asked, speaking from the phone.

Pierce turned to Trager. "Kill these fuckers, now! It's what you wanted, *mate*! It's why you helped me escape. Kill them now, and I'll forgive your faltering loyalties."

Trager raised his SIG Sauer and pressed it against Pierce's head, right between the eyeballs. "Shut the fuck up, Pierce!"

"What's going on?" Eloko stood, puffed up his chest to look big. "What's he talking about, Sergeant?"

"He's bluffing." Trager spoke through clenched teeth. He kept his pistol on Pierce's forehead, but his eyes shifted to Eloko and the four other soldiers in the room.

"Don't believe me?" said Pierce. "Check your operational accounts. Three and a half million dollars is missing. One million paid for Ponsonby's assassination, but the rest is Trager and my retirement fund—"

"*WHAT!*" shouted Walsh.

"The assassin would have succeeded if Trager hadn't lost his nerve and left me to rush a botched operation—"

"Shut the fuck up, Pierce—"

"Or what, you'll blow my brains out? You were going to do that, anyway. Just like you didn't want Molly to know about our little deal, in case she wanted a cut—"

"I'll fucking kill you!"

"You trained with the Navy SEALs, didn't you, Trager? *You* told me where to find their weapons cache in Cameroon."

"Is this true?" Eloko asked.

Pierce cackled. "Walsh knows what I'm talking about. I leaked the intel you provided me on your operations, linking Eloko to your diamond mine irradiation conspiracy. Detonating the drums in the tailings dams of your competitors, and blowing out the earthen walls at the same time, thereby flooding the entirety of the mines with radioactivity, rendering them unworkable. The CIA is hunting Walsh even now, because they know this too. A wanted terrorist just like me, or hasn't he told you—"

"Fuck!" Walsh swore down the line. "The accounts are fucking empty!"

It all went down within the space of three heartbeats.

Trager shot three soldiers through their chests, then raced for the exit.

Pierce threw himself to the ground, shattered the chair and freed himself.

Eloko lunged at Trager, but the Australian was a better fighter and clipped Eloko across the back of his head and sent him crumpling to the ground.

The last soldier raced to Pierce with his AK-47 raised.

Pierce was faster, rammed a splintered leg of the chair into the man's throat, spraying them both with thick, fresh blood. As the soldier collapsed, Pierce pulled the Glock 19 from the man's hand and turned to cover the room. Everyone was down except for Trager, who was long gone.

Eloko rushed to his feet and shot Pierce, twice, in the gut.

Before the pain hit, Pierce ran at the warlord and smashed his pistol down on his head. The warlord lost control of his muscles and crumpled onto the dank floor again like a sack of flesh and bones.

Pierce checked his naked abdomen.

No bullet holes.

No wounds at all.

Eloko had fired blanks.

"What's going on?" Walsh yelled through the line.

"You've lost." Pierce laughed again. "Eloko and Trager are dead." *Or soon will be*, he whispered to himself. "You're next."

He heard the line disconnect.

Outside, the sounds of gunfire spoke of a ground battle between Trager and Eloko's men. The Australian was doing most of Pierce's work for him.

Pierce grabbed a length of cord that had bound him, then used it to tie Eloko's hands behind his back. He checked the bandage on his arm, tore it away to find his earlier bullet wound was raw and infected.

He stripped the corpse of the soldier closest in size to him and dressed in his clothes and combat harness, then holstered the Glock 19 and grabbed three magazines. Pierce grabbed a fallen AK-47, ensured that it had a bullet in the chamber, then gathered up all the thirty-round banana-shaped magazines and slipped them into the pockets of his military fatigues.

With his adrenaline rush subsiding, and without warning, he vomited again, bringing up more blood and bile. The fever still gripped him, and his stomach ached like a fire was burning inside him.

With his stomach empty, he found bottled water and drank it all.

Eloko was coming round.

Pierce took the soldier's knife and cut away Eloko's clothes, so he was as naked as Pierce had been. The man likely hid many surprise potions and tricks in his garb that Pierce didn't wish to face later, and now he had solved that problem.

"Get to your feet!"

"No!" Eloko hissed like a snake from his prone position.

Pierce fired a single shot through his right shoulder.

The warlord howled like an animal as blood seeped from the wound. He struggled against his bindings.

"You don't need arms for what I have planned. Guess where I'll shoot you next."

The warlord struggled to his feet.

Pierce helped him, then pushed the man towards the door. Eloko would be his body armour.

59

Outside, it was early morning. Mist permeated the camp, reduced visibility and transferred the tall emergent jungle trees into outlines that stretched as much as fifty metres into the sky. Pierce heard the gentle flow of the Kadei River and saw its banks at the edge of the camp, and he found his orientation.

Pushing Eloko in the back, but keeping him close as a human shield, he moved forward. The only people he saw outside were corpses. Men, children, and women.

The camp was as Pierce remembered. The same huts, wooden houses with thatched roofs, storerooms and animal pens with goats, pigs and chickens. Litter and empty drums lay scattered everywhere. Campfires smouldered from the previous night. Where the soldiers had cleared the jungle foliage, the ground was orange mud.

"I'll make a deal," Eloko said as blood dribbled from the earlier glancing blow to his forehead and now trickled into his eye, forcing him to blink it away. The bullet hole in his shoulder oozed blood, but that wound didn't seem to bother the warlord as much. "I have diamonds. Millions in diamonds. You can be rich."

Pierce ignored Eloko, then pushed him forward again. He noticed another wooden building and knew from Derek Kiambi's descriptions this was the Bottle Room, the so-called crypt of souls that Eloko claimed to have absolute power over.

Pierce was still figuring out his next move when a missile streaked through the air from the misty jungle foliage and hit the Bottle Room, disintegrating it in a bright flash of white. They were close enough to feel the blast wave, but not close enough for it to harm them.

Eloko trembled.

Pierce grinned despite the sweat pouring off him. "What will everyone say, Eloko, now that your slave army didn't die when their souls did?"

"You should kill me now," Eloko raged. "Because you won't get your chance later. My soldiers are loyal and will protect me with their—"

His answer came as a series of bullets fired from the mist. Those bullets clustered in Eloko's chest, killing him. Suddenly the warlord became a burdensome weight, forcing Pierce to drop him face first into the mud. Then Pierce dived behind the cover of a hut as more bullets flew from the mist in his direction.

Readying his AK-47, Pierce heard shots come from behind him. The shots were aimed at the men who'd killed Eloko. Soon the bullets found their targets, and those men screamed from their own pain.

It had to be Rachel Zang in a sniper position, taking out

targets when they moved from cover. He'd guessed she had been the one to destroy the Bottle House with the Switchblade drone.

He glimpsed more men in the undergrowth, obscured by the mist.

Zang fired again.

More targets dropped.

Three soldiers rushed Pierce, appearing from the side of the hut, and were upon him in seconds.

Pierce raised his AK-47 and fired in time to tear a man's chest open with a spray of 7.62mm rounds.

A second man struck at Pierce with a machete.

Pierce responded by lifting his assault rifle as a shield. As the two weapons collided, he kicked the man's legs from under him, turned and pulled his Glock 19 from its holster and fired into the face of the third attacker, who'd hesitated, waiting for a clean shot with his M16.

The machete foe struggled to his feet.

Not fast enough, as Pierce shot him at close range through his heart.

Meanwhile, the sniper kept shooting, laying a covering fire for Pierce. Zang had come for him, waited until she had seen Pierce before engaging the enemy. Perhaps he could trust her. He wanted to.

Pierce readied his AK-47 as three children ran around the hut in a second ambush. They too held the old-model Russian assault rifles and soon lined up Pierce in their sights. The scene would have been comical in benign circumstances, enormous weapons in tiny hands, but they could kill Pierce as readily as any foe.

The boys hesitated, and Pierce could have killed them all with a sweep of bullets from his own weapon. But these kids couldn't have been over ten years old, and every child's life was more important than his. He dropped his AK-47 and raised his hands. "I won't hurt you. Do what you must."

A man speaking Sango caught the children's attention. All four turned as Dr Derek Kiambi stepped from the mist and spoke to the children in hushed tones.

Zang resumed her covering fire, dropping distant soldiers one by one.

Before anyone took a bullet, Kiambi directed the children behind one hut, out of range from their enemy. Pierce followed, lifting his fallen AK-47 and returning his own covering fire.

Soon Kiambi had the boys close to him, who hugged him around the waist. "Mr Pierce, I'm so glad they didn't kill you."

"Me too."

"We should leave."

Pierce laughed. "You were right. With the Bottle House destroyed, Eloko's men turned against him."

"They did indeed, and I saw it all. Oh, before I forget." He handed Pierce a radio with an ear and throat piece. "Ms Zang says you can talk to her with this. Channel three."

Pierce noticed Kiambi wore the same communication devices. Once he had the parts in place, as further bullets flew over their hiding spot, Pierce activated the speech pod, which he'd adhered to his dirty shirt. "Zang! Thanks for coming."

"You're welcome, my friend." He heard the noise of a rifle firing, both through the mic and nearby. "Most tangos are down. Many have fled. I can't see any more at the moment, so I'm coming to you. I'll need covering fire."

"Yes, ma'am," Pierce said with a smirk. He lifted his AK-47 and was careful not to point it toward any of the children.

"We came on a boat," Kiambi said. "I have rounded up as many of the children as I can, taking them there."

Pierce touched his forehead, feeling the fever burning inside him. His hands carried a faint tremor. "What can I do to help?"

"Don't let any of the children die."

Pierce nodded and noticed the shooting had ceased. Zang had proven to be an efficient sniper, yet he kept his AK-47 ready should they come under further attack. He got on the radio with Zang. "What about the radioactive drums? We need to mark them so we can get the US Air Force here and securely get them away."

"Already on it." Zang spoke through the mic. "Cover me."

"Roger that." Pierce laid down covering fire, not that anyone shot back. Eloko's men were dead or fleeing into the jungle.

The tall limber woman materialised from the fog, running in military fatigues, and armed with a Mk 17 set to sniper mode. When she was close, she ducked down next to him while he reloaded the AK-47. "Nice to see you in one piece, Pierce."

"Likewise."

"I take it the hospitality wasn't up to your usual standards?"

Pierce grinned as his fever seemed to burn hotter. "Let's just say this place will be lucky to get a one-star review on Google."

Kiambi rejoined them, having concluded his brief conversation with the three children. "I have about one hundred young ones ready to go. Ms Zang, the boat we came in won't be enough."

Zang nodded to three trucks parked nearby, with trays large enough to pack dozens of children into each, so long as they didn't mind close contact with each other. "If these are here, there must be a road out." She turned to Pierce. "New plan. First, we find that road. Second, we fuel the trucks and load the kids to drive them out. Third, we tag the radioactive drums with an infrared marker and call in their location to the CIA and JSOC, US Joint Special Operations Command. Fourth, we destroy any weapon stores before we leave. Am I missing anything?"

Pierce nodded, stumbled as his legs almost gave out under him. "Five, I find Trager." He described his torture and how he had convinced Walsh that Trager was a double agent.

Zang shook her head. "It's over for the Aussie. If he's still alive, he's on the run now, from us *and* Walsh."

"This isn't about retribution, Zang. He's the only one still alive who knows the locations of the two other radioactive drums in position in the mines. I can guess generally where they might be," Pierce said, remembering the six diamond mines Ponsonby had called out in his Cape Town speech, "but not specific coordinates within each mine."

Zang licked her lips and didn't speak for several seconds. "Pierce, you sure you're okay? I presume they tortured you?"

"It wasn't too bad." Pierce almost raised his hand to see if they were shaking, then stopped himself when he knew they were. He felt his tremors intensify from deep inside his muscles, threatening to consume him if he lost control of his body again. His stomach still cramped from the hallucinogenic poison in his body, and his mouth and throat were raw. But the fever was the worst, like an oven burned inside him.

Zang handed him her water bottle, which he accepted and guzzled. "No offence, Pierce, but you look awful. I should be the one to go after Trager."

60

Zang had seen Trager vanish into the jungle, too fast to take him out with her sniper weapon, but she knew which direction he had headed. When she reached the path that he had followed into the thick foliage, she spotted fresh blood on shin-high leaves. Trager was injured, which suited her.

Once she stepped into the thick rainforest and moved deeper inside, the interior opened like a vast chamber. It was easy to lose one's orientation because there was almost no light, and the jungle looked the same whichever direction she looked. The canopy one hundred and fifty feet above obscured the sun during the day and the stars at night, and with the exception of insects and birds, there was no noise. Only the jungle edges were thick with near-impassable vegetation, for the deep rainforest where she found herself now was a carpet of leaves and fungus, interspersed with the thick trunks representing columns and the dense green leaves above like a ceiling.

She followed the trail Trager must have taken, for there

were no fresh impressions in the fallen leaves anywhere else, and took off in a sprint.

Only minutes into her run did she see Trager, eighty feet ahead of her as he limped behind a tall, thick trunk with buttress roots providing him sufficient cover. She fired a shot from her SCAR Mk 17, missing him. Then she lost sight of Trager as he ducked down behind the roots for cover, and now his foxhole provided her foe with the advantage. Complicating matters, the layout of the buttress roots offered no straightforward path to sneak up on him, and she needed Trager alive, while she could not say the same was true for her as far as he was concerned.

With the stock of her SCAR Mk 17 pressed into her shoulder and her eyes lined up along the sighting iron, Zang took in a lungful of the humid air and approached with one cautious and silent step after another.

Following Trager to this point had been easy enough, but she reminded herself that despite his wound, he was special forces trained, a veteran of one of the most respected and successful covert military outfits anywhere on the planet. Sergeant Trager was a man who would have lived for weeks or months behind enemy lines in the battlefields of Taliban-controlled Afghanistan, killing insurgents in the night, and then disappearing before anyone knew he was there. He might do the same to her if she wasn't careful.

She took her time, watched for trip wires or disturbed ground where Trager might have booby-trapped a grenade. She didn't believe he'd had time to prepare such elaborate traps, but one could never be too careful with an opponent of his skills, calibre and battle-hardened experience.

Advancing in a wide arc around the tree, she glimpsed

his unmoving body. She listened for his breathing, but there was no noise.

Then she realised the situation was wrong. All she could see was his shirt and pants. It wasn't Trager, but his clothes mimicking him.

Gunfire exploded around her.

The SCAR Mk 17 was torn from her hands as a bullet hit and dragged it away.

She dived for the buttress roots, drew her HK45CT semi-automatic pistol and fired blindly towards where she thought the shooter had positioned himself.

Zang heard a grunt, a sound like a man punched in the chest. She moved, then raised herself up to fire again with three close shots towards where she'd heard the noise.

Trager had already vanished.

Then she spotted him racing for cover behind a second trunk, wearing nothing but his boxer shorts and boots, his back to her.

Zang exploded up onto her feet and sprinted after him, switched out the magazine in her pistol, then lined up the weapon and squeezed the trigger several times, shooting in his direction before he reached the cover of the next emergent tree.

Once again, she'd missed.

Then she realised how exposed her position was, and there was nowhere to hide.

Zang had no choice but to sprint and catch him before he decided to turn around and take a shot at her. He was wounded. She was not. She would be faster.

When Zang reached Trager's tree, he turned back as she'd expected, and pointed his SIG Sauer pistol towards her.

Propelling her body off the jungle floor, Zang kicked the gun from his hands. He grunted again, and she rolled, coming up with the pistol in her hand. She fired off the last of her rounds, missing him again when he moved too fast.

Trager recognised he was too close for her to reload or for him to reach his fallen pistol, so he came at her with fists and jabs. He didn't kick, and she saw why. His left leg was messy and bloodied.

Zang feinted and parried. She was faster, but he was stronger. All muscle, and bulkier and larger than Pierce, he was like a bear crossbred with a gorilla. Trager had mastered his discipline, fought while ignoring the pain of his many wounds, and kept coming for her.

Strike. Parry. Strike. Feint. They engaged for many minutes, and soon they were both panting from exertion. Then a fist from nowhere collided with her jaw and sent her reeling backwards, leaving her unsteady on her feet. She tasted blood in her mouth.

They separated for a moment. That was a mistake, because Trager drew his fighting knife from the sheath across his arm.

He came at her faster than she'd thought possible on his injured leg.

Zang moved backwards, then turned, and ran up the side of a buttress root and leaped over it. She spotted her fallen pistol, rolled to grab it and switched magazines, then chambered the first round as she came back up in a crouching position, down on one knee.

Trager appeared around the buttress root and raced towards her.

She fired twice.

Two bullets imploded his lungs.

Trager's eyes grew wide as his mouth made an O-shape, not at first registering the pain, then feeling it in its enormity. He stumbled, dropped the knife and fell onto his knees, and stayed there.

Zang got to her feet and stepped back. Ten feet was a safe distance.

"Fuck!" he wheezed. Then blood dribbled from his lips.

Zang figured he'd be dead in minutes. That didn't give her long to secure the information she required. "Trager! The locations of the radioactive drums in the mines. Where are they?"

The Australian looked up at her. His eyes became bloodshot, but that wasn't his problem anymore. He spoke in harsh whispers. "You know... once upon a time... I was a patriot... I wanted... to save the world."

"You still can."

His breaths grew shorter. His pupils dilated wider.

"Walsh and Ponsonby know... The *Cancri*... off the coast of Angola."

She kept her pistol aimed at his face. "The drums, Trager. Don't waste my time. Just tell me where the last radioactive drums are?"

He grinned as more blood poured out of his mouth. "Kill them for me... For Molly..."

His eyes rolled upwards, and he tumbled forward, dead as he hit the carpet of leaves beneath him.

Zang already knew his fate, but put a bullet through his head anyway. There was no point in taking unnecessary risks.

After she gathered up her weapons and equipment, she checked her own body for potential injuries, finding only superficial wounds, then marched back the way she'd come.

She reflected on her mission. It had not turned out how she'd expected.

Without slowing her stride, she made a call on her satellite phone and coded in, using a CIA encrypted network that would allow her to speak without fear of being overheard.

Her case officer answered almost immediately. "Reporting in already, Zang? You are okay, I take it?"

"Yes, ma'am. I'm good. I just called to say it's confirmed, Pierce *is* a patriot. He never was a conspirator in Walsh's scheme."

"Excellent," said the older woman on the opposite side of the planet. "Then he's perfect for what we have planned. More so, in fact."

61

Despite the cramping in his stomach, headache, fever and nausea, Pierce worked with speed. He ran mechanical checks on the three largest trucks and ensured their gas tanks and jerry cans were full. Next, he joined Derek Kiambi to round up all the surviving children and secure them in the back of each truck. Then a systematic reconnaissance of the camp soon revealed the road to Berberati. Lastly, Pierce gathered up what food and water he could find.

While completing his last task, his earpiece chirped. "You copy, Pierce?"

"Loud and clear, Zang." He felt the tension in his muscles lessen. Sergeant Trager could have killed her today, so knowing that she was alive brought a smile to his face. "You okay?"

"Yes, on my way back. Trager's dead. He didn't give me the location, but I discovered Walsh and Ponsonby will soon be on Polytope's *Cancri* mining ship in Angola. We can ask them."

"How did you find that out?"

"Trager wanted me to know. I'll be with you in a few minutes and tell you more."

"Good, we're ready to roll. And, Zang?"

There was a pause. "Yes, Pierce?"

"Thank you for coming back for me."

"You're welcome."

As Pierce returned to the trucks, he stumbled across Eloko's corpse. Flies buzzed around his wounds and orifices. The bullet charm around his neck prompted a chuckle from Pierce, for it had not made him bulletproof.

On impulse, Pierce returned to the torture room and searched the warlord's shredded clothes, finding a draw-string leather bag. He opened it to discover, as he had expected, several dozen uncut diamonds. He also found Eloko's Beretta APX. Pierce pocketed both and returned outside.

He found Derek Kiambi speaking to the children in a local dialect. Many of the kids wore blank expressions or were wide-eyed, suggesting they were in shock. These children had endured the worst horrors the world could subject them to; they would never be without the limitations that extreme trauma brought out in its victims. He might not be able to help them mentally, but physically he could make them safe again. Some children would reunite with their families or close relatives. Others would end up in orphanages or refugee camps, but that was a better future than slavery, soldiering and prostitution.

Kiambi stepped up to Pierce and shook his hand. "Thank you for coming back, Mr Pierce."

Pierce's stomach cramped uncomfortably, and he struggled to reply to Kiambi. His strongest desire was to lie down and curl into a ball until the pain subsided — if it ever did. Eloko's poison was as awful as the psychotic warlord had claimed. Through gritted teeth he said, "We'll soon reunite you with your wife and children, Kiambi, and deal with the man who has her hostage."

"You mean Mamadou? He's already dead, Mr Pierce." Kiambi pointed towards a fallen soldier with half his head missing. "That's him, there. He was one of Eloko's men."

"I see. Well, let's get you back home. And thank you for coming to get me and the children."

Kiambi's eyes filled with tears. "I never thought this day would come. I mean, I planned for it. I made friends with the children, looked after them where I could, knowing that if I were ever to get them away from this hell, it would only be because they trusted me. I thank God for the strength he gave me to get through this."

"Well, you did a commendable job."

Kiambi wiped his eyes with his dirty sleeve. "You must think me a weak man, to express my emotions openly."

"The opposite, in fact. I admire you." Pierce scanned the jungle, noticing that the mist had lifted, and guessed that Zang would return any minute now. "Kiambi, if you could do anything with your life, what would you do?"

He shrugged. "Reunite with my family. Rebuild my home. Give my children a decent education. If I had the money, I'd open an orphanage and a medical clinic in Berberati. Offer free services to those who can't afford to pay me. Our people say the Central African Republic is a beautiful country, but it is not. We have a long way to go before we can say our nation has recovered from the ravages of war, before Christians and Muslims put aside their hatreds and live harmoniously together again, as we once did."

Pierce grinned. "I thought you might say that." He passed Kiambi the leather drawstring satchel. "Use this to get you started."

"What is it?" He opened it, and his eyes grew wide. "Where did you find these?"

"Eloko had them. No one will come looking for them now. Zang and I will put you in touch with reliable buyers. Individuals who won't rip you off or steal them from you."

Kiambi took Pierce's hand and shook it. "My friend, how can I ever thank you?"

"No need to thank me."

Zang appeared, stripped down to a singlet top and combat fatigues and covered in mud like the rest of them. When she spotted Pierce, she grinned and raised an eyebrow.

"Well done," Pierce said.

"You didn't think I could do it? Take on a special forces soldier like that?"

Pierce laughed, appreciating the hurdles Zang must have navigated within the CIA for them to accept and consider her as competent as any man performing the same job she did. "I never doubted you, Zang. Just worried about you, as I would about any of my team."

She nodded and looked to the river and the submerged cage with the radioactive drums. "We need to call them in. I'll contact the CIA and JSOC, provide GPS coordinates, and mark them with an infrared beacon. An Air Force team will arrive a few hours after that to recover them."

Pierce's stomach cramped again, and he almost doubled over. He needed rest, but not until they had gotten the children away from this hellhole. "I want to be long gone from here by then."

Zang nodded. "You don't look so good, Pierce."

"I'll be fine."

She frowned. "Sure you will."

"Zang, I'm okay." He wiped the sweat off his forehead and the back of his neck, then stumbled on his weak legs.

She gave him a look that said she didn't believe him. "Sit down. Rest for a minute."

He obeyed and immediately didn't feel so woozy anymore.

"You should call it in."

Pierce raised an eyebrow.

"The CIA is starting to understand your innocence in this conspiracy. Calling in the radioactive drums will go a long way to supporting that belief."

"Ms Zang is right," said Kiambi. "You are a good man, and if my words count for anything, I'll tell your CIA employers that."

Resting his hand on Kiambi's shoulder and smiling, Pierce thought through Zang's logic. Her strategy made sense, but Pierce wasn't certain he trusted anyone within the Central Intelligence Agency right now, at least not until he dealt with Idris Walsh and recovered the missing radioactive waste canisters on his own. "Maybe, but I'm not coming in any time soon."

She reached up and touched him on the arm. "I never said that, but call it in. We'll also split the children between two trucks instead of three. You aren't in any state to drive."

He stared out across the ruins of Eloko's Anti-Balaka camp and didn't argue with her. For so long this camp had been his prison, a hell from which he was never certain he would escape. The smells he remembered from that time still lingered, of dampness and mould and the sweat of men.

The noises he remembered, of drunken and drugged soldiers who played loud, hate-lyric music on tinny boomboxes and who fired AK-47s into the night sky just for fun, were no longer there. There had also been the screams of young girls forced to perform acts they should never have to endure. Pierce was glad to leave this place, and that its source of misery was now no longer part of this world. This was not retribution or a reckoning, but the surgical removal of a malignant tumour from society, and the world was again a slightly better place than it had been this morning.

Wiping the sweat pouring off his forehead and feeling the heat of his skin, he noticed the children now split between the two trucks, and Kiambi and Zang standing at the front of the first truck and staring at him, waiting for him to make his move. The drive out would be difficult on the deteriorated and washed-out road, and there was always the likelihood of tripwires attached to grenades, and sentry posts armed with men who hadn't yet heard that Eloko was dead and had been a fraud. But with the help of Zang and Kiambi, they would secure them all in new homes and reunite them again with families where they could. He might have to live a solitary life, but he did so by choice. It didn't mean others had to do so too.

"Okay. I'll call it in, Zang. Then we move out."

PART IV

COVERT RETRIBUTION

62

Namib-Naukluft National Park, Namibia

The sun rose as a bloody red sphere over the dry savanna and craggy mountain range beyond. Feeling stronger than he had in days, Pierce stepped outside and onto the porch and enjoyed the fresh, dry air in his lungs. He stared off across the vast natural landscape and reflected that today was the first day since his poisoning that he didn't suffer a fever and his stomach didn't cramp.

The drive from Eloko's camp to Berberati was now little more than a foggy memory. During the bumpy ride, Dr Kiambi had checked Pierce over. He'd told Pierce there was little he could do other than place him on a drip, if they had one, and order him to rest, which he could do. Other victims who'd endured a single dose of the hallucinogenic poison recovered within a few days with no lasting effects. If Pierce had endured two or more doses, then Kiambi would not have been as hopeful.

Three days later Pierce found himself with Zang in a remote Namibian safe house. It felt more like a vacation retreat than a staging point for covert operations. As soon as they arrived, and after inspecting it, he slept for fifteen hours.

He woke refreshed the next morning, made himself an orange juice and a bowl of muesli and fruit, which he consumed heartily, then brewed two black coffees and took them out to the outdoor table.

Taking a seat on the porch, he removed his new Glock 19 9mm semi-automatic pistol and Eloko's Beretta APX from his pockets and laid them on the table next to the coffees. Pierce first stripped the Glock and cleaned it. Then he did the same with the Beretta, noticing the odd ordering of blank and live rounds. Once he'd cleaned the second weapon, he returned only one type of ammunition into the magazine.

With his work done, he finished his coffee, leaned back in his chair and enjoyed the view.

The other coffee he left alone.

Zang had told him the safe house belonged to a former CIA officer who now consulted to various Namibian national parks on anti-poaching and wildlife security, and who for the next few weeks was on a business trip outside the country. The former case officer travelled often and made extra cash by renting his property back to the CIA as a refuge for operatives lying low between missions in Africa. That was Pierce and Zang now, although he wasn't certain if he was still with the agency.

Or if he wanted to be.

His mind drifted back to when Daniel Eloko had shot him twice in the stomach. In that moment, Pierce had believed he was a dead man. On reflection, Eloko had a reputation for magic tricks, so a weapon loaded with a random combination of blanks and live rounds seemed inspired — but only from a twisted and macabre point of view.

He looked again towards the horizon of savanna grasses and sparse thorn trees and the mountainous peaks of boulders weathered over millions of years. The sunlight painted them in yellows, oranges, and reds. It had been some time since Pierce had enjoyed the natural beauty of the African landscape.

Rachel Zang stood some distance off, with a satellite phone adhered to her ear and the warm summer breeze blowing her long dark hair around her face. She brushed it aside often and, when she noticed him watching her, touched the back of her neck. Dressed in jeans, hiking boots and a striped flannel shirt, the clothes accented her height and slim frame. They were not too dissimilar to what Pierce wore.

Zang ended her call and walked back to their safe house. She sat on a deck chair opposite Pierce, sighed, and put her feet up on the table. Now the sun was higher in the sky and yellow, the weather turned hot. Soon a thin film of sweat glistened on her skin while the sunlight reflected off her emerald-green eyes.

He pointed to her coffee. "It was warm when I made it."

She laughed. "It's fucking hot here. Don't think I'll notice." She breathed in the strong coffee aroma before she took her first sip. He'd never seen her calm and at ease until today.

"Reporting in?" Pierce asked.

She nodded.

It had taken two days to reach Berberati and prepare Dr Kiambi with everything he would need to rebuild his life, or rather everything it was possible for them to provide. During Pierce's moments of lucidity, he'd put Kiambi in contact with David Nogambi, the UN Refugee Agency aid worker he had met in Cameroon, and a diamond trader in Abuja who owed Pierce a favour and wouldn't double-cross him in fear for his life.

They reunited Lifeway with her husband the moment she understood Eloko and his thugs were dead and could no longer threaten her. The soldier who had claimed her, Mamadou, had held Lifeway and her children as hostages, so there was no emotional connection to untangle. Pierced sensed neither Derek nor Lifeway Kiambi had believed until this moment that it was possible they might one day escape their nightmare. But they were together again now, and they had money and a purpose. Pierce hoped they prospered and no further tragedies marked the rest of their hopefully long and happy lives together. The love Derek and Lifeway expressed to each other left Pierce feeling empty in a manner he could not describe.

Then there had been the flight on the CIA's off-the-books Gulfstream G280 jet that transported Zang and Pierce to Swakopmund in Namibia. They never met the flight crew, and no one else shared the passenger cabin with them. Pierce had experienced similar covert flights, where no human interaction passed between the crew and the passengers. This maintained deniability and served to protect the identity of operators in the field, but Pierce had his suspicions that the powers back in Langley knew he was on the flight, which meant they had plans for him. On this tranquil morning, in this perfect retreat, he was about to press Zang on this matter.

She massaged her shoulders, perhaps to release the tension carried in her muscles. "You're looking much better."

He nodded. "I feel it too. The cramps and fever are gone, just as the good doctor said. So, what's the plan?"

Zang grinned. "What do you want the plan to be?"

He shrugged. "That depends."

"On what?"

"On what Langley's intentions are."

Her face softened. "You are no longer on our terminal list, Pierce, if that is what you are asking?"

"I figured that I wasn't; otherwise, this resort would be the opposite of nice."

"Pierce, you exposed Idris Walsh as the real traitor. I saw what Walsh and the others did to you, the tortures they put you through. And evidence we've uncovered elsewhere supports your story."

"Evidence like what?"

"Like the murder of a Colombian forger with a talent for creating realistic but fake news and surveillance tapes. Traffic cameras recorded Walsh in the same area at the same time police responded to a gas explosion in the Colombian's house two weeks ago. He was Walsh's man who created all the false intel he had me and the others chasing for months."

"Where is Walsh now?"

Zang shrugged. "He disappeared into Canada four days ago. Intel suggests he'll be on the *Cancri* tomorrow, as Trager said he would be. Satellite imagery confirms Rupert Ponsonby has been there for days, and our taps into his communications suggest he's waiting for Walsh to show up. Ponsonby also has eight South African mercenaries protecting him and the ship, not including Ponsonby's normal security contingent. All the mercenaries are former Recces and led by a rather nasty individual called Kurt Krige. You know anything about him?"

Pierce nodded. "Doesn't care who he works for. Once aided Janjaweed insurgents in their massacres of the Dinka people in South Sudan. The latest I heard was that he hired out his services to the Sinaloa drug cartels in Mexico. Not above killing civilians, women and children."

"That's the one. Did you know Walsh and Krige are friends? Have known each other for decades."

Pierce raised an eyebrow. "I didn't know that."

"The more I uncover from Walsh's past, the murkier it becomes."

For a long moment neither spoke. Pierce took Zang's cup and made them fresh black coffees. When he returned and placed her coffee before her, Zang was again massaging her shoulders.

"You okay?" he asked.

She smiled and nodded. "It's nothing. Just tension."

"A migraine?"

"No, thankfully."

Pierce sipped his coffee and stood by the door. "What about the radioactive waste?"

"We recovered the four drums in Bayanga no problem. They're now secure in an undisclosed facility inside the US."

"And the last two?"

"Specialist teams are scouring the planet looking for them. We have tipped off various diamond mines, those you said were mentioned in Ponsonby's speech, but we have to be careful who we tell, because we don't want fanatics finding the drums before we do. So far, nothing. But regular facial-recognition and radiological scanning data sourced from all the various major airports any of our bad guys might have used suggests they've only flown on minor airlines within Central or Southern Africa that don't record such things."

"There can't be too many mines to check?"

"But enough."

Pierce swallowed, then drank more of his coffee. "Why do I feel this is all leading somewhere?"

She looked up at him through bright, expressive eyes. "That's because it is."

63

Pierce moved to the railing and prepared himself for what Zang was about to say. She had an easiness about her, projected confidence and independence in equal measure, and yet Pierce sensed she was choosing her words carefully. He said, "Let me guess. You want me to extract from Walsh and Ponsonby the locations of the final two waste drums?"

Zang stood so she wouldn't have to look up at him, then stretched out the muscles in her back by raising her arms high over her head. "Yes, Pierce, that's right. That's why the CIA wants you to complete your mission."

"My mission? I didn't realise I had one."

"Your self-appointed mission. Since Kazakhstan, your single goal has been to bring Walsh and his co-conspirators down. Why stop now?"

"I was pursuing my own objective, which was my freedom, and I've achieved that. Why do I need to kill Walsh? The US has plenty of covert teams that could terminate him more efficiently than I could."

"Because you're deniable, and the CIA needs an off-the-books assassin with the right motivation. It's the perfect deep cover legend for you."

Pierce laughed without humour.

He realised how tired he was, of fighting, always operating at high alert, the never-ending pretence of being someone he was not when operating under a deep cover identity, and the persistent double-guessing of his superiors' motives supposedly on his side, but whose motivations were often greed and self-preservation. But what bothered him the most was his lack of choice. Once he'd believed the CIA would welcome him back after they learned about the hell he'd been through, but to deny him that choice now and diminish his role to that of a deniable contractor felt like salt thrown on a wound.

Pierce considered Zang's part in this murky covert operation. He didn't doubt her loyalty or patriotism and had witnessed how often she put her own life on the line to serve a greater good. He sensed that her intentions to help Pierce conflicted with her orders, but she wasn't the decision-maker in this moment, only their messenger. Perhaps that was how the CIA wanted it.

"You're upset that Langley doesn't want you back?"

Pierce snorted out a chuckle. "What bothers me are the lies. I don't feel any need for retribution against Walsh and Ponsonby. Sure, I'll kill them given the opportunity, and without hesitation, because it serves a greater purpose, but don't try to manipulate me emotionally into carrying out whatever mission you have mapped out. Give it to me straight, and then I'll tell you if I'm willing to do it."

Zang gritted her teeth and paced. "You want it straight, Pierce? I'll tell it to you straight. Ponsonby and Walsh are terrorists. Nuclear terrorists at that, so the worst kind, and that also means Polytope Diamonds funds terrorism. Your mission objectives are simple. First, find the last two radioactive drums. Second, terminate Walsh and Ponsonby with extreme prejudice. Third, sink the *Cancri*. In that order."

Pierce stared out across the African landscape and thought how peaceful it could have been here if they weren't having this conversation. "Yet the CIA wants it deniable, so nothing comes back to them?"

"Exactly!" She massaged her neck again. "It's not something you and I haven't done a thousand times before."

"Turn around."

She frowned. "What? Why?"

"Zang, turn around and sit on that chair."

She hesitated, then did as he instructed.

"You have another migraine?"

"Yes."

"I can fix that."

"How?"

"Trust me."

He didn't want to talk anymore and realised how long moments of silence brought him a temporary peace. It had often been that way during his incarceration in Eloko's camp. Days spent alone meant long periods without torture or interrogation, and he soon realised he needed them. Without speaking, his hands were on her neck and shoulders, massaging the rock-hard muscles. She flinched at first, but soon his nimble fingers worked the muscles until the tension went out of them. Working his hands brought a calmness to his mind, so he enjoyed the moment too.

Fifteen minutes later, when Zang loosened up, he looked at his palms with his fingers spread. There were no tremors.

"Wow! My migraine's gone. Where did you learn to do that?"

Pierce stepped back and sat opposite her. "I have my secrets. So do you, and I accept that. It's the roles we chose. But in missions we work on together, you can't hold anything back. Give it to me straight, or I just walk away."

She nodded and cast her eyes downwards. "That's reasonable. We need you to be deniable because others will see the bombing of the *Cancri* as an act of war against Angola and possibly Great Britain since this is a British company."

"Bombing?"

"Yes, you'll place explosives to sink it. Given your recent, albeit fabricated history, the CIA believes you make the perfect deniable operative to pull this off. Going after Walsh and Ponsonby for revenge is a scenario that no one will scrutinise."

"But that leaves me out in the cold when it's all over, with more governments and organisations putting out more kill orders in my name. Far more than I have already." An icy shiver ran the length of Pierce's spine. No wonder direct talks with the CIA hadn't happened. Communicating through Zang in this remote safe house was just another layer of deniability and distance if all this went wrong.

Zang stepped forward and touched him on the arm. "You're not alone in this. All the equipment and weapons you need are ready for you. Or should I say, ready for us. I'll be there with you, and I'll be with you when we escape. Afterwards you and I will return to the States as a team, where we will provide you with protection."

Pierce stared into her deep, emerald-green eyes. She never blinked nor displayed tells of concern or that she was trying to mask a lie. "Why are you coming with me, Zang? Doesn't that defeat the purpose?"

She didn't answer him.

"Langley told you to send me in alone, but this is personal for you too, isn't it?"

She looked away and lowered her eyes. "Mark," she'd never called him by his first name before, "I have a plan. A two-pronged attack, one of us striking from the air and the other from the sea. And I have a means of securing us on board with no one knowing. And the means to get us out again."

He sensed she still wasn't telling him everything. "Your superiors ordered you to send me in alone. So why are you helping me?"

She caught his stare and held it. "Because you and I are the same, and this is wrong, sending you in alone. We are just not alike because of our skills and experience, but also because of our motives. People hurt me badly when I was younger, and the same happened to you. I can see it written all over that mask you call your face. You hide your feelings well, but not from me. I see it because I wear the same mask."

"How do you know about my past?"

"I don't know your secrets, specifically, just as you don't know mine. But I can see how past trauma defines you as much as mine defines me. We understand each other, and I need people in my life who understand me. They don't come along that often."

"How do we get on board the *Cancri*?" Pierce asked, his body rigid.

Zang stiffened and stepped back. "Odel Nunes. Angola's Minister of Natural Resources. He's connected to all this, through regular bribes Ponsonby pays him. Ponsonby has been reneging on his deal, which naturally has upset Nunes, making him our way in. Nunes plans to meet with Ponsonby soon to secure his next bribe payment. The CIA therefore has arranged for Nunes's regular pilot to come down with bad food poisoning, allowing me to step in and replace him."

She explained the rest of her plan.

Afterwards, Pierce thought through her strategy and saw that it might work.

But he didn't tell her how he would alter it to suit his own needs once the mission was in play.

64

Pierce woke suddenly.

A foreign noise alerted him into consciousness.

Without moving, he listened again for the noise.

The safe house was dark this late into the night. The air felt cool after the day's heat, but still warm enough to sleep without sheets. He remained motionless, feigning unconsciousness until he recognised the noise that had awakened him.

The hum of the kitchen's refrigerator.

In his pyjama pants and bare chested, he tiptoed into the kitchen with his Glock 19 in his left hand. The refrigerator's rumble had changed frequency. This was what had woken him, so nothing of concern. Pierce opened the door and closed it again. The noise dropped off to an almost imperceptible purr.

A second noise.

He turned in a blur, Glock raised and lined up on the potential threat.

Less than two metres from him, Rachel Zang stood

wearing only a short T-shirt, her SIG Sauer semi-automatic aimed at his forehead. Her long arms and legs shone white in the starlight filtering through the windows.

They locked eyes, neither moving. Neither lowering their weapons.

She dropped her pistol and tore off her T-shirt. Naked, her slim but muscle-honed body glistened with sweat. Firm breasts seemed to point straight at him. Her shallow breathing grew in intensity.

Pierce's heart rate increased. The pace of his breathing soon matched hers.

She rushed him, jumped and straddled him around the waist.

Pierce dropped his weapon, his mouth all over hers. One hand gripped her firm bottom, holding her close to him, the other entangling her hair at the back of her scalp, pulling her head close to his. Their mouths entwined. Her breasts pressed firmly against his chest.

He carried Zang to her bed and threw her on it. She tore off his pyjama pants and pulled him down. Kissing turned into lovemaking.

Pierce soon felt lost in the intensity and urgency of the moment.

He had wanted this for too long.

65

F ifteen minutes later they lay panting on their backs, staring at the fan rotating overhead, with sweat dripping off their naked bodies. Rachel's long, slender left leg lay draped across his thighs. Pierce's hand rested on her belly, feeling the rhythm of her breathing. Her hand rested on his jaw, tracing the stubble that would be a beard soon if he didn't trim it.

She laughed. "That was... unexpected."

Pierce felt the palpitations in his heart. His stomach felt alive with fluttering butterfly sensations. "I feel I should call you Rachel now."

"That would be nice, Mark, but only during moments like this. On a mission, I'm Zang, and you're Pierce. Helps keep the boundaries clear."

They lay for a moment, not speaking, just feeling each other's presence and aliveness. He wondered if she felt the same palpitations and fluttering.

It had been too long since he'd last enjoyed the pleasures of physical intimacy. He'd recognised his desire for Rachel

Zang the moment they had met, and now that they had acted on their mutual attraction, he wanted more. He felt purposeful again, like he had rejoined humanity after being apart from it for so long.

"You liked me even when I was Irina."

He couldn't tell if it was a statement or a question.

"I did," he said, and realised he meant it. "I'm still trying to accept that you planned on killing me in Kazakhstan."

She sat as she tucked her long dark hair behind her ears. "About that…"

Pierce sat too, sensing the conversation was about to turn in an unexpected direction. "What is it you're not telling me, Rachel?" He tried out her first name. Speaking it caused his chest to heave.

She smiled as she rested her hand on his shoulder, just above the bandage over his bullet graze, which was healing without complications now that it had been properly treated and Pierce had commenced on a treatment of antibiotics. Both their bodies displayed the numerous cuts and bruises they'd endured over the last week, and older scars from past missions and traumas gained in the field. "Until we met, I honestly thought you were a terrorist." She looked away. "But it wasn't you who I was after. Not really."

Pierce raised an eyebrow. "What do you mean?"

"All this time, I've been hunting bigger fish. The CIA had Walsh under investigation for some time, suspecting him of corruption and misappropriation of funds. They placed me on the Trigger Man Task force to find out how corrupt he was, and…"

His hand traced the length of her thigh as her voice trailed away. "Did it come out, what I did before I joined the CIA? Did Walsh ever learn my secrets?"

She laughed again. "No, and that infuriated him. Nobody knows. Your past is locked up tight. You are a man of mystery, Mark."

"You don't know?" He'd expected his secret to be common CIA knowledge by now.

She shook her head and smiled.

"Good. That means I still have friends in Langley."

"You do. Most people think you are an asshole, but some still like you. I was told what you did in your redacted past contradicted the narrative of you stealing nuclear waste."

He didn't answer, not sure how he could.

She massaged the back of her neck, working the tension out of her muscles. "I'll get another migraine if I'm not careful."

Pierce laughed. "Sounds like a hint for another massage?"

"You are so good."

"Lie down. On your stomach."

She grinned and did as he asked. Soon his hands were upon her neck and shoulders, working the muscles with a firm massage. He felt again the rock-like hardness in her body everywhere his fingers worked.

"Wow!" she said, then flinched.

"It hurts?"

"Yes. But in a good way. Where did you learn to massage like that?"

"I could tell you, but I'd have to kill you, Rachel."

"Very funny!"

"Speaking of which..."

She moaned with joy as his hands worked the muscles around her neck and upper back. "You feel this is an appropriate time to become deep and meaningful with each other, Mark?"

"Why not? You're naked and completely at my mercy. So if you don't report to Walsh, who is your boss?"

"Ah, that's my secret, for now."

His hands moved down her back and kept massaging. Her muscles loosened. "But it's more than that, Rachel. Something is driving you. More than the job. More than patriotism. You said so earlier, that you've been hurt too."

"You mean, just like you?"

"How did you get into this business?" Zang's head turned to the side, and her eyes were closed. "Or is that a secret too?"

He looked at the wall and stared into nothingness. "I made a mistake. When I was a kid. People died, and I wanted retribution. The anger that fuelled me then was the anger I experienced in Kazakhstan, wanting to get back at Walsh and Trager for what they had put me through."

Her eyes snapped open, drawing his attention back to her, but she didn't move from where she lay flat on her stomach. "You experienced severe trauma as a kid?"

His hands moved down to the outsides of her thighs. "I made a choice that the adults in my life should have never let me make."

She nodded. "Now you blame yourself for what happened?"

He looked up and thought about her question for a moment. "Not anymore. After a while, I no longer sought revenge."

"Why not?"

"Every time I sought revenge, it never brought peace, to me or others. I didn't see the point anymore. I lost my way for a time while I was Walsh's prisoner, but I'm back to my old self again."

"What did you want then? Or what do you want now?"

Once again, her questions probed the core of who he was. He soon felt lost in his own dark thoughts. "Balance."

"Balance?"

"There are too many people with money and power in this world, whose only aim is to gain more money and power at the expense of others. Often at the cost of the lives of people without money or power."

She closed her eyes again, smiled as his hands massaged the insides of her thighs. "People like Walsh, Eloko and Ponsonby?"

"Exactly. Restoring balance to the world is the only path I've found that brings me contentment. How ticklish are you?"

"What do you mean?"

"Roll over."

She lay on her back, her hipbones and nipples pointed towards the ceiling. He took her left foot in his hands and massaged between her toes. Rachel didn't flinch, and he enjoyed the sight of her naked body laid out in front of him. "So not ticklish at all?"

"Not with you, it seems."

As his hands did their work, he noticed again old scars between her recent wounds. A knife wound on her left forearm. An indentation in her right thigh that might have been a bullet or knife wound. Burns on her right shoulder. Her skin told a similar story to his own.

"With me, it's all about daddy issues."

He raised an eyebrow. "I'm intrigued."

"My father. He's rich. You know, a penthouse in New York

kind of rich. An executive in the petrochemical industry. With my family, I experienced overseas assignments in Russia and Saudi Arabia."

"Is that how you speak Russian? Time in Russia as a child?"

It was Rachel's turn to raise her eyebrow. "So, Mark, you have seen my file."

"Parts of it."

She frowned, playfully kicked at him with her foot. "I won't ask how."

"You know all about me. It seems only fair."

"I know nothing about what you did before you joined the CIA."

He nodded and smirked. "I interrupted your story."

"I spent my entire life fighting with my dad. We didn't agree on most things, boys, my education, my friends, how I dressed, parties I wanted to go to, that kind of thing. Our failed relationship took a nasty turn while we lived in Riyadh, in one of those compounds where the Saudis like to lock in foreign workers. Our house servants were Filipino. I was friends with their daughter, Juanita. One day, Juanita's father angered our Saudi clients. Soon afterwards, the family disappeared, including my friend. I begged for my father to help, but he did nothing. I think my dad didn't care that the family was likely being tortured or killed for whatever crime they supposedly committed. Eventually I realised my father was heartless, cared only for himself, and cared only for others when it suited him. I'm sure it's why my mother divorced him and why I've rebelled against him ever since."

Pierce noticed that Rachel had not mentioned that her mother was dead. A point he felt not prudent to bring up until she did.

"Hence why you joined the Air Force?"

She frowned again.

"You don't like my massaging? I can stop."

She pressed her toes back into his waiting hands. "It's not the massage that bothers me. You are too good, and I no longer have a migraine. It's that you know so much about me, and that is bothersome."

"Not that much, I promise."

He pressed into the arch and bridge of her foot, which caused her to sink into the sheets.

"I don't know why I'm talking. I should just enjoy this pampering."

Pierce switched feet, kneaded the second foot.

After a minute, Rachel Zang spoke again. "My father wanted me to be a lawyer or an accountant. He even wanted me to be an economist of all things. He keeps telling me I could make high six figures by now if I had followed his advice. When I joined the Air Force, I didn't know he had contacts at the highest levels of the Pentagon. It was Dad who ensured my USAF career stalled."

"So you quit and applied for the CIA. Even though Dad had acceptances for you lined up at all the Ivy League colleges?"

"Yes, because of the secrecy Langley offered." She stretched all her slender limbs and yawned. "Dad believes I'm studying economics and working as an economic analyst for the State Department, just as he always hoped. If he knew I was CIA, and a field operative at that, I think it would kill him. But I can make a difference in the world working as a spy. More so, it seems, than I could when I was with the Air Force."

Pierce nodded. Her past fit in with what Valeriya and

Yebin had secured from her CIA files. Her every word seemed truthful, and her every action seemed supportive towards his goals and needs — except for the detail about her dead mother. That one omission he could understand, so why did he feel Zang was keeping a crucial piece of information from him?

Then again, he wasn't telling her everything on his mind either.

"Mark, I feel I must do a lot of good in this world before I can ever make up for all the bad things Dad has done." She reached up and pulled Pierce down on top of her, then kissed his mouth hard. "Talking about doing something good, ready to go again?"

66

Moçâmedes, Angola

In the early hours of the morning, Zang led Pierce to the property's airstrip, where a turboprop Cessna 208 Caravan waited. The aircraft's metal skim reflected the orange hues of the rising sun and looked fresh off the production line.

After proceeding through a series of pre-flight checks, she turned the craft onto the dirt airstrip and sped up until they lifted into the air. Because of the engine noise and wind rushing past outside, they rarely talked despite their headsets. Pierce sat in the co-pilot's seat and watched the landscape of savanna, grasslands, mountains and desert pass beneath them. At one point, they spotted a herd of elephants trundling through the desert, which brought a smile to both their faces.

A thousand kilometres later, after a single refuelling stop in Etosha National Park, they reached a third private airfield on the outskirts of Moçâmedes, an Angolan port city near the Namibian border. Zang taxied and parked their Cessna, then paid a hangar fee to store the aircraft, proceeded through customs and immigration, then they caught a taxi into the city centre. Moçâmedes proved to be a dusty metropolis, the houses spread thinly, and the most prominent colour for anything was that of sand. The only moisture seemed to originate from the ocean swells beating their waves against the city harbour.

As the taxi dropped them in the city centre, Zang leaned in and kissed Pierce hard on the lips. "This is where we say goodbye, Mark... or should I say Pierce... for now."

He reciprocated with equal passion as his arms slipped around the curve of her back and pulled her close.

Then Zang pulled away and locked her unblinking emerald eyes with his. "Last night was fun. I'd like to do that again sometime."

"A date, then, when all this is behind us."

Zang grinned, then recited an address for a lock-up garage where the equipment he'd requested awaited. She kissed him on the jaw, turned and walked away without once looking back.

When he was alone again, Pierce rented a Land Rover, then drove to the garage, reaching it by lunchtime. Inside and beyond the gaze of prying eyes, Pierce sifted through the various crates to ensure everything he needed was present. With the dry air and the temperature well over thirty degrees Celsius, he was soon sweating.

The weapons cache was more than he could have hoped for. He'd brought his Glock 19, Beretta APX and Ka-Bar fighting knife from Namibia, but he felt more confident that their mission would succeed when he discovered an M4 carbine, perfect for close-quarter battle, particularly after he fitted it with a suppressor.

Other equipment he gathered included light-intensifier goggles, binoculars, a combat rig and body armour, more magazines for his Glock, a wetsuit and a rebreather, so he wouldn't give away his position with bubbles breaking the surface, a heated dive vest, because of the frigid Atlantic water, an inflatable Zodiac boat with an outboard motor, a medical kit, flashbangs and fragmentation grenades, a dive watch with GPS locating, buoyancy bags for holding his equipment, several ropes, a REBS magnetic climbing system, and four MILA limpet mines with computer-controlled detonation systems. Every piece of equipment, he noticed, was available for purchase on the private market.

As he stared at all the equipment laid out on the wooden bench before him, Pierce reflected that powerful individuals inside the CIA had gone to great efforts to equip him. Failure was not an option here, and the CIA wanted him to know it.

After eating an MRE, or meal ready to eat, and drinking a litre of water, Pierce changed into a tan shirt, cotton pants, desert boots, sunglasses, a cap and a scarf tied across his nose and mouth. From this point forward, he would operate as if USAF drones and Pentagon satellites were recording his every move. Zang and he might work together tonight to achieve a mutually beneficial outcome, but that didn't mean she trusted him, or that he trusted her. While he might not prevent recordings of his upcoming actions, his disguise would prevent the CIA from conclusively linking him to today's extreme action should the powers in Langley again turn against him at some future time and use the recorded footage as leverage.

With the equipment stored, Pierce drove out past the

large container port with its many Panamax ships and over-head stacker cranes, then turned south towards the nearby Namibian border along the coast, separating the frigid Atlantic Ocean from the scorching Namib Desert.

Once Pierce neared the GPS coordinates Zang had provided as his staging point, he followed a trail down to the empty beach and drove along the sand for several kilometres, and past a rusted trawler wreckage home to thousands of seabirds, pounded day and night by breaking waves. So far, he acted as Zang had instructed and parked his Land Rover behind a dune. Then he inflated his Zodiac, prepped his equipment, and dressed in his wetsuit. With the cap, sunglasses and scarf obscuring his face, Pierce took his binoculars and scanned the ocean.

He spotted the *Cancri* two kilometres out.

Magnified, the diamond mining vessel resembled an oil drilling rig riding on the back of a container ship. Pierce knew the *Cancri* was a smaller version of the diamond mining vessels De Beers and the Namibian government operated further south for their own oceanic diamond extraction processes. *Cancri* had been a prototype that failed to live up to its design expectations, but that hadn't stopped Rupert Ponsonby from purchasing it at a discounted price and spending years refurbishing and redesigning it until it produced the diamond quantities he desired. Production rates weren't comparable to De Beers, but effective enough to be profitable.

As Pierce waited for the sun to set, he ate protein bars and chocolate and hydrated. He would need his energy reserves to swim the great distances expected of him this night in the chilled ocean currents.

With his meal finished, now was the moment he would break with the script and confuse the eyes in the sky.

He called Mackenzie Summerfield on the secure number only he knew.

She answered immediately, and they both cycled through a series of identification and duress codes. Langley would now try to hack into his satellite phone to listen to this conversation, because the directors on the seventh floor never liked it when field operators didn't play by their rules. He felt confident the encryption software Valeriya and Yebin had provided prevented the CIA from doing so, because the two hackers had never failed him before.

"How are you holding up?" Pierce asked as his eyes scanned the waves breaking on the beach. A pair of seals flitted through the surf, catching fish in their jaws and eating them just as fast. Heavy clouds formed on the horizon, and the breeze lifted, suggesting that a storm loomed.

"Better. The arm's healing nicely."

Mackenzie sounded tired, but this didn't surprise him, as her body would drain her of energy to heal her gunshot wound.

"Mackenzie, have the CIA contacted you now that they know you and I are innocent in all this?"

"No, but I must admit, I've made it difficult for them to find me..."

He waited for her to finish her sentence. When she didn't, he said, "What's up? I hear it in your voice that something troubles you?"

He heard her swallow. "Actually, there *is* a surveillance team watching me. They don't know that I know, but that could change. I'm thinking I need to go dark... I mean really disappear for a while." She spoke her words as a statement, but he could hear the question she wanted him to answer.

"I agree."

"You do? Why? Who do you think they are?"

"I can't know for sure, but I suspect they are our people, the CIA."

"What makes you say that? And why would they be watching me? And why should I run again?"

He described his last few days. Recounted the CIA flight from the Central African Republic to Namibia and now to Angola, and how Rachel Zang remained his only point of contact with their former employer. "Mackenzie, they're keeping me at a distance. I'm about to secure myself on board Ponsonby's mining ship, the *Cancri*, on their behalf. My mission objective is to find the final missing radioactive canisters, terminate Ponsonby and Walsh, and then destroy the *Cancri*."

"Interesting..."

Pierce frowned. "What's interesting, Mackenzie?"

"I've long maintained operational back-door hacks into the CIA servers. Langley has not been sitting around idly since your escape from the CAR, so they've already recovered the two missing canisters. Did so days ago. Found them in the diamond mines in South Africa and Botswana you mentioned last time we talked, so Zang lied to you."

Pierce shuddered as his fists tightened and his teeth clenched. This was the secret Zang had hidden from him, but why? With all the radioactive waste accounted for, there was no reason to send Pierce to the *Cancri* because an airstrike would be more effective at sinking the vessel than the single-man sabotage mission he had agreed to.

But perhaps this was no longer about Walsh and Ponsonby. Was this about Mark Pierce himself?

He said through clenched teeth, "Or she didn't know."

"They're setting you up, Mark. If you destroy the *Cancri*, you're committing an act of terrorism. That leaves you out in the cold and forces you to go on the run again."

Pierce felt as if he had just placed a few puzzle pieces into place and could see for the first time what the puzzle picture was. He didn't like what his mind's eyes saw.

He half whispered, "A deep cover, not of my making."

"What did you say?"

"Nothing important." He looked toward the sky for the drone he would never see, believing for a minute it might kill him now that he had figured out their scheme, with a hellfire missile he wouldn't see coming.

But the CIA had no reason to dispose of him yet. He was to be their deniable asset in the field, sent across the globe to do their dirty work wherever it suited them. He could perform any unsavoury task they asked of him, because today would mark him as a terrorist, and therefore no lines would ever be drawn connecting him to Langley. His future career path with no benefits for him.

What he did see were the first stars twinkling in the dark blue sky, for the sun had dipped behind the watery horizon, and the lights of the *Cancri* lit it up as an easy target.

"They don't want you coming in, Mark. They want to keep you in play as a rogue operative."

Pierce grinned. "I'd suspected that might be the case, Mackenzie, but thanks to you, now I know the truth. I came up with a contingency plan, just in case."

"Good. Help me sleep better at night and tell me your plan?"

67

Pierce spent eight minutes laying out his planned course of action. When he finished, Mackenzie responded, but with an unexpected question.

"Has Rachel Zang flirted with you?"

He found himself unable to answer.

"I'm not jealous, Mark. We're friends, not lovers. But I know you, and I know she is exactly your type. And I could tell when I met her, she had feelings for you too. Or maybe that's what she wanted me to think. Have you considered Zang as a honey trap, *and* is your new handler? There to manage you while you operate on the outside as a deniable CIA asset, rather than on the inside as you and I once did?"

"What are you saying?"

"I'm saying you need to keep that possibility in the back of your mind. What I'm getting at is that Zang is likely conflicted in her feelings towards you. But believe me, you'll be the one who suffers any consequences, not her, should this *Cancri* mission fail... or succeed. Or if the outcomes are not what the CIA want."

Pierce chewed on his lip for a moment, then said, "I agree, actually. I can't help but feel Zang wants to be on our side, but her ultimate agenda, and the agenda of the CIA, is not."

"Maybe." Mackenzie's breathing rhythm changed. "You are responding emotionally here, and you were the one who taught me never to let that happen in the field. Be careful, Mark. Untangle yourself from this mess, quickly, then contact me. Don't return to the United States until you clearly understand your situation, or until we get the chance to speak again. If you need help, I recommend you contact our mutual friend you rescued from Tigray, Ethiopia, all those years ago. He can help you. You remember who I'm talking about?"

"Yes. Good idea. What about you?"

"After what you've just told me, I've made up my mind. I'll go dark and disappear from the UK as soon as we hang up. My surveillance team are amateurs, so they'll be easy to lose. Contact me using the Manhattan method when you are secure."

"Sounds like a plan."

"I..."

She paused for a long moment, prompting Pierce to say, "You're hesitating, Mackenzie? What *don't* you want to tell me?"

She cleared her throat. Pierce knew she did this whenever she was about to sob or cry or otherwise hold back from expressing her feelings verbally. "Mark." Her words caught in her throat. "My behaviour in the past... I wanted to say... I'm sorry."

"You don't have to—"

"But I do. I was so angry with you when I believed you

had abandoned me, and all that time Walsh had imprisoned and tortured you. I could have helped you if I'd looked into it and tried to find you. Instead..."

"Forget it, Mackenzie. I'm not angry or sad or disappointed or anything. You did what you thought was right at the time. That's all any of us can do."

He allowed space in the conversation for Mackenzie to respond, but again, the line was silent for a long count of seconds.

"Mark?"

"Mackenzie?"

"It worries me that you *aren't* angry or sad or mad or frustrated. I've been through every emotion I know a thousand times or more since I last saw you in Morocco. So what about you...? What are you feeling, Mark?"

"Focused."

He knew this was the wrong answer as soon as he spoke, but couldn't find it in himself to correct his statement.

Again, Mackenzie cleared her throat. "Mark, either you're a saint and you understand yourself better than any human on the planet does, and you've faced all your demons and come out the other side as a content, emotionally balanced and self-aware man, or..."

He didn't respond, and now it was he who created the long, silent gap in their conversation.

"Or emotionally, you've completely shut down."

Pierce contemplated Mackenzie's observation. No one knew him better than she did, and he wondered if there was any truth in her analysis. His inability to respond meaningfully now had to be a testament to that.

"Look after yourself, Mark. I hope we meet again."

There was a finality to her words he didn't like. "Of

course we'll meet again, Mackenzie. Never doubt it. You be careful too. I'll come find you when this is all over. I promise."

"I'd like that."

He sensed she didn't believe him.

The call ended.

Hearing only the waves breaking on the sandy beach, and watching the growing storm clouds darken on the horizon, Pierce recalled the Manhattan method, a code directing Pierce to a YouTube video where they could leave comments under false identities. If Mackenzie established herself in a safe location, she'd tell him where that was by posting there. This video had over five hundred comments since Pierce last looked, so one more remark would go unnoticed, except by him.

He stared out across the sea. The storm clouds now produced rain and lightning, violent weather that would never reach these desert shores, but would cause all kinds of havoc for ships in those Atlantic waters. The lights of the *Cancri* were also prominent. Just how the CIA wanted it.

Rechecking his equipment one more time, and ensuring that he still carried Captain Eloko's Beretta APX, Pierce pushed the inflated Zodiac out into the frigid swell and powered through the waves.

68

Cancri, Atlantic Ocean

Despite Angola's proximity to Africa's equatorial regions, and his heat suit operating at full capacity, the Atlantic Ocean currents chilled Mark Pierce and caused his body to shiver. Seawater here flowed straight from Antarctica.

The water at least was clear despite the turbulent waves above and the night-time conditions, so Pierce could see at least a few metres ahead. He didn't use his torch in case anyone on the *Cancri* spotted him.

As he kicked his flippers, propelling him forward, Pierce glanced at the green illuminated readings on his watch to gauge how close he was to the *Cancri*. The mining vessel had been anchored to a single point the entire time Pierce had observed it from the shore. He figured its stationary position allowed its remote-controlled marine crawler to scour a designated seabed region, removing all diamonds from the surface sedimentation before it moved on. Assuming the boat hadn't moved in the last ten minutes, GPS guidance simplified Pierce's nocturnal swim because he didn't have to surface regularly to see where he was.

He had anchored the Zodiac dingy some three hundred metres from the mining vessel and marked its GPS location. With the storm and darkness, no one on the *Cancri* would see it at that distance, yet it remained close enough to serve as his lifeboat. If Pierce needed to swim back, he'd positioned it downstream, allowing for a gentler swim than the battle he endured against the currents now to reach the *Cancri*. Swimming in near zero temperature water with sufficient kit to weigh him down had nearly exhausted him, so this was not a feat he wished to perform twice.

As Pierce came within two dozen metres of the *Cancri*, he surfaced. Immediately rain and spray hit him from every direction. Swells were at least a metre high and battered him every few seconds. The *Cancri* rolled and lurched in the salty water as spray and rain splashed over its deck in every direction.

Pierce dived again and swam until he reached the underside of the submerged hull. Now he used his flashlight to find his way around, because its beams wouldn't reach the surface with the *Cancri* above him. His orders were to fix the three limpet mines to the aft, rear and centre of the hull. Figuring the US drone he suspected to be watching might track his infrared signature, or in case there were tracking devices in the mines, Pierce performed the task as requested. But the three mines would never detonate because back on shore, he'd removed all the explosives.

His muscles aching, he swam again until he found the slurry pipeline and winch cable, which tethered the crawler to the ship. Somewhere down in the deep dark, the crawler munched away at sand, gravel, seaweed, and diamonds. Pierce set the timer on the last MILA limpet mine for fifteen minutes, this one with the explosives still inside, then secured it to a cable looped around the tethering line, and watched it drop into the dark, inky depths.

He removed his flippers and fitted the REBS climbing system to his legs and hands. Then, climbing first underwater, he surfaced and magnetically adhered to the hull. Soon he clambered up the side of the *Cancri* like Spiderman. The spray and the waves pounded him while the roll of the *Cancri* induced nausea, but he kept moving. The thunder and rain, while exhausting him, muffled any noise of his climb.

As Pierce reached the top of the deck, he slowed and peered over the edge.

Through the rain and spray coming off the tumultuous ocean, Pierce spotted a mercenary clad in a black wetsuit with a Steyr AUG assault rifle and light-intensifier goggles masking his face. The man fought to maintain his balance against the roll of the ship and wasn't looking in Pierce's direction.

Pierce shot him through the head with his suppressed pistol.

When the body crumpled, Pierce climbed over the railing and onto the wet deck.

A wave washed over the deck and almost sent Pierce sprawling along its surface until his magnetic glove clamped against a bulkhead. He waited until the water surge passed over him, then released the magnetic charge.

Removing the REBS system, he climbed to his feet and searched for the dead man, finding him wedged under a set of stairs. He took the dead mercenary's radio and headset and donned them. The dead mercenary's companions would speak soon enough, telling Pierce their intentions and leading him to Idris Walsh. As more seawater washed up on deck, he threw the body and the rest of man's gear into the dark water and watched it disappear.

Suddenly, the distinctive noise of a helicopter rotor sounded over the raging winds of the storm. Then Pierce saw its lights emerge from the black clouds as it passed overhead. It was an Airbus H125 helicopter bringing Angolan Minister Odel Nunes to the *Cancri*.

Its arrival signalled to Pierce it was time to go loud.

Suddenly Pierce heard gunfire from the deck of the *Cancri*. For a moment, he thought he'd been spotted, and was under attack. But the concentrated fire was upon the helicopter.

Then Pierce saw that it had been hit, for fires now burned in its hull.

Zang was on board. It was losing altitude, and there was nothing he could do.

69

Rachel Zang had not expected the Angolan helicopter she piloted to come under attack, and now when the hull had taken multiple hits, and with the engine on fire, she knew it was only a matter of minutes before the craft crashed into the ocean with Odel Nunes and his entourage on board, killing them all.

But Zang had planned ahead enough to have worn a parachute, so while the helicopter was still holding steady, she opened the cabin door and threw herself into the dark, stormy abyss.

She deployed her parachute seconds later. The sudden deceleration, as the canopy unfurled, jolted her chest and neck and set her nerves on fire.

Then, as her descent slowed, she looked up. She feared the Airbus H125 would crash down on top of her, but the spinning hull raced past, the slowing blades passing only metres from her. For the briefest moment, a wide-eyed Nunes in the cabin focused on her. Then he vanished, and the darkness swallowed him and the helicopter wreckage forever.

Then the *Cancri* raced up at her.

Zang had given herself the barest minimal altitude to survive the fall. No sooner had her parachute opened did she collide with the structural steel beams of the *Cancri*'s processing plant. There was no elegance in her impact, which winded and stunned her, though she rolled in time, and no bones were broken.

Then the jolt from the impact of hitting the gangway surged through her legs and up through her torso like an unexpected punch to the gut. Her eyes watered, and her vision filled with tiny sparks of light.

Gasping for breath, she slid to a halt, only to realise she was now slipping further along the structure before dropping again.

Now the deck raced towards her, but her tattered parachute caught in the superstructure and slowed but didn't stop her descent. The second impact was like running into a wall, and she expressed her pain through animalistic grunts.

The *Cancri* lurched, and Zang slipped a third time, to be caught in a wash of chilled seawater, which sent her over the railing and down the side of the hull. Again, her parachute dragged behind her and caught only when her legs dangled mere feet above the crashing waves.

She hung for a moment, soaked and battered, swinging like a puppet. Sea waves and spray smashed against her again and again, sapped away her body heat and sent her teeth into a mad clatter. Every muscle stung from multiple bruises and cuts, and she was certain she'd passed out several times from the pain.

As the minutes passed, Zang regained her composure.

Biting down on her rising panic, she checked for broken bones or major bleeding and discovered that she was intact.

A corner of her mind registered gunfire from combatants engaged in a shoot-out on the deck. She had to return to the deck before someone found her and cut the chute, leaving her to fall into the ocean and die from hypothermia or a quick burst from an assault rifle from above.

She planted her feet against the hull and prepared to climb.

Then the chute cords shuddered, and her feet slipped.

She felt her body being yanked upwards.

And again.

Someone was pulling her up.

She fumbled for a grip on her belt as her fingers searched for the SIG Sauer semi-automatic pistol she'd holstered there, but it had slipped out during her fall.

Whoever had grabbed her chute dragged her higher still. She prepared herself for battle, not sure who she would confront once on deck again.

Then halfway up, the person dragging her stopped and left her hanging. This person fired a weapon, spraying bullets across the deck. A lull followed the shooting, so her saviour pulled her up again.

Whoever was pulling her up, they wanted her alive. It might be Pierce, but more likely it was one of Walsh's mercenaries. Zang prepared herself, knowing that she would have to fight for her life as soon as she was back on deck. She let them spend their energy lifting her while she conserved hers.

When she was near the railing, a muscular arm reached down and grabbed her hand, yanked her up and over the deck, then dropped her on the metal deck.

She looked up at her rain-drenched assailant dressed in a heated wetsuit and armed with an M4 carbine. "Pierce?"

"Zang." The former CIA paramilitary officer kicked over a fallen Steyr AUG assault rifle. "That was close."

She nodded as she gathered her breath and the weapon. "Well, I'm here now."

"You'll get reprimanded, helping a rogue operator."

"Probably. But I couldn't let you do this alone."

"I thought it was all a lie, you coming?"

"It's not. Not from me."

For the briefest moment, Pierce expressed relief. Then his expression turned unreadable. "Walsh has been busy. He, Kurt Krige and their mercenaries are preparing to abandon the ship. I've killed four of them. At least four are still alive. They killed a half dozen crew members and mining engineers."

Zang climbed to her feet and ignored her aching body, checked that the Steyr's magazine was full, and a bullet was in the chamber.

"What's going on here?"

Pierce passed her several spare magazines. "From what I can work out, Walsh and Krige stole half a week's worth of extracted diamonds and will soon make a run for it with the loot. Looks like they'll leave Ponsonby behind as the fall guy."

"Ruthless. How did you learn all that?"

Pierce touched his ear, showing a radio earpiece. "They don't know I'm listening in."

She caught Pierce's stare and nodded. His eyes were cold again, his emotions compartmentalised while he operated as a single-purpose killing machine. She too would be the same in the coming battle, but something else in his expression concerned her. "What's bothering you, Pierce?"

"The crew," he said as his eyes returned to the deck, searching for threats. "We need to save as many as we can before this ship goes down."

"The limpet mines, how long have we got?"

As if to answer her question, a water funnel erupted from the ocean as a cascade of spray, bubbles, and noise, drenching them with more chilled seawater.

"That was the crawler." Pierce wiped spray from his hair. "The three other mines I adhered to the hull, as you requested, are set to detonate in thirty minutes."

"That doesn't give us long."

"No, and our priority is getting the crew to safety." He gritted his teeth and wouldn't look at her. "During the earlier shooting, the surviving crew barricaded themselves somewhere, but I don't know where. We need to find them and get them into lifeboats."

She grabbed his arm and turned him until he looked at her. "Mark, sinking the *Cancri* is the right course of action. You know that?"

He said nothing.

"Ponsonby and Walsh are terrorists, and this is their base of operations. We are fighting a war against terror here, have been for decades, and it's bigger now than you could imagine."

Pierce nodded, but his face remained cold and expressionless. Zang had called him by his first name, broken their agreement on when to be intimate and when not to be, but she didn't care. She had to convince him of this important fact before he led them both down a path they might not walk away from.

After several seconds, he nodded as the rain pounded down on them both. Lightning flashed in the sky, and a roar of thunder passed overhead. "Okay, I agree with you, Zang. We blow this ship into a billion pieces, but I won't let the crew die. You take the aft. I'll take the fore. Call me if you find them before I do. You have a radio?"

She nodded, handed him a second communicator linked to hers. Pierce placed the earpiece into the opposite ear to the one eavesdropping on Walsh and Krige.

"Channel five, Pierce."

"Good. Be ready to evacuate in twenty. And remember, Walsh, Krige and at least three more mercenaries prowl these decks. They want everyone dead before they leave, and that includes you and me."

70

Pierce had no intention of saving the crew. They didn't need saving. The MILA limpet mines would never detonate, and Walsh and Krige had no intention of going after the crew so long as they kept themselves stowed away below deck.

Walsh and Krige only wanted diamonds, and from the overheard conversations Pierce had listened to via the stolen radio, the two men had secured over fifty million US in uncut gems and were about to make their escape. Another helicopter was flying in to collect them. With the storm still raging and water drenching every external surface, Pierce didn't believe the helicopter could land, but the mercenaries could still extract themselves from this vessel via drop ropes.

Twenty-one minutes was how long Pierce had to execute the last stage of his plan before the helicopter arrived.

The *Cancri*'s aft carried the ore processing and diamond extraction technology. That was where he had sent Zang, knowing she would find the crew bunked down in tool and storerooms. The fore held the bridge, executive quarters, and the helipad, and that was where Walsh, Krige and their surviving mercenaries had gathered. It was there that Pierce would kill them all.

He found he could move quickly under the cover of the structural elements that supported the many conveyor belts, pipelines, mechanical equipment, X-ray detectors and crushers. He spotted a mercenary guarding the door leading into the bridge tower. Light-intensifier goggles rested on his head but were not positioned over his eyes. Too many floodlights on deck and the semi-regular lightning bolts would have blinded him if he wore the goggles.

Pierce hid behind a noisy slurry pipe, lined up the soldier in the M4's sights, and ended his life with a single, suppressed 5.56x45mm NATO round buried in his skull. The blood spatter on the bulkhead soon washed away in the sea's spray and rain.

After doubling back and approaching the bridge tower from the starboard rather than the port side, Pierce lined up the second sentry and killed him the same way.

Stepping over the second dead mercenary and balancing against the erratic roll of the ship, Pierce snuck into the bridge tower. Five minutes had elapsed since separating from Zang, so he had time for caution. He took the stairs, covering every corner as he advanced. He kept his breathing even, his finger above the trigger, and his eyes lined down the M4 carbine's iron sights. The roar of the storm and the crashing water against the hull muffled any noises he made.

He reached the third of five decks before a burst of fully automatic fire sounded in the stairwell. Bullets and sparks bounced around Pierce. A round hit him in his chest rig and knocked him back against the wall. The pain was like a horse kick to the chest, and soon his eyes watered and lungs stung.

Before the shooter could get a second shot, Pierce retreated around a corner and waited. If he was bleeding out, he was bleeding out, for there was no way he would check his wound while another man hunted him.

Thirty seconds later, after the pain eased, and the foe failed to engage, Pierce figured his chest rig's armour plating had saved him from a serious wound.

But it hadn't saved him from his infliction.

His hand shook. His legs quivered.

Fumbling as he withdrew a fragmentation grenade from his chest rig, he pulled the pin and threw it up the stairs. Then he ducked into a room behind its steel door and used it as a shield. There came a flash, a compression wave, then noise and smoke.

Pierce pushed open the door with trembling fingers to discover his mangled adversary had tumbled halfway down the stairs. Blood dribbling from vacant eyes, ears and mouth.

Pierce stumbled over the body and continued forward. He tried not to think about his neurological state, because that never helped. His hands soon shook so violently he couldn't keep his M4 carbine still enough to fire it effectively.

So he slung his carbine over his shoulder and armed himself with the Glock 19.

Then Pierce remembered he had taken a bullet, and now might be the time to check it. He unlatched his chest rig, discovering the bullet hadn't penetrated the armour plates, but his chest was a mass of red bruises that would hurt more later, as he came down from his current adrenalin rush.

With shaking hands and legs that felt like jelly, Pierce refitted his chest rig and advanced again.

Zang chirped in his ear. "Pierce, are you okay? I heard shooting and an explosion."

"All good, Zang. Three Tangos down. Only Walsh, Ponsonby and Krige remain. Engaging now."

"Be careful. Any civilians in your area?"

"Negative. What about you?"

"Found them. Secured them in lifeboats. I'm coming to you now."

"Roger that."

With the conversation ended, Pierce reassessed his plan. He'd rather complete this part of his mission without Zang's involvement, but keeping her away was not an option now. Pierce estimated he had minutes at most before she reached him.

Minutes to complete what he had come here to achieve.

Pierce advanced up the stairs on legs that weren't as quick to respond as he expected them to be, but he still moved fast.

When he reached the executive quarters, he stepped inside.

Two bodies lay sprawled across the floor, one dead and one alive. The dead man was Khawuta, Ponsonby's ineffective bodyguard. The man who lived was Ponsonby, who squirmed and crawled behind his desk. "Don't shoot! I'm innocent."

"Sure you are." Pierce checked the room until he was certain they were alone. "Get to your feet, Ponsonby, or I'll shoot you now."

"Pierce?" Ponsonby struggled to stand. His eyes were wet with tears and his suit tattered and scuffed, but somehow the Polytope executive had kept his tie straight and top button done up. His hair, however, was drenched and plastered to his thinning scalp. "Walsh and his mercenary friend, they took the diamonds. Let me help you punish them; then we can split the diamonds."

Ignoring the man's pleas, Pierce secured the door, then took two detonator switches from his combat rig. One he placed in Ponsonby's hand, then wrapped packaging tape around the man's wrist and fingers so he couldn't release it. He left the Englishman's thumb free. The other detonator Pierce held in his shaking left hand and pressed down on the button. "This is a game of trust," Pierce said with a sly smile. "Press down on your button."

"What? Why?"

Pierce raised his Glock and pressed the muzzle into Ponsonby's forehead. "Do it, or I will shoot you."

Ponsonby complied.

Pierce flicked a switch on his radio transmitter. "Right, Ponsonby, I've armed three limpet mines I secured to the *Cancri*'s hull earlier. So long as one of us keeps our finger pressed against the button, they won't go off. I can release my grip, and so long as you hold yours, we're fine, and the reverse is true. But if we *both* release our grip, it's game over. The entire ship goes up in a fireball we won't be able to outrun. You understand me?"

Pierce smelled urine. Ponsonby had wet himself.

"Why the fuck would you do that, Pierce?"

"To keep each other alive. You now need me as much as I need you to survive this."

"Why?"

Pierce grinned. "I'll tell you later. Now move!"

They advanced into the hall and back to the stairs. Pierce kept Ponsonby in front as a human shield. Never once did Ponsonby's finger move off the button.

The next level brought them to the empty bridge. A prominent door provided access to the helipad seen through the bridge windows. Pierce heard a second helicopter, its blades whipping somewhere up above, through the darkness and the storm clouds and thunder and lightning. Walsh and Krige would appear here soon enough to make their escape.

Now it was just a matter of waiting.

"Hello, Trigger Man."

The voice came from the stolen radio earpiece. It wasn't Kurt Krige who spoke, who had given most of the directions on the overheard conversations, but the spymaster, Idris Walsh.

71

"Had to get in the last word, Walsh?" said Pierce. Conversing with the American spymaster served no purpose. There was no chance either man would let the other live out this night, so the permanency of their future actions made conversation irrelevant. Then Pierce guessed Walsh's intention, which was to distract him while Kurt Krige moved in to take Pierce by surprise.

"You were my biggest mistake, Pierce. Not killing you earlier was my undoing."

"You're right there." Pierce forced Ponsonby onto his knees, then hid them both behind the control console of the bridge. The Glock shook in his hands, but he'd still use it to take out Krige when he spotted the South African mercenary. The killer had to be close by, so he whispered in Ponsonby's ear, "Keep your finger on the dead man switch." He removed his finger from his own switch. "You're keeping us alive until I kill your partners in crime."

Drenched in his own sweat and shaking with fear, Ponsonby nodded in capitulation.

"Am I boring you, Trigger Man?" the spymaster chirped again over the radio.

"Walsh, I don't know why I'm complimenting you, but you were never boring."

A chuckle came over the radio. "You want to know what is boring? Your friends in Baku. Odd-looking man and his cute girlfriend with the nice tits and barbwire tattoos..."

Pierce said nothing, and neither did Walsh. His foe's intention would be to provoke distress, anger, maybe even rage, but Pierce held his tongue, because he already knew Valeriya and Yebin were dead.

"They're boring, Pierce, because I killed them. They wouldn't talk, so what else could I do?"

Despite his rational mind telling him to keep his cool, every muscle in Pierce's body tensed as he fought his urge not to race forward and throttle Walsh until his eyes popped and his swollen tongue lay limp in his dead mouth...

Revenge.

Not a calling, but a weakness.

Walsh wanted — needed — Pierce's rage to consume him, to turn this battle of wits, skill and strength to the spymaster's favour as Pierce lost control.

"You think you will kill me tonight, Trigger Man? Avenge their deaths?"

"Yes."

There was a long silence. Pierce listened for sounds of a man, for Krige, but with the roll of the ocean and the howling winds blowing spray across the bows, and Ponsonby sobbing next to him, it was hard to hear anything else.

"You came all this way, for revenge. For retribution."

"What did you call it, Walsh? Covert retribution?"

"Exactly!"

Pierce chuckled. "This isn't about retribution. This isn't even about stopping your plans. My friends are dead, so you can't use them against me. Also, your plans to get rich by radiating the world's diamond mines died in Central Africa, when Zang and I destroyed Eloko's operations and informed JSOC and the CIA where you hid the radioactive canisters. All six canisters."

"Then why are you here? You want the fifty million in diamonds I'm going to walk away with? I can hide forever with that kind of money."

Pierce looked to Ponsonby, but the Englishman would have only heard Pierce's side of the conversation. Ponsonby wasn't reacting to anything but his own fear. "I have your executive friend with me, Walsh, but I guess he's worth nothing to you now?"

Walsh laughed. "No, you're right there. I kept him alive so he'd take the fall with the Angolan government, but I see Minister Nunes didn't survive contact with you either."

"You can thank Rachel Zang for that one. Another good CIA operator you betrayed."

More laughter erupted from the spymaster. "Zang's working for someone else, Pierce, or didn't you know? She was a CIA plant, inside *my* operation. It's why she needed to die in Kazakhstan... Oh, going by your silence, you didn't know?"

Pierce nodded but didn't answer. Walsh's words rang true, considering that Zang had withheld important information from him. But that was a minor issue he would deal with another time. Again, Walsh was looking for the right button to push in Pierce to make him lose control, but it wasn't working.

He heard the helicopter again, hovering somewhere up

above in the darkness. He had to presume they had snipers on board, ready to take him out if he stepped onto the helipad, but also knew the rain and wind would make a clean shot almost impossible. Pierce glanced at his hands, shaking like a ribbon in the wind, and knew he would never get off a clean shot across any distance, at the helicopter or at the two men he still had to face.

Where the hell was Krige?

"This is about putting you down, Walsh. As long as you live, you'll keep betraying people, playing them like pawns to sacrifice, only so you can get rich. Tonight is about taking you out of the equation."

"How very fucking noble of you."

The bridge door burst open as Krige rushed in.

72

Krige fired his Steyr AUG, but Pierce was ready and ducked as the volley of bullets thundered past and sent fracture patterns through the bridge's viewing glass.

Pierce returned fire, but his shaky hands betrayed him, and two of his bullets went wide.

The third shot was a fluke hit, knocking Krige's rifle from his hand.

Within seconds Krige closed the distance between them, slapped Pierce's firing arm aside as a fourth bullet ricocheted off the metal roof. His other hand struck towards Pierce's throat, which Pierce only blocked at the last minute with a pivot of his body and forearm, sliding the blow effortlessly away.

Now they engaged, like two giant tigers clawing each other for the kill.

Pierce soon found his rhythm, anticipated strikes, and blocked them with a fluid motion. But shakes still gripped his muscles, and his arms and legs felt like rubber. He resorted to kung fu parries, a loose and limber style that turned his strikes into a dance, slipping his legs and arms between Krige's powerful limbs and diverting them away. The roll and pitch of the *Cancri* threw both men off balance multiple times, but they kept on their feet. To fall was to surrender to the other and die.

Pierce tried for an incapacitating strike many times, but Krige anticipated his every move, except he blocked with force rather than finesse. A grin etched on his grizzled face when he realised Pierce couldn't control his shaking.

Another strike. Another parry. Then a fist found a path through the melee and hit Pierce in the chest exactly where the earlier bullet had struck him.

The force sent Pierce staggering backward, and the pain was worse than the initial gunshot. He choked for air and almost blacked out.

From the corner of his eye, Pierce spied Walsh on the helipad, reaching for a dropped rope hung from the buffering helicopter above, an old Atlas Oryx used in great numbers during South Africa's bush war with Namibia many decades back.

Pierce tensed and returned his focus to the hand-to-hand combat. Strikes were to kill. Blocks were to stay alive. His body soon surged with the heat of anger, for he felt consumed with the need to punish this man.

Then he realised he was wrong and focused his mind. He let go of his anger and felt his body respond as it should.

He was in control again.

Krige came at him, confident because he believed Pierce was beaten.

He didn't see the uppercut, a clean and fluid motion from Pierce's right arm, that surged up and impacted Krige's jaw, a blow that shook the mercenary's brain inside his skull and rendered him unconscious.

Walsh hooked himself to the drop rope.

Pierce skidded across the bridge, past the still cowering Ponsonby, and scooted up his Glock 19. Once on his feet, he ran as he aimed at Walsh, but with the rolling deck and ocean spray, he stumbled, and his shots went wide.

Walsh had the straps around his chest now, ready for the helicopter to sprint him away.

Pierce raced across the helipad, threw himself at Walsh and grabbed him around the waist as they both lifted into the air. He fumbled for a grip on the wriggling spymaster, reached to a pouch on his belt and unbuckled it. Then Pierce slipped and fell back to the helipad.

Three tins slipped with Pierce and bounced with him.

"*NO!*" Walsh screamed.

Pierce rolled with the impact.

Walsh disappeared into the darkness as the helicopter made good on their escape plan.

Two tins went over the lip and dropped into the chilly ocean water.

As Pierce stumbled to his feet, Krige appeared. The mercenary staggered across the rolling helipad. His mouth bleeding profusely, he lifted a semi-automatic pistol.

Pierce was faster, raised his Glock and fired until the magazine emptied, and the slide locked into place.

Full of holes, Krige took two more steps, then collapsed to his knees as torrents of blood gushed from his mouth. Then he tumbled forward, and he too disappeared into the rolling ocean waves.

Pierce staggered to his feet, scooped up the last fallen can.

Now Ponsonby stood on the helipad with him. "You got the diamonds?"

"Yeah." Pierce let Eloko's Beretta APX drop to the helipad and slide towards Ponsonby. He pretended he didn't see it fall. "You want these diamonds? They're all we have left."

"Of course I do, you oaf. I'm finished here. I'll split them with you if you get me away."

Pierce watched Ponsonby for a moment. There was a glint in the Englishman's eye that hadn't been present before, a hunger. The man looked dishevelled, his suit torn and scuffed, his face bruised and his skin dirty with grime. But under the broken facade of executive self-entitlement lay the animal that would follow any dark scheme to its despicable end in order to maintain his wealthy status.

Pierce grinned despite the rain pounding against his face. "Tell you what, why don't you have them all. If you can reach them."

Pierce flung the last can into the churning ocean swells.

"*NO!*" Ponsonby screamed, just as Walsh had.

Pierce stepped to the edge of the helipad. He looked down. Through the rain and dark clouds, he saw the ten-metre drop into the churning ocean. A survivable distance to fall.

"You. Fucking. Asshole!"

He heard the hammer of the Beretta cock.

Pierce turned to find the weapon lined up and in his face. "What about the dead man switch, Ponsonby? You forget about that?"

Ponsonby shuddered and jumped backward. He no longer held his thumb over the fake detonator, and neither did Pierce. "You...? You fucking lied to me?"

"Needed to keep you on your toes."

"You ruined everything."

The Englishman lined Pierce up in his sights, but he never had the chance to fire the weapon. One second his eyes were wild, like a cornered animal. The next the front of his face blew apart in a storm of flesh, blood and brain matter, and he toppled forward as another wet mess upon the rolling helipad.

73

Rachel Zang held her arms steady as her eyes stared down the length of her Steyr AUG assault rifle, and the roll of the *Cancri* threatened to knock her off her feet. The smoking barrel spoke for the half dozen bullets she had fired into the back of Ponsonby's head, pulping his face and skull into a putrid pool of muck. But now her weapon was trained on Mark Pierce.

The man she had been intimate with now stood unconcerned on the lip of the helipad.

Up high, the roll of the ocean swells was more noticeable, the winds felt stronger, and the spray still chilled her. Pierce could fall at any minute, drop into the ocean and disappear. Why didn't he step away from the edge?

"Ponsonby was about to shoot you."

Pierce laughed. "Zang, he was supposed to."

She sucked in an involuntary breath and asked herself, had she misjudged him? Too much time under torture and incarceration in Central Africa. Had it broken him? "You want to die?"

The former CIA operator laughed. "No."

"Then what the hell do you want?"

He scratched the back of his head in a casual gesture, even though his legs fought against the elements to hold himself upright. He hadn't raised the Glock 19 in his right hand, and she wondered where his confidence came from. What did he know that she didn't? "Pierce, it's been over thirty minutes. The limpet mines didn't go off?"

"Did you get the crew off safely?"

She listened to the inflections in his voice and watched his facial muscles. "You really care about their welfare, don't you?"

He nodded, then looked down into the water. "I can't set them off. No explosives inside, you see."

"What are you playing at?"

Pierce laughed, but his chuckle was of a man who cared for nothing. "You're playing me, Zang. You and whoever it is you really report to in the CIA. You don't want me to come in. You're 'enhancing' my legend, turning me into a disgraced operator who's gone off the reservation. Killing Walsh, Ponsonby and Krige, then sinking the *Cancri* sends exactly the message you want the world to know about me. You want me to be *your* terrorist. But what exactly you have planned for me next... I'm not sure I want to know. I don't want your deep cover. Walsh made me live one long enough, and I'm out."

Zang swallowed and adjusted her aim. Mark Pierce had guessed the CIA's motives perfectly. "Then what do you want? We can re-negotiate?"

He shook his head. "I'm going to disappear for a while. But to do that, I need everyone to think I'm dead. I don't want anyone to come looking for me. That weapon

Ponsonby had, the Beretta, it was Eloko's. It's loaded with blank rounds."

Zang adjusted the weight on her feet. The rolling swells picked up, and so did the wind, forcing her and Pierce to adjust their footing and balance again.

"You have a drone overhead, watching all this. When you shoot me, you need to make it convincing."

"Me? Convincing?"

Pierce nodded. "I need you to shoot me, Zang. Not actually shoot me, but make it look like you did. When you do, I'm going to fall into the ocean and disappear. Can you do that for me, *Rachel*?"

Zang hesitated, uncertain what to do. Now it was him using her first name, making it personal. Intimate. He broke the rules too.

She had her orders, and until this moment she had believed everything was progressing as planned. Then she remembered what her boss had once said about the infamous Trigger Man. No one can control him, and if you try to manipulate him, do so with extreme caution.

"There is a bigger operation at play, Mark, with bigger stakes than you can imagine. Come in, and we'll debrief you."

"We?" Pierce cocked an eyebrow. "I don't think so. This is what I'm going to do. I'm going to raise my Glock and point it at you. But you are going to fire first, and I'm going to fall into the ocean."

"And if I don't shoot?"

"Then I might shoot you."

Pierce went for his gun.

Zang fired over his head.

He was convincing as he staggered backwards and dropped like a stone into the raging swells below.

Racing to the lip of the helipad, Zang looked down, but the Trigger Man was nowhere to be seen. The churning ocean currents had already claimed him.

Her satellite phone rang.

She answered as wind and sea spray numbed her face. "Yes, ma'am."

"What the hell happened?" her boss asked from half a globe away. She'd watched everything, as all the action unfolded, seen through the infrared lens of the Predator drone Pierce had correctly guessed about. Storms didn't stop the CIA from spying on anyone.

"Pierce... He... was about to shoot me."

"So you shot him?"

It took Zang a moment to answer, but when she did, the lie came easily. To hell with their real operation. To hell with the bigger picture. They'd find another way, and Mark Pierce deserved her respect and loyalty.

He needed time to find peace again, and she would give it to him.

"Yes, ma'am. The Trigger Man is dead."

EPILOGUE

ONE WEEK LATER...

Edinburgh, United Kingdom

For six days straight, Mackenzie Summerfield had kept herself on the move. An unknown group hunted her and had tracked her from Nottingham to Leeds and finally to Edinburgh in Scotland, where she found herself now. This wasn't the amateur group she had spotted earlier and told Pierce about, but a far more sinister and ruthlessly efficient team. This second group's intention didn't seem interested in merely reporting her movements back to Langley. Rather, Mackenzie sensed, they actively hunted to kidnap or kill her.

She had no obvious proof this was the group's intention, except that on two occasions in Leeds, tinted-windowed vans had slowed while passing her when she was alone on the streets. Her skin had prickled, and her stomach had churned with metaphorical butterflies each time she'd barely diverted fast enough to foil a snatch. But that only meant the team would change tactics next time they came for her.

Escaping Leeds by bus, then train had been more luck than good tradecraft on her behalf.

Now she was in Edinburgh, at the height of winter, with snow falling regularly and daylight lasting only a few hours each day. The arm she had taken the bullet was in a sling but still ached and gave her away as an easy mark from a distance, but it hurt worse not to mobilise it. Plus, she feared the stitches would unravel if she moved it too much or too quickly, and she couldn't afford to bleed out.

Somehow, this evening, she'd found herself darting through the University of Edinburgh on foot, and with the sun now far below the horizon and the teaching semester at an end, the campus was empty, and she was alone.

But she could only deal with what was in front of her, so Mackenzie pulled her overcoat closer around her body and pressed on. The kitchen knife in her coat pocket gave her some comfort that she might fight her way out of any future confrontations she would inevitably face, but nothing else did.

A man of medium height stepped out of the shadows and appeared on the path she was taking. He wore a parka and jeans, but she couldn't see his face because the angle of the streetlamp cast his front in a silhouette.

Her heart beating fast, Mackenzie turned to retrace her steps and flee. But three other individuals, all men, and all imposing, had snuck up behind her.

She turned back to the first man, the obvious leader of the group. Her only option now was to talk her way out of this situation, if that was even possible.

"Ms Summerfield, surely you recognise when the game is up?"

He spoke with a Middle Eastern accent, but that was all she could ascertain, as she could still not clearly see his face.

She said, "It's a mistake threatening me like this."

He stepped closer, but she still couldn't see his face. "It's not a threat. It's a kidnapping."

"Who do you work for?"

The man shrugged. "Does that really matter?"

"One hundred per cent it matters."

"Then I guess you're going to be disappointed."

She reached for the knife in her pocket, but it was too late, as the men behind her had snuck closer. One foe now wrestled her good arm into an immobilised and twisted position behind her back. Their grip hurt, and she struggled until another man jabbed a needle into her neck.

Suddenly, as cold fluid flowed into her, Mackenzie became both dizzy and exhausted and knew she'd be unconscious or dead in seconds. She didn't know which she feared more.

The man who was in charge stepped forward, and she could see him now. There was nothing remarkable about him except that he was clean shaven, both on his face and scalp.

"Why?" she asked with a slur. It was the only word she could speak, as every muscle in her body numbed and tingled and no longer felt they belonged to her own body.

"Mr Pierce, of course. If we own you, we own him too."

ACKNOWLEDGMENTS

Thanks to Bodo Pfündl and Friedrich Reher for sharing their first-hand experience in South Africa; Kashif Hussain, Ross Sidor, Deep Ranjan Sarmah, Kenneth Karcher, Ann and Ian Short, Brian Drake, Steve Lepperand and Bob Adamick for general feedback; and Dori Barrett, Terrill Carpenter, Don Shetterly and Roxy Long for early reviews and feedback on the manuscript.

Thanks also to my editor, Alice Latchford, for her work in tightening up the manuscript you have in your hands, the entire team at Inkubator Books, and Shirley Khan for her review of the manuscript.

And special thanks to Bec Short for always being there at my side and constant encouragement.

This book was one hundred percent written and edited by humans. No artificial intelligences were involved.

ABOUT THE AUTHOR

Aiden Bailey is an international bestselling thriller author from Australia. Formerly an engineer, he built a career marketing multi-national technology, engineering, and construction companies. His various roles have included corporate communications with the Australian Submarine Corporation, technical writing for several defence contractors, engineering on an outback petroleum pipeline, a magazine editor and art director, and engineering proposal writer for the Royal Australian Air Force's surveillance and intelligence gathering aircraft and drone enabling works. Aiden has travelled widely in six continents and his experiences are the basis of many of his stories.

Did you enjoy *Deep Cover*? Please consider leaving a review to help other readers discover the book.

www.aidenlbailey.com

ALSO BY AIDEN BAILEY

The Trigger Man

Deep Cover

Printed in Great Britain
by Amazon

40586939R00270